Mia Raven

Norma Lopez-Stewart

Table of Contents

I would like to dedicate this novel to my wonderful husband, Gregory Stewart, who saw my dream and worked endless hours on this project.

To my family and friends who encouraged, supported, and believed in my vision.

About the Author

Norma Lopez-Stewart was born in New York City but spent most of her life in Reading, PA, and now resides in Tampa, FL. She's an author with a great passion for storytelling. She has worked on a series of strong female leads, entitled, The Dark Days Chronicles, in which she uses her Latin heritage to bring her characters to life.

Prologue

New Orleans 2058

Before The Dark Days

The money was rolling in for the executives of the Human Cell Cosmetic Corporation. Their main corporate offices and laboratories were located in the business district of New Orleans.

Electronic Billboard Advertisements were displayed everywhere with gorgeous women hiding the subliminal messages.

Billboard Commercial

The look of beauty is in your hands, enhance a better you with the latest in beauty treatments and procedures that will make a better you. A doctor in one of our advanced technology treatment facilities can safely perform any procedure.
Affordable plans to suit any budget. Why wait to become the better you? Call us right now to schedule your appointment and transform yourself into the beauty you always knew you could be. Standard retina scan required for payment.
#-010-666-818#8

This new craze exploded everywhere. The market was saturated with testimonies of satisfied customers and how the procedures changed their lives.

A Child by Design
Human Cell Cosmetic Corporation
Advertisement

Welcome to a new breakthrough in evolution technology. Where you don't have to guess what your child would look like. Think about it, your child with those beautiful blue or green eyes blond hair, alabaster skin like silk. Now it is possible to safety change an embryo's DNA. It's what you deserve, a perfect child. So, let us help you have that special baby, by your design.

All major credit cards are accepted, retina scan or payment plans to suit any budget. Call us right now to schedule your appointment; soon to be mothers don't wait.
1-800-222-6666

<u>A Child by Design</u> was another procedure developed by a group of scientists from the Human Cell Cosmetic Corporation. Customers flocked to these clinics for these mind-blowing procedures. A Child by Design Clinic Specialists could create miracles by giving couples what they wanted. Couples raced to these clinics to have the child of their dreams. Brown eyes could be changed to any color of the spectrum. Trillions were spent on these procedures. The company spared no expense into luring people into the hands of sharp fast-talking sales personnel. They offered

easy payment plans, great incentives that people found hard to say no to.

New Orleans, home of beautiful people, rich culture, music, mystery and intrigue was made famous by these corporations. Animated signs lit up the city with entertainment. The job market was booming. Television commercials offering great jobs and incentives. Benefits too good to pass up, as college graduates raced to New Orleans to take advantage of the job opportunities. New Orleans was one of the fat cats of America, raking in huge amounts of money.

The tourist industry couldn't keep up with the demands as crowds of people from all over the world came to enjoy Old Town. The French Quarters was kept untouched keeping the authenticity in the mist of all the new modern constructions. Old Town was its own little city within a larger one. The trolley cars were still operational. Small jazz clubs could be found on every corner along with the wonderful Cajun food, the palm readers and curiosity shops full of colorful dolls, beads, masks, all kind of trinkets people love.

Clinical Trials – Costa Rica

Millions traveled to Costa Rica for a chance of making money from the human trials. They were promised health benefits for the whole family, tricked into participating in certain programs. Young albino children especially were recruited for scientific experiments.

Like any popular treatment, other companies jumped abroad in other South American countries. Laboratories popped up everywhere with wonderful gifts and incentives. The demand was great and extravagant gifts to entice pregnant women were offered.

Another large corporation recruited in Africa along with the smaller islands and other neighboring countries. Mexico and even China had their own companies, hitting the competition hard. The years of experimentation began to change families, as each generation became lighter and people of color died out and were no more.

For many years, their corporations amassed great wealth, especially when new enhance procedures were developed and people became addicted to the new fads.

August 7, 2242, the world was thrown into chaos, as death knocked on the doors of the poor as well as the rich. Bodies littered the streets of every town and city in the world. There was no place to hide as the beast spread like locusts bringing down the mighty cities.

Huge incinerators burnt diseased bodies to keep from further contaminating other resources. While people moaned and buried their dead, another monster emerged, the Purest Movement.

When the Purest Movement invaded the cities and towns these huge corporations were destroyed. Bombed, set on fire, anything that resembled technology was targeted. The Purest believe that God was punishing the world for their vanity and greed. Thousands of city buildings were burnt down with people still inside.

New Orleans' business district smoldered in ashes for months. Pockets of fire re-igniting, making recovery worst as people fled for safety. Television stations were bombed, cell towers came crashing down. Companies that made electronic products were burnt to the ground.

The world went silent as each country tried to salvage what wasn't destroyed. Those survivors of the Dark Days struggled to make sense of their own safety as the deadly pestilence killed billions throughout the world. The Purest Movement spread their deadly seeds of self-righteousness, condemning those who would not join their movement.

New Orleans

The city was obliterated by fires and bombings, so much was destroyed. Things seemed hopeless as people began to dig themselves out of the rubble. The Purest group moved through cities taking what they wanted. The future of this once great city looked bleak, until the tribal groups began to move in. They began to stabilize the city and electing an Overlord to petition the Inner Cities for supplies. This was the new beginning…

Chapter 1: Raven Moon

Esmeralda Estate

Two Years Earlier

"Why am I always the last one to find out about these things," Falu bellowed. "I swear to God if it's the last thing I do, I'm going to shut down those operations. So, where the hell is this woman now?"

"We don't know Falu. After the match she just disappeared," Max replied.

"Fabulous… just fabulous! I leave for a couple of weeks, and the city goes to shit. Look Max, I don't mean to sound like a prick. I just spent two weeks trying to convince Jesse Quintanilla that we are ready to move forward, and I come home to this bullshit."

"I understand you worked hard on that presentation, what do you want us to do? I mean, come on. How many brown-eyed women are there in New Orleans? I'm sure someone must have seen her," Max responded, worried his brother was going to blow his lid again.

"I have an idea," Ricky interrupted, trying to come up with a solution, "Why don't we take the picture that is on the posters and make some of our own. Like, with a reward or something?"

Falu pondered the suggestion for a moment. "That sounds like a good idea, I also want you to put pressure on Jim and Eric. Those bastards know more than what they're saying. I want those posters out and distributed as far as possible… they could be keeping her out of the city limits, slimy bastards. So, let's get this done as soon as possible before something else happens."

New Orleans after the Dark Days became a haven for some of the worse criminals, a hiding place for the lowest form of scum. The human slave traffickers were the biggest drug and human enslavers. They were dangerous and ruthless when it came to their operation. Sex was sold openly like hot dogs at a hotdog stand. New Orleans, the city of mystery, jazz, along with the richest food, became one of the most notorious cities feared by many. The degradation was overwhelming as families struggled to survive, looking over their shoulders, watching out for vultures that would prey on them.

However, the winds were changing. A new movement was sweeping the dirty streets of New Orleans. People were beginning to have faith that the once famous city of New Orleans could be restored to its greatness.

When the tribal communities began to buy land and move in the territory, things began to change. The tribal communities brought with them a higher standard of living.

The tribal communities were very spiritual, highly educated and moral. They were dedicated to serving their families and communities. The communities were made up of all classes of people and races. They brought with them their drive and commitment for the greater good of men and women. The communities knew that educating their children would enrich their way of life.

They raised strong men and women who defended their land and communities with their blood. Outsiders feared the tribal people and didn't understand them. Therefore, they made up wild stories. The tribal communities treated their women like gold, knowing they were the givers of life and the nurturers of their families. They guarded their communities with the same passion they guarded their families. Their strength began to bring back order into the beaten-down city. Finally, it was beginning to resemble the great and beautiful city it once was; full of spicy food, music and mystery that came from the soul.

The overlord of New Orleans was a tribal member. Everyone feared the name of Falu Moreno Vega; he was young and ambitious. His father was known as the King of New Orleans and his tribe. Falu was called the Prince. But when his father passed away, he was renamed the King of New Orleans. He was feared for his massive build and brute strength. A beautiful man with an intensity that would make anyone bow to him. However, his secret weapon was knowledge. Falu was highly intelligent, which made him more dangerous. He used his knowledge to keep control, and out of fear of the mighty overlord, the city was beginning to rise from the ashes. He vowed to make his father's dreams of making New Orleans a proud city to live in and entice business and growth to a fading society.

Present – Somewhere on Route 79

Rosa watched as her teenage son CJ wiggled in his seat, "Honey, we need to stop," she said to her husband. "Henry, the children are hungry, and they have to go potty."

Kathy shifted the baby from one leg to the other, "That's a great idea; we've been on the road so long without a break."

Henry pulled the beat-up school bus off the street and down a small path that used to be a campground. The tables were still sturdy after all the years of neglect.

"Don't go far, children," Henry yelled to his son CJ, who took off running toward the wooded area.

"I've got to go to the bathroom, dad." Henry watched his son disappear into the woods. Henry and his brother-in-law Marcus had been traveling for weeks trying to find work, and a place to settle. They heard there was plenty of construction work in New Orleans, so they packed all their belongings, and families on a hope, and a dream.

The two highly skilled men had been out of work nearly a year. Neither one of them was able to work in their profession. Henry was tired of working odd jobs and not having enough to feed his family. He hated sleeping in the converted school bus, trying to keep thieves from stealing the little they owned. Henry looked older than he was. All he ever wanted was to make a decent living and provide for his family.

Kathy brewed some tea after building a small fire on the old, rusty grill. She used the last of the bread to make sandwiches for the children.

Rosa sat quietly, looking out into the distance, "What do you think? I feel we're making a huge mistake," Rosa said, tired of traveling. "I mean, this is a huge city, we're going to get lost here." Rosa held back the tears she had been suppressing ever since Henry announced they were moving to New Orleans.

They were small-town folk from a place where everyone knew and supported one another. "I know you're scared Rosa, but I have to believe there is something better out there, for our children's sake. If we don't take this chance, I feel like we'll never know if we made the right decision. Trust my brother… Henry, wants the best for you and his family," Kathy said with a smile. She believed in Henry and her husband Marcus.

"I wish I could be like you, I worry about everything, but I'm trying." All they could do was hug each other. Their lives have been very hard.

CJ loaded his bow and watched as the wild pigs ran back and forth. Slowly, he pulled back on the bow and aimed, sighting his target. He let go of the arrow, but the thirteen-year-old CJ missed, arousing the rest of the pigs. He watched his meal run deeper into the woods. "You brats," he said to himself, "come on piggy, piggy, one of you is going to make a wonderful meal."

He decided it was worth running after them. He tried tracking them down a small path, then lost them when a huge tree blocked his path. He began to move the tree limbs, when he realized there was someone trapped underneath. Curious, he removed some more of the branches until he could make out a human underneath. It was a woman. He touched her face to see if she was still alive. Afraid and not knowing what to do he ran back to the others who were ready to sit down to eat.

"Dad, come quickly. There's a woman, I think she's still alive," he yelled, his heart racing. Henry followed his son down the narrow, heavily wooded path with the others right behind him. Henry reached her first and checked for a pulse. "Is she still alive, dad?" CJ asked. He had never seen a dead person up close.

"She's still warm," Henry raised her head, slowly putting his jacket underneath. His hands were full of blood.

"Henry… she needs a doctor," Marcus said, staring at the injured young woman.

"She's bleeding! I need something to stop the bleeding," Henry said, desperately looking for something.

"Henry, where have we seen this woman before," Marcus asked, staring at her.

"What are you talking about," Henry replied as he wrapped her head with a piece of Rosa's apron.

"Think, man; remember when we were at the post office, you pointed to that poster of the beautiful dark-haired woman. The missing person poster. Remember, you said it would be nice to have that kind of money, the reward."

Henry could only stare, "I think you're right, it's her… the woman in the poster. Holy cow, you know what that means?" his eyes lit up.

"Would one of you tell us what you're talking about," Kathy asked, wondering why they were so happy.

"This means we are in the money, sister, Falu the overlord of the city, he has a huge reward for this woman. We are going to take her to him and collect the reward," Henry replied excitedly.

"I'm with you brother. This is the break we've been waiting for," Marcus added, smiling for the first time since they left home.

"Are you crazy," Rosa exclaimed, "Falu Moreno… the man is a beast. Have you not heard all the horror stories about him?"

"But Mama, we can't just leave her here," CJ exclaimed, kneeling next to the woman, touching her hair. "Her hair is so nice; dad, her hair is as black as a raven."

"Yes, son. She is a natural child, born without being altered. You remember the pictures in the history books that I showed you?"

"I don't know, dear… what are we going to do with her?" Kathy questioned, tired and grumpy.

"Look, we have a choice. We either take a chance and bring her to Falu… or drop her off at the nearest hospital, which is probably forty miles further. CJ is right, we can't leave her here. We may be poor, but we are still God-fearing folk, and this is the right thing to do," Henry argued, trying to convince the terrified and confused women.

"I'm with Henry," Marcus added, "Falu's estate is closer than the hospital."

Between the four, they carried the young woman, whom they had wrapped in an old blanket. Rosa cut up some strips of cloth to bind her head, hoping to stop the bleeding. "I hope you know what you're doing, Henry. I don't want to spend my life alone, waiting for you to get out of jail," Kathy said, fussing.

"Why would Falu send us to jail, we didn't commit a crime? Now have a little faith in your God, I think it's time things go our way," Marcus replied.

"Sister, I know things have been hard for all of us, but I have a good feeling about this. Falu has a lot of construction projects going on. Even if we only get a recommendation, it would be worth the trip to his estate."

Kathy was still not convinced, but she said no more. She silently made a prayer. CJ and his mother kept a close eye on the young woman. They managed to stop the bleeding but hoped they could get her to a doctor in time. "Marcus, maybe we should take her to the hospital instead," Kathy offered, nervous.

"Kathy, I'm with you," Rosa agreed.

"Falu has many people at his employment, and his estate is vast. He keeps a doctor in the house for his men."

"How do you know so much about him?" Kathy questioned curiously.

He smiled, "Everyone knows the mighty Falu Moreno. He takes good care of his men. We found out a lot about the Esmeralda Estate… it's common knowledge."

It was getting dark by the time they reached the boundaries of the estate. They could see the main house from the road. The guards stopped them at the gate, one of the armed men stepped out of the guard house. Rosa's eyes were wide with fear; she held her baby tightly in her arms.

"State your business," the guard demanded.

Henry swallowed hard, fishing for the right words. "We're here… to see Mr. Falu," he finally said. "We have someone he's looking for," he pointed to the back of the bus.

When CJ uncovered her, the guard ran back to the guard house to call the main house. "I want you to follow me," Angelo said when he returned, jumping into a small car making his way up the road toward the main house.

The floodlights shined brightly on the French Château style mansion over 62,600 square feet over 13.6 acres of land. Angelo made a left turn before he reached the main gate taking them toward the back of the mansion. They went through another set of gates past the stables and warehouses. Finally, he stopped by a loading dock and motioned everyone to follow him inside. They saw two men waiting with a stretcher to carry the woman inside.

The women and children watched wide-eyed in wonder at the beautiful lounge area they were escorted to. "Welcome to Esmeralda, please make yourself at home, someone will be with you soon," a young woman said. The women sat the children on the floor, they were afraid to let the children sit on the clean furniture with their dusty clothes. The men looked at each other, now wondering if they'd made a mistake bringing the woman to Falu.

Falu was surprised to hear that someone had found the woman who resembled the one on the posters they sent out two years ago. When they uncovered her, he was astonished. "Who is she?" He asked, confused, "bring me the men who found her." Falu pulled the blanket off of her, checking out the condition of her clothes.

"It's not her Falu, this is someone else," Max said, puzzled.

"Yeah, but who? We know it's not the Quintanilla woman. I've met her; she is well and very married."

He could read the fear on Henry and Marcus' faces when they walked into his office holding their hats, pale and scared to death. "Mr. Falu, my name is Henry Forman, and this is my brother-in-law Marcus. We travel with our wives and children. We stopped to rest and eat when my son CJ happened upon this young lady in the woods. There was a huge tree branch covering her, and we noticed that her head was bleeding." Falu came from behind his desk and stood in front of them, towering over the two men.

"Oh my God," Dr. Peggy said, "what do we have here?"

"A mystery of some sort… take care of her," Falu said, his voice echoing throughout the office. "What brings you people into my city? And how did you know to bring the girl to me?"

Henry looked at Marcus, "Sir, we are builders by trade," Marcus explained, "We heard that there may be work here, so we decided to take a chance and move to your city. We are just looking to make a living and perhaps a better way of life for our families. We saw the woman's picture on the wall of the post office in our town."

Falu stood with his arms crossed, staring at the two very frightened men. "How do I know you two didn't hurt or rape this woman, and now you want to collect a reward?"

Henry's jaw dropped, he was almost in tears. "Oh my God, no… Sir, I swear on my children, we never touched the woman… she was hurt when we found her… please believe me," he pleaded.

"We have our wives and children with us… we are God-fearing people, please believe us, our intentions are good," Marcus added.

Falu stared at them intensely, "Well, we'll find out after the doctor examines her…" he walked closer to them. "Ricky is going to get you settled for the night… if what you claim is true, then you have nothing to worry about," he turned to Ricky. "Get them fed and make sure they are comfortable for the night." Falu walked away, leaving the two men terrified.

Ricky laughed, trying to put them at ease. "Don't worry about Falu, he just doesn't trust many people. Now follow me, and don't worry, you are our guests for the night."

Ricky ushered the families to the guest rooms. They were so overwhelmed that Rosa started to cry when she walked into the beautiful rose-colored room with light green floral prints. The king-size bed was adorned with oversized pillows in different shapes. "I can't sleep in that bed," she cried.

"Why not, is there something wrong?" Ricky asked, not understanding her reaction.

"Well look at us, we're wearing rags... I must be dreaming. This is a dream," she turned to look at her husband.

"Mrs. Rosa, I understand you're uncomfortable, but please, it would be an insult if you didn't enjoy my cousin's hospitality. The bathroom is through that door if you wish to shower or bathe. Please accept that these are your rooms for today," Ricky gestured. "I will send one of the girls with some clothes for you and the children. The sofa is a sleeper for the two little ones, we will have it set up for them. I'm sure we have plenty of clothes that will suit you. When you are finished, our cook is preparing a nice meal for your family. Take your time and enjoy the evening."

They looked at one another, exploring the stunning room. The children ran into the bathroom with its oversized bathtub. "Look Dad, real soap… and there's hot water too." CJ took his little brother by the hand and filled up the tub with bubbles. Henry laughed, listening to his boys enjoying the water.

Rosa was still afraid. She found a warm robe and pressed it against her cheek. "Well, I guess we can't insult him," she said, making Henry laugh.

Kathy and Marcus enjoyed watching their baby splash in the tub happily. Kathy started to cry. "What's wrong, honey?" he asked concerned, kissing her forehead.

"If we should die tonight, I shall go happily," watching her baby play in the tub." Cassie knocked on the door before entering with an arm full of clothes for them to try on. They were impressed with the quality of clothing and shoes they had to choose from.

"Take what you want, we have plenty. That little one could use some nice things." The baby's blonde hair shined as she cooed, wrapped in the soft oversized towel. "Dinner will be served in fifteen minutes; I hope you enjoy your stay."

Meanwhile, Falu couldn't help but stare at the young woman who lay motionless in the doctor's examination room. "How is she, Dr. Manny?"

"Well, I've done some preliminary testing and an examination on her… she has a mean cut on the back of her head. We did a scan and found nothing broken or any other injuries."

Falu uncovered her to look at the rest of her body, he smiled. "She's tribal…" He examined her closer, "what in God's name is she wearing?"

"I know, I was trying to figure that out myself," Peggy said, as she handed Dr. Manny the vial of blood.

"I'm going to test this… Peggy's going to check her to see if she's been raped. When I get back, we'll do another scan just to make sure we didn't miss anything."

Max joined Falu as he stood by her side. "Man is she hot… but what in hell is she wearing, these are strange clothes for a tribal woman… looks like what the young men wear on a hunt."

"Hey, she would look good wearing a sack of potatoes," Falu said, grinning.

Peggy laughed at the brothers. "You two are thinking with the other head… she's amazing… look at those legs and thighs, oh and don't forget the breasts. I'm sure you haven't overlooked those, and come here," she drew open her eyelids. "They are brown and yes, her hair is really black."

"Damn, damn, damn, she's hot!" Max said. "Falu check her tags to see if you can figure out her name and what tribe she's from."

Falu pulled her sleeve up to check her tag. Every tribal person wore a tattoo on their upper arm. It was a brand to let other tribal members know where they were from. This was done when they are teenagers. "Well, that's strange… hmm, something's missing."

"What do you mean, what's missing," Max asked, he didn't know how to read tribal branding.

"Normally the first line has her tribal name… hmm very befitting, Raven Moon. The second line is her given name: Mia, which should have been a tribal name."

"What does that mean? Was she exiled maybe," Max asked.

Falu shook his head, "I don't know, it could mean they left the community, but not the lifestyle. There could be many reasons."

"Well, I'll tell you what, she has great taste," Dr. Peggy interrupted, "those boots are high quality, store-bought and she's clean… her hair… smell it."

Falu touched it; bringing a strand to his nose, "Hmm, roses… her skin is flawless like a doll…" he picked up her hand and examined her fingers, "she has a callus on her index finger."

"Interesting… I also found this, a small bow with arrows. Oh, and this knife attached to her thigh,' Peggy said smiling, "she's a girl after my own heart, now you two will have to give my girl here some privacy. I'm going to check for semen. Boss, hand me that rape kit over there." Peggy placed her legs in the stirrups and draped the sheet around her.

"You need help," Falu uttered, smiling.

"I don't think so boss… this won't take long," she turned the light on her and adjusted the clamps, but stopped, "oh well, not long at all." The guys were surprised she was done so quickly.

"What happened, you didn't even open the kit thing here," Falu asked, confused.

"Don't have to boss… she's as pure as the driven snow."

"Are you sure? How old do you think she is? More or less…?"

"Falu, I know what I saw, she's a full-grown woman… around her early twenties, and I'm sorry to disappoint you, but she is a virgin."

Falu couldn't help but smile, "That's almost unheard of, in a tribal community, a woman like her, come on. She would have been married by now, have had a baby or two. Hmm, something is not right here," he stared at her, "sweetheart, who are you and where the hell do you come from?"

"I guess we'll find out when she wakes up," Max said. He could see Falu was intrigued with the woman. "So, it's safe to tell our very scared visitors that they are off the hook, since no raped occurred here."

"Yeah… I'll talk to them so they can sleep in peace. I think I scared the shit out of them."

"What else is new, brother. It's a good thing though, people tend to respect you when you scare the shit out of them."

The families enjoyed hot baths and a wonderful meal they provided for them. Nevertheless, the women were still concerned about the young woman they brought with them. Ricky waited for them to finish before he announced that Falu was ready to speak to the men. The men and CJ were ushered back into his office. Falu did a double-take when they walked in, clean-shaven and their new clothes made a big difference. "Please sit, gentlemen," they looked at each other nervously.

"The woman you brought me is not the same person in the poster." Henry looked disappointed. He was really looking forward to the reward money. Falu continued, "I am going to give you the reward anyway… had she not been found, who knows what would have happened to her. We are taking good care of her… now." He threw a bag with twenty gold coins inside to each of them, and tossed a shining gold coin to CJ, his face lit up. "What kind of work do you do?"

"I can frame, drywall, cement. I can do just about everything to build a house. Marcus is a great roofer and electrician. We have a lot of experience, we are just looking for a chance to prove it."

"Alright, tomorrow, take this note to the construction site that bears my name. Find Eli, the foreman, he'll set you up with work and give you a place to live. It's a trailer but they are very nice and comfortable, the community is safe, they even have a school nearby. I'll check up on you in a few weeks to see if you are as good as you say you are."

They couldn't believe their luck, thanking Falu a hundred times for everything. When Henry saw his wife, he started to cry as he showed her the money. She joined him full of tears. "I told you we had to take a chance… now we have jobs and a place to live," Henry explained, breathing a sigh of relief.

"Really?" Rosa laughed with tears, "oh my God, after all this time living in that cramped bus, well I don't know how to act."

"We each have a place to live, and there's a school for CJ. We have more money than we ever had. No more hungry bellies, and my beautiful wife shall have store-bought clothes. We can save some of this money so the kids can get a good education."

Max stared at his big brother, "That was a good thing you did," Max said, "you always amaze me when you show your sensitive side, I'm proud of you."

"Well, it is what our parents would have done; you know Pop was ruthless, but when it came to family and kids, he was a big softy."

"Hmm, you're right. We know the truth about Pop. To the outsiders he was fearsome, but the minute he came through those doors, Mom wore the pants. You will follow in his footsteps one day."

"You are absolutely right Max, but I don't think Pop would have wanted it any different. She ruled at home and he loved it. However, I'll kill you if you tell anyone about my soft side. I can't have you distorting my reputation of a mean ass sonofabitch" Falu said. Max laughed, slapping him on the back.

Dr. Manny returned, carrying the negatives. He held up the x-ray to examine the film when Falu knocked on his door, "Come in, boss."

"So, what do you see? Is she going to be alright?"

"As far as I know, no broken bones, she has a concussion," he took a deep breath, "that's what worries me. I guess we'll see when she finally wakes up, and that won't be until tomorrow possibly. I gave her something for the pain, so she should sleep comfortably until tomorrow. I didn't want her to wake up in the middle of the night confused. Kenny is going to be on guard in case something happens, he's instructed to call me."

"If you need me, just call, I'm going to check on her before I crash for the night," Falu suggested. He stood before the beautiful woman; he couldn't help staring at her. Max watched his brother admiring Mia as she lay motionless. Falu picked up her hand and kissed it. She was like a doll, hair black as night. He was tempted to kiss the sleeping princess.

Falu was a strongly built man, six feet four, with muscles just like his father. Falu ruled the city with fear following in his father's footsteps. His golden blond hair and steel gray eyes sent chills up many spines. His brother Max took after his mother's family, shorter slimmer built with the same coloring. Max watched him with curiosity; he had never seen his brother so fascinated about a woman before. "Ah, what are you up to, bro," Max said, still at the door. Falu smiled and he touched her long hair.

"She's tribal, she intrigues me. You know Max, I met the other woman Brydus when I went to the Inner Cities and I said to myself. That is one lucky sonofabitch, because that woman was gorgeous and now… this beauty falls into my lap."

"Falu, you're not thinking of keeping her are you… she belongs somewhere to someone."

"I know, at least I'll know who she is and who she doesn't belong to… she's not married or engaged."

"How do you know that?"

"Because no tribal man is going to let his woman running around with an outfit like that, you should know that by now. Someone would have laid claim on her even as a young child. Think about it bro, she's natural born. Men in a tribal community would have claims on her from birth. Once a couple is committed it's like their married. Now, as for me… I kind of like the rugged sexy type, a strong woman."

"My brother, I know what kind of women you like, a little slutty and very sexy. Let's face it, you're a pig," they chuckled.

"I am who I am, I can't help it. I enjoy women." "You know I tease you, but it's not your fault women flock to you the way they do."

He turned to Max surprised, "Max, you're so full of shit. You get laid more than anyone I know."

"So, I learned from you, big brother."

"Sure, blame me for your whorish ways. Love 'em and leave 'em, Max."

Falu continued to stare at her. He bent down to trace her beautiful features. "Max, is it possible to feel a strange attraction to a person you've just met? I haven't even heard her voice to see if it's a voice you want to listen to forever. She's beautiful, Max a piece of the past, and she's here."

Max stood by his brother and could see what his brother saw. The need to want and be loved. "You know what Pop taught us, he said when he met our mother he knew she was the one for him. Mom wasn't a tribal woman but, yet he fell in love with her."

"Hmm, maybe you're right, but you have to admit Mom was special, and Pop adored her. So, my little Raven Moon, I guess we'll find out more about you tomorrow," he kissed her, excited to know more.

The girls attacked him the moment he opened the door, asking him a million questions about the injured girl. Falu only laughed at their curiosity and assured them he didn't know much of anything about her.

Ivette and Tina waited for Betty to finish with Falu. They were anxious to hear what he said and how he felt. Ivette was nodding off when Betty finally returned to their room. "Did he say anything else?" Ivette asked, jumping up from the bed. Betty closed the door quietly; she could not contain her excitement.

"I think he's interested, all I could get out of him was her name… Mia, and it was the way he said it that led me to believe he's very interested."

"Wouldn't that be awesome, he's tribal and she is too. They would make such a perfect couple," Tina said, dancing around the room.

"But we don't know if she's staying," Ivette added.

"It doesn't matter. He will follow her wherever she goes. I can tell when I saw her," Betty said, agreeing with Tina. "You never know… she may be the one, let's keep our fingers crossed girls," Tina said, crossing both hands.

"I think she's the one… I can feel it," Ivette said smiling."

Falu tossed and turned all night, thinking about the young woman sleeping peacefully one floor below him. The next morning, Falu was in the worst mood ever. He had a room full of contractors bidding on a construction project. He couldn't believe the amount of applications and proposals he had received in such a short time. Another building project was ready to break ground, and the word was out that he was still looking for a construction company to manage the work.

"What the hell is all this shit," he bellowed, "Dammit Ricky, have you looked at some of this garbage? How am I supposed to trust people with such a huge project if they can't even spell proposal," he threw it across the room.

"Hey, calm down cousin, I just got these. I didn't have time to go through them and sort them out. What do you want me to do with these people waiting to see you?" Falu went to pour himself coffee but there was none. He slammed the door to his office. Max stood by his office door. "What's wrong with you, bro? You're barking louder than usual," Max said, knowing Falu hated having so many strangers in his estate. Falu ran his hand through his hair in frustration. "You need a damn secretary Falu, someone who will keep all your appointments and put all your shit in order," Max commented.

Falu turned to Ricky who was still waiting for his orders. "I'm sorry, Ricky, look man, I'm just a little on edge about this project, and there's no damn coffee!" They laughed at his outburst. "I'll be alright, it's just me bitching."

"If you had a secretary, maybe you'd have fresh coffee when you wanted some," Max said, throwing another jab at his idea.

"Yeah maybe that sweet young thing in Dr. Manny's office… you never know she may be looking for a job," Ricky said, trying to lighten the mood.

"Sure, then this place would really go to shit. I'd be so busy banging her every time I get a chance," Falu said, laughing at the visual.

"See, that's why you scare the crap out of women, you're a vile pig with only one thing on your polluted mind," Max added.

"I'm just stating a fact. I wouldn't be able to keep my hands off her… at least I'm an honest pig," they laughed, "all right, Ricky I need you to call the guard house and tell Tony not to let anyone pass. If they have a proposal, they can leave it with him. We'll collect them later. I have this blueprint to finish and I would like to finish that today. Max, you're in charge of interviewing the contractors. You know what I'm looking for, they're waiting in the library. And dammit call down for some coffee."

"All right, I'll interview these fools and look through these proposals. I'll set aside the ones that have a solid plan. Oh, I had ordered more coffee before you came in barking away," Max said, "but in the meantime… think about what I said… a secretary."

Falu shuts himself off from the world when he's working on a project. He kept trying to focus on the task at hand, but he always ended up thinking about the girl. Falu had a fantastic mind and had a way of working out things in his head. The blueprints he composed were like second nature to him. The last visit with Jesse Quintanilla turned out to be the best yet. He was surprised when Jesse invited him into a private meeting. That's when Jesse discovered just how valuable his talents were and how important Falu was to New Orleans and the regrowth of the country.

Falu took a break; his eyes were tired from lack of sleep which made him concentrate harder. He picked up the 8 by 10 picture of his parents to remind him why he was working so hard. He remembered fondly when Max took a picture of his parents. Like always, they couldn't keep their hands off each other. He'd never seen two people so in love.

It was a beautiful summer day, the whole family was there, and Falu had just finished school and was preparing to study aboard. Max caught them kissing, sitting on a huge rock by the lake. Max surprised them by taking the picture. His father's arms were around his mother's waist, and she had her arms around his neck. They smiled when they saw Max. He took the picture, and that was one of many family get-togethers he never wanted to forget.

For two years, he couldn't bear to look at any pictures of his parents, hating the fact that God took his parents too soon. His mother died in such a horrifying way. Her murder almost turned him into a bitter man. It was then when he saw himself in the mirror and realized that he had to see his parents, dreams come true.

"Well Pop, we're on our way… this is for you."

Chapter 2: The Awakening

Dr. Manny and Peggy went about their daily routine. He used his flashlight to check Mia's pupils and see if there were any changes in her since the night they bought her in.

"I checked her vitals; they are really good. She's stable; when do you think she'll come around?" Peggy asked, making a notation in her chart.

"I'll give it a few more hours. There is a drug I can give her to bring her around, but I really hate using it, so I'm giving her some time to come around on her own."

Peggy continued to put things away. Falu and Max stopped in to see how she was doing. Staring at her as she slept, Falu was concerned. He had worked all morning but couldn't get her out of his thoughts.

Peggy went to walk some specimens downstairs to the lab. When she returned, Mia was sitting on the edge of the bed; her head was down, and then she turned to glance at Peggy. She stood up with a look of panic on her face.

"Oh shit," Dr. Manny said, who was right behind Peggy.

"Hi, I'm Dr. Peggy," she walked towards her slowly.

Mia looked around for a way out; she sprung toward the open door before Peggy had a chance to finish her sentence. Manny tried to stop her, but she tossed him aside like a small child. "Call Falu!" he yelled to Peggy as he followed Mia down the hallway.

Peggy appeared at Falu's door out of breath, "Come quickly, she's up and going crazy. She ran upstairs."

Mia's mind was racing as she tried to open doors to find an escaped exit. She flew up the stairs to the third floor, hearing voices echoing from the bottom floor. Meanwhile, Falu and Max were following behind. Mia ran like a wild woman, hair flying and eyes confused. Her heart was pounding so fast that she felt as if her head would explode. She ran head-on into Raymond's chest, one of Falu's guards, falling back on the floor. He struggled with her, but he underestimated her strength and went headfirst into a glass door. Angelo tried to stop her by trying to kick her legs from under her. But she was quick; she flew into him and rammed her fist into his nose, spattering blood all over the place. The girls screamed when Mia burst open the doors to their suite. She looked around and found a broomstick and started to swing it like an expert. All Mia saw was a giant man coming toward her. She pointed it at Falu as he crept towards her.

"Take it, easy baby, we're not going to hurt you, cálmate, nadie te lastimará, mi amor." Falu continued to close the distance between them. Mia swung at him, and the broom broke as it crashed against his arm.

Without a weapon, she looked for a way to escape, saw the double doors to a balcony, and struggled to open the heavy doors. When she looked back, Falu was coming toward her again. Finally, she opened the door, climbing onto the edge. Mia looked down at the swimming pool below, thinking twice about jumping. "Stop! Porfavor, nadia te vas se dano," (*please! stop, no one is going to hurt you*), Falu shouted as he grabbed her from behind in a bear hug. Mia struggled with him, elbowing him repeatedly in his ribs. He had her around the neck, and with his legs, he tried to pin them together to keep her from kicking him. "Dr. Where the hell is that sedative? She's killing me," Falu cried, not wanting to put any more pressure on her neck since she was struggling feverishly.

Dr. Manny managed to get her thigh still enough to inject her with the sedative. Falu was sweating hard, watching her slowly close her eyes as she finally stopped struggling and went limp. "Damn it to hell," he yelled, feeling the pain in his ribs as he carried her downstairs.

"What in God's name is she made of," Peggy said, attending Angelo, who was bleeding from a broken nose. The whole estate was reeling about Mia; they wanted to know who this strange woman was.

When Mia woke up, she was strapped to the sofa in Falu's bedroom. Falu was raising hell as Dr. Manny tried to bind his throbbing ribs. "Man! That shit hurts. This bitch hits like a man," Falu yelled, cursing up a storm.

"Well, you're lucky there not broken," he replied.

"Holy shit, man, they feel like it."

Mia made her presence known, "Sueltame cerdo!" (*release me, pig*), she screamed in Spanish.

"Did she just call me a pig? How did she know," Falu said, laughing at his situation.

"Alright… now try not to put any more pressure on them," Dr. Manny advised.

Mia began to rattle her handcuffs and yell at the strangers, "Sueltame bestia!" *(release me, beast!)*

"I think she's talking to you, Falu," Max said; he chuckled. Falu ordered everyone out; slowly, he walked toward her holding his ribs… Mia had stopped struggling and lay quietly.

"Hables espanol?" he said. Mia rolled her eyes in anger.

"Let go of me, you idiot!"

"Oh, so we speak English now, that's interesting, hm."

"Why do you have me tied up like an animal," she said angrily. He knelt next to her.

"Maybe if you stop acting like an animal, I wouldn't treat you like one," he uncuffed her, letting her sit up.

"What is your name, and where do you come from?" He watched as her eyes filled up with tears and go blank for a moment.

"I don't know… I can't remember," she looked around to see if something was familiar to her, "are we related… who are you to me?"

"So, you don't remember anything," he asked again.

Mia started to cry, "I don't know… I don't even know my name," tears rolled down her pretty face.

Falu felt sorry for her, "You're a tribal woman. Your name is on your arm; we call it tagging," she looked at the marking on her arm and couldn't understand it. "Your name is Mia, does the name ring a bell?" she shook her head no, "Your tribal name is… Raven Moon… your given name is Mia," he smiled. "You were hurt; that could have something to do with your memory." Falu could see her getting angry. He sat back on his bed, feeling the increasing pain in his ribs. "My name is Falu, I am the overlord of this district and this city, and you are in my home. You belong to me now."

"I belong to no one!" she yelled, making herself clear, "if you are not my husband, then I am a free woman," she jumped up, pushing him back into the bed, racing out of the room. She found the staircase. Mia was terrified and confused. Her mind was cloudy.

Falu radioed Max, "Damnit, Max, she's on the run again coming your way."

"I'm on my way," Max raced up the top of the stairs and waited for her to come toward him. She could feel the pounding in her chest as she ran down the stairs. The pain in her head was overwhelming. When she reached the second landing, she stopped…slowly walking toward the mirrored wall. She reached out to touch the mirror, looked at her image and fainted.

Max reached her first, "what happened," Falu asked, picking her up and throwing her over his shoulder, feeling the pressure in his ribs.

"That was the weirdest thing; she just stopped when she reached the mirror like she'd never seen herself in a mirror before."

"That's impossible. Tribal communities have the best of everything; the women especially are spoiled. There must be another reason, something may have triggered her memory, and it caused an overload."

"You're probably right; she had a blank look on her face."

"I'll tell you what, if she hits me in the ribs one more time, I'll bust her in the jaw. I will have to handcuff her to the bed before she hurts herself even more," Falu said, "call doc so she can check her over."

Falu sat in the dark, waiting for her to wake up. He felt her stir in the darkness, "Mia, I know you are scared, but I'm tired of your shit. You have to trust me. I can't let you leave the estate… first of all, because you don't know who you are, and this city will eat you alive because a woman like you would bring a lot of money to some unscrupulous people who would sell you to the highest bidder for sex. You may be strong and able to fight, but you can't whip everyone's ass."

"You're just saying that to scare me."

"If you don't believe me, you can ask the girls… you'll be staying in their room. They have no reason to lie to you."

"You can't keep me here," she replied sarcastically.

"Listen to me, Mia. I will keep your ass handcuffed to a bed if I have to. You can do it the easy way or the hard way; it's your choice!"

"What will you do with me then?"

He smiled in the dark, "Mia, I bought you for forty pieces of gold. You figure it out... you belong to me," he whispered, "now until I decide what to do with you, the girls will take care of you."

Mia was defiant, but the girls embraced her. They fixed a small area in the room so she had her own space. Mia thought hard about her situation; however, when the girls began to tell their stories, she became frightened. Betty brought her some food. She hadn't realized how hungry she was until she ate the sandwich and drank the green tea.

The girls smiled and tried to make her feel welcome and comfortable. Her bed had brown silk sheets with a lovely crimson comforter to match. They took one of Falu's t-shirts for her to sleep in. That night they stayed up curious about the dark beauty. But Mia had a difficult time sleeping, wondering who she was. Her mind was racing until the early morning when she finally fell into a deep well-needed sleep.

"Wake up, sleepyhead, it's a bright and beautiful morning, sugar… breakfast is served."

Mia woke up shy and timid. She could hear them talk and giggling from the outer room and couldn't resist the aroma of fresh brew coffee, sausage, eggs, toast and oatmeal.

"Good morning, sugar, come and join us," Tina said, waving her over. Mia found herself in the middle of gossip; they laughed and giggled, making her feel part of the group.

"You are the talk of the town Mia,' Betty said; she was a beautiful redhead with pretty green eyes.

"Why, am I the talk of the town?" Mia asked, confused with their statement.

"Well, it's not every day we have a tribal princess in our midst, a fighting one to boot," Ivette explained, "you hurt some of the guys when you tried to leave yesterday."

Mia looked down at her plate, "I'm sorry; I didn't know what I was doing. Will I be punished?"

"Don't worry, honey, it happens. People get hurt all the time, but Falu was in so much pain we couldn't do anything last night," Tina added, "poor baby, I felt sorry for him."

"So that means he'll be really horny tonight," Ivette replied.

Mia almost choked on a piece of toast. "You have sex with him… are you his wives," Mia was confused. The girls couldn't help but giggle at how naïve she was.

"Sugar, we don't mean to laugh at you. I guess we should enlighten you about our situation here. We're all his girls; we take turns having sex with him," Tina explained.

Mia shook her head in disbelief, "So you don't mind that he sleeps with all of you… what kind of place is this?"

"We're his kept women… it beats life in the street or getting abused by strangers," Betty added.

They spent the rest of the morning reciting horror stories of what happens to beautiful women that have no protection. Women who are forced to go into the brothels to make a living. Mia was surprised by their personal stories and found herself crying along with them. She realized that Falu was telling the truth, that life outside the estate was dangerous. Especially when she didn't even know who she was or where she came from.

Mia tried really hard to understand the girls and those around her. They set up sessions with a therapist to help her to regain her memory. Dr. Manny and Peggy saw her for the headaches. The first two weeks were crazy for her. She refused to come down for dinner even when Falu ordered her to. But he was extremely busy to deal with her and decided to address the matter later. The girls loved teaching her new things; every day, there was something to teach her that would surprise them. The first time they put her in front of a full-length mirror, she started to cry. "Is that really me," she touched her face.

"That's all of you, sugar; now you see why the men stare at you." Mia stood five feet eight, long black hair, a beautiful oval shape, huge brown eyes, and very well defined lips. Her camel-colored skin was flawless, with strong muscular legs. Thighs and full breasts that would tantalize any man. Her fanny was like steel that was only enhanced by her small waist. The girls laughed as Mia tried to walk in high heels. They helped her walk in heels that were too big for her. But Mia enjoyed trying to dance to the Latin and soul beats. Ivette taught her some steps, and to their surprise, she caught on right away.

"Come on, girl, shake what the good Lord gave you, woohoo, go ahead," Ivette shouted. They were singing and dancing so loudly they didn't realize Falu had been watching them for a while, enjoying the view. When Tina noticed him standing at the door with his arms crossed, she ran to turn the music off.

"Hey… how long have you been standing there," she asked nervously.

"Long enough," he cocked his head to the side as he focused on Mia, who was frozen in place. "What in the world are you wearing, woman?" he asked, frowning.

"Ah, she doesn't have any clothes of her own, so we tried to dress her in some of ours," Ivette said. She couldn't figure out whether he was angry or just tired.

"She looks ridiculous. Gino is coming tomorrow morning; make sure she gets everything she needs," he looked at the girls and shook his head. "You girls get whatever you want. We'll make a trip to the city this weekend and have some clothes made for her."

"Thank you, Falu; we'll make sure she gets what she needs," Betty said excitedly. They loved to shop.

"Mia, I need to speak to you," Falu said sternly; she followed him into his room. He couldn't help but stare at her breasts squeezed in Ivette's shirt. "I'm sorry I've been neglecting you. I've been really busy. Tina will take care of you. Make sure you let her know what you need… you know, girlie stuff," she looked away when he took off his shirt. She tried not to look at him, noticing the fading black and blue marks on his side. His muscular chest and shoulders rippled as he moved.

"Can I ask you something," she said.

"What can I do for you, Mia?" he replied, smiling, seeing the reaction to his naked chest. She stepped back against the door, "Well, I feel as if I should be doing something around here. I'm not one of your… girls or a servant… I was just wondering what my purpose is here."

He smiled, closing the distance between them, "So, do you want me to tell you the truth or make up some story you want to hear," he chuckled.

She was annoyed by the smug look on his face, "What do you mean the truth? Of course, I want to know the truth," she said argumentatively.

He pinned her against the door, coming painfully close to her face, "The truth is that you will be my woman…" he whispered in her ear, "eres Mia, you will be mine."

She pushed him back, "You're insane. I don't know what you've been drinking, but it's making you dizzy."

He grabbed her wrist. "Think what you like, Mia; you will be mine…" he kissed her hand. Mia tried to control the butterflies in her stomach, not realizing how much he affected her. She pulled away from him and rushed out of his room, listening to his laughter as she slammed the door.

"I hate him!" she yelled, going into her room.

"That's not good. Tina, go talk to her," Betty pleaded.

Mia was lying down on the bed when Tina sat next to her. "Hey sugar, don't let what he says shake you up; Falu is… well, he's really sweet. He is a powerful man, and sometimes he could be a little forceful… but he has a good heart."

"He's so full of himself, and it burns me up. I just want to punch him in the face."

Tina tried not to laugh, "He likes you, Mia, he looks at you and sees a strong tribal woman, and I think that's what he likes about you."

"I don't like the way he makes me feel… I get this feeling in my stomach and nervous… he looks at me like I'm a buffet table."

"Well, he is a fine-looking man. With a great muscular body. Woo, it's natural to feel a little gritty when you're near him."

"How do you do it? How do you have sex with him! Do you love him?"

Tina searched for the right words, "I do what I can to fulfill his needs. I love him because he doesn't look at us like whores. To him, we are his girls, and he takes great care of us. Falu has never beaten us. In fact, it's been the other way around. If someone tries to hurt us or disrespect any one of us, he is the first one to go after them. So, we feel very safe and guarded with him. It is an honor to be one of his girls. Women all over envy us, and they have every right to be. We live like queens in this palace. We are not denied anything. So, if I can comfort him and keep him company for a while, it is so little for what he has given us in return. He gave us life, and he is trying to protect you from those horrors out there, especially for someone as unique as yourself."

"I'm sorry, I don't mean to complain. I'm just confused. I don't like it when he comes near me. But I guess I can put up with his nonsense for a while," she smiled. Tina knew what Falu saw in the beautiful woman. She had no idea how she affected men and how powerful her sex appeal was. But her innocence was written all over her face. The other girls listened at the door.

"Look, you can ask us anything. We just want you to see what we see," Tina said, brushing the hair away from her face. "We are here to help you, and someday you will regain your memory, I promise."

"I am grateful. You all have been wonderful to me. I couldn't ask for better friends…and teachers," she laughed.

"That's all right, sugar; we love having you here, don't we, girls?"

"Yes, it is our pleasure," Betty added.

Falu's Bedroom

Tina laid in Falu's arms after sex; sometimes, he would cuddle with the girls before returning to their room. Tina tried to make him relax, running her finger along the curve of his chest; he always made them feel important, not just like sexual objects.

"Falu… do you know anything about Mia? She doesn't seem to know too much of the world… when she looked in the mirror, she started to cry."

"She's a tribal woman… from an Afro-Latin community or both, I believe."

"Could you be, or could she be related to you?"

He nuzzled her neck, holding her from behind, playing with her breast. "She is not my kin. I know all my family members, even those who lived in other communities. My father kept us well educated about who we were and where we came from."

"Are they still around? I don't remember anyone visiting you."

"When my father died, my uncle moved our people west. They have huge vineyards… where do you think I get all that great wine from. Anyway, back to Mia… she's a mystery, but once her memory is restored, I can find out where she's from. I will seduce her with my charm."

Tina laughed, "I envy you, Falu. You know your family history. The only thing I remember about my family is how poor we were and how mother worked herself into an early grave."

"You know Tina, I will always care for you and the other girls," Tina kissed his cheek and smiled. Falu was such a handsome man, but his serious nature made his features hard. However, when he smiled, he could bewitch any woman with his beautiful, brilliant smile.

"We like her a lot, but there is more to her than we know."

"I know, and I can't wait to find out... take care of her for me, you know I'm so busy; show her the ropes. Get her whatever she wants. I want to keep her happy."

"Don't worry; she's in good hands. We call her our little sister."

"No doubt, I almost laughed when she tried to wear high heels and dance salsa, it was cute. It will be to my advantage if she regains her memory."

"Falu, what if she's married?"

"She's not married; believe me, I'm a man. She wouldn't have made it to the wedding bed a virgin. She is a big mystery, and that's what scares me. But as long as she's in our care, I think she'll be alright."

"She's a beautiful woman, but we'll turn her into a goddess."

The girls watched as Mia slept, they knew Falu liked her, and he had plans for them. "We have to prepare her for him. Teach her how to dress, dance and be flirty; it's like she's been living in another world all her life," Tina said, speaking in a loud whisper.

"Did he say anything else? I tried to get something out of him yesterday, but all he did was laugh at me," Ivette frowned.

"I know she's the one. They are from the same world. She is strong just like him," Betty chimed, "somehow, we have to show her not to be so nervous around him."

"We have a lot to teach our little sister, our beautiful little sister. I can't wait," Tina said, smiling, "when we're done with her, he'll be like a puppy dog waiting to be petted."

"I hear you, girl, just like a puppy, and we all know how he loves to be petted." Ivette laughed.

Chapter 3: The Girls

The girls were up early the next morning planning for the day. Mia always seemed to sleep later because of the pain medicine she took for the headaches. They gathered together outside on the balcony. Ivette closed the double door. "I have a plan. I was thinking about it all last night," Tina smiled.

"Well, spit it out. She is the one, right," Betty asked excitedly.

Tina sipped casually on her coffee, smiling. "I am 100% sure she is the one."

"Are you sure? Did he say so? You didn't say anything last night?" Ivette asked curiously.

"I know, but I had a chance to remember some of the things he said. The way he said her name like very endearing; the man was hooked. He has plans for Mia, and so do we. We all agree to prepare our little sister for him, right," Tina said, finishing her coffee.

"Oh hell yeah," Betty interjected.

"By the time we're done with her, he won't recognize her. Ivette, you work on her dancing; you know how much Falu loves to dance."

"I have a great idea. I'll get him to put a pole in the middle room, men love that stuff, and with the sweet booty she has, it will drive him up the wall," Ivette said, moving her hips, "yeah baby."

"That's a great idea, honey, I'll work on her clothes, and Betty, you're good with make-up. We will sex her up and turn her into his sex kitten," Tina laughed. "It is time he has someone to love, and she is the one who will fill that position. She just doesn't know it yet."

"Then we have some work to do," Betty said, giving each other a high five.

The door swings open, and sleepy Mia walks out into the balcony, hair messy in a sexy way. "Did I miss the party," she said, eyes still half shut. The girls looked at each other and laughed.

"Sugar, you're just in time," Tina replied.

Gino laughed as the girls emptied his truck full of lovely women's garments. He always did well when he came to the Esmeralda Estate, but today the girls went through everything, even the sexy lingerie he's been trying to peddle. They walked out with an arm full of clothes for Mia. Tina was satisfied with their purchases grinning at the other girls.

Mia was excited about all the pretty clothes the girls picked out for her. She was almost in tears when Ivette surprised her with a music pod full of over ten thousand songs in English and Spanish. "What is it," she exclaimed.

"It had recorded music, sweetie, songs of love, to dance and party; here these are the headphones so you can hear them."

"It's small," her eyes lit up when she heard the first song, "this is great, thank you."

The girls made her try on the clothes they bought for her, purposely picking out clothes that were a little provocative and revealing. But when it came to the baby doll lingerie, she was confused. Tina insisted she model for them. "Come on, sugar, move that booty; that's what men like."

Mia tried not to fall off her heels as she paced around the room in a red peek-a-boo baby doll outfit. The girls cheered her on, caught up in the moment until she heard Falu clapping, grinning from ear to ear. Mia froze for a second until she ran into the bathroom to cover up.

"Hey baby, where are you going," he cried as she slammed the door behind her. His eyes were dancing with lust when he saw how beautiful she looked half-naked. The girls enjoyed her embarrassment. Falu stood outside the bathroom teasing her. "Hey baby, come on out and model for me; I want to see what I'm paying for," he laughed; he could hear her causing up a storm on the other side of the door.

"Go to hell, Diablo!" she yelled. Falu was amused, and the girls began to fuel the situation.

"Come out, sugar - big daddy's waiting for you!" Tina called out to her. Mia pulled open the door.

"Can a girl get some privacy around here," she slipped past him, covering herself with a towel and locked herself in her room.

"I rather enjoyed that," he said, teasing her. Mia leaned against the door, her face flush, embarrassed. She wanted to slap him. He always looked at her as if he could see through her clothes.

For weeks the girls worked with Mia, and she enjoyed having the girls around. They were teaching her how to dance, and she spent hours listening to her music pod. At night, she would fall asleep to music, and when she began to sing, they soon realized that she had a great voice.

Mia felt lost; she tried not to think about Falu and his strange ways, wondering why every night one of the girls would go to him, and it didn't bother them that he slept with other women. She was puzzled at the relationship they shared.

Tina took a shower after being was Falu; she sat at the edge of her bed rubbing lotion on her arms. Mia stared at Tina curiously, "Tina, does it bother you that he had sex with all of you...? I mean, why he doesn't marry one of you."

Tina tried to make her understand, "Sugar, Falu has a very strong sexual appetite; we share him because we have a contract with him."

"A contract, now that is bizarre? But doesn't it bother you? You girls are so beautiful."

"Falu is a super lover, and we're not the only women he sleeps with. He has tons of women after him. Many of who want to marry him to become the mistress of this estate."

"But Falu is no fool; he knows what he wants," Ivette said, joining the conversation.

"I'm sorry, but when I have a boyfriend, he better not be looking at any other woman," Mia stated; the girls giggled.

"That a girl Mia; fight for your man," Ivette cheered.

"I will kick his ass, whoever he is," she laughed, "I'm just being silly. I don't know anything about love, I think."

Mia fought the way he made her feel whenever he came near her. He was very generous, and the power he excised made her stomach do flips. It also made her angry with herself for feeling the way she did. At night her dreams were about him, a sexual dream that made her wake up feeling embarrassed that he had invaded her dreams.

She began to spend more time in the gym. The estate had a great gym with weights and machines, workout bags and even a sparing ring. She took advantage of it and found that she felt better when she finished a good workout. Little did she know that Falu was watching her with hungry lust; he purposely stayed away from her, afraid he would take advantage of her while she was still sick. He'd reminded himself of the argument he had with his brother about seducing the beautiful Mia.

Every Thursday night, the gang would meet to relax and play a few hands of poker at the nightclub that was located in the basement. Five thousand square feet designed with tables, three full bars, pool tables and other games. There was a stage for bands and a nice size dance floor. Falu wanted a safe place for his men to unwind. Then there was the woman who constantly fought to get an invitation. Most of his men bought their own women, but plenty of single men were always looking for a good time. He also contracted musical groups and bands to come and perform. There were people knocking on his door to entertain his men, and with a good word from Falu, their careers would soar.

Falu looked forward to his poker night. It gave him a chance to catch up with the gossip train that goes on in his estate. Ricky and Dr. Eli were the first to set up; also joining them was Max. Falu was always the last one to set up his chips. They played for real money, and most of the time, Falu was the big loser. But he didn't care; he just enjoyed relaxing and the company.

"Okay, bitches, I'm not leaving this table until I win back all my money from last week," Falu said smiling, lighting a blunt.

"You say that every week and you always lose, brother," Max said, looking at three of a kind in his hand.

"That's because you douchebags cheat, don't think I haven't noticed," Falu said, passing the blunt to Max.

"You're so full of shit, man, you get buzzed and forget how to play," Ricky said, laughing. He was already feeling the effect of the cannabis.

"Yeah… I'm going to be watching you two… I trust doc, but you two assholes… hm, I have my eyes on both of you," Falu said, losing to his brother again.

"You're not concentrating, my brother… your mind is on sweet Mia, and you can't think straight," Max chuckled, "keep thinking about her; I'll keep taking your money."

"Falu, my man, he's right. You do have Mia on the brain; why don't you just pop that cherry and get it over with,' Ricky teased.

"What's wrong with you dickhead," Max said defensive, "she's a tribal woman. She should be treated with respect, Ricky. Falu, you can't possibly be thinking of forcing yourself on her," he looked at Falu, who rolled his eyes.

"I don't want to force myself on her but damn it – she's so hot, I got a peek at those juicy tits, and I almost lost it."

"Your brother's right Falu," Dr. Eli explained, "I am aware the woman is very beautiful, but you can't force yourself on her while she's sick, and she'll lose respect for you... unless it's just a piece of ass you want, then it doesn't matter how she feels."

"I can't believe you guys think I'm this unfeeling asshole. That I have no restraints when it comes to a hot, sweet sizzling, smoking woman."

"Falu, you are my brother, and I love you, but you can be a big asshole, especially with women."

"Why would you say that? So, I enjoy women, so what," Falu said, lighting another blunt and passing it to Ricky.

"Bro, promise me you'll wait until she well; she deserves that much," Max pleaded.

Falu grabbed Max by the neck playfully. "You remind me of mom; she would have said something like that. I promise I won't force myself on her, but... I will try to seduce her because..." he paused for a minute, "she will be the mother of my children." Everyone was shocked.

"Are you serious? Did you just say the m-word... are you fallen for her?" Max asked excitedly.

"I'm saying... I'm in love with the sexy bitch. I can't get her out of my mind... but you're right. I want a willing partner. I love the way she's playing hard to get; she calls me the devil, and when she speaks to me in Spanish, I just get tingly all over, and it doesn't matter if she's cussing me out. It just turns me on. I wonder where she gets those terrible ideas from," they roared with laughter.

"Then it's settled… you will respect her and not rape her."

"God, baby brother, I have plenty of women. I don't need to rape her; you need to stop smoking; it's getting to you. When did I ever have to rape a woman?"

"That's right, you have plenty of women hanging from your dick, and you have the girls," Max said, satisfied with his promise. Max liked Mia and didn't want her to have the wrong impression about his brother.

"I think you made a wise decision; Mia is in a delicate emotional state right now. I have a strong feeling she will regain her memory; it just may take a little time," Dr. Eli said, expressing himself as a professional.

"Well, I hope so because my balls turn blue every time I'm close to her. She had gotten under my skin, and all I want to do is plunge my charley deep between those beautiful firm thighs."

"And this said by the man who is running this city, cousin, you are one of a kind." They laughed. It was a great night as they continued to enjoy the evening. Falu dragged himself upstairs and called one of the girls into his room.

The girls continue to help Mia adjust to life at the estate; she would get frustrated sometimes and longs to be alone away from all the craziness. She enjoyed the view from one of the terraces that are located off the West wing. From there, she can see all the activities going on Bourbon Street.

The cool night breeze felt good against her face as she tried to imagine herself walking through the farmer's market and visiting some of the stores. She was so preoccupied she didn't hear Falu when she came behind her. She jumped at his presence. "Damnit, you scared the shit out of me," she yelled at him.

"What are you doing out here? It's after midnight." Falu laughed, but he could tell she was annoyed that he interfered with her peace.

She rolled her eyes at him. "I didn't know I had a curfew," she replied with sarcasm.

"So here I am trying to spark up a nice conversation, and you're giving me attitude."

That was her defense mechanism when it came to Falu, "I'm sorry you just have this way of bringing out the worst in me."

"Oh yeah, and why is that," he inched closer to her. He touched her arm with his finger, and she began to feel hot.

"Please don't do that; it bothers me."

He kissed her neck. He felt her stiffen. "So is that better," he said, teasing her. She moved away from him. When Falu put his hand behind her neck and pulled her to him, she was shocked, not expecting him to come closer. She was frozen in place, trying to recover. But before she could react, he forced his mouth on hers parting her lip to send a bolt of electricity through her body. He held her in a steal grip until he let she had to come up for air.

"Oh God, what are you trying to do? What if I'm engaged or something, and here you are taking liberties with me, what would I tell my intended."

"You don't have to tell him anything because if he comes near you, I'll break his neck," he wouldn't let her go, "he'd have to come through me first," he released her. Mia could still feel the effects of his kiss on her lips.

"You're ridiculous. What makes you think I want you to kiss me?"

"Your mouth says no, but your body doesn't lie, and those lips of yours are made for kissing, and I intend to use them… a lot."

"I don't want to argue with you, and I don't want to be one of your girls, waiting and begging you to take me to bed to have sex, so go rub your dick somewhere else."

"Oh really," he tried not to laugh, "enlighten me, what do you want?"

"Well, I don't know what I want, but it's not you or this crazy arrangement you have with them," he corned her by the ledge.

"You don't know anything about the contracts we have together. They serve me, and I take care of them and their needs. They want nothing, and they pleasure me whenever I want… but you're different, Mia. We will have no contract between us because none will be needed. You may not be part of that club, but you will share my bed and all that comes with it."

Mia's mouth dropped. "You're that sure," she asked boldly.

"Mia, I guarantee it, you will be my woman, and you will come to me… willingly… get used to it, sweetheart."

Mia was so angry she pulled away from him and escaped towards her room; when she tried to slip into her room without waking the others, they heard her muffled cries.

Tina tried to comfort her. "Sugar, what's wrong? You can tell me, honey… I hate seeing you so unhappy."

Mia wiped her eyes, "I feel like a fool; I don't know why I let him get to me."

"To whom are you referring, sweetie?" Tina continued to caress her hair.

"The beast… he kissed me and… I started to feel strange."

"Oh, he kissed you," Ivette asked, popping her head up, "you said he kissed you. How?"

"What difference does it make? He kissed me, and… it wasn't bad, and I'm so angry with myself for not kicking him in the nuts." The girls laughed at her.

"What did you expect, sugar… you're beautiful. Why wouldn't he want to kiss you?" Tina asked.

"Wait until you get a taste of his joystick," Betty said, teasing, "you'll pass out."

"Stop teasing her, Betty… look, don't feel betrayed; enjoy it, your young body is just reacting to pleasure, sex is very pleasing, and his really good at it," Tina wanted to assure her what she felt was normal.

"I don't want to seem like a baby; I'm just so confused and all these feelings… I hate it when he touches me."

"Hey Mia, don't worry, soon you will get your memory back, and you and Falu can work things out… okay, sweetie. Now go to sleep; tomorrow's another day," Ivette tried to comfort her.

But sleep didn't come easy to Mia; she could still feel the force of his kisses on her lips and how her own body reacted to his closeness. The hard chest muscles and the steal grip as he held her in place. What kind of devil was this, she thought. Why did she melt at his boyish smile and lose control in his closeness?

The morning came really fast; the aroma from breakfast forced her up and out of bed. The girls were already on the second cup of coffee when she dragged herself to the table.

"Good morning, bright eyes... you look like shit this morning," Betty commented, looking at her bloodshot eyes.

"I didn't get much sleep last night," she tried to force a smile.

"Well, after breakfast, we were going to go swimming. Maybe that would wake you up; it's a beautiful day," Ivette said, "I'll let you use one of my bathing suits."

Ricky knocked on the door, interrupting their breakfast. He walked into the terrace where they were having breakfast. "Damnit, I thought maybe I'd catch you girls naked or something," he teased.

"Don't you wish, you pervert!" Betty teased.

"Well, I'm just the messenger; Falu wants to see Mia in his office as soon as possible."

"I'm not going to his office," she wrapped her robe tighter.

"Hey, I'm not going to be the one to tell him that if you don't come to him, he will come to you, and it won't be pretty. He threw his hand up.

Mia becomes frustrated, "Alright! Tell him I'll be down as soon as I get dressed."

"Good girl, we don't want to upset the boss, do we. See you, girls, later, maybe next time, hm, you girls can put on a show for me," Ivette threw a pillow at him.

Mia had to calm herself before she entered his office. He was all business-like when he looked at her. He grabbed her and led her down the back stairs towards the stables. Tony is wiping down a beautiful dark brown mare. Mia's eyes light up the minute she sees her.

"Oh, aren't you the beauty," she says to the horse as she rubs the mare.

"She's two years old, a real beauty… do you like her?"

"What's not to love Falu," she said, looking her over.

He enjoyed watching her smile. "Good, I'm glad you approve… Tony saddle Mia's new horse."

"Mine, she's my horse," she said excitedly "are you serious?"

"Try her out…" Mia climbed on the horse as if she were born on one. She rode the young mare around the yard slowly until the horse got used to her.

"Damn, she looks good on that horse. She knows her animal," Tony said, watching with approval.

"I knew she was a horse woman," Falu says, watching her go back and forth.

"So you think that will get you in her pants," he smiled, and all the men teased him.

"I don't know… but I'm trying," he chuckled. Mia felt the freedom as she rode her horse, knowing this was part of her life. She could feel the horse's strength between her legs, and knowing how to control it made her feel alive again. "So, how does she ride?" Falu asked, enjoying her look of happiness on her face.

"Like a dream, she's superb."

"So now you have to give her a name so we can get her register," Mia looked at her and smiled.

"Lucky that's your name… because I'm lucky to have you," she said, petting her.

Falu wanted to be part of her happiness. "You can ride her anytime, excise her daily but don't leave the field unless you have someone with you; it's dangerous," he put his arm around her shoulder, feeling her tense at his touch.

"So, what will this gift cost me?" she said, looking up at him.

"What, can I give you a gift… do I have to want something in return?"

"It's an extraordinary gift Falu. What I'm I suppose to think?"

He pulled her by the waist against him from behind, pressing up against his chest. "Except it, as you wish, what I want from you will come later," he kissed her neck, sending all sorts of sensations through her body. Falu noticed the reaction and pulled away. "Our turn will come, baby; you and I are meant for each other," he kissed her passionately before letting her go. Mia can't deny her growing feelings for him, she dreams of him at night, and she gets angry when she sees him with other women. She hated not being in control of her feelings.

Chapter 4: Outside

The girls waited anxiously for Mia to return, "she's been gone a long time; what do you think is going on?" Ivette said, looking to see if she was coming.

"The more time they spend together, the better. Remember, he kissed her, and he doesn't kiss women unless he really likes them… I can't wait," Betty said, putting a sheer veil against her face.

"This is it, girls, we are on our way to having our own place and business… as much as I love it here, it's time he found true love. I will miss him terribly, but there are plenty of fish in the sea," Tina said, happy things were working out as they had planned.

"We have to prepare our little sister for his sexual appetite; I don't want her to be scared. You know he could be so demanding," Ivette said, wondering how they would accomplish that task.

"Somehow, I think she can handle him; once she wraps those legs around him and rides him hard, he won't look at another woman," Betty laughed.

"I think you're right, sugar; I have a feeling she's going to rock his boat as soon as she gets a taste of his joystick," they laughed high, fiving each other.

Mia loved listening to her music pod whenever she got a chance she was plugged in; she swaged her own beat on the balcony. The girls had the music blasting when Max knocked on the door. "Hey, girls, it is I, the king of your hearts," Ivette turned down the radio, "how you 'all doing? I have some guys coming up here to install your dance pole," he looked over at Mia dancing on the balcony.

"About time, sugar; we're on a time schedule here," Tina replied. The girls were excited.

"Hm, can someone tell the princess to put on some clothes? I guarantee you there will be some accidents if they see what she's wearing," Mia wore shorts and a t-shirt that was too small for her.

"Don't worry, sugar, we'll take care of her; we have a lot of work to do," Tina said, giving the girls a look only they understood.

Mia took to the pole like a pro; the girls made it a game and watched as Mia learned all the tricks to pole dancing; every day, they tricked her into practicing. But Mia didn't realize how she affected men with what she wore and how she walked and spoke to them. They were ready and willing to give her whatever she asked.

***

Down Bourbon Street – Geraldine's

The trip to Old Town was something the girls looked forward to. Falu always got them a fancy car to ride in, and they loved seeing all the new stores popping up all over the city. They headed downtown Bourbon towards Geraldine's place, which was located at the end of the road in Old town, the French Quarters. Mia found the streets fascinating, especially since people stopped to stare at her. She rode next to Ricky, who appointed himself her tour guide. He went on and on about the old and new businesses and how their crews worked to improve certain parts of the city.

The pink neon sign displayed Geraldine's name shining brightly. She had a large display window with pictures of women wearing sexy exotic clothes and some mannequins with dresses and party clothes. Nico met them at the door for their scheduled visit. Falu was his best customer, so they always scheduled a private shopping session whenever he wanted. The girls disappeared towards the back of the store, which had more of the clothing and delicate wear.

Nico was always delighted when Falu and his girls came to shop; Falu always dropped a load of money. Nico stared at Mia, who looked around as if she was in a different world. "So who is this beautiful creature," he asked Falu.

"This is Mia; I want some special clothes made for her," Falu said as they watched Mia touch all the leather goods.

"She is magnificent," Nico exclaimed with delight.

"She's natural born; what you see is what you get," Max said. Mia picked up a whip and began to feel the handle in her hand.

"Would you like to try it out, my dear… we have some cans outside you can practice with," Mia looked at Falu. He just shrugged his shoulder. She stepped outside, cracking the whip. They could hear the sound of the whip as it connected to the cans outside. "Fascinating, Falu, who is she," Nico rubbed his balding head, adjusting his Peabody glasses.

"She's my new girl; I want you and Gerry to design some sexy eye-popping outfits for her. I want everything, clothes, boots, jackets, the works. When we go out together, I want heads to turn."

"Oh, my friend, heads already turn, I bet, but she will be our muse. My creative juices are already flowing… ah, one thing, do you mind if we take pictures of our creations, she will make a beautiful model."

"I'm sure she won't mind… where's Gerry? She's usually down here busting my balls."

"Oh, she'll be right along; she got caught up with something and is just finishing up."

Mia loved the way the whip was handled and the sound it made when it connected with the cans. She lined up the can again and noticed movement behind her. Two men had jumped the fence and were standing behind her; she never turned around. "Oh, my friend… those two are big trouble," Nico said; they could see a concerned look on his face.

Falu saw the two men behind her and didn't move. "Just sit back, Nico and enjoy the show," Falu suggested. Nico was confused that Falu wasn't outside, scaring them off. Ricky and Max found some chairs and placed them by the window to watch the attraction. Falu crossed his arms, watching Mia, who was getting ready.

"My friend won't… anyone go to help her; maybe you can scare them away?"

"Nay, she's getting ready to open a can of whip-ass on these douchebags," Falu said, remaining calm.

The two came closer to her; they wore dirty leather jackets and red bands across their heads. "Hey, you with the pretty ass want to play hide and seek. I can show you where I want to hide my dick stick," he said, rubbing his crouch.

"Yeah, or we can play sandwich a long time, baby," she turned around to glare at them; they were surprised but became even more excited; they saw her in all black. She wore two-piece fitted pants and a shirt that exposed most of her flat, tight belly. She smiled as she turned around to face them.

"So you want to play…show me what you got," she smiled, dropping the whip and waving them on.

"This is going to be an easy lay; come on, baby, I'm so horny," one of them lunges forwards to grab her, and she grabbed his arms and twisted in such a way that it snapped.

It was so quick it took him a little to realize she had just broken his arm. He fell to the ground yelling from the pain. When his second man saw his friend on the ground, he flipped out and went for her neck. She twisted from his grasp, ploughed her elbow into his neck; her palm came crashing on the bridge of his nose, bleeding all over the place.

"Oh snap… holy shit, did you see that? Woo, Lord, that was nasty," Ricky said, enjoying the action.

"That's what they get for messing with our girl." she kicked the legs out from under him and came crashing down on the ground, hitting his head. His friend continued to scream profanities at her. Mia dusted off her clothes, picked up the whip as if nothing had happened and came inside.

"You alright, baby, didn't you break a nail," Falu said as she closed the door.

"I'm good; they may need a doctor."

Nico was dumbstruck. "So, how did you like it," she looked at it and handled it in her hand.

"It's good, but it has to be tailored to the person," she put it down and walked away, looking at the leather jackets hanging in the front of the store.

"Falu, where did you find her, God, she didn't even flinch."

"Yeah, that's my bitch, a girl after my own heart… and will someday be the mother of my children," Falu said proudly. Max and Ricky went outside to clear the men from the back yard kicking them around some more for messing with Mia.

"The girls come back carrying arms full of clothes and shoes, heading towards the front where the leather goods are displayed. They chatted about the clothes they picked out, measuring some against Mia. She loved the feel of some of the delicate materials.

Falu felt the sting to his butt as Gerry slapped his behind, "You bastard, where the hell have you been!" she gave him a big hug, barely coming to his chest; she was five feet nothing, brassy, abrasive and didn't care who she offended with her temperament. "Look at you, you handsome devil," she laughed loud and scary.

"I've been busy," he said to the small Jewish woman.

"You know if you're giving your business to someone else, I'll kill you," she threatens with her boney finger.

"Come one, baby; you know you're the best. You and Nico always do me right."

"Yeah, don't think you can come in here and sweep me off my feet with your sweet words, muscular arms and all the rest of you."

"I bought my new girl so you can outfit her, "Gerry swiped off her glasses as she watched Mia try on jackets with Max and Ricky.

"Holy shit Falu is she the real deal? You know there a lot of girls dying their hair that color."

"Oh, she's all real from her head down to the toes, brown eyes that would melt you in place."

Gerry cleaned her eyeglasses again. "Damn it, Falu, you have got to be one of the luckiest sonofabitch I know; look at that ass, it's like a steal and those tits, you better watch out; they might poke your eyes out," they laughed.

"Falu wants us to dress her," Nico said, happier than he's been in months.

She looked a Falu with one eyebrow raised. "Mmm… interesting, so sweetie, what do you want… sexy or slutty,"

"A little of both, baby," he put his arm around her shoulders.

"You're my kind of man, Falu; I tell you what. You will be the most envies man this side of the Mississippi, Nico, my measuring tape!" she started to measure herself.

"Hm, nice small waist… you must work out your tits are really firm," Gerry said, feeling them up; Mia looked at Falu, surprised. "What a fabulous ass, nice round and juicy," Gerry could keep all the measurements of everyone she sawed for in her head. Gerry and Nico had been in business for thirty years. When Gerry is finished with Mia, the girls drag her to the other side so she can try on some shoes.

"Falu, those eyes, what a sight. I can make some really nice hats or headpieces."

"Anything you say, honey, you're in charge."

"You damn bastard, she has eyes for you, I can tell; a woman knows these things… it's all in the eyes. If you screw things up with her, I'll really hurt you."

"I told Falu we may want to get pictures taken if it was alright with him,"

"I have some great ideas for a clothing line you have inspired an old woman."

"She needs some riding gear; you know what I want; I have thirty gold coins; this should get you started."

She weighed the purse in her hand, "Don't worry, love; I know what you want; let me create my magic… I should have something for her to try on in two weeks."

"Thanks, Gerry… I want my girl to look hot."

"Oh, don't worry about that… she's going to give you a permeated boner, you pig, always thinking with that one eye bastard."

He laughed, "You know me all too well, Gerry; I wonder if that's a good thing."

She touched his chest. "I know my men; you are hot and nasty."

Max enjoyed teasing Mia about the two strangers she just beat up. She laughed at his antics and jokes as they rode home together. Falu liked listening to her laughter. It made him feel good; she was always so tense around him.

Every day it became harder to stay away from her, so he welcomed all the work he was doing. Sometimes he would watch her sleep. She looked so peaceful, and he wondered what was going through that pretty head of hers. He caught up to her and handed her a pair of riding gloves. They felt like butter against her skin. "You shouldn't have," she said.

"Do you like them?"

"Yes, their lovely."

"Enjoy what I give you, Mia," he winked at her and rode ahead, leaving her more confused than ever.

The girls continued to play dress her up with Mia; she laughed and enjoyed the sisterhood among them. Falu would show up now and then and just stare at their craziness, and every night he would call one of the girls to his room to service him. Mia found it hard to understand their relationship. The girls were all so beautiful, yet he did not commit to any of them.

Mia sometimes wandered around the huge estate, the landscaping, tennis court or the two swimming pools and pool houses. The house was equipped with a steam room, and sauna, and it had a club in the basement they called the Gentlemen's club. Mia found it funny because none of the men were gentlemen. Sometimes she would sit outside in one of the lounges and listen to the music; when she recognized one of the songs, she would sing along. It would transport her to the stage, giving her time to think about her situation. Falu made her nervous because of the way he looked at her, and sometimes at night, when he called for one of the girls, it would make her jealous, and she didn't understand why.

A familiar song came on, and she found herself drawn to the club. When she entered the club, it was dark except for the stage; like in a trance, she walked up to the stage and swayed to the song's rhyme as the pretty young girl sang the R&B song. Max was the first to notice her and approached her. "Mia," she turned around quickly, "Hey honey, what's up couldn't sleep," she smiled at him.

"Yeah, you could say that; I heard the music, and I just wanted to see who was singing. I hope that's alright."

"Sure, um, ah, why don't you sit with me and have a drink."

"I think I will… thank you," he ordered drinks and turned his attention to her.

"So, what's on that pretty head of yours?"

"I'm just confused as to what my reason is for being here," she sipped on her drink.

"I understand you are confused, but what's really bothering you," she smiled and looked at him, wondering if she could trust him with her feelings.

"It's your brother… he makes me feel so weird, and I don't understand the relationship with the girls."

He reached for her hand. "Mia, it's not what you think. The girls take care of him and love him dearly… it's like dating three women at one time but not on the same day. It is a temporary situation, one day, they will go their separate way, but they will always remain friends."

"So when he's finished with them, he will just set them aside, isn't that cruel?"

"No, honey, I know it sounds tricky, but there is a contract between the four, and they are happy with the situation. When Falu finds the woman he wants to be with, he will set them up with their own home and business. This is not a forced arrangement. They can leave whenever they want… you understand," Max didn't want to go into Falu's intentions towards her. He knew that he was falling for her, but she was already confused, and he didn't want to complicate her any more than she already was.

Chapter 5: Reyes and Esmeralda, Max and Falu's Parents

Reyes met Esmeralda on the way to the market, running after a neighbor's son who touched her inappropriately. The young man ran right into the steel wall that came out of nowhere. The young man bounced off his chest and onto the ground, where Esmeralda commenced to beat on him. Reyes couldn't help but laugh as he watched this beautiful golden eye petite woman punch him until she was satisfied. When she finished, Reyes picked him up by his collar and made his apologies to her. She smiled as the young man dropped to the ground. He sprung to his feet and ran for his life. Esmeralda stared at the beautiful, strong man who was a tribal man. His hair braided down his back, and he wore a t-shirt that showed off the massive muscles in his arms and chest. She had to look up, shielding herself from the sun and realized how tall he was.

"Are you alright? He didn't hurt you, did he?" she could only shake her head, "I don't think he'll be bothering you anymore."

"Thank you. Had you not stopped him, I would have continued to chase him and make a fool of myself," she couldn't look at him; she was nervous even talking to him.

"I'd been watching you for a while, and I saw him. He was very bold to touch you like that. All I can say is that he has good taste." He was flirting with her as she looked down at her feet.

"I don't know what to say, but I don't allow men to take such liberties with me."

"Oh, I understand perfectly. My name is Reyes, just in case you wanted to know."

"I've seen you before at the fresh fruit market," feeling foolish, she thought, not knowing what to say.

"Why didn't you ever say hello then?"

"Well, if we weren't formally introduced, I would have looked like a fool."

"So now that we have been introduced, we're not strangers," he said, watching her cheeks turn red.

"I better get home, I'm late, and my parents worry. It was a pleasure meeting you."

"I walk you home?" he said in his deep sexy voice, his steel-gray eyes pierced into hers. "I, I only live down the street; please don't go out of your way."

"Don't deny me the pleasure of walking with you; it's not out of my way."

He insisted on walking her home. Everyone stared at her with his big presence, his muscular body gleaming in the sunlight. People moved out of the way as they walked down the short distance to her home. Esmeralda felt as if everyone was watching them, but she didn't want this moment to end.

He stood over her, looking down at her, and she wanted to melt on that spot.

"Well, Ms. Esmeralda, I hope to see you again soon. It would be my pleasure," he took her small delicate hand and kissed it. When he turned to leave, it was like a part of her went away with him.

Esmeralda couldn't get the handsome Reyes out of her mind and her dreams. She needed to find out more about him and where he came from. Every day she ran past the marketplace to see if she could catch a glance of Reyes. She found it hard to concentrate on her dancing when all she could do was think about him.

Esmeralda was the youngest of three siblings. Her older brother Carlos dreamt of being a rancher, and when he turned eighteen, he went out west to join a large ranching community; within two years, he was married and settled. Her sister was two years older, but she was wild and difficult, so Esmeralda was the one her parents counted on whenever they needed help.

The family was well established in the community. They were hard-working people who had earned respectably. Esmeralda's father owned La Cantina, a nice restaurant where he served a decent meal at a great price. He was once a lawyer but gave up his law practice to take over the family business when his mother became too old to cook. Cooking was in his blood. All six children learned how to cook well. But it was Candido who had his mother flare for the kitchen. Candido worked in the kitchen and his sister Emily took care of the front.

Esmeralda took after her mother; she had her golden eyes and thick blonde hair; Zorida dreamt of being an international dancer but was too poor to afford the elaborate costumes. Travel was too expensive, so she taught dance and worked as instructed for a few years until she meant Candido. He came for lessons and stole her heart with his sense of humor and style. They married a year later, and as a wedding present, he bought the dance studio for her mother, Madame Zorida. Little by little, she turned it from a medium rated studio to a full-blown dance school. She was the one that encouraged him to follow his heart and do what made him happy. Now instead of coming home to an overwhelmed husband, she came home to a happy man who loved taking care of his children and associating with his customers.

Esmeralda was the only one who followed in her mother's footsteps. Zorida saw her gift when she was three years watching her child dancing and singing with her father. Esmeralda was a daddy's girl; his eyes lit up when she walked into the room. Esmeralda practices every single day after school. When she graduated, her mother sent her to the dance academy up North, where she shined among the freshman student. But just when her dreams were coming true, her mother was diagnosed with an old disease MS. It was a difficult blow for the very close net family.

She came home to help her father deal with his wife's illness. Even with all the problems, her mother's attitude was positive, and she insisted on going into her office to make the best of the situation. Esmeralda was there to help run the business and to take over the classes under great protest from her mother. "Mi carida hija, you don't have to give up your dream because of me." Esmeralda adored her mother; she was smart and strong even when her illness kept her from doing what she wanted.

"Mama, this is my life, you and Papa… I love this life; this is where I belong."

"I just wished so much more for you, I wished the same for your sister, but she has her own agenda. You know she's pregnant."

"I know, Mama, but please, you shouldn't stress yourself over Mariana; she'll be alright… and you'll get to meet your grandchild."

"I guess you're right, my daughter, before I die."

"Mama, please don't speak like that; people live a long life with MS, don't give up hope."

Zorida saw the frightened look on her daughter's face. "Esmeralda, please sit; there is something I need to tell you." Esmeralda sat next to her holding her mother's hand in hers.

"I've had this sickness for a long time… I just never told your father you know how he is. He cries every day now as it is… but I've known for some time now," tears ran down Esmeralda's cheeks. "I want you to promise me something," Esmeralda couldn't speak from the lump in her throat, "I don't want to be hooked to machines; I want to be at peace with my family at my side. You will abide by my wishes, mia amor," with great sorrow, she agreed.

Esmeralda lost her loving mother a month after her sister gave birth to a handsome son. The whole family grieved bitterly; her father was inconsolable and shut down The Cantina for a while. It was the little baby who bought him out of his depression.

Esmeralda hired a manager for the school and helped her father get back on his feet. Mariana married the baby's father, and they moved in with Candido to help out. Esmeralda continued to teach the junior classes and opened the other side for the adult private lessons. Every day as she walked home, she'd hope to get a glance of Reyes; it's been a year and a half since their encounter, and she still couldn't put him out of her mind and heart.

When she saw some of the people from his tribe and her heart began to race, but again she was disappointed. Mariana fought with her every time she tried to set her up with someone in her husband Guillermo's family. "Tony has been asking about you; how about if we double date this weekend?"

Esmeralda was barely in the door when Mariana started in on her. "I'm going to have to decline, Tony's nice, but he's... how should I say... so arrogant."

Mariana, like all ways, started in on her; it was like a broken record. "There's nothing wrong with Tony... you're the one who pushes everyone away."

"Sis, can I make my own choices in men? Please just leave me alone!" she tried to head to her room, but Mariana blocked her way.

"I'm trying to help you! You're stuck on that tribe, asshole... open your eyes. You know they think they're better than us. They come to the square turning their noses at us as if their shit doesn't stink. Wake up and stop dreaming! There's a bunch of men who are kissing your ass just to touch your hand, and you act like you're this princess."

Esmeralda felt a stabbing pain in her heart. "You're going to find yourself alone, waiting for a dream! Still dreaming of a man who would never give you a second look, wake up already, will you, before you end up like Titi Emily, alone and desperate."

"I'm a grown woman; I dream about whom I want to… and love who I want to love. Stay out of my LIFE. Look after your own kid and leave me the hell alone," Esmeralda pushed passed her and slammed the door. A tear rolled down her eyes as she felt her heartbreaking little by little. *Maybe she was right,* thought Esmeralda; he hasn't been around in so long, why she couldn't get him out of her heart.

Esmeralda continued to work late nights; business was good, she thought about applying to the Dancing School of the Arts again, but she thought about her father and how he would feel if she left. He still cried when he'd have one too many beers. He would seek her out and cry on her lap. He would kiss her cheeks and say she has her mother's golden eyes.

It was right after she finished her fifth-grade ballad class when her new manager Rosita announced she had a new customer who wanted a private lesson.

"Querida, he's asking for you," she said from the door.

"I'm tired. I can't take on another student. Give him to Karen. She makes him feel welcome."

"I know she would love to make this hunk. Hell, I'd make him feel welcome if I wasn't married. But you know what, boss, I'm not going to argue with him. Maybe you can tell him yourself you're not taking on any new students. He won't take no from me."

Esmeralda turned to her in frustration. "What I'm I paying you for if you can't tell some dude, he's going to have to request another teacher."

"I know, but I remember you saying, Rosita, I am here for you if you have a difficult customer, I will handle it… remember."

Esmeralda tried not to laugh. Rosita was comical at times. "Ay, ay, ay… tell him to wait in my office; I'll be with him in a minute." Esmeralda went into the bathroom and washed her face with cool water, and brushed her hair back with her hand. Esmeralda made a face at Rosita as she entered her office and ran into a steel wall. When she looked up, it was Reyes smiling at her with his pearly whites. She almost passed out. "Reyes," she finally found her voice, "Um, please have a seat."

"How are you? It's been a long time," he said, looking better than ever. Her heart was beating a mile a minute.

"I have been well, and yourself," she tried to sound casual.

"Great, now that I'm back home… I heard about your mother's passing. Sorry for your loss. I know it is a terrible thing to lose a parent so young. Our community had her in high esteem; she was a great woman."

"Thank you. It was really hard on my family. She was a strong force in our lives."

"My only regret is that… I wasn't here to… to offer you a shoulder to lean on."

She smiled. He was so handsome she could hardly keep her eyes off those lips that she wanted to press against hers. "I wish you were too. I could have used a strong shoulder to lean on. But let us get on with the business at hand; what can I do with you, I mean for you?"

"I need you to teach me to dance, I'm getting married, and I don't want to look like a fool on the dance floor."

The smile melted from her face. "I… I see. Well, I can partner you with Karen; she's a wonderful instructor," she tried to feel happy, but how can you smile when your heart is being broken into a million pieces.

"It has to be you… she's around the same size and weight… please, I wouldn't be comfortable with anyone else," he pleaded.

She had to be professional, "Well, if you insist, it's customary that both bride and groom practice at the same time. When do you want to begin."

"Well, my bride dances very well; I'm the one who needs lessons. I want to arrange an hour a day. I can't wait to make her my bride, and the sooner I can learn the different dance moves, the sooner we can get married," he smiled, and she just wanted to slap the smile from his face.

"Everyday… nobody takes lessons every day, and the only time I have is an hour before closing."

"Good, then I'll take it; I will meet you here at five for my private lessons. I can't wait," he didn't even let her reply. "You've made me very happy. My bride will be so happy when I can swipe her off her feet during our wedding ceremony."

Esmeralda watched as the man she loved walked out of her office. She couldn't hold back the tears anymore, all this time waiting to see him just to find out he was getting married to someone else, and why was she surprised. He had to be the most beautiful looking man on the earth in her eyes. His sex appeal spilled over. When Rosita came in with his contract, Esmeralda was drying her eyes. They were swollen and red.

"Querida, what's wrong?"

She shook her head, "It's nothing… I'm just tired, that's all."

"Oh my God, Esmeralda, that's him… he's the one that you've been dreaming about for all almost two years. Mi Dios querido, now I can understand why he's gorgeous. I almost fainted when he spoke to me with that sexy voice and those bedroom eyes. Oh my, it's getting hot in here or is it just me," she laughed, and Esmeralda burst into tears again. "Oh, I guess I'm not helping any, but what's the problem? He's taking lessons, and so you're going to be a dance with that hunk every day… I would be jumping from the roof with happiness."

"Rosita, I love you, but you have to learn when to shut up. He wants lessons because he's getting married."

Rosita understood what all the tears were about. She came around her desk to comfort her. "I'm sorry, Querida, I know it must hurt,' she held her for a long time.

"Please don't tell anyone… I feel like a fool as it is," she sniffed.

"I promise… everything's locked up. Do you want me to wait for you?"

"No, I'll be alright, I just have a few things to finish up, and you go ahead. I know how your husband worries when you're not home at a certain time… and Rosita… thank you for letting me cry like a fool on your shoulder."

"Anytime, boss, that's what I'm here for. You pay me well."

Esmeralda tried to get some paperwork done, but the news of his coming nuptial threw her for a loop. She had to pull it together and not let him know how much she loved him. Tomorrow night when he came for his lessons, she would be his teacher and conduct herself accordantly. She turned off the rest of the lights and said goodbye to Harold, the night watchmen.

It was dark out when she stepped into the street. Down the familiar, she went oblivious of anything that was going on. When she passed French Café, she heard her name being called. When she turned around, it was Reyes running toward her. "Oh God, why is he torturing me," she said to herself.

"Hey, let me walk you home," she wanted to slap his face and tell him he was killing her. "Oh, I don't want to detent you; it's not far."

"I know, but I can't let a pretty girl like you walk alone at night. You must promise to let me walk you home after our late lesson."

"Really, Reyes, it's not necessary," she wanted to run away from him.

"I insist if anything happened to you, I wouldn't be able to live with myself, so don't try to protest."

And so it was every day after their excruciating hour of pretending she didn't care for him, Reyes insisted on walking her home. Every night she cried herself to sleep. Emeralds loved feeling him against her. His strong, powerful arms and chest felt like a dream against her. She was nervous about tonight's lesson. It was the tango and very suggestive. But he insisted on learning all the steps, and tonight they were going to dance it straight through. She positioned herself in his arms during the introduction. It was like magic; they danced like they'd been dancing for years. He didn't miss a step, and she came alive in his arms as he tossed her around on the dance floor. For a minute, she forgot he was engaged, and then during those intimate moments in the dances, she became his. Rubbing her thighs against his, feeling his chest against her breast, she could feel the heat coming through her feet. When the music stopped, they were both out of breath. He held on to her a little longer than he should; his eyes melted into hers.

"That was excellent. I really don't know why you're taking lessons; you're a great dancer."

"I'm a quick learner, and you're a great teacher." Esmeralda wondered what kind of woman would let a man like him take lessons alone.

"So, Reyes, tell me about your bride to be" she wanted to know who she was giving him up to.

"She is the most beautiful woman I have ever seen; she is smart and very talented. When I look at her, I want to make love to her day and night."

Esmeralda rolled her eyes. "Well doesn't she sound… perfect," she tried to keep the sarcasm out of her voice.

"She is to me; I can't wait to see her every day."

"Wow, it must be hard for you to be apart," she now wished she never asked about this perfect woman he was describing.

"It is very hard; every time I say good night, I want to turn back and sweep her off her feet and take her home with me."

It was getting hard for her. Every evening she was around him, she suffered wanting him so badly and not being able to tell him how much she loved him.

She needed something to take her mind off of him, so she took her sister's advice and decided to go on a date with Tony. He had been trying to ask her out for a while now, but it did not go well. Everything he did annoyed her, and she couldn't help comparing him to Reyes.

The Monday during the dance session, Reyes was not his normal charming self; he was abrupt and serious. "What is wrong with you, Reyes, we went over this before, and you did it perfectly," he pulled her into his chest. "I want to dance something romantic like the tango we danced to the other night," she tried to pull away, but his grip was like steel.

"Reyes, you don't have to practice the tango. You know the steps; now let's try this again," she was not going to put herself through that again. He let go of her and walked away.

"I'm sorry… my mind is elsewhere."

"Is there anything I could help you with?" he looked at her and turned his face.

"You wouldn't understand; you're just a woman."

"Oh really, of all the pig-headed things to say," she scolded him.

He tried not to smile. "I'm sorry it wasn't met that way, it's just that I saw my future bride talking to someone else, and I got jealous, and so I'm starting to feel unsure."

Esmeralda sat next to him, knowing the strong feelings of jealously that flow from her heart. "I'm sure it was innocent."

"It was, but sometimes you just love someone so much it hurts when you're away from them, you understand me."

"I do understand," she wanted so much to hold me and kiss him and make him forget about this other woman who had stolen his heart. All she could do was sit by and watch the man she loved marry another.

"Do me a favor Esmeralda... put something soft, slow and dance with me. I want to make sure I know what to do when I hold my bride in my arms and make her forget everything but me," she put on a slow romantic bolero, and he brought her onto the dance floor. The lights were dim, and she could feel his strong muscles against her and his strong arms. She couldn't help running her hand up to his powerful arms. He pressed his face against her head, and for the first time, she didn't care about anything. Only that she was in his arms, and it didn't matter if he was getting married; only that he was hers for this moment.

She felt his mouth close to her ear; his soft breath woke up her senses, letting her body sway to the rhyme of the music. Esmeralda was flooding with air as he carefully made her forget the world. He found the curved of his neck, and without any hesitation, she began to breathe faster, lost in his arms and in the middle of the song. Just as it was going to climax, he captured her lips and sent her reeling into another dimension. She felt his manhood pressing against her as his kisses became more demanding. She pushed him away.

"Oh my God, Reyes, what are we doing! Shit," she ran to turn up the light.

"I'm not sorry, Esmeralda; I've wanted to do that for a long time."

"Please leave. I can't do this with you, Reyes. You're going to have to bring your bride with you if you want to continue lessons." Reyes just looked at her and smiled. Let me walk you home."

"No, please… I know my way."

"I will wait for you, don't argue with me," he walked her home in silence until they reached her house. "I won't be able to meet for our next few lessons, but Friday, my bride will know my true intentions," he grabbed and kissed her once more, leaving her breathless before he left. She was stunned, standing on her porch, wondering what had just happened. She went to her room confused and closed her eyes, trying to remember how wonderful it felt kissing and holding him, but it would come to an end this week when he brought his bride to meet her.

Esmeralda stayed busy the rest of the week. She was going crazy with Tony and her sister nagging her for another date. She needed to get herself in the right frame of mind to meet with Reyes and his bride. She started to feel guilty loving him so badly and having to pretend not to care. By Thursday, she was a nervous wreck. She couldn't concentrate and had Karen take over some of her classes.

Friday was a strange day. Karen was sick and cancelled all her afternoon classes, leaving her alone with the pending visit and his bride. Esmeralda went to freshen up when Rosita came knocking on the bathroom door. "Querida, your man is here accompanied by a stunning creature."

"I'll be there. Give me a minute," she powered, her eyes holding back tears.

Rosita was entertaining them in the outer lobby wanting to take a peek at her competition. Reyes was dressed in a white shirt and gray pants. He was sharply dressed and more handsome than she remembered. His bride had long hair the same color as his and was tall and slim. When she turned around, she got a good look at the stunning woman. She composed herself the best she could and went out to greet the woman who had stolen her man away. "There she is," Rosita said. Esmeralda put on her professional face and walked onto the dance floor. "Esmeralda, meet Nedra; we're not here for a dance lesson," he said; she was confused. "I have to use your bathroom. Keep Nedra entertained, will you," he rushed away.

"So you're the dancer he raves about. You should be faltered. You are very beautiful, but I can't understand why he wanted lessons he didn't need."

"I'm sure he only means it in a very innocent manner. A lot of people take lessons to improve their style or learn new dance steps," she wanted to change the subject. "So when is the wedding day?"

Nedra looked at her strangely, becoming angry. "Reyes! Get your ass out here now!" Esmeralda braced for the worse. Reyes walked toward them, smiling as if he got caught in the cookie jar. "Reyes, you didn't tell her! What's wrong with you?" Nedra turned back to Esmeralda, who was totally confused by the outburst. "Tell her!"

"Nedra's my sister. I did not lie to you about dancing with my bride at my wedding," Esmeralda had tears in her eyes.

"What are you saying?" her heart was breaking in so many ways, and she felt like a fool.

"Esmeralda, two years ago, when I met you, I knew I wanted you to be my wife. I just wanted to know if you felt the same way about me. It wasn't clear until our lesson on Monday when you responded to my advances."

Esmeralda's mouth went dry. "You jerk!" he wasn't expecting her reaction. "You made me believe you were getting married to another," tears rolled down her cheek, "I cried every night after our lesson, and others could see my heartbreaking in a million pieces. Were you so blind!"

"I told you," Nedra said smiling, "I told him over and over to tell you how he felt."

"I didn't know how you felt about me! I wanted you to get to know me better before I ask you to be my wife."

"You know how I feel right now…I feel like slapping your face for putting me through hell, and yes… I will marry you," she fell into his arms.

His sister clapped her hand, laughing. "It's about damn time. I'll be waiting outside; you two need to talk." Reyes didn't want to let her go; she couldn't stop crying as tears of happiness rolled down her face ruining her makeup.

"Why did you stay away so long," she asked, confused.

"I went away to school. I was on break when I met you and… I wasn't free at the time. I ended my engagement and went back to school praying all along that you would still be single."

"Every day, I would go past the market to see if I could get a glimpse of you."

He kissed her again passionately, "Come on, I want to ask your father for your hand in marriage."

"Now, can't we wait a few days?"

He picked her up with ease. "I waited long enough; it's going to happen tonight."

Esmeralda waited patiently as Reyes spoke with her father. Nedra tried to engage her in conversation. "Don't worry… Reyes knows what to say."

Esmeralda sat across from her, "I just realized I don't know anything about him."

"Well, brace yourself," she looked at Esmeralda, "my brother has had many women, all tribal women… he was engaged with Carmen Padilla and a very beautiful woman. And with all her beauty, there was something lacking. She was… how should I say spoiled rotten, and every time she didn't get the way, she ran back to Mommy and Daddy, who always came between them.

Reyes hated it, he broke it off, and she, of course, did not take it very well. I remember the day her parents came to interject; they had their noses up in the air. My brother is a lot like my mother, very strong-headed, and nobody messes with Mama. Anyway, Carmen sat between her parents as they began to complain about how terrible my brother treated her. She cried into her handkerchief, feeling like a victim. My mother let them have their say. I saw my father going towards the living room, and he stopped. Oh my God, he said to me, your mother is going to make arroz blanco out of them. I better interfere.

If there's one thing you don't do is mess with mama's baby birds, she went up one side, and down the other so swiftly, they didn't see it coming. She spoke in two languages… it was beautiful. Two weeks later, he ran into you again. He had seen you before and always made comments about how pretty you were. He saw you running after some boy and followed you to interference. He was so happy, Esmeralda, he said sis, I finally spoke to the woman I want to marry."

"But I didn't see him after that… I looked for him."

"He was sent back to finish school; my parents are professors. Reyes is very smart and knew that education was important to our tribal community. He told my parents he had fallen in love with a non-tribal woman after he broke off his engagement. My parents, they are very liberal, and they wanted him to be happy and didn't care who he married as long as he finished school.

He'd ask me every time we went to visit if you were still single. My parents would laugh and say she's waiting for you, son. He would get very happy… you are nothing like Carmen. The way you took care of your mother and father, and all the sacrifices you have made. That is what my family looked at, and you make him happy."

Her eyes started to tear up, "I've been in love with him since that day we met, and he insisted on walking me home."

"Anyway… he didn't know how you felt about being with a tribal man. We are proud people, and others think we are arrogant, but that is not the case. We are proud of our heritage and who we are as people."

"That was never the case; I just thought I wasn't pretty enough for him."

"At you kidding me, you're gorgeous; he thought he'd have to fight off suitors."

"I had many asking, but there was only one, and I still can't believe he's here… I feel like this is a dream."

When the door finally opened, the two men were laughing and embracing each other.

"Well, Reyes, I have to tell you…" his eyes were tearing "you have the best," her father hugged her.

"I promise I will always take good care of her."

Esmeralda was nervous when she set out to meet his parents. They invited the family to come for a picnic celebration. The first thing she noticed was how beautiful everything was; the houses were beautifully built and constructed. The streets were clean, and the stores were beautifully painted. Most of the homes had a lovely garden in the front yard. The whole community was well organized. His parent's home was a beautiful colonial style home, richly painted in blue and white like the rest of the homes. The front porch had all kinds of plants, stone pottery and a set of fancy wicker furniture. The house was large and airy that opened into a large living room with beautiful hardwood floors and a stone fireplace. The walls are decorated with rich colors and beautifully painted pictures. She felt the warmth of family as she entered his home.

His parents went out of their way to make her and the rest of the family feel comfortable and welcome. Rocio, his mother, was a tall, status woman with long, almost white hair. She was a stunning woman with powerful presents. His father was more laid back, full of jokes and hardy laughter, tall, and for a man his age, he took great care of himself.

They were impressed to find out that her father had been a lawyer and where he went to school. His grandmother couldn't stop hugging her. She was in her eighties. But still kept on getting up early in the morning to make coffee and breakfast for her family. She was sharp and very wise.

Everyone looked to her for wisdom. During dinner, when everyone sat down to eat, his grandmother stood up and looked at Reyes. He was her favorite of her ten grandchildren. "Mi hijo lindo, mi vida y corazon, I had a revelation… your firstborn will be a male of great importance, and he will be exceptional. Favoring his father, and it was all possible because of the match you made. She will be your goddess; the children she brings forth will bring us great joy." Reyes gave his grandmother a hug and kiss. "Te amor," she said to him.

That afternoon she meant Carmen, she was very pretty tall like him, but she was a bit snobby. Carmen tried to engage her in an intellectual conversation. What she didn't realize was that even though she had her mother's talent, she had her father's intellect. Esmeralda was extremely bright; she loved to read and had many heated discussions with her father about social issues.

Esmeralda loved the community gathering; however still very busy with the dance studio and did not have time to plan a wedding, so she left most of the planning to his family. Mariana protested about everything. Even though she was the maid of honor she still fussed about the dress, the food and anything else that came to mind.

The wedding would take place in the community plaza, and all who wanted to attend were welcome. Candido didn't care as long as his little girl was happy; he insisted on catering some of the food and the wedding cake. Candido loved the tribal community's' closeness; it reminded him of his birthplace, where everyone looked after each other, and the people stood together when it came to important issues.

Mariana was prepared to take care of her father on her own. She was pregnant again and was going to show when the time the wedding came around. It would be a huge event not just for the community but for Esmeralda's family and friends.

Reyes tried really hard to stay away from Esmeralda; his passion for her was getting the best of him. She never discouraged his advances and had no problem giving herself to him, loving him so much. Reyes waited for her every night when she was done at the studio to walk her home and spend some time together.

He had his dreams; when they sat on his parents' porch one evening, he expressed what he wanted to do. Esmeralda couldn't help but stare at him whenever he held her and turned his face towards the sky. He wanted to restore the integrity of New Orleans and its beauty. He had researched and read everything he could get his hands on about how beautiful the city was before the Dark Days.

For Reyes' birthday, Esmeralda found a rare book on the History of New Orleans. It had beautiful colorful pictures and a gold binding. When he wrapped it, he became emotional. "Oh my God, baby, it's beautiful, she sat on his lap as he paged through the large book, but after a few pages, he began to breathe heavily. "Baby, if you don't get off my lap, we're going to have problems," he started to laugh.

"Good because I have another surprise for you," she whispered in his ear.

"Baby, I'm a hot-blooded man. Stop, or you're in trouble."

"Just follow my lead. Say good night to your family because you're not coming home tonight."

Esmeralda made him stop at a small Inn they passed every time they went back and forth. He smiled as they stopped to get the key to their cabin. When he opened the door, the room had a big sign that said happy birthday, a bottle of wine chilling by the bed. "Why you naughty girl," he pulled her him crushing her to his chest, taking her breath away. "I've been waiting for this moment for so long, but I didn't want to pressure you."

"Well, you have a strange way of proving you want to wait… I know I don't want to wait any longer." Esmeralda changed into a sexy little nightie driving Reyes crazy.

That weekend was magical for both of them; she knew this was where she wanted to be for the rest of her life, lying in his arms. He was passionate and sometimes demanding, but she matched his eagerness.

When they were finally married two months later, she was already pregnant. He laughed on their honeymoon as he held her head in the bathroom. "Baby, I'm sorry, but this will pass."

Falu was born seven months later; he came into the world kicking a screaming. The spitting image of his father, just like his grandmother had predicted. He often said that it was his build up waiting for his wife. Falu was named after Reyes' grandfather, who passed away, and Falu became the reason for living in his family's home. Falu took over their lives; he could talk before he could walk properly. His parents fought with them to care for the little guy who was growing so fast, strong and animated. When he was two, Esmeralda was pregnant again, and again she was sick almost every day for the first three months. But his family didn't mind having Falu turn their household upside down.

When Rocio saw how intelligent he was, she taught him how to read; he could read and do calculations by three. He would read everything and anything, and it made them laugh. Falu could do no wrong in their eyes.

When Silva was born, he spent more time with his grandparents, who encouraged their grandson to learn, getting him interested in all subjects. He would sit on his grandfather's lap while he read to him. Falu also enjoyed his visit with Candido, his other grandfather, who let him put his little fingers into the dough or let him stir things in the kitchen. He would tell his Abuelito he was going to be a cook just like him. But his grandfather Candido had other ideas and a different agenda for his grandson. He wanted to make sure he went to a good school; he still had connections.

Reyes made his mark in the city. When Falu was six, he moved Esmeralda and his children to a beautiful estate right outside the city. He began his quest to make changes in the city. He petitioned the Inner Cities to consider his city as part of the network, and in turn, they made him the Overlord of the City and the providence. This title gave him the power to make changes and establish order in the city. Under Reyes, he established a military force to clean out some of the bad elements in the area, but there was still so much to do.

When Candido became ill, Esmeralda spent time nursing him; her sister and husband worked the restaurant and didn't have the time with her four children underfoot to care for him. Reyes is concerned with his father-in-law's health, and his wife hired a nurse to look after him. Their youngest son Max clung to his mother and cried whenever she was out of his sight. Reyes continued with his quest to restore his city. As his son Falu grew, he too wanted to follow in his father's footsteps wanting to see his father's dreams come true.

Falu loved his tribal community along with his sister Silva who married at seventeen. His aunt Nedra and her husband bought land further west. They wanted to establish another community, a winery, and it was growing.

Falu was sent to school in Europe to get a more rounded education; his father wanted him to go to the same university he graduated from.

They called Reyes, the king of his tribal community and New Orleans, and his son Falu, the prince.

Chapter 6: Revelation

This was Falu's busiest season; the sooner they could break ground for the construction of the levies before the weather turned and construction would slow down. Falu was like a dragon when it came to his projects; he pushed his workers and his foreman to get the work done. His main goal was to entice new business to the area to make New Orleans a place where people wanted to visit and spend their money. He had entrepreneurs banging on his door for permission to open a new business, but not all of them had the best interest of the city.

When Falu needed to entertain someone special, he always turned to his girls to help him organize and serve his clients. The girls were only too happy to help and get involved in the activities. Mia always refused to come down whenever Falu asked.

He tried to understand that maybe she was afraid, so he would order her to dinner with him on one of his private terraces. At first, she refused and begged Tina to go in her place. But Tina would argue with her, dressing her up in a sexy outfit and scolding her about being so difficult. "When Falu asks you for something, you are not supposed to argue. Believe me, sugar; you don't want to see that man when he's angry. Now you're going to have this special dinner and smile, even if it's killing you. Please, Mia, I've seen him angry, and it's…it's something you do not want."

"I'm not afraid of him," she said, pouting.

"Then maybe you should be because he can make your life very difficult. Now you go and be nice, be a good girl." Mia looked at herself in the mirror; the white dress clung to her every curve.

"But look at me, this… half of my breast is hanging out!"

"That's what they're for, sugar, for him to look at. Do me a favor and keep him happy. Tame your mouth, you have no filter when you speak to him, and I sometimes cringe at the things you say to him."

"All right, but I want it noted that this is under protest."

"Under protest or not, you listen to him and say yes, sir, and okay, honey, you have an attitude with him all the time."

"That's because he likes to bait me… and, well, I feel funny when I'm near him, my stomach."

"Those are love butterflies, honey; it's normal."

"Love butterflies, I don't know anything about love, and he has enough women loving him."

"Hm, sounds like the green monster to me," Tina teased. Mia was surprised.

"What are you saying?"

"I'm saying that you like him, and it makes you jealous when you see another female flirting with him." There was a knock on the door. "Now that's Ricky; you remember what I said. Smile, you have a beautiful smile; use it."

Ricky escorted her to dinner. He commented on how pretty she looked and warned her to behave herself. When she walked out on the terrace, she was amazed at how handsome Falu was in his olive green shirt and black pants. He was clean-shaven, and he had a glow about him she had never noticed. The butterflies in her belly were fluttering a mile a minute. She tried hard to disguise her feelings and remain unmoved. Someone worked hard at trying to make the place romantic, and they did a beautiful job, from the flowers to the music. Mia felt like the main meal.

"Have a seat… you look amazing," he said with lust written all over his face, "wow."

"Thank you," she said, "you look really nice too." They had a wonderful spread laid out for them, "so what's the occasion," she asked?

"I think this meeting is overdue, don't you think. I've been very busy, and things are going to get even busier."

"And what does that have to do with me?" she said with an attitude.

"Why are you so defensive all the time? This has everything to do with you and the girls. I need you and the girls to help entertain some of my clients. Help me organize some of the events; you know, help serve food things of that nature.”

“So let me get this straight you want me and the girls to strut around your clients, serve them food and drinks… I presume you want us to look nice, wear some sexy clothes.”

“Yes, my girls always look nice. Is that too much to ask of you?”

“First of all, I’m not one of your girls; I’m not your cook or your servant.”

Falu gave her a side glance as he cut into his steak. “Mia, I clothed you, fed you, and kept a roof over your head. That’s the least you can do for me,” he was trying really hard to keep his temper under control. Mia saw the look on his face and remembered what Tina had said to her.

“Fine, whatever you say…”

“Good, I’m glad you finally see things my way. Now can we enjoy our food? Cook made this especially for us,” he winked at her.

“Falu, can I ask you a question? This has been bothering me for a while?”

“What’s keeping you up at night, my love?”

“Well, the girls, why haven’t you married any of them? I can see they have feelings for you, and you for them?”

Falu rolled his eyes, his whole attitude changed, and he became serious again. "Mia… my relationship with the girls is none of your business. But if you must know, it's because I'm not in love with them. I care about them. I would kill for them. I enjoy their company. They make me laugh, and it's just sex. I take care of them, and that's that."

"How do you have sex with someone almost every night and not form a bond," she was rattled on.

"It's just sex, Mia, that's all. I like to have sex… a lot!" Mia went silent; she could tell that it hit a nerve with him. "Is there anything you need to say to me, Mia?"

"Sometimes, you can be such a jerk."

Falu chuckled, "You bought up the subject about the girls. The woman I want is sitting right in front of me, so stop playing matchmaker." They ate in silence for a while; Mia began to relax after her second glass of wine.

"Falu… I don't want to be your whore."

Falu choked on what he was drinking and started to turn red. "What are you talking about?"

"I don't want to be your first or fourth lay of the week. I don't have a contract with you, so why should I be made to join your little sex club." Falu knew this would come up, and he understood her reasoning. "You say I belong to you. I'm really confused at what that means."

Falu sat back and tried to relax. "Querida, I know you are confused, but let me explain something. Ricky used to date this really whacked-out chick. I mean, after what happened to her, it's a wonder she can function. However, I dated her older sister… at one time. I thought she might be the one. We hit it off, and she's one hell of a woman Rosalina. Anyway, she was always on me about reading my fortune. She wanted to know if we were right for each other after having some hot, heavy sex one night. She insisted on reading, and something very interesting happened. She started to become excited and began to rumble like chanting. I wanted to freak out, but I remind cool. She started to laugh, and that's when she told me that my soul mate would be a dark woman. A beautiful dark-haired woman with dark brown eyes… I told her she was full of shit. Where was I going to meet a true-born woman? That was unheard of; she said the cards don't lie. I thought it was crazy until a strange woman came to town, a dark hair dark brown-eyed woman. I later found out that she was the wife of a very important man. I met this woman, and she was extraordinary. I was hooked."

"So you think I'm her, the woman in the cards?"

"Mia, I've been around, traveled abroad, and you are the second woman I've met. When you were bought here, I felt the draw. Because you are sick, I don't blame you for not feeling the same way for me."

But Mia felt the draw as he spoke about his ex-lover; the green monster was killing her. She wanted to throw something at him. "So what about this woman? Are you still in love with her? It seems as if you two were meant for each other?"

"That was a while ago, we are still a really good friend, and she's married, happily married with a handsome son and another on the way." Mia thought about the other women in his life, and she became jealous. She tried to finish her dinner without throwing something at Falu, who sat across from her. After the servants cleared the table, Falu led Mia towards the gardens where they could be alone. She wanted to enjoy his company, but she couldn't get past the women. Everywhere they went, women flocked to him. She could not let herself be a victim of heartbreak; she would keep her feelings for him guarded.

"Falu... I appreciate everything you've done for me, I love Lucky, and the girls are wonderful. But I'll be going home as soon as I regain my memory... there's got to be someone missing me... somewhere."

"Believe me, I want nothing more than for you to regain your memory, but it doesn't change anything about us," he pulled her roughly into his arms. "You belong to me. I can feel it in my soul. The only reason you aren't in my bed right now is because you don't remember. But hear me well, you will be my woman, and you will come to me willingly," he held her head and kissed her forcefully. She tried to pull away, but he kept her in a stolen embrace. He kissed her again, and the sensations were overwhelming. When he kissed her neck, he heard soft moans escaping from her denying lips. She was breathless when he stopped kissing her and let her come up for air.

"You're mistaken if you think I'm coming to your bed willingly," she said, almost in tears.

"Mia, my love, you can talk all the shit you want… if I wanted, I could take you right now, and you would enjoy it because you are hot-blooded and steaming, just like me. Once you taste the joy of sex, I guarantee you that you will be more than willing to come to me. I also know that we will share something special and wonderful. But don't test my patients, my love. I can be a brick if you push me."

"I feel nothing for you, your disgusting the way you walk around thinking that every female wants you."

"Then your body is betraying you, baby. Soon, my love, we will be enjoying more than just kisses. I will be exploring the most intimate parts of your body… and you will be completely mine."

By the time Falu walked her to the room, she was upset. When the girls tried to question her about the dinner, she lay in bed and covered her face with her blanket. Like before, he called one of the girls to him.

Mia struggled with her growing feelings toward Falu; every chance he could, he would come after her, kissing and touching her in places that drove her crazy. The girls knew that something was bothering her, but they didn't pressure her to reveal her feelings or thoughts.

They continued to teach her the latest dance steps. They even bought in an expert dance teacher who immediately fell in love with her. They glided across the dance floor like they had been dancing for years. It was by mistake that they discovered something else about Mia. She could sing. Her sultry voice hypnotized them sometimes, they would start to sing all together, and they would shut up and let her carry the song. It gave them goose-bumps when she hit those scales. She learned a lot of the songs on her music pod. It didn't matter what language she could stay in tune with.

Falu's men sometimes hung out by the pool outside their room to hear her belt out a song. He was also captured by the songbird's voice and didn't mind as long as they did their job. But Falu was becoming more frustrated by the day with Mia; he wanted her so bad sometimes that not even the girls could cool down the burning he had for her. He let her know who was in charge whenever he could.

It was Mia's last fitting for the clothes that Falu had commissioned for her. She was saddled and ready to go when Ricky and Max reached the stables. To her disappointment, Falu would not join them on this trip. They made fun of her when they saw her hair wrapped up and sunglasses. She wore green shorts and a yellow and black striped half shirt. The two looked at each other and wondered if maybe they should let her know just how much she would attract attention. They would have it to watch her closer. She rode down the main street as if she belonged. She loved watching the interaction with the people as they made deals and haggard about price and the wonderful smell of the spices and flowers as they rode by.

Gerry was excited to see them; they had been working hard creating a clothing line, especially for her. "Come in, my darling child. I have some really beautiful things I want you to try on. You two can give me some feedback and tell me if Falu will like what I have created for this beautiful creature."

Nico came from the storage room holding an arm full of clothes with different fabrics and textures. Mia tried on one scandalized outfit after another. Ricky and Max couldn't help but stare at her; however, she didn't mind the provocative clothing. Nico took pictures of her in different poses. He was like a little boy who had just got a new toy.

"Girl, your ass looks delicious in those pants," Gerry teased. Mia was getting used to Gerry touching her. She wanted to make sure everything fixes properly and that every line was in its place. The clothes looked as if they were sown right on her. Some of the clothes had plunging necklines and strange cuts for the back to highlight her sexy rear.

"So what do you think, boys, did I or didn't I deliver," Gerry asked, smiling.

"You always do, Gerry. I especially like the leather outfits; I think Falu will like those best," Ricky added.

"I know my shit, and I know my beautiful model, God, what I wouldn't do for a few like her."

Max always enjoyed Gerry; she was funny, "Ricky, I have to go across the street and pick up my package Mia. I should be no more than five minutes. Stay with her, Ricky," Max instructed.

"Take your time. I have to wrap some of the outfits for you to take with you. I'm excited to hear how my boy likes them,' Gerry said, ensuring they were wrapped correctly. Nico instructed Mia on how to care for the leather garment, but her mind was on Max, who was taking too long. Mia walked towards the front door where Ricky was looking to see if Max was coming.

"Something's wrong, Ricky," she said. Ricky was also worried; he motioned her towards the door.

"Gerry, lock this door behind us," Ricky advised them. Gerry and Nico looked at each other afraid; they always felt safe in their location, but sometimes things happened. Ricky ran across the street where Max was supposed to pick up his package. When he returned, he was troubled. Mia looked around to see if he was down the street. "They said he picked up the package a while ago," she could see the worried look on his face.

With caution, they walked down to the end of the street where there was an old empty warehouse; when they turned the corner, they saw a pair of legs. Max laid on the ground, pale and out cold. Mia reached down carefully to see if he was still breathing. It wasn't a robbery; he still had his package and his clothes.

Mia felt a cool breeze behind her and saw a shadow out of the corner of her eye. With Ricky in view, she motioned to him. He nodded back to her. From the rafters, someone jumped towards Ricky, but he moved, and the man fell to the ground. Within a few minutes, they were in the middle of a full-blown fight for their lives.

Ricky fought like a madman with two men while Mia was crushing bones with a few others. She managed to flip over one of them and landed in front of a tall man who pushed her out of the way and knocked one of the men onto the ground. The three of them fought to overcome the six attackers until the attackers lay on the ground bleeding and broken.

"Max finally came to Mia's lap. She was trying to get him to wake up. He woke up swinging. "Max, it's alright, it's over," she said, calming him down; he sprang to his feet, embarrassed and angry.

"I heard a woman crying for help, and they jumped me from behind the bastards." Gerry and Nico had summoned the sheriff. When they arrived, the men were all tied up needing medical attention. Ricky and Max thanked the tall man that jumped in to help them.

"My name is Kumar. I heard the shouting and realized you were in trouble," he kept staring at Mia as if he knew her.

"I think Mia was kicking ass, but I'm glad you jumped in," Ricky said, "I'm Ricky, and this is my cousin Max, and this beautiful woman is Mia."

"I was more than happy to assist."

Max tried to clear his head as he shook Kumar's hand. "I want to invite you to meet my brother Falu; he would like to meet you and thank you for coming to his woman's aid."

Kumar was stunned. "It would be an honor to meet Falu; I've heard many great things about him."

"Good my friend, right now I better get back home to get my head checked."

News of the attack reached Falu before they entered the gate, Falu met them at the entrance, and he reached for Mia holding her face in his hands. "Are you alright, and do you need to see the doc?"

She smiled at him, "I'm alright; I wasn't hurt, just glad to be back. Max was hurt; he should see the doc right away," he kissed her and smacked her hiney."

"I'll talk to you later," It didn't take Falu long to wonder who this tall stranger was. Max introduced them.

"I am honored to finally meet you; I've heard so many wonderful stories about you."

"Don't believe the bull shit. I'm sure half of the stories they say about me are not true, but come and join me for something to eat."

"Falu, there is something I need to talk to you about. Can we speak in private," Kumar asked. Falu became defensive.

"My office… Ricky, come with me," Falu led him down the hallway towards his office. Ricky closed the door behind them. "Please have a seat," Falu sat across from him. "So, what's so important?"

Kumar looked at Falu and then towards Ricky, who sat to his left. "It's about Mia," he could see the tension in Falu's face right away.

"You know Mia," Falu asked; he put his guard up. Ricky moved his chair closer to Kumar.

"I've known Mia for 15 years." Falu was surprised. "I've been searching for her. When she disappeared, we feared the worst."

"And who are we? And who are you to her?" Falu was trying to remain calm.

"Her family, Mia's parents and younger brother Teek, they are beside themselves looking for her."

"You still haven't told me what your relationship with her is," Falu asked, crossing his arms.

"I was her teacher, and two years ago, I married her aunt on her mother's side."

Falu finally began to relax. "Mia was found in the woods a few miles from here; she was hurt and has lost her memory. We have been working with her on this problem."

"No wonder she did not recognize me. I didn't understand what was going on, so it explains a lot. What I do know is they've been watching her for a while."

"How do you know," Falu asked.

"I saw her riding in and followed to see where she was going. She didn't seem to be distressed, and I was relieved. But as I sat down across the street next to the post office, I noticed a few men gathering out front, looking at the store she had just gone into. I started to get suspicious. I hid but kept them in view; when Max came out of the store and went into the post office, I saw the plan in motion. I watched Max when he ran across the street towards the warehouse. I waited a few minutes, and when he didn't return, I went to find him when I saw Ricky go into the post office and run back to the store. I crept towards the warehouse and saw Max lying on the ground. Mia and Ricky were attending to him. When the men jumped from the rafters I jumped in, they were trying to kidnap her."

"What the hell? I'm glad you were there to help out. She doesn't even seem fazed with the episode," Falu said, concerned.

"You have no idea how relieved I am that she is with your friends. Do I have a story to tell," Kumar smiled. Falu began to relax. They ordered food and drinks for the four; Max had joined them after the doctor checked him over.

"Her father and I have been searching for her. We feared that Jario may have taken her, but let me start from the beginning so you can understand where I'm coming from. Mia's mother's name is Solana, a beautiful red-haired tribal woman daughter to great teachers. By the time Solana was seventeen, she had her certification to teach the younger ones. Now Mia's father Naphtali… that man is something else; he was adopted into the tribe. His parents died when he was a year old, so he came to live with his aunt."

"So what is the tribal name? She doesn't have it on her arm?"

"Rivera-Negron, that's the tribal name. His aunt loved Naphtali and raised him like her own, and Naphtali Arroyo grew up to be a great businessman, very business savvy. He knew how to sell and buy and always made a profit. He was an honest man who loved to wheel and deal. Solana has been in love with Naphtali ever since she was like fourteen. But he never approached her because he was five years older than her and always felt he needed to bring something to a relationship besides his good looks.

Her father was overprotective, and when other young men came around sniffing after his daughter, he would drill them to the point that they were afraid to come back. Anyway, one day she stopped Naphtali at the market and asked him why he never asked her out. He was surprised, always wanting but never daring to make his move. Young men always surrounded her, and he never thought he had a chance with her. But once he got the invitation, there was no stopping him.

They began to see each other, and it got really hot and heavy. He asked her father for her hand in marriage, and for the first time, her father didn't have issues with the young man she chose. However, Solana had also caught the eye of someone else. Jario Mundo was the son of the Warlord, and like his father, he was a son-of-a-bitch. Jario's father, Gilberto, was a cruel man, and he wanted Jario to follow in his footsteps, and he did. He grew up a bully to those he could beat and took what he wanted. He came aggressively to Solana and scared her. When he went to speak to her father, he flipped out on Jario, yelling he already had two wives and had four children, and she was already promised to someone else.

Well, it was like a slap in the face to Jario. He demanded that the elders decide. However, big papa wasn't having any of it; her father persuaded the elders to vote against him. Jario failed to get what he wanted and was publically humiliated, which sent him into a rage. He hated Naphtali but was afraid of him. Whenever he came around, Jario disappeared.

Three days before they were to be married, Solana was raped and beaten in her own backyard. The whole community was up in arms. Naphtali was away with his friends who kidnapped him for his bachelor party. When he returned, they had to tie him up and keep him tied down for three days. Solana sent him back the ring with a note saying that she was damaged goods and would release him from the marriage.

Jario's father petitions the elders again for her hand in marriage. Solana's father was so angry and hurt at what happened to his daughter that he took the petition and burnt it right in front of Gilberto's front yard. Naphtali was finally released after promising he would not kill Jario. He went straight to Solana's, who was terrified to leave the house after the trauma. When he saw her, he broke down and cried at her feet. Her pretty face was bruised, her lip broken, and she had a cut on her left eye. He said, "I promised to protect you, and I failed," he put the ring back on her finger. She couldn't help but cry as he knelt and held her hand. "We will marry as we plan. If not, he wins. But before we marry, I will fight for your honor." That no one will take from him, Naphtali called him out as custom, beat the man so bad he was begging for mercy."

"I would have killed him, no doubt," Falu stated.

"He wanted to; however, she didn't want her marriage to start with blood on their hands. Afterward, he did something very strange. He moved his family and hers fifty miles away. They settled and started a community of their own. They settled right outside of Georgia.

"Georgia, now I know why she does carry the tribal name. How the hell did they manage to be in this territory? Georgia is a hundred miles away?" Falu asked.

Naphtali was very bitter after what Jario did to his wife; it took him a long time to get it out of his system, which is why he moved away. He started their community, and within a year, it was thriving. They adopted others into the community and opened stores and a great trading post. Two years later, Mia was born, she was born under a clear full moon. Mia was a beautiful baby. They rejoiced when they found out about her color; they felt very blessed. However, Solana was very scared that someone would come and steal her away. Naphtali moved his wife and newborn to the outskirt of the community; only members of the community knew Mia's identity, and they protected her from outsiders. No one was allowed to speak about the beautiful dark-haired, brown-eyed child.

I met Mia when she was five years old. She was bending down by a small brook letting the water flow through her fingers. I had never seemed such a beautiful sight in my life. She stood up boldly and said, "Hi, my name is Mia; who are you," in her tiny voice. I went down on my knees and bowed to her. She was amazing. Mia smiled, took my hand, and walked me to her house, where her father and mother were crazy looking for her. I was fascinated by the child and wanted to know about her culture and people.

Her father and I became close friends, and I moved close by. One night while we talked, I suggested that I teach her the arts. I spent thirteen years in Japan as a boy, where my father taught English, and I got lessons in return. Afterwards, he moved us to Taiwan and Laos, where I continued my lessons. I became a master, but when my father passed away, my mother and sister decided to move back home to New America. They settled somewhere up North with family, and I went on my journey for peace, and that's how I met the family. Mia was a hard student; thinking she was a man, whenever we spared, she hit like one."

"Well, I have news for you she still thinks she's a man," Falu said. They chuckled.

"She practiced day and night to the point that her mother had to force her to come in and eat. I had never seen anything like that in my life, but that disciple made her fast and strong. Her mother fought with her because she refused to wear woman's clothes. She liked the freedom of the shaco, the clothes the young men wore when they went hunting."

"Well, that changed, the girls have her in high heel swing on pole, but something strange happened. She passed out when she saw her reflection in the mirror; we didn't know what that was about?" Falu asked curiously.

"Believe it or not, that was her mother's idea; when she was about four, the other kids made fun of her because of her long black hair and brown eyes. They teased her, saying she didn't bathe. The kids called her dirty bird; she would run home angry, staring in the mirror for hours crying because she wasn't like the other children. She couldn't go into some areas unless she was covered up. So her mother got rid of all the mirrors except for one that she kept in her personal belongings. It was hard, but Solana was determined to keep her daughter safe and happy. Solana was paranoid, especially when Mia was very young.

"How did they manage to end up this way," Falu asked.

"Well, Mia always tried to cover her appearance; she had to fight her way out of situations when men hit on her. One crazy guy broke into her room and tried to rape her. Needless to say, I don't think he would ever have children after she finished with him. She was only fourteen. Another time two men jumped her in the woods. We watched her beat the living daylights out of those fools. Afterwards, we finished them off, you know, just to make sure they got the message.

Something happened when she was seventeen. Naphtali and I went hunting. Jario's older son Ivan came to the trading post with one of his younger brothers. Mia was picking up some things with her mother; when Ivan saw Solana, he stopped her and stated he knew her. I think Ivan was seven when Solana left the community. She was horrified. He was the spitting image of his father, and she panicked. When Mia saw her mother in distress, she approached Ivan, who turned a few shades of red with anger. He made his first mistake by grabbing Mia by the arm. She took him and his brother and made them eat dirt.

Anyway, there was a huge commotion the store owners chased them out of the area. Two weeks later, Ivan and his brother came with twelve others to claim Mia. They said that she belonged to the tribe. Mia went ballistic. I had to keep her locked up in her room. They had been hunting for them ever since, claiming that she belonged to the community. They wanted to make her some kind of princess. Ivan would be her mate so that they could have children that look like her, to restore color to their people. So when she came up missing, we thought they had taken her. We actually went to see if they had her; when we didn't find her, we started to look elsewhere."

"But it still doesn't explain how they made it out here. It's a long way from Georgia to New Orleans," Falu asked.

"Well, we moved a lot because Solana was scared to death they would come in the middle of the night and take Mia away. She was also afraid they would kill Naphtali. He was determined they were not getting his daughter, which is why they went into hiding. "

"Kumar, what are your plans for Mia? I have become very fond of her," Falu explained.

"That's an understatement; he's in love," Max teased.

Kumar smiled and nodded. "What's not to love? She is exciting and super sexy. Mia is twenty years old, and the only other man she let get close to was a young man named Nelson Robles. We used to call him Zorro because he wore black all the time. He was crazy over her, and she liked him."

Falu was displeased, "I don't think I want to hear this," Falu's face changed.

"I think you should… it's important to understand who she is. One day Zorro came to visit; he wanted to be alone with her; they decided to walk down to the market. They talked and flirted with each other. When this dude came out of nowhere, he started to follow them, making rude remarks at him, calling him a puss and a dickless asshole. Taunting him of what he would do to Mia, making sexual innuendos. So instead of Zorro standing up to the guy, he apologized, taking Mia by the elbow. She pulled away from Zorro. She called the man out, and he laughed. Mia attacked this dude, destroying him. Zorro just stood there and did nothing. When she finished with the guys, she walked away from Zorro. She snapped. I tried to calm her down, and she started to cry from anger."

"Damn, what kind of man apologies after they insulted you in front of his girl," Max said, "he was a puss…man, please, Falu would have killed him."

"Mia never spoke to him again; he was a sissy boy with a lot of money. After that, they moved west. To be honest, I am relieved that she is with you. I know she is safe. I would tell her parent and put their mind at ease. Solana is very stressed out, and Naphtali doesn't want to leave her alone too long."

"Good because I wasn't ready to let her go… we are tribal, and I know she's the woman I want."

"So let me ask you, have you been intimate?"

Falu laughed, "No, but I'm working on it. Why do you ask?"

"You are in for an experience... if she is anything like her mother and aunt... make sure you take your vitamins. They are very sensual," they all laughed.

"I think I don't have problems in that department," Falu replied.

"I tell you what; I think you are just what she needs in a man. But I warn you not to go easy on her. Show her who the boss is, or she will lose respect for you. She needs a strong hand. Well, my new friends, I think I should be going. I must inform my family that their daughter is well and safe. Her father will be very happy."

"Why don't you stay the night and leave in the morning? Come on, enjoy our hospitality, and you are welcome anytime," Falu offered happily.

"Thank you, my friend. I shall enjoy that. I will be back again to keep an eye on her; I have a few weeks before I have to go back to my wife."

Chapter 7: Good Girl

Falu had Mia watch closer after they interrogated the attackers. He found out that someone had paid them to kidnap Mia. A scientist wanted her DNA, and ran some experiments on her. After tracing the source, they found him working out of a homemade laboratory that looked like something out of an old horror movie. He was arrested and sent to prison for attempted kidnapping. The four other women he had locked up were released and taken to the nearest hospital. However, one of the doctors got away.

Mia hated that she had to be escorted every time she went outside the estate's perimeters. She felt like a child, which led her to argue consistently with Max and Falu's crew. But Falu was afraid that someone might get the wrong idea with all the visitors coming to see him.

As the weather became warmer, the girls spent more time outdoors by the pool, one of the cooks was always at the grill cooking burgers or hot dogs and the drinks were plenty.

The girls loved to dance and sing along with the music. Sometimes, they would get carried away. By mid-evening, the music was pumping, and the laughter grew louder until they noticed Falu at the bar staring intensely at Mia. Mia wore a tiny black and white string bikini that left nothing to the imagination. It took the girls a minute to gather up all their things and head upstairs. When Falu finally made it upstairs, they had already bathed and were in bed. He stopped at the door with a fake smile on his face. It wasn't the first time they partied at the pool, and he didn't seem to mind. "Funny thing happened," he stated, "I wondered where half of my crew were. They seem to be M.I.A. I couldn't get them to do a damn thing, so I took a stroll to find out what the hell was so interesting in at that side of the house. Guess what I found… would any of you care to take a crack at it," the girls looked at each other confused, "Let me enlighten you… Mia, you were in this black and white bathing suit just showing off what the good Lord gave you!"

"What did I do wrong? I was having fun just like everybody else?" she snapped with an attitude.

"Damn it, Mia, you were shaking your ass in bathing that was too small for you! Get yourself a decent bathing suit before I kill someone. Get yourself together, woman. I have people coming in a few days, and I don't want to be embarrassed by having half your shit hanging out."

"Don't worry, Falu, I'll make sure she gets one tomorrow," Tina volunteered.

"Make it happen, Mia…" she turned her nose up at him, "one day; I will spank some sense into you," Falu said, shaking his fist at her. Like always, he called one of the girls to his room.

"Why does it always have to be about him," Mia whined.

"Because he's the boss sugar, mine yourself, honey, he means what he says. Tomorrow, we'll try to get something he'll approve of."

"God, I feel like a child. He doesn't own me," Tina and Ivett laughed at her childlike pouting.

"According to big daddy, he does own you," Ivette giggled.

Mia hated when he scolded her, she wanted so much to hate him, but something about him kept her bound to him. She was angry, especially when he was around, so she spent a lot of time in the gym banging out her frustrations.

Glen was always available to help her work out and helped her get sparring partners. Johnny Boy was in charge of the free weights and holding the punching bag when she pounded into it. She loved torturing the young man, and he always complained about her.

The control room had all the cameras in all the hallways and most rooms. Next to the security room was the largest meeting room, where Falu held his monthly meetings with his crew. Max bought Tony some sandwiches, fruit, and chips. Tony always lucked out; he got to eat all the leftovers.

"Hey, what are you doing," Max asked.

"I am watching my girl. I love watching her workout," Tony said, biting into the sandwich.

"Is that Mia," Falu said, standing behind him.

"Yeah, boss, watch, this is some funny shit; holdup, let me turn on the mic so we can hear."

Mia laughed at Johnny Boy.

"I hate holding this bag for you… you're so angry,' he said, whining and complaining. They watch as Mia kicks the bag sending him flying across the room.

"Get your ass up and hold this bag like you have a pair of balls in those pants," she yelled at him, making everyone laugh.

"Come on, Mia, you ain't right. Every time I hold this stupid bag, I go home with black and blue marks, have Glen hold it for you."

"What a puss! All you had to do is put some backbone into it," she turned to Glen. "So, who do you have for me?"

"I have these two guys that I had to pay them to spar with you, so go easy on them… please." Mia smiled at him and asked him to help her stretch. They watched as she danced around the ring, teasing them.

"She's such a damn show off," Max said.

"Yeah, but she can kick some ass. I still feel the side effects in my ribs," Falu said, touching them.

"That's what I live for, to watch her in action… come on, look at her move, it's like poetry," Tony said, getting excited.

"I'm glad you found some entertainment, but keep your eyes and ears open. There'll be many people coming through those doors, and some of them aren't people I'd take home to meet mama. But I need their products, and I aim to get them."

"I hear your boss. Got to watch my girl. I'm always on guard."

Tina and Betty made all the arrangements for the pool party. Falu had some important clients coming that he wanted to impress. The investors were scouting a location to open a Jazz Club and were serious about coming to New Orleans. Falu wanted to put some figures on paper and seal the deal. This was the kind of business Falu wished to bring to the city. He tried to restore the beauty and establish a reputation for good food and music.

The band was setting up, ready for the evening. Tina and Ivette hung decorations and lights and Betty took care of the food and table arrangements. Betty was in charged that his guests were comfortable, escorting them to their tables.

The girls wore beautiful fashion bathing suits, and their hair and make-up were applied with expertise. Falu was happy with their work; he knew he could count on them to make the place look festive. He wore a white cotton shirt and tan shorts down past his knees. He wanted to fit into the summer scene. "You girls did a great job, and you look fabulous," he kissed Ivette's temple, "but where's the princess? I want her down here."

"She'll be down, she was nursing a headache earlier and was in the shower when we came down," Ivette said, assuring him she was on her way.

"Alright, now when Mr. Landis arrives, please make sure he's comfortable he's a nerves shithead, but he's the money man, and I want this business signed and sealed before he leaves my door."

"Don't worry, we'll take care of him," Betty said, rubbing her hands; she loved when they entertained outside guests. They always had so much fun.

"Good, I know I can count on you girls. Just keep the food and drinks coming."

The music started as the guests were ushered to the pool area. The girls ensured they had plenty of food and drinks and were seated comfortably. "Your women are so beautiful Mr. Falu," Mr. Dennis Landis said, hoping not to offend Falu, he was afraid of Falu. Landis was an older gentleman with a round belly and receding hairline. He was nervous to be so close to Falu but was star-struck. All he talked about was seeing the mighty Falu, the King of New Orleans.

"Thank you, Dennis. They are some of the most beautiful women in these parts."

"You're a lucky ma, ma… man," Dennis rose from his chair slowly, mouth wide open. All four of his guests followed his gaze, "Holy cow," Dennis rubbed his eyes. They couldn't help but stare at the beautiful Mia wearing a scandalized pink Brazilian bikini, her hair piled on her head with tiny curls caressing her flawless face, long dangling red earrings, and red lips. Falu fought to keep the stirring in his pants in check.

"Dennis, that's my woman," Falu said.

Dennis went pale and started to sweat, "Please don't kill me, Falu. She's a true beauty," Falu chuckled as the other looked away when Falu said she was one of his girls.

"Do you want to meet her?"

Dennis's eyes were wide, "Really?" Dennis started to sweat again.

"Sure, I'll call her over so you can meet her… you know she'll be singing later tonight." Falu waved her over, but she pretended not to see him. She grabbed a food tray and began to pass something out. She could see his eyes boring into her as he got closer; he held her gently by her elbow, whispering for her to follow him. When he introduced her to Dennis and his guest, he started to stutter. When she smiled at him, he turned bright red and started to shake.

"Oh my, pl… please…forgive me. I feel like a fool," he didn't know where to look, staring at Mia's breast and then her hypnotic brown eyes.

After the introduction, Falu excused himself and pulled her inside. "You know I'm beginning to think you retarded, or you just like pissing me off."

"What did I do now? You said to get a bathing suit in my size I did. You said to make sure we look nice… I looked in the mirror, and I asked some of the guys. They said I look nice… what more do you want," Mia replied, annoyed.

Falu laughed, "What do you think the guys will say, Mia? Look, maybe I should have been a little more specific… you look amazing," he caressed her cheek, "I just don't want others looking at what belongs to me."

"When did this happen? When did I suddenly belong to you!" She answered sarcastically. He stared at her for a few seconds and pulled her into his arms. "You were born for me… your future is with me, and the only reason I haven't made mad love to you is because… I don't want to force you… I want a willing lover." She could feel his erection pressing against her. He tipped her head back, kissing her holding her in such a way so she couldn't move; she was trapped in waves of sensations and heat, "Yu eras mia ahora y siempre."

Mia was frustrated with her own passion. "Now put on one of those doohickeys women use and cover-up what belongs to me." Mia was blushing when he finally let go of her, and he smacked her hiney before it left her shaking. It took her a while to get herself together to join the others. She wrapped herself in a surah before stepping outside with the others. She looked at Falu, who winked at her.

She hated herself for allowing the feelings to surface every time he kissed her, wishing he didn't stop. When his lips touched her neck, it turned her to mush. When he whispered softly in her ear it drove her crazy.

The party was a success, during one of her songs, Dennis couldn't contend himself. "I do anything you say, Falu, sign any contract you want, and I know you'd properly kill me, but if you can allow Mia to sing at my place now and then, I would give you a piece of the profits." Falu smiled as he watched Mia on stage singing a heartfelt Spanish song that always gave him chills when she sang.

"There's no need for that. I'm sure she'll enjoy singing. If you follow me, we can have these papers signed and notarized tonight."

"Yes, anything," he said, unable to take his eyes off Mia as she belted out the song's chorus, "I've heard from many that you are an honest man Falu. I'm very happy."

That night after the party, she went for a walk to her favorite place where she could look out into the busing city. She didn't want to be present when he called one of the girls to his room.

The night air was cool against her skin. She felt like she could breathe again. The stars adored the night skies. It was a clear night. She listened to her music pod; it played a song of love and hate. She hummed to the song, lost in the lyrics and the rhythm of the music, relating to the song's intensity. Mia closed her eyes and could envision being on stage singing the song when she felt a pair of hands on her shoulders and flinched.

She turned abruptly to see Max's smiling face. "Oh my God, Max, you scared the shit out of me!"

"I'm sorry I called out to you, but you didn't hear me. I was securing the area. What are you doing here so late?"

"I just needed to think, I love the girls, but sometimes it gets crowded."

"Well, I can understand that, but they mean well."

"It's beautiful out here. I like watching the city's heartbeat."

"What's on your mind, or should I say who?"

"Are you assuming I'm thinking about that whore brother?"

"Who else," he chuckled.

"I don't want to talk about him…" she fought back the tears, "What about you, Max, who holds the strings of your heart." He smiled. Max couldn't help, but he understood why Falu was crazy about Mia like her. He sat close to her watching the moon shine on her beautiful face.

"No one special, but I'm having a good time looking… tell me, Mia, why the mention of my brother brings you close to tears."

"I'd hope you didn't notice," he hugged her. "When did he become this huge entity who incites fear in people."

"Oh, I guess he was born with it … they used to call my father the 'King of New Orleans', and he was the prince. Falu was always larger than life …"

"So, do you always hate living in his shadows?"

"Oh hell no, not at all. I wouldn't know what to do if he hadn't taken control." He hugged her neck playfully. "Look, Mia, underneath all that power, there is a man who needs someone to love him, and you're that woman."

Mia started to laugh, "You're kidding me, right? I mean, women are not something your brother is lacking, there are always some women hanging from him, and I'm sure they are more than willing to give their heart if he asks."

"But none of them is pulling on his heartstrings, and he wants you, Mia. What about you? How do you feel about him?"

"Max, I truly don't think it's my heart that he wants. I don't know how I feel… my mind gets foggy, and sometimes I just don't want to think… what he does behind closed doors."

"Well, I know this: when my brother loves someone, he gives his all and has his heart set on you."

"I don't know what will happen when I regain my memory, Max. What if I'm involved with someone else, and it's hard to know… I just don't want to be hurt."

They continued to talk for a while, unaware that Falu was watching in the shadows, every time he heard her laugh, a surge of jealousy ran through his body. Horrible thoughts began to creep into his head. What if Max was in love with her too? They never had the same taste in women, but Mia could change anyone's mind. Falu tore away before he made a fool of himself. He loved his brother, and his brother would never disrespect him. But if she had feelings for him, he didn't know how to deal with the knowledge that she preferred his brother instead.

The thought made him angrier as he reached his suite. He waited for Mia on the balcony with the doors wide open to avoid missing his presence when she came by. He was not going to let her get by him. "Where have you been?" he said sternly. She tried to make light of the situation, but inside she was afraid of him.

"I was on the terrace getting some night air with Max."

"Oh really, doing what," he said accusatorily.

"What do you think we were doing?" she answered sarcastically.

"I don't know, but you better tell me something soon."

"Falu, why are you being such an ass," she tried to leave, but he grabbed her by the wrist.

"You don't know what kind of an asshole I can become, Mia. But you were the one with my brother all lovey and cozy."

She tried to pull away from him, but he held her tighter. "If you knew where I was, why'd ask," she said under clenched teeth, "Do you think there's something between Max and I?"

He pulled her to him, "I don't know what to think. Every time I come around you, it's like you can't wait to get away from me," he yelled.

"Maybe because he's not trying to get into my pants… Max respects me, Falu, and all he did was talk about you, defending his big brother. You should be glad, you have such a loyal brother." She tried to leave, but he pulled her into his embrace.

"I want to know, do you have feelings for my brother? Be honest with me, woman, because I can't take lies."

"I do… have feelings for Max, but not like where the dirty mind is going. I like Max a lot. He is one person I could talk to and be myself… but I… my feelings lay elsewhere."

"Thank you for being honest, there isn't anything I would do for my brother, but I'm not going to pretend I don't want you in every way. I don't just want what is between your legs… I want everything…, especially your heart," he pressed his lips to her ear. "There is no other woman for me but you… I know you'll come to me when ready," he whispered. She tried to pull away again.

"How could you say that when you screw any women who shakes their ass at you," she said, becoming angry.

He pulled her back. "You'll understand when the time comes… as I said, it's just sex. Now go to bed before I change my mind and drag your pretty ass to my bed."

Mia cried herself to sleep, she had to put up a wall. The pain was insane, and she could always count on her indifference to keep herself straight. She wanted to believe that she belonged to him, that he cared, but she was convinced that he probably said the same thing to the girls. How else would he get three fabulous women to sleep with him every night? She could still feel his kiss on her lips, and instantly her body began to betray her.

Chapter 8: True Feelings

Mia was angry all the time. She tried to control her attitude, whenever she was around Falu, it came out in spades, and he caught the brunt of it. Most of the time, he just laughed at her and blew kisses, making her even more furious. Once a week, she would accompany the girls to the nightclub when they had a live band. Sometimes depending on the band, they would ask her to sing.

Falu wasn't around as much as he wanted to. He was working hard, trying to get these projects on the way to the interview late in the evening.

It was Betty's birthday, and they decided to celebrate it in the club. Falu gifted her choice of band for the night, food, and drinks. Mia was late nursing a headache; she arrived wearing a black leather outfit that turned heads. All eyes were on her. She smiled at all the activities, the dance floor moved with dancers, and the main bar was backed up. Mia made her way towards the back bar when she bumped into Falu, who was waiting for a drink with a woman holding him from behind. She didn't notice him until she stood right next to him. "Oh my God," she said when she saw him. He tried to hold her arm, and the woman let go of him moving away.

"You look really nice, baby," Falu said.

"Too bad I can't say the same about you. You look like shit."

"That's because I didn't get a chance to shower and change. I just came down from the office," he held her by both arms.

"You smell like some of your whores. Now let go of me."

"Come on, baby, let's not fight. Let's dance." He tried to pull her to the dance floor.

"I don't want to dance with you. I know how you dance with these women digging your hands down their shit."

"Woo, baby! You're a mean bitch when you're jealous… Come on, Mia! Daddy loves you only."

"Oh my God, Falu, you're ridiculous." He was so powerfully built, that she always had difficulty pulling away from him. He tried to hold her close.

"Relax, woman! Just dance with me. I swear I won't molest you on the dance floor." He smiled.

She finally pulled free, "Kiss my ass!" She yelled at him.

He watched her disappear into the crowd. "Baby, I love you… hum…I love that woman," he said aloud. He was in great spirits and smelled himself.

Maybe she was right.

After a shower and a change of clothes, he returned to the party. He could hear Mia's sultry voice singing an R&B song with the crowd wanting more. He loved listening to her sing, but sometimes he would get upset watching how she moved on stage.

Max and Ricky waved him to their table with three girls sitting comfortably drinking and smoking cannabis with the guys. When Falu sat down automatically, one of the girls moved closer to him. "She's on fire tonight, man," Ricky said, moving to the beat.

"I can tell the crowd is pumped …" Falu said, drinking the shot Max poured for him. The girl moving closer to him began to touch and rub herself against him. "Not now, baby… I have a bigger fish to catch tonight." Mia began to flirt with the male band player when she finished singing, and her laughter drove him crazy.

"Calm down, brother. She's just having fun," Max said, knowing his brother well.

"Well, guess what, if she's going to have fun, it will be with me tonight. So sweetheart, move over because my bitch is sitting with me tonight, and she doesn't play fair." Falu made his way toward Mia, who was in the middle of a group of men. When they saw him coming, they moved aside. Mia's smile faded when she saw him coming toward her.

"I have a table for us, come on," he didn't wait for her to reply as he pulled her by the hand. "You're sitting with me tonight," he pulled her along.

"Says who?" she stopped him.

"Says me… I'm tired of watching you flirt with every son-of-a-bitch here." Mia was not pleased with the seating arrangement, especially when the other women at the table glared at her. The first fast song they played, she pulled Max unto the dance floor. Falu sat back and smiled; he knew she was playing with him. Ricky took his turn dancing with her until a slow song came on.

"My turn," he said before she made it back to her seat. He held her tightly, drinking in her essences; she could feel his rippling muscles against her. "I better not catch you dancing slowly with anybody. Seriously, I will hurt someone." She felt his breath against her neck and wanted to pass out. Mia could feel his lust rising against her and couldn't help swaying to his rhythm; he knew how to dance so well, like music was part of his soul. Mia was lost in his arms when the music stopped. She was still trying to compose herself. Max was surprised that Falu behaved himself on the dance floor.

"See, I told you he can do it," Ricky said.

"What are you talking about, Ricky, love," asked one of the girls at the table. "Is that Falu's woman or something?"

"Yeah, and you better watch it. She'll kick your ass," Ricky said, laughing.

"She's mean, Ricky. When she glared at me with those crazy brown eyes, I thought I would turn to stone." She snuggled closer to Ricky, "You three dance so well. I wish I could dance like that."

"That's because my mother and grandmother were professional dancers. Max explained that they owned a dance studio, and she taught us how to dance," Max explained.

Falu made her dance to all the slow songs with him. However, Mia's attempt to stay aloof was not working. At every turn, he whispered in her ear, singing the words to the love song they were dancing to. She felt the hard chest muscles against her and wished he was hers, completely. For a moment, he was. But she wondered how many other women he whispered those sweet words to.

Mia felt uncomfortable sitting close to him and trying to keep her composer. "I'm not feeling well… I'm going to my room."

"Are you sure? I'll walk you," Falu said.

"Why, I know where I'm going?"

"I understand that, but I want to walk you anyway," he took her by the hand and walked her outside. "Why are you so bitchy every time I try to be nice to you?" She didn't want to tell him the truth, that she was madly in love with him and the only way she could get day by day was to lash out at him.

"I don't know, Falu, maybe I'm getting my period, who knows," she cried.

He walked her to her room and started to laugh. "You know Mia… I know what's wrong with you," he had this smug look on his face, "And I know just the person who can give you a fix. You need sex, baby, long-lasting, hot smoking sex," he laughed.

She wanted to slap him, "I can't believe you said that."

He kissed her. "Lighten up, baby. I know you're frustrated," she was silent. He held her hand, becoming serious. "I know you think all I do is sleep with different women, and you don't understand my relationship with the girls. But until we are in a physical relationship, it takes all I can do to stay away from you. The decision is in your court."

"Falu, I don't think you could be with just one woman. I don't want to get hurt, so the best thing for me is to stay far away from you."

He pulled her closer. "Mia, you're driving me crazy, but I'm chalking it up to your sickness. You will be my woman in every way… do worry, it won't be long," he kissed her. "Now go to bed, sweetheart, think about what I said, dream about me, baby."

How it would feel to be with him was never far from her thoughts. But it still killed her, knowing he was with other women. Maybe it is better that she didn't know. It was bad enough remembering the kisses and the sensation he gave her. She would rather not know the wonders of being with him and later suffer betrayal.

Falu continued to entertain his vendors, arranging a special business dinner party for Steven O'Hara, who had the steel he wanted, and Brandon Price, owner of the largest cement company in the area. Falu wanted the exclusive rights to as much steel and cement as he needed. He needed to lock in at a reasonable price as these two men were the shadiest he had ever dealt with. He planned to sign a contract and assign one of his men to overlook the operation.

The girls made all the arrangements, from cocktails to dinner; they took charge of making sure the guests were taken care of as perfect hosts. Mia was unhappy as she had gotten into a huge argument with Falu earlier and refused to participate in hosting his party.

"Sugar, please get dressed and come downstairs. You've been pushing your luck. Don't make things harder for yourself."

"I know what you're saying; I hate that smug look on his face!"

"She's right, Mia," Betty added. "He gave you an order. Now, all we have to do is entertain them until dinner. The servants will take care of the rest."

"Alright, but I'm not happy about this," she said, frustrated.

"Mia, this is very important to him, and it's important to us," Ivette said, finishing up the makeup. "Now be a good girl, get dressed, and pass out some drink."

Betty was surprised when she met Brandon Price. He was a heavy set man with a bald head. He wore five heavy gold chains that made him look like he didn't have a neck. Brandon wore diamond rings on almost all his fingers. The woman he traveled with was dressed in seedy clothes, a tight purple satin dress with most of her breast exposed. Like him, her jewelry and makeup were overdone, making her look more like a cartoon character. White powered face, purple eye shadow, and bright red lipstick. Betty wasn't aware that he was bringing someone else and had to rearrange the seating and let the cook know they may have one or two extra guests.

Brandon was impressed with the sophistication of Falu's estate. Every room he passed was just as exquisite as the next. "Hey Falu, my man, how are you?" they shook hands. "This is my lady Monet. She's a beauty, ain't she?" Falu smiled and knowledge her. He could tell she was once a beautiful woman.

"Falu, your women are sexy. We have a lot in the comment, brother. We both love beauty, look at my Monet, a face like an angel… look at these tits, and they're really not like those fake shits you see around… Hey, anytime you want to, you know… just say the word," he laughed loudly. Monet is seen to be in a daze.

"Thank you, Brandon, for your very generous offer, but as you see, I have my girls who satisfy all my needs."

"You are one lucky bastard. Look at this, you live like a king… you have a true gift."

"I see you're doing well yourself, but I'm concerned, Brandon… the price of your cement is going up… you wouldn't be robbing people with your prices. I would be really disappointed if that was the case."

Brandon's color drained from his face, "Oh course not, Falu, I wouldn't do that to you… I'm a fair man, and my prices are fair."

Ivette poured him another drink. "Good because if you force me to bring in my own company, I will run your ass into the ground."

"Oh no, my friend, I promise you I will give you my best, at a great price… that is why I'm here." Brandon was terrified; he knew that if someone could close him down, it was Falu and his crew.

"Now you're talking. Just don't disappoint me," Falu said, ensuring, he knew who he was talking to. Brandon was very shady.

Steven O'Hara did not shock Falu when he entered wearing a fur coat, looking like a pimp, considering that the temperature outside was hot and sticky. He also dressed flashy with rings and chains everywhere. He had tattoos on his neck and fingers, a ring on his eyebrows, and diamond studs in his ears. "Well, now that we're here enjoying the cocktails, dinner will be ready soon," the girls served drinks and trays of cheeses crackers.

Brandon was a loud man who liked to boast about everything he had. He wanted to fondle the woman he bought with him. Steven couldn't take his eyes off the girls. He followed Tina with his eyes every time she came with drinks. "I wish I had known we could bring a guest, I have some beauties of my own." Falu watched them closely. He wanted them to relax so they could strike a good deal.

They laughed and agreed to negotiate and have a tentative agreement before the night was over. Steven's eyes popped out when Mia strode in wearing a scandalized outfit that looked like something she should be wearing to bed. It was a sheer black catsuit with a netted top that barely covered her breast and hips. Tina almost dropped her tray when she saw Mia. She tried walking in front of her to cover her up, but it was too late. Falu had a full view of her, and he was not happy. He recovered enough to talk to the two men, drooling over her. "That's my new girl Mia," he signaled for Tina. "Get her the hell out of here before I kill her," whispering in her ear. Tina pulled Mia aside and told her to stay in her room, not to do anything until they arrived.

It took Falu almost two hours to get his guest to focus on business. Brandon kept throwing Monet in his face for an hour with Mia during dinner. Steven chimed in, making crude remarks about what he would do to her. The more they talked about Mia, the angrier Falu became until he blew up and threatened them. The room went quiet, and Steven gave him a price he could live with within a few minutes, and Brandan gave him several tons of free cement with his first order.

Tina was nervous and worried about Mia, who had calmly gone to bed. The girls were frustrated with her and repeatedly told her not to make him angry. But she always pushed him to the edge, and now they didn't know if they could save her from his wrath.

"Sister, you done pissed him off. I could see it in his eyes. It spelled out the murder," Tina said, pacing nervously.

"I'm not afraid of him. He'll get over it, you'll see."

"Little sister, we always warned you, don't let the breast out of the box. You are truly in some deep shit," Ivette added.

"If you are trying to scare me, it's not going to work," she tried to put on a brave face.

"No, we tried to scare you before it came to this. I don't know what we're going to do," Betty said. Mia saw the fear on their faces and knew they were truly afraid.

"What can he possibly do to me? Don't worry about me. I can take on the mighty Falu. I'll be alright," she had to convince herself.

It was after eleven when he asked his guest to leave, they had wanted to stay and suck up more of his food and liquor, and Falu wasn't in the mood. He was fuming again when he made it to their suite. The girls heard him coming up the stairs and prepared themselves. He pushed open the door looking for Mia, who was in bed. "Where is that bitch," he said, clenching his teeth. The veins on the side of his neck were bulging. "Mia, get up!" he yelled. She peeped at him from beneath the covers.

"What do you want?" she asked, scared.

"Don't play stupid with me, woman. Get your ass out of bed and get in my room right now!"

"I'm tired. I'll talk to you tomorrow," she was scared.

He walked to her bed and pulled the blanket off her, grabbing her by the wrist. With ease, he put her over his shoulder. Mia was not excepting him to toss her over his shoulder like a sack of potatoes.

"Are you insane? Let go of me!" she screamed. Falu threw her on his bed, slamming the door behind him.

"I told you not to push me! Now you're going to pay!" Falu grabbed her by her wrist and put her across his knee, pulling her underwear down. Mia was in shock. Everything was happening fast as she tried to wiggle out of his grip. But the more she wiggled and screamed, the tighter he held her, spanking her soundly on her behind. Mia screamed every time he made contact yelling all the obesities that came to her mind. Tears sprang to her eyes. When he was finish, he threw her back in his bed and pinned her down with his body.

"From now on, you will sleep with me and learn how to please your man. Do you understand me?" he yelled.

"Is that how you get your kicks raping and beating woman," she screamed back to him.

"I'm not going to rape you, Mia. You will give yourself to me, willingly!"

"Never... I'll never submit to you!" She screamed between sobs.

His mouth was close to her ear. "That's all right because I'm not going to make it easy for you to say no, watch and learn, baby," she could feel his muscular body stiffen as he kissed her and sucked on her neck and breast. Mia stopped struggling and let him have his way as he continued to kiss her neck and breast. The girls continued to knock on the door, hoping he would open the door and let her go. When he finally opened the door, he still had this wild look.

"Come on, Falu," Ivette said smiling. "Let's have some fun," the girls pulled him along, trying to calm him down.

He had to laugh at attempting to take his mind off Mia, who was still crying.

The girls took turns teasing him and making jokes, getting him tired to leave Mia alone. The music didn't conceal all the laughter coming from the next room. Her pride hurt more than the spanking she had received from the man that made her knees turn to jelly.

Mia cried, feeling the helplessness of wanting him, knowing that the significance of their relationship was about to change if she gave into him. "I can't give into you, Falu. If I do, I will lose," she said to herself.

A few hours later, Falu returned to the room. She laid still in the dark. He took a quick shower and lay beside her, pulling her close and trapping her in his embrace. Mia found it hard to sleep knowing he was so close. Every time she moved, he'd snuggled closer, and his manhood pressed against her. Finally, in the early morning, she fell asleep. When she woke up, he was gone… she took the opportunity to jump in the shower. The warm water was refreshing against her sore bottom. She was surprised at the marks Falu put on her neck and breast. "Shit," she said, trying to rub them out. "Damn you, Falu," she cried, frustrated.

The girls were already eating breakfast when she finally came out of the room. Her eyes were swollen from crying. Tina saw the marks on her neck. "How are you this morning, sugar? Did he… you know," she asked, looking at her crotch.

Mia nodded with tears swelling up again, shaking her head no. "We tried to calm him down last night, but we don't know how long we can keep him away from your…yummy," Betty said, shaking her head.

"He said… he said he wouldn't force me, but he wasn't going to make it easy."

"That doesn't sound good, Mia. I honestly don't know how you're going to keep him away. By the look of those marks on your neck, I'm pretty sure he is putting the pressure on you," Ivette said, feeling sorry for her.

"If I give in to him, then he wins," tears rolled down her face. "It has to be on my terms, not his," she argued.

Betty looked at her and laughed. "Well, now you go, girl. Not that it's going to work."

"Sweetie, you're a going to be a very up-tight woman when he turns on the heat," Betty said, concerned at how long it would take before she gave in.

"I'm already frustrated. I do get those feelings…you know… down there, he drives me crazy when he starts to kiss."

"The problem with you two is that you're both stubborn… God help you both, sugar." Tina fussed at her, taking a bite from her toast.

"Come on, let's do something fun, it's a beautiful morning, and the swimming pool is calling me," Ivette chimed in, trying to lighten everyone's mood.

"You girls go without me. I'm staying in today," she said sadly.

Tina hugged her, wanting to make her feel better. "You'll be alright, sugar. Try not to think about it too much. I mean, how long can he stay mad at you?"

Mia decided to spend the day inside, on the balcony listening to music, out of Falu's sight. She could trace the black and blue marks on her hiney.

Falu spent the morning reviewing all the new contracts and finishing the latest figures. All morning he answered Ricky and Max with short sentences avoiding eye contact and short tempered. They wonder if his meeting last night didn't go as he planned. Ricky rolled up the floor plan for the courier to pick up. Falu stood up and walked towards the picture window in his office. "What's eating you, man? Was the meeting a bust yesterday?"

Falu broke the pencil in his hand and smashed it against the wall, running his finger through his hair. "I blew up on Mia last night."

"You blew up on her. How?" Max asked, concerned about Mia's condition.

"She pissed me the hell off, and I gave her a spanking."

Ricky locked eyes with Max and laughed, "No shit, you took her over your knee… and spanked that sweet ass?" Ricky joked.

"Yes… I did, and it felt damn good. She'd been pushing my buttons, busting my balls for a while now, so last night it came to a head."

"Is she alright…" Max asked.

Falu rolled his eyes at his brother, "Yeah, little brother, you're always on her side, aren't you?"

"I like Mia a lot. I can't help protecting her… you do know it's a brotherly affection I have towards her, don't you?"

"I know, Max, but leave Mia up to me. I have to show her who wears the pants and whose balls are bigger. I'm turning up the heat, she's sleeping with me now, and it won't be long before she'll beg Big Daddy to ride my pony."

"Just be careful with her. Mia is very confused about her feelings for you."

"Well, I'm going to try my best to make things really clear. She already knows how I feel about her."

"So, what happened at the meeting that pissed you off?" Ricky asked.

"Everything was going well. I had those assholes relax, you know. They were blowing hot air up my ass. I made it clear I wanted this wrapped up tonight. So my sweet songbird comes downstairs looking like a two-bit whore with this peek-a-boo shit on. I turn red. It took me about two hours to get these douchebags to focus on the meeting. All they talked about was what they would do to Mia, asking me for a chance with her, pissing me off. I wanted to break their necks. I mean, granted, she looked beautiful, for the bedroom with me. I asked Tina to take the bitch out of my sight. Then asshole Brandon started to grab his shit trying to push the woman he was with at me."

"Ah, that big chest woman wearing too much makeup. I've seen him riding around with her," Ricky said, frowning.

"Yeah, I had to threaten them. I said I would beat them bloody if they continued to talk about my future wife. That chicken shit Steven started to sweat and apologized a hundred times, offering me a better price than I anticipated. But I warned them, if they start any shit with me as they did with Terry Owens, I will kick them out of my city. I'm not putting up with his price hikes."

"So you got what you wanted, and you still beat Mia's butt," Max remarked.

"Max… we had this huge fight earlier; I warned her about flirting with the guys and watch what she wears around them. What she wore last night was meant for the bedroom, and she knew it. She will not disrespect me like that anymore."

"Honestly, cousin, I can't wait until you pop that cherry. Obviously, she's crazy about you, and I've never seen you obsessed with any woman before. So get the getting, you'll both feel better."

Max shot his cousin sternly, "I know she likes you, but she's as bullheaded as you are. Honestly, I can't believe the girls didn't run interference for her."

"Oh yeah… they did. They pulled me into this all night orgy. I was one tired son-of-a-bitch this morning. The girls were worried as shit when I burst the door open of their room. Anyway, they did manage to calm me down and wore my ass out," they laughed. "So now, I'm in charge. I love that woman, but she will live by my rules."

Chapter 9: Love Test

Mia was getting ready for bed when Falu appeared in her bedroom. "Are you hard of hearing? What are you doing?" he asked sternly.

She got butterflies in her stomach right away. "I'm getting ready for bed. I didn't sleep well last night," her eyes huge with fear.

"What part of your sleeping with me from now did you not understand?" He grabbed her by the wrist and pulled her towards him. "Get to stepping, woman," he dragged her along behind him, pinning her to the door. His mouth was inches away from her face. "You don't listen well, do you? Now get your ass in the shower!"

"But I don't …" he cut her off.

"Do you want me to help you undress?" he said forcefully, she nodded. He undressed quickly and stood naked before her. She stared at his beautifully built body, well-sculptured abs, strong, wonderful, and defined thighs and legs. She turned away when he caught her staring. He turned around, smiling at her discomfort.

The three head shower hit his body in all directions when she shyly entered the shower. Her heart fluttered when she watched the water gleaming down his magnificent body. He handed her a bar of soap. "Lather me up, baby," he ordered.

She was confused, "What?"

"What part did you not understand? Take the soap and bathe me, woman," Falu smiled as she nervously washed his massive chest, legs, back, and shoulders. When she thought she was finished, he turned to her and smiled, "You forgot a spot."

Mia was mortified, "You're kidding, right," he shook his head no. She looked down at his erection and closed her eyes.

Falu laughed.

When she was done, he took the soap away from her. "Now it's my turn," her jaw dropped, and her eyes grew large. Falu took his time moving the soap over her breast and body, enjoying every moment. Mia looked away, wanting to punch him in his grinning face. When he turns her around to wash her back. He leans into her, pressing his chest and manhood against her back. Mia couldn't take it anymore, pushing him away and escaping his grasp.

"Can you be a bigger asshole," she uttered, wrapping herself in a towel and heading toward the door.

"Hey, where are you going?"

"I'm getting something to wear," she looked perplexed.

"Not necessary, baby."

"Really, Falu? Don't you think you've done enough?"

"The shit just started, baby," he slammed the door shut. Falu picked her up and threw her on the bed, fussing with her hands tying them to the bed.

Mia struggled to get free. "You said you wouldn't force me, now let me go!"

Falu laughed at her, "He trapped her legs down and pinned her underneath him. "There's more than one way to have sex, my love," he kissed her taking her breath away. Mia thought she was going to faint. Falu traveled down to her neck, breast sending waves of sensation throughout her body. Mia wiggled under the pressure of his lips that had stopped at her tight belly. She begged him to stop, making him laugh louder as he pried her legs apart and found his target. Mia started to scream as he skillfully drove her into a frenzy of passion. Mia was in tears when he finally let her go. Her legs shook, and she started to cry. She had never experienced something so intense before, and he knew she would react to this type of stimulation.

Falu left her tied up and went for one of the girls. When he came back, he cleaned up and watched Mia, who lay in a ball, with her legs pulled to her chest on her side. When he lets her go, she punches him in the chest. "I hate you!" She yelled at him.

"That's not what you were saying a while ago," he reached for her and pulled her towards him, holding her tightly from behind. "Listen to me, my princess. Sweetheart, I know what lays beneath that cool exterior," he whispered close to her ear. "There is a sweet, sensual, hot woman that's dying to come out. When she does," he teased. "What you just experienced is nothing compared to what's to come… my name will be on your lips," he chuckled

"You're a sick prick." Mia tried to block out the sensation as he touched her in places that made her blush. She wanted to give into him, to feel the sweet sensation he had awakened in her.

Falu was gone by the time Mia woke up. She tried hard not to think about the night before. The girls held breakfast for her and saw how distress she was. "Sugar, my dear girl, I don't know how much longer you will be able to hold off. Maybe you should see Peggy today about getting you on some birth control," she looked at her strangely.

"Mia, you weren't screaming, 'help me' last night. Falu knows what he is doing down there, and he wants your yummy really bad. It's only a matter of time before you give in, honey. So, if you don't want a baby, you better go for that shot. It's good for six months," Betty advised.

"Oh God, I don't know what to do. I don't want a baby," she whined.

"If I were you, I would just enjoy the ride. He has this big anaconda, and he knows how to use it," Ivette teased, putting a wine bottle between her legs and poking her in the arm. "Open wide, baby. I'm coming for you."

"Get away from me. You're disgusting," Mia laughed. Ivette chased her around the room with the wine bottle between her legs. Betty and Tina screamed with laughter.

"Help me, somebody," Ivette cried. "An anaconda is ravishing me. Help me, someone! Who will save me?"

Mia tried not to laugh. "Stop! It's not that I don't want to… that's the only thing I can control right now."

"You have it, sister, but I also know he is putting the pressure on you. As far as I know, I don't remember a woman he had to chase. But remember this… the man can go all night. We can testify to that, and he is very determined to get what he wants." Mia became quiet. Her mind wandered back to the night before when he fondled her to the point of screaming. She knew he enjoyed her discomfort, especially when he'd lie on her and kiss her breasts and sensitive spots.

"I better go see Peggy… I think you're right."

Mia realized she didn't have much time before giving in to his lust. She wanted him the worst way, but it had to be on her terms.

After consuming much wine, they turned up the music and headed for the pole. Ivette had been giving her lessons, and Mia was caught up in the moment. She took to the pole like a pro, bumping and grinding with the music.

"Go girl, make that pole part of you, yeah," yelled the girls. Ivette joined Mia at the pole.

Tina laughed so loud that she fell off her chair facing the ceiling. When she looked back, Falu was standing at the entrance, arms crossed, watching them act crazy. They stopped laughing when Tina turned down the music. "I'm glad everyone is having fun… Mia, run a bath for us." She looked at the girls for support. The master bathroom was adjacent to his room. It was fashionably done in black and navy blue with a huge old-fashioned claw tub and crone fixtures. Mia hurried to put the bubbly liquid into the tub and placed some towels by the bench near the tub.

When Falu took off his clothes, she saw the red marks on his back. "Get in. I need you to rub my shoulders, I was picking up cement bags, and I'm beat." Mia slipped in behind him. He enjoyed her closeness as he leaned back, feeling her breast against his back. "Sweetheart, rub my shoulders. They are so sore I can hardly move them." Mia tried to massage his back and shoulders as hard as she could, but her small hands were not doing the job. He turned around and was on top of her, smiling when he saw the shock on her face as he lay between her legs. "Now this is cozy," he pulled her towards him and kissed her passionately. "Man, I sure needed that." Mia could feel the heat rising inside of her. "You looked really sweet on that pole. Just pretend that pole is me," Mia tried to push him off her when he wouldn't move, pulling his hair. "Damn it, woman! Alright, let go of my hair," he laughed. He tried to wrestle with her, rubbing himself against her and laughing at her anger. She pulled his hair again and managed to free herself. "You're such a fake, and I know you want me to throw you on the floor and make sweet love to you," he teased.

She wrapped herself in one of the huge towels, "Diablo socio!" She yelled at him.

"I know, baby, but you still want me," she could hear him laughing as she slammed the bathroom door. She ran to their room to get dressed. Tina knocked on the bathroom door to see if he needed anything.

"Hey, is everything alright?" Tina asked.

"Come in," he gave her a devilish look. "I love teasing her."

Tina smiled and sat on the small stool, "She's young Falu, very stubborn but so sweet."

"You're a good woman Tina… I've been thinking about you girls for a while now. You girls have been so good to her. I have a surprise for all of you. I'm building some condos, beautiful three bedrooms, two baths, and nice balconies. It has hundred-twenty units." Tina's eyes grew wider. This is what they have been waiting for. "The condos are over fifteen businesses… I want you girls to be the co-owners and use one of the storefronts as an office. Each one of you will have a pick of your own place. Some of the units are already spoken for… I know the three of you are very fond of each other."

Tina's eyes became misty, knowing this was such a gift. He was always so good to them; they wanted him to be happy and in love. "Oh, Falu! Do you love her?"

He smiled at her. "I… adore her, she's my equal. Do you think I'm making a mistake?"

Tina swelled with emotions, "I see the way you look at her, it's more than lust, but she is confused. Is there anything we can do to help her understand?"

"You girls have been wonderful to her, and believe me. I appreciate everything you've done. She needed a friend, and you all embraced her."

Tina knelt by the edge of the tub, pushed his hair back, and hugged him. "Thank you, Falu. You have been a life saver to all of us, and you deserve to be loved. I have a strong feeling she's mad about you too."

"Has she said so?"

Tina didn't want to betray her. "Let's just say her protest has to do with something deeper, a woman knows… it's just a matter of time."

He touched her arm. "You know I'll always take care of my girls… you were there when I needed you, and now it's time to let go and allow you, girls, to move on with your lives, find that special person. Whatever you need and want, I will give you." Tina cried with happiness.

That night the girls celebrated with wine and tears as he played with Mia in his bedroom. All the pain and hardships were behind them. Falu selected them to be his special girls now, they made plans for their future.

The following morning Mia crawled out of bed with her hair in a mess of curls wearing only a robe. She walked toward the table and poured herself a cup of coffee. "Girl, love the look," Ivette said, teasing her.

"Yeah, you look like shit," Betty added, feeling sorry and guilty for her.

"I feel like shit," she tried to eat some toast.

"Tough night, sugar," Tina asked.

Mia pulled her robe tighter, "God helps me. He wouldn't let up! I wanted to slap him so he would leave me alone. We wrestled all night."

"Sugar, don't forget you have your appointment with Dr. Eli this morning."

"Ah! Is that today? I almost forgot," she put her hair in a ponytail. "I'm not changing. I'm going just like this. She headed towards his office barefooted in her robe. His door was opened when she appeared at the entrance.

"Mia, honey, come in," he said, happy to see her. She walked over to his sofa and laid down. He sat across from her.

"So, honey, how are you feeling these days?"

She took a deep breath and covered her eyes. Remembering what he did to her the night before. He teased her with the threats he promised, he would make her feel weak with desire but wouldn't give in sheltering her heart. "Dr., he's sucking the life out of me. What I'm going to do?" she cried, frustrated.

"What do you mean?" He asked curiously. She stood up and walked towards him opening her robe and flashing her breast. He almost dropped his glasses. "Oh my…ah, I see." He turned his gaze away.

"They don't stop at my belly. You get my meaning."

"Ah… I see…okay," he said nervously. "Why don't you sit back down, and we can discuss this." Mia covered herself back up and curled into a ball on the sofa.

"Mia, how does it make you feel when he does… you know?"

"I'm so ashamed of myself, Doc,' she started to cry. "He makes me sleep with him. I like feeling his strong muscular body against mine, and I feel so special…I think I love him. When he kisses me, I lose my mind."

He could hear the frustration in her voice. "Mia, there's nothing wrong with loving him. It's a natural and normal feeling. Tell me, why do you feel ashamed?"

"Because I feel… I feel tingling down there. But I won't give in to him… I won't give him what he wants… I mean, I want to. Heaven, help me! Doc, I want him to make love to me, but …"

"But what's stopping you…?"

"I watch him with the girls, and aside from having sex with them, I don't see him kissing them or touching them as he does me… he tells me he wants me. I'm afraid if I give in to him, he'll stop… kissing me, touching me… and wanting me. Can you understand that."

"I doubt that, sweetie. He doesn't have that kind of intimate relationship with the girls like he wants with you."

"I love feeling him pressed against me at night. He reaches out in the middle of the night and makes me feel safe and… wanted," she added. "He cares deeply for the girls, but it's just sex between them."

Mia jumped off the sofa, walking towards him, clearly upset, "Well, what does that mean? It's just sex. Make me understand what that means because I don't understand that phrase for the life of me. It's not what I want… I want love and passion. I don't want to be his fourth day sex partner."

"Calm down, Mia. I understand you completely, my dear, but there is an understanding with the girls, not you. You are not under that agreement."

"That's bullshit, then where do I belong? When he gets tired of me, what will he do? Toss me out like other girls? I deserve better, and that is why I don't feel like spreading my legs to him… it has to be on my terms. And I know he's not making things easy, but… I won't settle for less," she started to cry again.

"Oh sweetheart, please don't cry anymore," he put his arm around her. She cried on his shoulder. "Mia, lie down and relax. Let me tell you about the girls. Maybe it will help you understand who Falu is. Many people misunderstand him," he sat behind her in his chair.

"Behind all those muscles and strength lies a highly intelligent man. I had the pleasure of knowing his extraordinary parents. I actually knew his mother, Esmeralda's family. Falu's mother was a dancer and went to a prestigious school up North. Her mother was a dance instructor and a wonderful woman. Esmeralda was the youngest of three and followed in her mother's footsteps. Esmeralda was a beautiful woman. She was warm and loving and a devoted daughter to both her parents. Her sister needed help caring for her when her mother became very sick. Esmeralda would take over after working all day, spending hours by her bedside. Mariana was very jealous of Esmeralda's popularity. Esmeralda was madly in love with Reyes, but Mariana would call him all sorts of names trying to discourage her relationship. However, no one would pull those two apart, and their romance was superior. Esmeralda had these huge golden eyes and honey-colored hair. Max favored her a lot and his sister Silva."

"Wait, so there's a sister? They have a sister… he never mentioned her."

"Silva and her family left with their aunt. They run a huge winery in the west. It was the best move for her. Falu was the golden child. He was the spitting image of his father, the Warlord of his tribe and became the Overlord of New Orleans. Reyes came from a family of professors, extremely bright and charismatic. Reyes' family loved Esmeralda, so when Falu came along, it was a celebration. As a young child, Falu was like a sponged calculator. He would do calculations in his head when he was three years old. Esmeralda became pregnant again when Falu was two years old. Sick most of the first three months of her pregnancy, she had no problem letting the family help. Falu's IQ was off the charts, and his abilities to learn and absorb information were extraordinary, but it didn't stop there. He was athletic and very competitive. He blew through school and was sent to college abroad. But in his junior year, his father passed away of a brain aneurism, and he lingered in a coma for a while before he died. I had never seen anything like it before, and the funeral was monumental. They morn his death for months, but Falu was forced to leave his mother and go back to fulfill the dream his father had for him. Five years later, he graduated with a Ph.D. Max went for two years abroad and got really homesick, came home… he was a true mama's boy. Mariana's husband moved his family to Savannah after the father passed. Esmeralda took over the dinner, not having the passion for dancing anymore. She sold the dance studio and told me she would never dance again. Her dance partner was gone, and so went the desire to dance. She lived for her children and reached out to the community she loved so much. After Reyes' death, the city became very unstable again, some bad elements moved into the area, causing many problems. Esmeralda was still a very attractive woman and caught the eye of one of the worse felons that roam in this area. When Esmeralda refused his advances, Winston Clark was determined to have her regardless of her rejections for him. Falu and Max spent a lot of time at the Inner Cities inquiring about what he wanted to accomplish. He knew that the streets were not safe, and he put a bodyguard on his mother against her wishes. One night Winston Clark came into the diner demanding something to eat. He had been drinking and tried to kiss Esmeralda…she slapped him and shamed him in front of everyone. He laughed and promised he would come back and settle the score. They were troublemakers, always acting up when Falu was out of town. They knew he was dangerous, but they were also stupid. There were riots in the streets that week, and Esmeralda closed the diner early. These thugs broke windows, ran people down, stole, and burned everything in sight. That's when he came for her. He killed the guard and broke down the door. Esmeralda fought him. The place was a wreck. Winston raped her and beat her savagely. She was a petite woman and wasn't strong enough to defend herself. Two doctors worked on her, but the injuries were so extensive. The hospital did not have the equipment to save her life. It was explosive when Falu and Max found their mother in that condition. Max was inconsolable and cried like a baby, but Falu held his anger. The whole city was at their door praying, bringing food, and doing what they could. On the third day, as Falu and Max held her hands, they felt the life slip away from her." Doctor Eli removed his glasses and wiped his eyes. Mia used her robe to wipe her tears. "The last thing she said to Falu as she caressed his face was to take care of Max. She knew that Max was going to need him. Falu's face was like a stone as tears ran down his young face… he let out a deep cry from the depth of his soul. I was there, I think his cries were heard throughout the city, and Max became sick. Falu had to make all the funeral arrangements, and they buried her next to her husband… they were too young to die. After the funeral, Falu had a call to arms. Twenty thousand men and women came to his aid from all parts of the city and neighboring towns. They swept through the streets looking for every vile, undesirable man, woman, and teen. They went door to door, bringing them into the streets, and were given an hour to gather their things and leave, never to return. Winston Clark and his gang were not so lucky and were handed over to Falu. He beat him so bad that people turned away. All the pain and suffering poured out of him. Tears for his mother and the way she was murdered blinded him, and Winston's plead for mercy fell on deaf ears. He made it known to everyone that this kind of crime would not be tolerated anymore in his city. Then he slit his throat. The rest of the gang came before a firing squad. Their bodies were dumped in the swamp somewhere."

Mia cried for him. She understood he had to always be in control and why he had to always be strong for everyone. "Were the girls with him to comfort him, they take great care of him?" She sniffled.

"Oh no, the girls came much later. They were Max and Ricky's idea. Because Falu worked so hard, he had little time to socialize and was always frustrated. Ricky and Max came up with this grand idea; if he got laid occasionally, he wouldn't be such a ball-buster. He agreed with the idea.

Ricky and Max made all the arrangements. They auditioned hundreds of women.”

“Auditions… what do you mean, like sex, they had to have sex with him?”

“No, sweetie, they went on dates to see if they were compatible. They narrowed them down to twenty women. Out of the twenty, Falu chose five that he liked. Falu saw the connection between Tina, Ivette, and Betty. He had already made up his mind to pick Tina. When he overheard Ivette crying that she had nowhere to go, Tina and Betty were comforting her and held on to each other. Falu had been listening and watching them from the beginning. He gave two of the other women money and sent them away. The girls held on to each other for support. He paced back and forth, looking at them, watching the girls’ nervous faces. He looked at them, said he couldn’t make up his mind between them, and said he wanted to keep the three. There were tears of joy and happiness. Mia, he has changed the lives of those women in such a way they could never repay him. He will always care for them even when they go their own way. That is why their relationship is based on just sex. The girls would love to see him in love and happy.”

Mia hugged Dr. Eli. “Thank you, Doc, for giving me a little background on Falu. It helps me understand him and why the girls feel the way they do. I don’t know what’s going to happen once I regain my memory. I know I have a home and family. I don't know if I want to stay with him… I do know that I don't want to be his fourth day lover. Do you think he'll keep me here by force?"

"I don't think so, but I know he's hoping you to stay. I know he has strong feelings for you and will persuade you to stay with him."

"Doc, please don't tell him what we discuss. I don't want him to know my intimate feelings."

"My dear, this is between a doctor and his patient. I'll only let him know your progress. He always asks me how you're doing. Mia, don't be hard on yourself for liking him… he really is a great man."

Mia laughed, "I'll consider that while I kick his ass." Mia tried to understand Falu and what he expected from her.

Chapter 10: Boys Will Be Boys

It was always a treat for Falu to get away from work and enjoy some time with the boys. The work had been crazy in the field, and he looked forward to playing poker with family and friends. Like always, he was the last one to the table, and everyone else was buzzed when he got comfortable.

"I'm in. What are the stakes?"

"You ask the same question every week, Falu. Everything's the same," Ricky said, teasing him.

"Well, asshole. I need to know if things have changed," they all laughed, "I'm hot today, so don't cry when I take all your money," he chuckled.

"You always say that boss, but you always lose," Dr. Eli teased, laughing at him.

"Hey, I may be unlucky in cards, but I'm a love machine with the women… speaking of women. How is my little passionflower?"

Dr. Eli almost choked on his drink. "Oh my God… so Mia comes for her weekly visit late as always. She walked in with her hair in a ponytail, barefoot, wearing her robe as she had just rolled out of bed. She lies down on the sofa. Alright, everything's cool, so I proceeded to ask her how she's feeling, and she says… he's sucking the life out of me. I ask her what she meant… so this beautiful woman walks up to me, rips open her robe, and flashes me… I am staring at these beautiful breasts… my glasses fogged up, and I didn't even notice the marks she was trying to show me. I think she forgets I'm a man," they roared with laughter. "I'm sorry, boss, but I started to sweat. I turned away and asked her to please lay back down." Falu nearly fell to the floor, he was laughing so hard. "It was amazing, but I wasn't prepared," Doc added. "Hell, I'm still in shock."

"She does have an amazing rack. So… does she talk about me?"

"Now come on, boss, you know that there is a thing called patient confidentiality, and I gave her my word as a professional that I would not mention who or what we discuss in our sessions."

"Doc, I'm not stupid. I know my baby mentions me."

"I don't know how you can do it… sleeping with her every night and not sex her up. You must have nerves of steel," Ricky said, already buzzed.

"Are you serious? I would have forced her long ago if it hadn't been for the girls. It's very frustrating for me, but it's a game, and I'm not making it easy for her."

"How do you know she wants you, Falu. I know you never had problems with women, and she is making you sweat," Max asked, teasing him.

"It's all about the chase, brother. I know she wants me, but she doesn't fight that hard… but I want her to say, 'come to me, big daddy.' It's only a matter of time."

"Well, I hope so because you're a mean son-of-a-bitch when you're frustrated and horny," Max interjected.

"What do you know about frustration, you're like a rabbit jumping from one hole to another, and you got the damn nerve to talk about me…bitch you get more tail than I do," Falu teased.

"Alright, I gotcha, but I'm not biting anyone's head off, "Max said, lifting his shot glass. "Let's toast to the women in our lives."

"Here, to the women we love and my living doll!" Falu shouted.

Falu was in a great mood when he finally made it to bed. He watched her as she slept peacefully, taking a lock of hair to his lips and kissing her cheek and forehead. She wiggled close to him. "Te amo," he whispered. He removed all his clothes and climbed into bed, pulling her into an embrace, her body molded next to his. He can't fight the impulse to kiss her lips. She moaned in her sleep, opening her mouth to touch his tongue to hers. He held her face in his hand as his kiss became more demanding, trailing down her neck and sending steaming sensations through her body. She moans softly, pressing herself closer to him while he plays with her breast touching her nipples, feeling them grow hard under his touch. "Soon, baby, you will come to me soon," he pulled her close, feeling her sweet body in his arms.

The Party

The house was buzzing with people coming to see Falu; he was busy getting his projects off the ground. But his mind was not far from Mia, the headaches were getting worst, and Dr. Eli was thinking of putting her on another type of medication. Mia had been with him for four months and had adapted to life at the estate.

The girls were preparing for another huge event. It was an annual party Falu had for all his vendors. Tina was in charge of all the arrangements, making her feel important. She went over a food list when two men asked her to see Falu. She argued with them, they seemed out of place, and she did not recognize them from the regular vendors Falu did business with. This concerned her because they were giving her a hard time. Max heard the conversation and interjected. "I'm sorry I heard you wanted to speak to my brother?" They looked at him strangely.

"You are tribal?"

"Yes, you have a problem with that?" Max became defensive.

"No, actually, it's perfect. My name is Ivan. I have come for Raven Moon."

Max's eyebrows went up, surprised as they boldly asked for her, "Oh really, and how are you connected?"

"She is promised to me, and I have come to claim her," Max remembered the name from Kumar. He ushered them into the library away from the others. Falu had just finished meeting with Ricky when he interrupted them.

"Falu, you have visitors."

Falu didn't like the look on his face and concluded the meeting. "What's up?"

"Some assholes are claiming Raven Moon as his bride," Max said, physically upset.

"Really, who let them in?" The concern they got past security.

"I don't know, but I have them waiting in the library. I'm ready to snap their necks," Max said, clenching his jaw.

"Alright… do me a favor and take them to my office. Ricky, please bring Mia." Falu prepared himself mentally for the meeting. His relationship with Mia was better since her last doctor's appointment, and they could speak with each other without arguing.

When Falu walked into his office, the two stood up. They had no idea that someone like Falu was meeting them. They greeted him warmly. "Mr. Falu, we have heard many good things about you. I am Ivan from River-Negron tribal community, and this is my brother. Like you, we are tribal kinsmen. I heard that one of our members was in your care. We have been looking for Raven Moon for a long time."

"Mia is with me. What is your relation to her?" He already knew but was interested to see how they would present themselves.

"She has promised me. My father is the Warlord of our tribe; we were supposed to marry, but her family took her away from us. I have come to claim the woman I love and fulfill my promise to her."

"Interesting, why would Mia's family take her away and not want you with her? I'm just asking."

"Well, you know, young love. Her father doesn't think any man is good enough for Raven Moon. She is very special, as you can see. But we love each other, and that's what counts."

"I can understand that a woman like Mia… hot blooded and all, will drive any man to distraction. You know, in the sack and all, I bet she gave you a good ride," Falu said, waiting for their reaction.

"Once you taste her sweet nectar, it's hard to be with anyone else," Ivan implied. The door opened, and Mia walked in wearing a form-fitting outfit, boots, and her hair in a perfect curled ponytail.

"Am I interrupting something?" She asked, smiling.

"No, baby, come in. I have something to give you." Mia looked at Ivan and his brother strangely. They followed her every move.

"I wanted to give you the list of songs from Sol y Mar and Crazy People. They want you to pick some songs for you to sing."

Mia smiled, excited they wanted her to sing with their bands. "Wow, I can't wait. They both play such great music."

"How is the setup going?"

"It's going great. Everything is coming together," he kissed her forehead.

"Well, baby, you take your time," he kissed her and tapped her hiney before she left. Max and Ricky stood by the door, watching their reactions.

"As you can see, Mia has no idea who the hell you are, and I'm supposed the turn her over to you... it's not happening,"

Ivan was getting upset, the veins on his neck straining. "Mr. Falu, I understand your concern over Raven Moon, but as you know well, it is the business of the tribal community to take care of its own. She is like a goddess to us, and we believe that she will restore the true nature of our people and is very valuable to our community for our future."

The more Ivan tried to explain, the more Falu wanted to jump over his desk and smash him in the face. "Damn… I've never heard so much bullshit in my life." The brothers looked at each other. "I would have respected you more if you came with the truth. That she's a hot woman, and you want her."

"Mr. Falu, do try to understand, this is a tribal dispute, and as a tribal member yourself try to see our side of the story also," Ivan explained.

Falu came from behind his desk. "Let me try to make you understand this, Mia is my woman, and I don't give a shit about restoring the true nature of anything. She belongs to me, and she shares my bed every night."

Ivan's anger was evident, he was beginning to argue, and it wasn't sitting well with Falu and the rest. "I understand your attraction to her. She is a very beautiful woman and …"

Falu cut him off. "ENOUGH! You have insulted my intelligence with this bullshit story so let me come straight with you because I'm tired of the bullshit. You entered my home first of all without permission. I know the story behind Mia and why her family left your community. Rape and assault is ugly, and if you think you can come here to scare me into handing her over to you, you're sadly mistaken."

"Mr. Falu," Ivan replied. "There are two sides to every story, and I see you have heard just one side of it."

"There are no sides when it comes to rape and assault. Mia is my woman, my future wife, and will be the mother to my children. You would have to come here with an army to get her away from me. Now, I suggest you leave my presence before I lose my temper," he turned to his guard. "Get these assholes out of here and out of my city."

Ivan flashed his brother a scared look. "I'm sorry if I have intruded. Please forgive us. We shall be on our way."

"I never want to see your damn faces in my city again. Get it? You have been officially warned. Next time I won't be so nice."

When they were ushered away, Falu showed his nature, "Max, please find out who the hell let them in," he yelled.

"They came in with the kitchen help posing as waiters. That's why Tina was confused and argued with them before I stepped in."

"Alright, I don't want any unauthorized person on this property. Make sure you pass these douchebags' pictures around."

"Falu, is this the guest list?" Ricky asked, looking at a list of a hundred names.

"Yeah, take that to the guard. They don't get in if they don't have an invite."

"But you have Benny Hops on this list. I thought you couldn't stand the shithead?"

"I can't, but if I don't invite him, his brother won't come, and I need his brother's limestone. He was the only one I didn't get to renegotiate prices. I really need to speak to him and get that price down."

"You know Benny is going to hit on Mia?" Max said, concerned.

"I'm counting on it, brother. Then I'll have Teddy where I want him. You know how he protects that punk ass brother of his."

"But Mia will destroy him…he's a joke," Ricky added.

"I know. I'm counting on that too. I know his stupid ass will not resist saying something to her, and if I know my girl… she will beat the shit out of him. Teddy will come to his brother's defense. He will do anything to keep me from killing him."

"Well, I can't wait to see that. He is so slimy and nasty, and I hate it when he tries to talk to me," Ricky made a sour face.

"Now you know how I feel. He follows me around like a puppy," Falu whined.

Falu worked late into the night. When he came to bed, Mia was fast asleep. After a quick shower, he lay down and was content to just hold her. Mia stirred when he pulled her close.

"Late night again," she said, smiling.

"Yeah, baby, just tying up loose ends for tomorrow. I heard you had another bad headache?"

"This afternoon, but the new medicine doc gave me works really fast… the only thing is that it gives me strange dreams."

"Anything I should be concerned about?"

"No, not really. The dreams aren't scary, just strange people talking to me. Falu, who were those two men yesterday… it's like I had seen them before."

"In what sense do you remember them, from your past or in just passing?"

"I guess it was more like a feeling they kind of creeped me out."

Falu laughed. "Yeah, they were strange, but you don't have to worry about them. They won't be bothering anyone."

"Well, that is nice," she snuggled closer to him. He turned her to face him, kissing her tenderly. She returned his kisses until his kisses became more demanding. "Falu…"

"What is it, baby," he said, breathing heavy and running his hand to cup her hiney.

"I think you may want to stop."

"Why baby, I just want to touch you,' he said, pouting like a small boy.

"Honey, I have my monthly,"

"Baby, you've had your monthly since I met you. When are you going to let me love you, Mia?"

"You're so sweet when you're begging. I've been thinking about it… maybe after my monthly."

"Damnit, how long is that going to take?" He asked, kissing and teasing her.

"It will take a couple of days…" she smiled, knowing how much he wanted her.

He kissed her shoulder. "Well, I already waited over four months. What's a couple more days."

"It won't kill you."

"I know, but having you so close and me being horny all the time…is killing me."

"Poor baby," she teased.

Falu was content with holding her and did not need to call the girls to satisfy his sexual appetite. Mia was in heaven, she was ready to give in to him, he stopped pressing, and their communication was bringing them closer. He had also stopped sleeping with the girls.

Tina ran around like a crazy woman, ensuring everything was done, while Betty made sure the food was ready and the guest was finally arriving. Ivette ushered guests to the tables as they entered. Everyone was seen to be having a good time, and Tina finally got a chance to relax and enjoy the party.

She searched for Mia, who was scheduled to sing with Sol y Mar.

Benny was excited to be invited to Falu's house, and it wasn't every day he had that honor. Since his older brother had so many connections, he always took advantage of his social network. The first place he headed was to the bar. He tried to strengthen out his wrinkled brown shirt and his yellow tie. Benny considered himself a ladies' man. He was a fast talker and felt he was entitled to everything. Max was checking the liquor behind the bar when Benny spotted him.

"Hey, bro. What's up! Where's your brother, man? I haven't seen him?"

Max didn't want to tell him the truth that Falu tried to avoid him as much as possible. "He's around. Falu's a busy man."

"Man, this place is beautiful. It's nicer than last year."

"Well, you know my brother. He loves beautiful things."

"Damn, I wanted to know if he'd let me poke one of his girls. They are perfectly fine, like delicate flowers, you know. I especially like that one over there with the big tatas," he pointed to Ivette, who always wore clothes that covered up her breast.

"Let me give you some friendly advice, don't mess with Falu's girls, he doesn't like it. There are a lot of other women here you can hit on. Ivette is off limits."

"But he has three girls. How can he satisfy all three…? I can help him with that," he laughed, wiping his mouth with the back of his hand. Max rolled his eyes, wondering why he thought Benny would take his advice.

"Falu has four girls, so watch yourself. Don't go after Mia."

His eyes grew larger, "Mmm… Mia, that means mine… sounds juicy," he chuckled.

Max shoved a drink in his hand. "Don't even think about it, just drink and be happy." Benny scans the room when up comes Mia to sing a love song. "Oh my God, am I seeing things? Who the hell is that hot bitch?" Benny perked up.

Gary, the bartender, laughed as Max ran his hand through his hair in frustration. "Is his funeral boss? Let it be," Gary said to Max.

"This guy is a dick," Max added, helping Gary set up the bar.

"I'm going to introduce myself; you know I have a way with women."

"Benny, you need to go home, get rid of that cheap ass cologne, shower, iron your clothes, and maybe you can get 10 feet closer to her," Gary said, amused that he would try to speak to her.

"Man, you don't know anything about women. This cologne is a women's magnet. Women love the natural male scent. They know I'm a macho man, unlike you, sissy boys. Watch and learn, young bucks." Gary shook his head and laughed.

Tina was dead on her feet, glad to have a few minutes to enjoy the wonderful news. The girls were ecstatic about having their own place and running their own business. Ivette cried like a baby when Falu gave them the news yesterday. The condos were ready, and five new businesses moved in. Tina waved Mia over after her set. "Sugar, you sound better and better. Have you heard the news about our condos?"

"Yes, I'm excited for you, but why do you have to leave…? Who am I going to talk to?" she whined.

"You are always welcome, my little sister, anytime."

They watch Ivette running towards them, "Oh my God," she said out of breath. "That crazy stinky guy is after me," they stood up to see who she was talking about.

"Oh no, not him again," Tina said, rolling her eyes. "He is nothing but trouble. Keep your distance from him, Mia. He's a slimy piece of shit." They watched as he came towards them. The girls turned their backs to him, hoping he'd go away.

"Good day, my lovelies. Don't you all look lovely tonight?" Benny said, licking his lips. The girls tried to ignore him, but he stood close to Mia. "So, I hear you're

Falu's new girl… you know him, and we go back a long way."

"What is that foul odor," Mia cried. Tina and Ivette laughed at the faces Mia was making.

"That's my manly scent, baby. It's the musk of a real man; you get my drift." Mia turned away from him.

"Benny, you need to leave us alone before Falu sees you," Tina warned him, hoping he would go away.

"Bitch I'm not talking to you!"

Mia pushed him back, sending him crashing to the floor. "Don't you ever talk like that to her! Now go away, or you'll get hurt," she warned him.

Benny smiled as he stood back, "Hey, I'm sorry, please! I get a little excited when I'm near beautiful women."

"Well, this is a private conversation, and I wish you would leave us alone," she glared.

"You have the most beautiful eyes," he blew a kiss at her.

"And you're going to have black and blue ones with a spot of red if you don't beat it!"

"Sure, doll face. I will catch you later, my sweet. When you're in a better mood." Benny backed off, blowing kisses at Mia. As the girls talked about their plans, Benny continued to stare at Mia, winking and blowing kisses her way. After a while, he returns to the bar and has a couple more shots.

"Gary, that is one beautiful woman, and those brown eyes just melt you down."

"I told you not to mess with any of the girls," Gary said, enjoying his disappointment.

"There is a big difference between you and I, sir... I know what women want, her mouth may be saying no, but her body is saying yes."

"Seriously, dude, you need to back off. The room is full of nice ladies. Why do you want to mess with Falu's women?"
"Because I can, and for that beauty, I will take my chances with the big guy, now I'm going to make my swift move, and I'll be in the back with her in a few minutes." He swallowed his drink, wiping his mouth with the back of his hand.

Mia and the girls were engrossed in conversation when Benny crept back near her, whispering something to her. She took his wrist and twisted it behind him, flipping him over on his back. The other guest came to see all the commotion as they watched Mia pick Benny up by his shirt and punch him in the mouth, knocking him backward.

Falu heard the commotion and smiled, "That's my girl," by the time he reached Mia, Benny was on the floor bleeding from his mouth. Falu picked him up by the hair, "Your toast, buddy. Get your ass up and get out of my house! Falu picked him up from the floor and pushed him towards the door."

"Come on, brother. What did I do wrong?" He begged, "She's a sweet babe… I just wanted to go in the back and get me a little." Benny braced himself, seeing the look of murder on Falu's face, regretting what he just said.

Falu snatched him by his shirt and pulled him off his feet. "I will break your narrow ass in two assholes." Falu was just a few inches away from his face.

Teddy was right behind Falu, begging for his brother's life. "Please, Falu, I know he's retarded. Please don't kill him. He's the only family I have left… Look, let us make a deal. I will give you the bottom price. I'll sign whatever you want… but please spare his life." Falu let go of him.

"Wait right here. I've got to see what kind of damage your prick of a brother did." Falu walked over to where Mia and the girls stood. She was ready to argue with him when he put his arm around her. "Are you okay, baby?"

"You don't want to know what he said to me, and I want to rip the skin from my arm where he touched me," Mia glared at Teddy and his brother. Falu held her in his arms.

"Next time he touches you or comes near, you hit him harder. You got me." She tried not to laugh.

The party continued, and Falu got what he wanted, but Benny continued to bother Mia the rest of the night, winking at her and blowing kisses. Mia was on cloud nine when she was singing with the bands. Falu danced with her, having a great time. He was so sweet, whispering words of love in Spanish. He would kiss her when they danced to the slow love songs. But towards midnight, the headaches had returned, and the music and noise were making it worst. Falu knew something was wrong with her when she wouldn't finish her set. He pulled her in his arms. "Come on, Mami, tell daddy. What's wrong?" she rested her head on his shoulder.

"The headache is back. I need to lie down," tears rolled down her cheeks.

"Do you want the doc to look at you?" he held her face towards him, wiping the tears from her eyes, and kissed her tenderly.

"I just need to lay down. The new medicine he gave me works really fast."

"Alright, come on, I'll walk you to the room."

"You don't have to, baby. You have guests."

"You're more important than my guests. Come on, baby, I'll tuck you in," They walk arm and arm towards their quarters, stealing kisses along the way. "I'll look in on you later. Try to rest." He looked at her sweet face and wanted to tell her how much he loved her. He kissed her on the lips and forehead before he left.

The party raged on, and the music was nonstop as people danced, enjoying the festivities. The girls were celebrating their new future and prospects. Betty brought fresh drinks over for the guys who were playing pool. "My feet are killing me," she said. "I think it's time for the heels to come off," she said, rubbing her feet.

"Do me a favor, love. Can you check in on Mia? Make sure she's alright and doesn't need to see the doc."

"Sure thing, I'll look in on little sister." Betty sang one of the songs she had heard Mia singing earlier, "Rainy days make me think of you." All the lights were off when she reached her room and changed into flats. The balcony doors were open, which was strange. They never left the doors open at night. Betty opened the door to Falu's room and immediately felt something was wrong. "Mia!" She turned on the small light by the bed, looking around the room. The bed was slept in, but Mia was nowhere in sight. She began to panic, checking the other bathroom and her room. She ran frantically downstairs, searching the club and looking for him. Falu knew right away something had happened to Mia.

"What's wrong, Betty? How's Mia?"

She could hardly speak, tears rolled down her cheeks. "She's... she's gone. I couldn't find her anywhere," Falu rushed to his room, trailed by his brother. He radios down to Tony, who was in charge of security.

"Boss, I haven't seen her. Did you check to see if her horse was still in the stables?"

Falu sat down, trying to keep a cool head. "Lucky is gone, Falu. She must have slipped out when Kevin and Joe were bringing out the horses," Ricky explained.

Tina knelt by Falu's side, "Something happened to her, she left all her clothes and her music pod… she never goes anywhere without it… and I know for a fact that… that she is in love with you."

"Did she tell you that?" He asked sadly.

"Yes, Falu, she was happy she told me that just this morning."

Falu forced a smile. He wasn't ready to let her go. "Max… I'm going after her… get my tracker. She will have to tell me to my face that she wants nothing to do with me." "Well, I'm going too, she's my friend, and I'm not ready to lose her," Max replied.

Chapter 11: Lost Now Found

It was dawn by the time Mia found herself in familiar surroundings. She had been wondering for hours, trying to find her way back to her parents' house. The small one-story house lay deep in the woods, surrounded by tall trees and overgrown bushes.

The outside light was still on. Mia stared at the house that was once her home and realized how small it was. She saw her brother's tiny face in the window. "Mother, father, it's Raven Moon. She's home," he yelled as he ran out of the door towards his sister. She picked him up and hugged him tightly, "Raven Moon look at you… you look different. You look beautiful." She saw her parents at the door, tears running down their happy faces. Her mother was thin, and her father had a cast on his left arm.

"I was hurt and didn't remember who I was. I'm so sorry I can only imagine how worried you all were," Mia cried as she held onto her parents. "Father, what happened to your arm?"

"Don't worry about me, sweetheart. Ivan and his brother tried to kidnap Pony Boy, but we fought them off, didn't we, son?"

"Yeah, we showed them who's the boss," he smiled proudly.

"They came after me. Ivan and his creepy brother… but the man I've been with chased them away. It's not safe here anymore. We have to pack. I don't have much time. He'll be here for me soon."

"Who, my love… Falu?" her mother asked.

"You know of him?" Mia asked, surprised.

"We knew you were with him. Kumar found you and told us you were safe," her father explained.

"Then why didn't you come for me?"

"Sweetheart, he told us you lost your memory. You didn't even remember him, and you were safer with Falu than you would ever have been with us," he said, holding her tight.

"Well, it's not safe here anymore. Pony Boy, help father pack just important things. Hurry!" Mia looked around the shabby two-bedroom house and began to help her mother gather important items.

"Mia, you look wonderful, like a woman in love. Are you in love with this man?"

She looked at her mother. They were always so close and could always talk about anything. "Yes, mother, I am in love."

Her mother looked into her eyes, "Have you two… you know."

Mia looked away, embarrassed. "No, not yet, but I've been thinking about it a lot. I think he loves me too… he's a strong and good man, mother."

"Good, I'm happy you found someone worthy of your love. We've heard many unbelievable things about him."

"Well, you'll be meeting him soon."

"Oh, really, are you sure."

"I'm very sure he'll come for me."

Raymond had a hard time tracking Mia's trail. It looked like she was going around in circles until he isolated her path deeper into the woods. The small house was hard to see through the tall trees and thick bushes. "This can't be the place," Ricky exclaimed.

"There's her horse," Falu said, not knowing what to expect. His heart was pounding as he looked for any sign of Mia.

"Raven Moon, come quick, there's a giant man outside with some other big men," Pony Boy cried from the window.

"Stay here, Pony Boy, and help mother, please. Let me talk to him first." She could see the stress on his face when she opened the door. Falu could hear the beat of his heart echoing. Until she put her arms around him, he held on to her and didn't want to let her go. "I got this surging pain in my head. It was as if my whole life flashed before my eyes. I remembered everything, my family. I freaked out, wondering if they must be going crazily worried about me. I panicked. I had to find out how they were right away."

He held her face towards him. "You should have waited for me. it was dangerous for you to leave in the night."

"Help me, Falu… please," she started to cry, "help my family, they're not safe here… they tried to take my brother to get to me."

"Listen to me. I'd do anything for you… why don't we bring them to live with us."

She shook her head, "My mother couldn't handle that kind of life; ever since she was raped and beaten, she's been afraid of strangers. Falu, I'll do anything you want."

"You'll come back with me today… you'll come to me willingly?"

"Yes, whatever you want… but how can I live in luxury when they live like this."

He looked at the small house that needed so many repairs. "Look, I have this ranch only twenty-five miles from here. It was a get-away place my parents used when they wanted to be alone, and they'll be safe there."

She kissed him and held him close until she could hear his heartbeat. "I knew you'd come for me."

"Oh, did you now," he grinned.

"How many times did you tell me you'd track me down and kick my butt," she smiled. "Come and meet my family."

Pony Boy was starstruck with Falu and the rest of the crew. He pulled Max into the back yard showing him the little chicks and ducklings he was feeding. While Solana made coffee Falu took the opportunity to speak to Naphtali about Mia.

"Thank you for taking care of my daughter. Kumar told us you were looking after her, and she was under a doctor's care. I don't know how I could ever thank you for all you've done for her."

"Well, to be honest, I had selfish motives… I love her. The minute I saw her, she stole my heart."

Naphtali smiled and shook his hand. "You have my blessing. I could tell she has eyes for you too… she was so sure you'd come for her."

"I'd go to hell and back for her, and I think she knows that."

Pony Boy couldn't stop talking. He was so excited to have the company he didn't know what to do with himself. "I think you are like the ranch. It's beautiful with lots of horses and animals you can take care of," Falu said.

"You mean more than one horse?"

"Yeah, and you can pick your very own horse, but you have to take care of him," Falu explained, knowing he would jump at the chance.

"I will, I promise," he ran outside to tell the others.

"Mr. Max, I will get to pick out a horse. My very own."

"You are a lucky young man. What is your true name?"

"I am named after my father. When I turned 10, I picked my tribal name."

"It's a great name. I think you will do great."

"I can't wait." He ran off excitedly.

"The ranch has everything, a great marketplace not too far and even a school. You will be in charge of everything and want for nothing."

"We appreciate your kindness, Mr. Falu," Solana said.

"It's the least I can do, Mia. You will have to give your father Lucky, and someone will bring her back… you can ride with me."

"It will give me so much peace of mind to know you are safe, but we have to make sure someone is not lurking around and following you to the ranch," she said, concerned.

"Don't worry. Raymond is a pro and knows what to do. The ranch already has caretakers and security. The head housekeeper will take very good care of all of you. And don't worry about Mia. I'll take good care of her."

Mia said her tearful goodbyes to her family, but she knew they were in good hands. "Don't worry. They'll be fine. How about if we visit in a few weeks," Falu said, trying to reassure her.

"That would be nice," Mia said, leaning her head against his chest. She felt safe in his arms and was now committed to him. She would be one of his girls, but if that's what it took to keep her family safe, it was worth it.

It was mid-morning when they reached the estate, and Mia could hardly stay on the horse. She remembered Falu helping her upstairs and laying her on the bed. When she woke up the next morning, she was confused. Falu was not in bed. When she wandered into the outer room where they ate breakfast every morning, the place was empty except for the dance pole. Everyone was gone. The room she shared with the girls was empty, and all the furniture was gone. The room seems so large. It looked sad without the girls' pictures and decorations all over the walls. Mia was confused, wondering what was going on. She went downstairs to Dr. Eli's office, but it was closed. She felt like she was in a dream, but as she neared Dr. Manning and Peggy's office, she heard music. Peggy was at her desk making notes in someone's chart when Mia interrupted her.

"Dr. Peggy," she jumped. "I'm sorry, I didn't mean to startle you." Peggy was truly happy to see her.

"Mia, oh my God, how are you feeling? I heard you got your memory back. I'm so excited for you."

"Yes, it came back all at once."

"Great, I know the guys were so happy."

"Speaking of the guys, where is everybody? The girls are gone, their rooms are empty."

"Oh yes, they're moving. Honey, I thought you knew." Mia wondered if she wasn't losing her mind. Peggy senses her confusion. "Falu had been preparing for the girls to take over a project he was working on. They are going to be running a housing complex. It's very exciting for them." Mia took a deep breath. She wandered about herself, where she belonged now and how much she would miss the girls.

She waited for Falu. Everyone was gone, the estate felt eerie and empty. She wasn't feeling well, and the sight of her parents still haunted her. She remembered that day they were getting ready to move. Naphtali knew the house was not livable. It was only a place to rest until they decided where they were going. Her mother was sick and had no energy to go any further. She told her father that she would go hunt for some food for the evening. Mia tracked a herd of wild pigs and was in the process of shooting when a huge branch fell on her; all she did was look up and put her hand up to shield herself from the blow.

Mia went to her favorite place, the balcony, where she would sit for hours and watch the movement outside the estate's entrance. It was getting late. After eating something, she waited for Falu to come to bed, but she couldn't keep her eyes open after a few hours. The next day, movers brought a super king-size bed for the outer room, and they were moving furniture in and out. When they were finished, the girl's room was turned into an audio room with a great sound system and millions of songs. Mia was in heaven. She put on headphones and let the music take her away. She dreamed about Falu, how handsome and strong he was, and how he made her feel when he held her in his arms.

Mia moved to the beat of one of her favorite songs, closing her eyes to the world. When the song ended, she opened her eyes. Falu was standing at the door with a huge grin. Her heart melted when she saw him leaning against the threshold. "Where have you been?" She cried, relieved he was back.

"I've been watching you for the last few minutes and enjoying the view," he wrapped her in his arms. "I thought it was clear that the girls would be released from their contract when we became a couple. It's just you and me, baby. Come, we have to talk." Falu pulled her behind him and sat her on the edge of the bed. He kissed her passionately, laying her back on the bed. She was lost in his arms and embrace. He moved his hands skillfully, touching her in sensitive places, arousing her ready to be his. Falu turned her over as she closed her eyes, enjoying the sensation. She had dreamt of this moment when she would commit herself completely. There was nothing between them now. Lost in her heat, it startled her when he held her down and smacked her on her hiney.

"What, are you crazy? What did you do that for!" She jumped off the bed.

"Don't you ever pull some shit like that again, or I will spank you raw next time! Now come back to bed and let's get busy," he said, smiling and patting the bed.

"Oh-hell-no, I'm not in the mood now," she refused to come to him.

Falu laughed at her teasing. "Come on, baby. Come to daddy," he winked, making her angrier.

"You are so sure of yourself, aren't you?" she said with her arms folded.

"You said you would do anything… now come here and let me rock your world, baby."

"I knew that would come back to haunt me." She couldn't resist his smile.

"That's my baby; I've been waiting for this moment for a long time. Now you're mine." Mia fell into his arms without protest.

Falu made his move taking his time and making each moment count. He was not surprised when she moved his hand to those places that made her cry out with pleasure. He wanted her badly and waited until the moment was right to plunge into her sweetness. He was in heaven as she joined his rhythm, arching toward him. He removed her clothes, letting the light bathe her body. His heart was beating faster, using her lips to awaken that passion within the walls of her sexuality. "I said you would be mine," he chuckled. "I will take what a man could only take once. Mi amor," He cursed in Spanish, enjoying every touch as she explored his strong body, opening herself to him completely. All the months wanting him, she guided him inside of her, moaning softly, not caring about the pain that was substituted with pleasure.

"I knew it would be this way, Falu," she cried, wanting him more than ever. Mia tensed when she felt that rush that made her lose control for a moment, and her breathing became rapid. Falu chuckled, amplifying his passion before letting the sensations' waves pulse into her.

"Te amor Mia mi vida," he whispered in her ear. All the nights he dreamt of her wanted her badly explored at that moment. He lay on top of her arms wrapped so sweetly around his neck. She held on to him, feeling him pulsing inside her, enjoying the sensation. He had awakened something in her, and she was not disappointed.

"Mia," he whispered, "There's so much I want to teach you, my love."

"Huh, I'm ready," she smiled.

Falu woke up in the middle of the night watching Mia sleep. He pulled her closer to him, kissing her neck and teasing her with his lips. "You're punishing me, aren't you?" She said playfully, pulling away from him.

"Why would you say that, sweetheart? All I want is to be close to you?"

"Sure, baby, that's what you said an hour ago. You think I'm your new toy?"

"You are, and yes, you are my new toy, and I am punishing you for making me wait so long, knowing all along you wanted me."

"You see, that's why I made you wait so long because you're so damn cocky."

"I promise I'll leave you alone... for tonight... but tomorrow is another day."

They spent days getting to know each other better and tasting the sweet nectar of their love. When it was time for Falu to go back to work, he had a hard time leaving Mia lying contently in his bed. It was more than he could ask for, the woman he'd been dreaming of was with him, and the projects were on the way to breaking ground.

Falu was whistling when Max opened his office door, holding a bunch of papers to sign. "Well, you're in a good mood. It must have been nice taking two days off. Now you got to pay the piper."

"To hell with you, brother. I was on my honeymoon," he had a huge smile on his face.

"You're glowing like you just got laid."

"I had my Mia fix for the morning. Now I'm taking your advice. I'm hiring someone to take over some of the office duties, so I can spend more with my muñeca." (doll)

"Alright, now you're thinking, I'll put the word out."

It took Falu two weeks to finally get someone suitable. He had women of all ages interviewing for the part-time position. Some of the women came in with arterial motives wanting to give him sexual favors, one of the girls stripped during the interview. Max laughed throughout the whole presentation. He dismissed the ones who came in with overly sexy clothes. Finally, he found a sweet middle-aged woman who knew how to run an office. Mrs. Turner was the wife of one of his crew members. When he came in the following morning, she had turned the place upside down. Everything was organized, his office was clean, and he was happy.

Mia enjoyed her life with Falu. They did a lot of things together, her favorite time was when they had picnics, and they would go into the forest and sometimes make love under the trees and forget there was another world beyond the woods. They would visit her parents whenever Falu got a chance to get away. Her father had taken command of the ranch and loved every minute of it. Her mother had gained some weight and was teaching at the nearby school. Ponyboy worked with his father and couldn't be happier.

Even though everyone knew Falu and Mia were together, they still fought over the women who constantly threw themselves at him. Even at the clubs, when they went out together and she was asked to sing, the women would take the opportunity to take their chances with him. When she returned to her seat, some half-naked woman was circling his table. When they saw her glaring at them, they would take off. Falu always knew when she was angry. Her eyes gave it away.

"Hey baby, you sound great," he tried to kiss her, but she pushed him away. "What's wrong?" he grabbed her face and kissed her anyway.

"Every time I turn around, some skank smells your ass."

"Baby, what do you want me to do? Tell them to stay away from me, or my woman will kill them."

"For starters, you don't discourage them. You smile and grin, and you don't say anything. For instance, when you're in the field, you let all those half-naked bitches hang around wearing hard hats. How cute, there you are smiling, without a care in the world."

"So now you're checking up on me… are you jealous, my love?"

"Do I have a reason to be? If any of the guys in the bands talk to me for more than a minute, you have a fit."

"Hey, I can at least admit that I'm a jealous asshole because I love you, and it drives me crazy when I see you flirting with other guys. There I said it in front of my family and friends." Mia tried to stay angry at him; he was like a little boy.

"Mia, what he's saying is that his balls are in your pocket," Max laughed.

Falu's life was full now that he and Mia were together. He was obsessed with her and wanted her all to himself. He kept a close eye on her when she left the estate, unaware she was still being watched. Mia made herself busy, and she missed the girls terribly. Sometimes she would spend the day watching as they managed their business throughout the day. She was happy that Ivette found herself a little boyfriend that made her feel special.

It was Ivette's birthday, and they decided to go for a late lunch. Falu and his crew had an appointment with the engineer not far from where they would be eating. Falu had arranged a special cake made for her, and drinks and food were on his tab. Mia loved being around the girls again. They teased her terribly about sex and how much she was glowing.

"Look at you, sister. He must be giving it to you really hard," Ivette said. They laughed at Mia's expense.

"You were right about his sexual appetite; he's always poking me with that thing."

They were lost in each other's company and did not notice the four men and two women standing behind them. The girls were laughing and carrying on as if they were the only customers in the place. George, the owner, kept the drinks and food coming. The music came on a Mia and Ivette were on the floor dancing, laughing having a great time.

"I hope you are still practicing your pole dancing; you know how it turns men on."

"You got that right. Every woman's bedroom should have one. I especially like it when he dances on it, and I reward him handsomely," they giggled.

Mia stumbled into the bathroom and didn't notice someone following her. Two women were waiting for her when she finished as she stepped out of the bathroom stall. One of them looked like a man with a crew cut, rings on her nose, and a tattoo that said *hot shit* across the left side of her neck. The other was a tall thin woman who wore a leather vest and tattoos down her arms and the back of her neck. Mia washed her hands but was aware of the two women staring at her. She watched as the heavier woman inch her way toward her. The woman looked at her with lust all over her face, blowing kisses at Mia while she was drying her hands. "Mum, sweetheart, you're a pretty little thing, with a nice, sweet ass," she touched her hair.

Mia smiled as she finished drying her hands. "Thank you for the compliment," she tried to leave, but the tall thin woman blocked her path.

"Are those your real eyes, sexy thing," asked the heavier woman coming in closer from behind.

Mia glanced over her shoulder, rolling her eyes. "Excuse me, ladies I would like to join my party."

"Well, why are you in such a rush, pretty thing," the heavier woman asked. "Why don't you stay and play," she came close to her smelling her hair, "God, your beautiful," she tried to kiss her, but Mia put her hand up. The thin one comes around her, grabbing Mia by the neck from behind, while the other puts a knife to her face. "We're going to go out the back way, my pretty thing… so play nice. I don't want to cut that pretty face of yours." They were confused when Mia smiled. She head butted the tall thin woman in the nose with the back head, grabbed the knife from the other woman, and stabbed her in the shoulder with her own knife. Mia pinned her to the wall, still holding the knife in her shoulder.

"As you can see, ladies, I play dirty," she smiled. "It's dangerous to play with knives. You may have an accident." Mia pulled the knife from the woman's shoulder and watched her slid to the floor. The thin woman tried to grab her leg as she walked out, but Mia pulled her by the hair and punched her in the face knocking her back on the floor. The heavier woman just sat there on the floor, staring into space.

When Mia came out of the bathroom, she had blood all over her shirt and pants. The strange men saw the blood and attacked her. However, they didn't anticipate her fighting abilities as they flew into the counter and chairs. The girls started to scream, watching Mia fight the four men trying their best to subdue her. George came behind the bar with a gun, but someone hit him with a pool stick over the head. He stumbled back and fell on the floor. Mia was fighting like she was taught, with fearsome quickness remembering all the lessons Kumar had her practice over and over until it became second nature to her. One of the men grabbed her from behind, covering her face with chloroform. She struggled with him as he held her around the waist. When she moved her face towards the door, she saw Max coming towards her in slow motion before everything went black. Max punched the man in the head, grabbing Mia before she fell to the floor.

When Mia came to her senses, Falu was holding her. They had the four men and women on the floor tied up. The women were kicking and screaming obscenities. "You all right, baby? I saw blood on you and went crazy."

"It's their blood," she said, shaking her head. Falu helped her sit up. "Who the hell are they, and what did they want from me?"

"Well, the heavier one, she was the mastermind behind this… they just wanted you to join their organization."

"What! Are you kidding…? Why would they think I want to join their group?"

"You see, the big guy, that puss over there, the one crying. He spilled the beans when Max's body slammed him. They were going to brain - wash you into joining them. The skinny bitch had seen you before and thought it would be cool to have someone like you in their group."

"Oh my God, how are the girls? Did they get hurt?"

"They are alright. Tina hit one of them with a chair, and Ivette screamed in the middle of the street. We were going out the door when we heard her screaming for help."

"I feel terrible I ruin the party… those bitches." She looked at the one she stabbed in the shoulder. She was crying as they tried to stop the bleeding.

"Come on, baby. Let's go home."

"No," she protested. "This is Ivette's birthday, and why should we stop celebrating over a few assholes."

Ivette hugged her neck, "I was so scared we saw blood, and I freaked out."

"I'm alright, Ivette, but I don't want you to give up your day over this. Baby come on, I'll be alright," she begged him.

Falu held her tight, "We have to get you something to wear. Now you know why I don't want to let you out of my sight."

"You worry too much, but I love you for it," she kissed him.

"Alright, guys. Let us take this party to Pablo's. We can't let a little blood keep us from celebrating," Max cried. "And you two, get a room. Damnit!"

After buying something new to wear, the party went on all night long.

Chapter 12: Life Is Good

It was official, Falu and Mia were a couple, and he watched over her like a hawk. As Falu became more demanding in bed, Mia met him with the same force and intensity. He would get concerned when he came home after being in the fields and didn't find her right away. He was not happy until he saw her smiling face that lit up when she saw him.

In his free time, he was able to take her out to different clubs where she was always asked to sing. Falu became more obsessive about her. He made sure that everyone knew she was his woman. Falu always went out with his crew, when they all gathered together, it was one big party. **Club Rico Suave** was the hot spot. The owner was one of Falu's closest friends. When they came to the club, Rico kept the best rooms open.

Rico Santiago fell in love with Mia, and he couldn't content himself when she got up to sing. "Papi, your woman, is fabulous. Where did you find such an exotic creature? Puto malo! Honey, if I wasn't gay, I would steal her from you," they all laughed. Rico always said what was on his mind.

"I don't think you're her type, Rico. She likes my guns which you are lacking."

"Yeah, Papi, I'm sure she loves more than your guns. She's enjoying that pistola between your legs."

"You got that right," Falu winked at him.

"You are happy, Papi, I can see it all over your face. She must be taking care of you."

"I'm really happy, Rico. Mia is everything I want in a woman. I'm in love with her, and for the first time, life is good."

"My customers like her. I think we need to talk about having her sing for the best damn club here. What do you think puto? We have a deal?"

"It's up to her. I'm not her manager, just her whore man."

Rico laughed, "I hear you, my friend, son-of-a-bitch, you lucky puto."

Mia enjoyed the attention when she sang. The crowd showed their love with applause and song petitions. But Mia had issues with women that were always hanging around Falu. It was seen like every time she turned around, one was trying to get in his pants. They would sit on his lap or offer to give him a blow job just to get his attention. They constantly argued because he always made a joke out of her jealousy.

"You have no respect for me or my feelings!" She yelled, "How would you like it if I let some of the guy's paw all over me?

"I would kill them and kick your ass for letting them."

"Oh, how quickly you want to kick someone's ass, but when it comes to you, it is perfectly okay!"

"Baby, please, it doesn't mean anything. They are just being friendly," he laughed, but Mia was fuming with anger.

"Okay… that's fine, so when someone comes rubbing up on me, it doesn't mean anything. They are just being friendly."

Falu's smile faded, "So you want to be responsible for someone getting a beat down?"

"Falu… you need to learn how to be in a relationship. Set some boundaries with these bitches, because I don't like it, and I will not tolerate this shit. So, you pick, either you act like you want to be in a committed relationship, or you can continue to be the male whore you were. But I won't be around because I think I deserve better."

Falu was speechless at first, "Mia, you would leave me?"

"Falu, I love you, but I know me. I am a jealous woman. I will leave if you decide you want to sleep with other women. I need a man who is devoted to me and me to him, and if not, we may as well end this right now."

"Mia, I haven't been with anyone but you since we've been together. Come on, baby, I don't want to be with anyone else. I thought you knew that. Sweetheart, I promise you I will do better, but if you ever leave me, I swear on my parent's graves I will hunt you down."

"You don't get it, do you? It's still a joke to you, and I would leave you because… I lived four months being angry all the time when you slept with the girls, and I loved them. It was crushing me to pieces. How do you think I will feel if I catch you with some skank hanging from your dick?"

"You know you have a way of painting a picture. Listen to me, Te amo, l love you more than life. I understand your feelings, and I feel the same way. I would probably go to jail for killing someone. Just give it time, my love. The more people see us together, they will get the hint. I promise you. Now come here, my princess," he drew her into his arms and kissed her passionately. "However, if you think you're running away from me, you're crazy. I will hunt you down and tie you to my bed."

"You are so dramatic," she scolded him. "Look, I understand that some habits are hard to break," she put her arms around his neck. "Just don't blame me when I slap some bitches around, and you will be on a sex diet. See how you feel about that?"

"Hey, never that," he held her from behind, kissing her neck.

"Just think about what I said. Now come and join me in the shower, sweetie. Maybe you'll get lucky."

"Lucky… shit, you belong to me. So don't before get it!"

Rico's club was jumping like usual on a Friday night, and everyone bought a date. They were having a great time drinking and dancing. Like always, Mia agreed to sing a few songs. The club was full of women trying to get with the guys. Max's date was angry with him because he knew all the women in the club who always came to say hi to him. They welcome him with a kiss on the cheek. Mia danced with Falu's crew; every time Max danced with Mia, his date would catch an attitude with him.

"Why are you dancing with her? That's your brother's woman, it's bad enough I have to compete with all these other bitches. Now, I have to compete with her too?" Beth argued.

"Had I known you were going to be such a bitch? I would have left you behind. Chill out and relax! You don't want to dance, so guess what, that's why we come here to dance and have fun." Max scolded her. "Don't stress out about Mia and Falu. To them, no one else exists."

"Max is right. Chill and have a good time," Ricky said, passing a joint to Max. When Falu and Mia danced to a slow song, it was like they were alone in their bedroom. Falu knew how to bump and grind to the music. It was very provocative and sexual, and they didn't care.

"You guys should get a room if you're going to practically have sex on the dance floor, damn it!" Max chuckled, passing the joint bad to Ricky.

"They are disgusting," Beth said, rolling her eyes.

"No… they're in love," Max replied with the same attitude. "Now shut up, you're ruining my buzz."

Falu made Mia sit on his lap, blowing smoke in her face. An hour later, Mia was drunk and stone. It didn't help when the guys blew pot smoke in her direction. Falu held on to Mia, who could hardly stand. "Come on, baby. I'm getting a tattoo, and so are you. I designed a beautiful raven for you, and I'm going to put your name on my arm so all the women can see that I love you."

"Aw, how sweet, you do love me," she said in her inebriated state.

"Max, I'll be next door at Papo's. The rooms are ready if you guys need to crash." He threw Mia over his shoulder. "Yeah, baby, it's going to be where no other man will dare to go, or I'll kill him."

Papo was happy to see Falu." Que pasa mi hemano," Papo greeted him; Falu laid Mia on the table.

Papo was nervous as he looked at the picture Falu drew. It was a beautiful picture of a black raven with blood red letters spelled out Property of Falu underneath. "Boss, I don't want her coming back to me kicking my ass, I'll leave town for a while, and I've seen her fight."

"Let me worry about Mia. If there's an ass to be kicked, it would probably be mine but go ahead. I give you permission… right here above the booty, so when she wears those low riders, they can see who she belongs to," he said, slapping him on the back.

"Oh, and what a nice booty it is," Papo said, trying to keep his hands from shaking. He bent down to whisper in her ear, "Please don't kill me, Mia." Mia moaned something and turned her head.

Falu's heart with Mia's name came out beautiful, but Papo had to calm himself down and swipe the sweat from his brow a few times to ensure Mia's tattoo came out perfect. When he was done, Falu congratulated him. "You did a great job, my man. I love it."

"I'm glad you're happy. I was really nervous," Papo said, wiping the sweat from his brow again.

"You do great work, now let me get my very drunk woman to our room," he threw Mia over his shoulder again and walked the block to his room, laying her on the bed. "You belong to me, querida. You just don't know what you've done to me."

Falu and the rest of the crew were downstairs early the next morning eating breakfast when something flew past

Falu's head. Mia was steaming with anger, "You asshole! How could you?"

Falu laughed, knowing it was coming, "Hey baby! Look, I have your name on my shoulder, baby. What's the problem… ? I think it looks sweet."

"I didn't give you permission to put your name on my body. That's the problem," she stomped back upstairs. The crew made fun of Falu as he laughed with the rest of them.

"Brother, you better do some serious ass kissing," Max teased. "Right below the tattoo."

"She'll get over it," he said, finishing his mimosa. "I better start now."

They made kissing sounds as he followed her up the stairs. "I love it. She's going to kick his ass one day," Max chuckled. "Hit him hard, Mia!"

"I'll put money on that, my money's on her," Ricky added.

"I put some money on that too," Tony agreed.

"You men are all dicks putting bets on their relationship," Beth finally said, sounding off.

Max gave her a side glance, "It's not what you think, those two are madly in love, and I am forever grateful to my girl Mia."

"What are you talking about? She just threw something at his head!" Beth cried.

"You don't know my brother. Since my parents passed, he's had a lot of responsibilities. He had a lot of women, but Mia kept him grounded and extremely happy. As long as he's happy, he's not stressed out, and he won't work us to death," Max explained.

She rolled her eyes, "You think too much of this woman," she replied sarcastically.

Falu crept upstairs toward their room, where Mia lay on her stomach. He walked in. "It better be room service!" She said. He stood by the door in case he had to run.

"Hey, muñeca, mi amor… don't be mad at me. Look how nice your name looks on my shoulder."

"Falu, you're lucky I love you, but next time, if you want to mutilate someone's body, use your own."

He jumped next to her on the bed, playfully kissing her, "Baby, I adore you. I want us to get married and have children together. I know it hasn't been easy to love me… but one thing I know… we were meant for each other." He touched her lips with his finger. "My mother had one lover… my father. And my father was just like me, wild with so many women he didn't know what to do. Every time he turned around, some woman was offering herself to him. But one day, he fell in love with my mother, on the road to market… one sunny day, and he waited for her for more than a year. He was a lot like me, trying to fill that void with women. But when he met my mother, he said she was all he needed. They loved each other in such an insane way. People envied them."

"Is that right, lover boy?" she said, teasing him.

"I remembered as a boy watching them dance and kiss when they thought we were asleep. He'd… said her name in such a way I knew it came from his heart even when he worked long, hard hours. Father always made time for her." Mia touched his face tenderly. His face was sweet as he spoke about his parents. "My father died the last year of college… and she never took another man even though she had many suitors.

She was angry with God because He took my father too soon. I could hear her crying and speaking to God about how they were supposed to grow old together and bounce grandchildren on their laps. Mia, I know how my parents felt because I feel the same way about you. I'm sorry if I'm possessive. I know my father was the same way as my mother. He would not feel right until he knew where and if she was safe." Mia kissed him, she always became emotional when he spoke tenderly about his parents. She knew he missed them. "So please forgive me if I display that same kind of love for you… there may be a time when you must tell me to back the hell off, and I will understand." Mia looked at him with different eyes. He was so tender when he wanted to be understood. "Te amo mi vida," he kissed her shoulder.

"Man, you really know how to kiss ass… I liked the tattoo when I got a good look at it. I just wish you would have asked first. I don't mind having your name on my ass, and my name does look rather good on your shoulder."

"Para simple me amor, I will love you forever. Now, do you forgive me for being an ass?"

She stared at him for a minute with her big brown eyes, "You're so damn cute when you beg… but I have other ways of punishing you."

"Ah, baby, come on, you don't mean that," he pinned her down in the bed, kissing her neck, fondling her breast. She responded to his touch.

"You are not getting in my panties this morning, so don't even try."

"Are you sure about that?" He wrestled playfully with her, making her giggle, trying to pull off her shirt.

"Oh, I guarantee it," she cried, laughing at him.

"Alright… let me just kiss you and hold you," he grinned lustfully.

Beth didn't understand the relationship between Mia and Falu's crew. She was jealous of the way Max referred to her and how they spoke so endearing about Mia. Beth sat quietly, not saying much as they finished their breakfast.

When they were ready to leave, Falu appeared, carrying Mia down the stairs on his back. They were playfully kissing and hugging each other, and Beth thought it was strange. "Well, I see you sold out," Beth said, sarcastically.

Mia looked around to see who she was talking to, "Excuse me are you talking to me?"

"There's no other female around." Falu wanted to step in, but she motioned him not to.

"If you have something to say to me, make it clear enough so I can understand what the hell you're talking about?"

"An hour ago, you wanted to take his head off, and now you're all up his ass."

Mia tried not to laugh, "First of all, it's none of your damn business what I do with my man."

"Your weak, a sellout, you walk around here all high and mighty, and you ain't shit."

Mia was taken aback by her words. Max heard the argument and joined them. "What the hell's going on here?" Max said, surprised Beth was attacking Mia.

"Just let her talk… so when I put my foot up her ass, you'll know why," Mia said, smiling.

"I'm not afraid of you… take your best shot," Beth fronted.

Mia crossed her arms and stood where she was, confused, "First of all, what did I ever do to you. Tell me before I knock your ass out?"

"I watched you all last night, dancing and needing attention from all the men. I've known women like you in the past, and I realize how manipulating you are and your kind."

Max pulled her by the arm, "What the hell has gotten into you?"

"No, Max, it's alright. Let her get it off her chest," Mia said, her eyes boring into her.

"That's his woman, not yours. Why are you always defending her?" Beth yelled.

"Max, my brother. Handle your business, please," Falu tried pulling Mia away.

"Hold up, baby. I don't think she's finished, and I want to hear what she says."

Beth looked at Max and shrugged her shoulders at him. "You make a life for women like me hard. I've been interested in Max for a long time, and yesterday I felt like a second fiddle around you. I don't like it, keep your hands off other men, and don't be a pig thinking you can have all the men to yourself."

"My, my, my… I didn't know you had such low self-esteem that you had to attack me with your stupid bullshit. Max is

a dear friend of mine, and I love him like a brother, so deal
with it bitch." Her mouth was tight, and her fist clenched.
The men try to stop what could turn into a fight. Falu tried
to calm Mia.

"You have no right to talk to her like that," Max said,
angry inches away from Beth's face.

"I felt like a fool watching you dance with her like she's
your woman last night."

"Baby let's get out of here before I kick this jealous
bitch's ass," Mia said. As they walked out, they could hear
Max and Beth arguing about the night before.

She turned to Falu. "Do I manipulate all your time?"

"Don't worry about her baby. He needs to dump that
crazy bitch."

"But she truly has a problem with me, I don't get it. I
tried to talk to her, and she just sat there like she didn't want
to be bothered."

"She didn't want to dance, he asked you… it's her loss."
Mia felt bad the confrontation stayed with her all afternoon.
That afternoon, she searched for Max. If there was someone
she loved and counted on, it was him. Max was in the
exercise room when she found him. He was on the weight
bench when she looked down at him.

"Hey Max. Can we talk?"

He smiled at her, "I hope what Beth said didn't upset you."

"Well, my first reaction was to kick her ass… but then I started thinking… maybe it's true. I do enjoy dancing and carrying on with my friends."

"Mia… it's not just you. It's any woman I talk to… but she doesn't like you for some reason."

"I'm sorry if I caused you any problems with your girl."

"My girl… Mia, you know me better than that… Beth is just a booty call. She came to me. I didn't even invite her, she just gravitated toward me. I can't be with anyone who doesn't love our Mia… that's what we call you, our Mia. You keep my brother in line, and I love it… but mostly because… you love him. I cut psycho bitch loose."

"Alright, but I still feel really bad."

"Sweetheart, I'm glad she let me see where she was coming from, I can't deal with someone like her."

Mia felt lonely without the girls and had no one to talk to about her feelings. The last time she went to visit, they were so busy. Falu had been working on the new design for the western solar grid and spent much of his time on the presentation. So, she spent most of her time practicing with some of the local musicians who fought over her to sing with their group. She was booked in some of the clubs, and her fans followed her.

Mia came live on the stage, when she sang her slow soulful songs, Falu was always there watching her. She loved seeing his face in the crowd, but their happiness would soon be challenged once again by Falu's past.

The twins were back, and they had a plan. They wanted Falu and were determined to bring him back into their crazy world. Sonia and her sister sat in the dark watching Mia on stage for days. They had been watching the strange woman mess with their meal ticket. Sonia was not happy, she tried to get information about Mia, but the only one who would speak to them was Max's ex-girl, Beth.

When the twins left two years ago, they planned to take over Mississippi and Alabama. But things didn't go as planned, and they are now hunted by a deal gone wrong. Falu was the only place they knew would be safe. However, they were not expecting her. Sonia thought the black bitch that had her claws into him, with a bottle of whiskey in her grips. She needed a plan to separate them so she could trap him into being their protector and meal ticket once again.

After Mia's set was over, the twins left and headed toward the estate. Carmen fought with the guard that wouldn't let them through. The twins wore him out, and he finally gave in but not before alerting Tony that they were coming.

Falu was ready for a night full of lovemaking. He had set Mia up all evening, whispering sweet words, getting her in the mood for hot sex and lots of loving. He carried her up the stairs on his back. They laughed as Mia kissed his neck and ear, sending chills up and down his spine. "You've been a bad girl. Wait until I get you upstairs."

She giggled, "Well, it better be good because I'm extremely needy tonight," she teased.

"Oh, I got something for you, baby. Big daddy's been ready." When they entered their suite and turned on the light, the twins were half naked on the bed. "Hey, big boy, we're back," Sonia said, giggling, flashing her breast.

Mia was in shock. She looked over at Falu, who was turning bright red with anger. "I told you about leaving your trash around," Mia said, giving Falu a dirty look before walking out the room.

Falu was beside himself. "Get out of my room! Now," he yelled, flared with anger.

"Oh, come on, baby, since when have you turned away from a three some," Carmen teased, throwing her shirt at him and reaching to grab him.

"I want you both out of here now!" He bellowed. Max heard the yelling from his room, and when he saw Mia walking down the back stairway, he knew something was wrong. Max walked into a shouting match between the twins and Falu, who had Carmen by the wrist, pushing her out the door, "Get these bitches out of here before I kill them.

"You promised my brother you would look after us! You lied to a dying man," Sonia yelled back. Max managed to calm the girls down, but Falu was fuming. "You're a liar. You promised my brother we would always have a place with you, and now you're kicking us out."

"I said I would care for you, not have you in my bed. I swear to God, if you ruin my relationship with Mia, there will be hell to pay." He walked away, trying to cool off.

Mia was outside on one of the terraces, and she couldn't get the vision of those two women wearing her clothes on their bed. "Mia," she didn't even turn around, taking a deep breath. "Baby," She could see how angry he was; she touched his face. "Are you alright?"

"No, I'm not," she avoided his eyes that were smothered with anger. He put his head down, "They seem to know you really well."

He held her by the waist from behind. "That was a long time ago when I was young and stupid. Jack, their older brother, was my best friend. We went through school together. When I went to college, he'd come and visit. We'd hung out all the time. We were like brothers, the four of us. I could always count on Jack. He saved Max's life more than once. He was one of the men who were badly injured defending my mother. After my mother was buried, even with his injuries, he fought side by side with me. The wild twins lived with us, and he kept them in line when he was around. But after a year, his wounds wouldn't heal, and we found out he had a disease from some woman. It was deliberate, she knew she was sick and waited for him to be stinking drunk and infect him. He had no idea… I watched him dying. It was horrible. Max cried like a baby, we were all really close. Anyway, he made me promise to take care of the girls. They were the only family he had left. We buried him next to our parents."

"So what do you own them, was screwing you part of the bargain?" She spouted.

He pressed her against him tightly, "It's something that may have happened one night. When I woke up, she was in my bed naked. I kicked her out of my room, she went crazy picking on the girls. I asked them to leave. I told them they could return only if they learned how to behave."

"Well, they're back, so now what, what are you planning to do with them?"

"We were cool for so long. I mean, we all hung out together, never causing trouble, but they seem to have something against the girls."

"Falu, I know you feel obligated to help them, and I'm not opposed to you helping them. But I'm not the girls. I will not put up with their shit… I will seriously hurt them."

"I know, and it scares me sometimes. I realized you don't fight women unless they come after you. And I know your strength firsthand, and you can easily kill someone, whether male or female."

"Look, as long as they respect us. I don't have a problem with them."

He turned her around and kissed her passionately, "Te amo, Mia."

"Te amo mas," She kissed him with the same fire. "Are those bitches out of our bed? I want to get down and dirty with you," she smiled.

"Damn… that's one hell of an invitation," he dragged her behind him.

Mia tried to understand that Falu had a different kind of life than she did. Even though they were both tribal people, she was sheltered most of her life, and they moved so much that it was hard for her to make long-lasting friends.

Most of the time, she stayed close to her mother, who was always afraid that someone would try to kidnap her. The Warlord wanted to force Mia to marry his son, so the war began. To be part of the family that violated her mother when she was young made Mia angry and bitter toward that family.

Mia held on to Falu after they made love. She didn't know how she had lived without him all these years. He was part of her now. Sometimes, she would get emotional when they were together, just holding each other. It usually made her cry when he would open up and reveal his feelings. She knew he had a lot of hurt and pain in the past and tried to understand that part of his life.

She made him feel like a million bucks. Mia was smart and didn't put up with his bullshit. She was his equal and made his life exciting. He longed for her when they were apart.

Chapter 13: The Twins

The twins were wild and crazy. They drank too much and were very promiscuous. Wherever they went, trouble brewed, and they didn't care who was hurt along the way. When they were younger, there was always so much drama. Jack was their older brother, he was thirteen when the twins came along. Jack was his mother's right hand, and he worried when she became pregnant with the girls. The doctors had warned her not to have any more children. Her heart was not strong enough. So, Jack grew up fast, he took on adult responsibilities to help his father, a sweet, quiet man who didn't have much to say but took care of his family.

When the twins were born, it consumed their lives. They were not identical twins, but they were extremely demanding from the beginning, and Jack feared for his mother's health. Jack worked after school at the supermarket and brought home formula so his mother wouldn't have to breastfeed. His father, Jack Senior, helped at night when the colicky girls cried. The girls became a hand full as they grew older.

One day Jack senior went fishing and was never heard of again. Jack senior loved to fish, and he would travel to really dangerous areas. That day Jack had to work and did not accompany his father. That was a decision he regretted for the rest of his life. The girls were seven when their father disappeared. They were mean and disrespectful.

Jack and Max were in the same classes at school, and after a while, they became very close friends. Jack admired Falu and followed him in places, and Falu was more than happy to teach him the ropes. He became a regular at Falu's grandparent's home, and they treated him just like a grandson. It was through Falu's grandmother that Jack's mother, Holly, became the middle school's head cook. They loved her. She was sweet and passionate and always put 100% into what she did. It also allowed her to work when the girls were in school. But as they grew older, they became more defiant and difficult. They would cut school and go off with the boys and other kids to party. They always found someone to buy them liquor. They would escape through the bedroom window at night and come home wasted.

Jack was the only one who they listened to. He would chase them and spank them, especially when they made his mother cry. It tore him apart to hear his mother crying in her room. She missed her husband, who, after months of searching, everyone gave up.

Jack would kneel down beside his mother and hold her. He could see how tired she was and how much the girls took out of her.

Carmen was the worst of the two, and Sonia just followed and did what her sister wanted her to do. When Reyes gave him a job in security, Jack was overwhelmed with gratitude. As an employee, he was able to move his mother and sisters into a better neighborhood. Holly loved the house. It was clean and had a pretty nice front garden, and the place was closer to her job.

But the girls were blossoming teenagers growing fast. On some occasions, Jack caught the girls in bed with their boyfriends. He was always throwing someone out or chasing some boy away. Carmen and Jack would get into screaming matches. He warned the girls constantly that their mother was sick. Holly worked the extra hours, and the stress was not good for her. After a scolding from Jack, they would promise to behave. The girls would calm down for a few days and help around the house, but it didn't take long before they were up to their old tricks. When the girls were teens, Jack was dating an older woman with two young children. He would go and visit her now and then, help her out, and in return, she took care of him.

Jack and Falu had become very close friends. They had the same temperament, and Jack liked Falu's no nonsense approach to things. They enjoyed hanging out and running after girls. He became a part of the family.

Life was good for Jack. He ended his relationship with the older woman and was in love with Camilla, a beautiful petite woman closer to his age. They were engaged to be married the following spring. But the woman he was involved with in the past would not let them live in peace. She made life impossible for Jack and Camila, so she called off the engagement and moved away.

Jack was devastated, and when Reyes asked him if he wanted to stay at the men's quarters, he jumped at the offer. The four became inseparable. They helped Jack get over the breakup, giving him work that would take his mind off Camila.

However, the girls continued with their destructive behavior. At the age of seventeen, Sonia left home and was living with a really abusive man. After a few months of beatings, she moved back home. Carmen was happy. She missed her sister. Carman took her to wild parties, letting her know what she was missing. Hanging with a rough crowd.

Jack tried to keep the peace between his mother and sisters. They would bring their friends to the house when their mother wasn't home and steal whatever they could. One night while Jack was bringing his mother some groceries, the two girls got into a huge fight with the boy next door. Sonia threw a rock through their window and hit his grandmother. Tired of their bullying, the quiet young man was calling them out in the middle of the streets. The girls cussed and laughed at him. The whole neighborhood was looking out their door, watching the fight. Jack and Ricky parked their car and tried to break up the fight. Jack spoke to the young man and agreed to let him handle his sisters.

Jack calmed his sister down, dragging them into the house, when he noticed his mother was nowhere around. He searched the house and found her on the floor in her bathroom. She had fallen and hit her head.

She lingered in the hospital for days, going in and out of unconsciousness. His mother had suffered a heart attack. He sat in her room, watching and listening to the monitors they had attached to her, keeping her alive. Jack prayed for his mother to recover, but the doctor's prognosis was not good. Her heart was too weak, and all the added stress from the girls was not helping. She passed on a pretty Sunday morning. She told him she was going to be with her husband. She mentioned having a dream about him knowing she didn't have much time. She had him promise to take care of his sisters.

Reyes and his family paid for her funeral. They were his strength when he broke down at the burial site. For weeks he refused to speak to his sisters, blaming their behavior for their mother's death. Only after Esmeralda's murder did Falu ask Jack to move his sisters into the estate. They were running with a really bad crowd again, and they were getting ready to sweep the city clean of criminals causing most of the problems.

Jack was injured during one of the sweeps, but while in the hospital, they discovered the true nature of his injuries. His friends were unaware that he had been seeing his old girlfriend, and that she had given him a sexually transmitted disease. She was bitter from the breakup and still in love with Jack, but she was very angry when he left her for a younger woman. In fear he would do it again, she paid a witch for a potion that would make him stay with her forever. Everything has a price, and keeping him with her took on a deeper meaning in the spiritual realm. Until death, she had no idea that it could kill him in the process.

His best friends stood by him as he fought for his life, asking Falu to take care of the only family he had. Falu promised to do what he could. So many lives had been lost, it was the least he could do. The girls would come and go throughout the years whenever they broke up with a boyfriend or ran out of someone to sponge from, and they came back to Falu. The last time they came for a visit, they fought with Falu's girls, and he asked them to leave.

Carmen remembered the special night with Falu. It was one of those crazy nights of drinking, pot smoking, and dancing. She had her eyes on Falu for years, and she was going to take advantage of his drunken state to worm her way into his life. But when he rejected her advances, she was crushed. He had the girls, and they seemed to be in the way. Carmen hated the girls, they had him, and all she could do was pretend to be his friend. Now they were back, and another woman took the place of the girls.

Ricky didn't trust them and asked Tony to keep a closer eye on them after the fiasco in the bedroom. Falu had them hustled into his office. Carmen wore clothes that were too tight and ill fitting. She dressed in reliving clothes and loved to wear heavy makeup with her signature blackberry lipstick. Her look made her stand out, especially with her platinum color hair. The girls had similar looks, but Sonia was an inch taller and thinner.

"Have a seat, you two. We need to talk," Falu said. Ricky and Max join the two as a backup.

"What's up, baby? We came to say hello, and you treat up like shit," Carmen said, smiling and spreading her legs.

"I was hoping for some action." Her sister laughed along with her.

"Who the hell wants that foul, nasty ass shit? It's a miracle it hasn't fallen out," Max said sarcastically.

"Oh, you're so funny. Don't you wish you had some of this?" she replied. Max turned up his nose.

"Cut the shit. I'm here to inform you that things have changed, I'm in a serious relationship, and for once in a long while, I'm happy. I am warning you, don't mess with my woman. She is not like the girls you tried to bully around.

Mia will seriously kick your asses. Now, what in the world brings your sorry asses back here?"

Sonia turned up her lips. "Ah, we're broke and have no place to go. We thought maybe we could hang out here for a while until... well, I don't know whenever."

"Falu, you're the only close to family we got. We have nowhere else to go," added Carmen.

Falu eyed them back and forth. He knew they were telling the truth. "My problem with you two is that neither of you knows how to live with decent folks, so it's going to take me a while to find a place for you to live."

"But what about us living here? This place is huge," Carmen protested.

"Oh, hell no, you are not staying here. I have plans for my family and crew, and I'm sorry, but you two are not part of that plan."

"That's not nice to say. Come on," Carmen said, jumping from her chair.

"Yeah, that's some dirty shit, man, you ain't right," Sonia added.

"I will find you a decent place to live, float you some money, and what you two do from there is up to you."

"Come on, Falu. Who turned you against us?" Sonia whined.

"You only have yourself to blame. You create pandemonium everywhere you go. If that's possible, I would like to be friends with you two."

Carmen turned her gaze away. It wasn't what she expected, "Guys, that's all we want, to belong just like everyone else. I'm sorry, we're not here looking for trouble, it's really dangerous out there, and some shady people are looking for us to kill us," Carmen confessed.

Falu tried not to flip out, "And you two are bringing this shit to my door. What kind of trouble are you talking about." Falu asked, frustrated. The girls looked at each other.

"I say we give them money and send them on the way. Wherever they go, trouble follows, and I think they should own up to their mistakes," Ricky suggested getting angry.

"True that cousin," Max chimed in. "You two have no filters, sleeping with any dick that comes your way. Stealing and acting like fools. I say turn them out in the streets and let them hustle like everyone else."

"Come on, Max, give us a chance. Those people don't want money. We… saw a lot of things, things people kill for. They want to kill us," Carmen said, looking guilty.

"So, where are these folks from?"

"Ah…Alabama… the Nelson Cardona family," Carmen said, watching the look on Sonia's face. Sonia recovered quickly and nodded her head, agreeing with her sister.

"I've never heard of them, but if you say it is true, my offer has not changed," he crossed his arms in front, knowing they would object to anything he proposed.

"You're a liar. How could you lie to a dying man?" Sonia yelled, throwing a fit, "You promised."

"Sit your ass down," Max snapped and stood in front of her stopping her from throwing things around like she was in the habit of doing. "There's no broken promise here. You are grown ass women able to make a decent living and have a normal relationship. You choose to act like an animals, both of you."

"Really, Max," Sonia balled up her fist.

"Good, go ahead, take your best shot. It better be a good one because your ass isn't waking up until next week bitch."

"Alright, that's enough. I think I am more than generous. That's what I'm offering to take it or leave it." Falu concluded.

Carmen smiled and nodded, "That's cool, man. I understand and we appreciate everything you do for us," she winked at her sister.

"Good, then we're on the same page. We have an understanding," Falu said, waiting for them to acknowledge.

"Sure, anything you say, big boy," Carmen replied, smiling.

Ricky slammed the door behind them when they left. "You don't believe them, do you?" Ricky asked.

"Not as far as I can throw them. Ricky, contact Jeffery Cohan and have him find something for the whack-a-doo sisters. If they're in trouble, I don't want it coming to my doors, and I'm not shedding blood for their stupidity."

"I'll get right on it. The sooner we get them out of here, the better."

"I want something outside the city limits and away from decent people. I don't want to ruin anyone's neighborhood because of those two."

The twins looked for a safe place to talk away from prying ears. "Carmen, why did you tell them the Cardona family was looking for us? They're nice people. Now, what if they come here and they question them?"

"Calm down, sister. I had to tell them something, and the Cardona brothers would never come down here. Now we have a window of opportunity. He wants us out of here because we're a threat to his precious black bitch. She's been in his ear, and I bet money on it."

"So how are we going to do this," Sonia smiled wickedly.

"I have a plan. We are going to make her stay here a living hell. We'll hit her hard, and in a few days, she'll be packing her clothes," they laughed, giving each other a high five.

"Alright, operation, pack your clothes bitch and get to stepping," Sonia added.

Mia tried not to bother Falu, who was working nonstop on the solar grid. She would run her horse Lucky and hit the gym in the morning. The twins studied her routine. Mia was doing pull-ups on the bar when the twins entered the gym, pretending to work out. They looked at each other and giggled as if they had a secret joke. Mia ignored their remarks.

Tony took over for Franklin at the security booth. "Huh, this doesn't look good. How long have the twins been in the gym?"

"They just got here a few minutes ago. I've been watching their moves. Turn the audio mikes on," Franklin flipped the switch. Mia continued on the bar when Sonia jumped on the bar, trying to pull herself up.

"Wow, this shit is hard," she said out loud. Carmen grabbed her legs to help her sister with the pull ups. They fell to the floor laughing. Mia started to stretch, warming her limbs. Carmen crept closer to Mia, who was on the floor doing a split. "Mia, that's your name, right? My sister and I were thinking. A pretty girl like you, have you ever been with a woman?" The guys laughed.

Mia looked straight in Carmen's face and grinned as Carmen waited for a reaction. "Why do you ask? Are you interested?"

Carmen blinked, confused, "Well, you know Falu does like to watch girl-on-girl action," Sonia replied, sitting next to Carmen and playing with her sister's hair, "It's a real turn on," Sonia added.

Mia gave them a side glance, "The only action Falu wants right now is between my legs, so you skanks need to find another man to focus on. He is off limits to you two."

"Tell them, girl, make them run with their tails wagging," Tony cheered from the booth.

"Woo, we have here a tough bitch," Carmen laughed. "There's a ring right behind us. Why don't you show me how tough you are?"

"You don't want to go there with me?" Mia smiled, wishing for a reason to kick their asses.

"So, what do we have here…a chick, chick, chicken," Sonia sang, making chicken sounds.

"Don't do it, Mia, don't let them bate you," Franklin said.

"Oh, this is not going to be pretty," Tony added.

"Alright, if you insist, however, I have one slight request," Mia grinned.

"Sure honey, what could that be," Carmen smiled brightly, glad Mia went for the bate.

"I've never fought with twins. I just want to know how it feels to fight you both at once… that's if you're not afraid." Mia's eyes became slits.

Carmen laughed out loud. "Anything you say, sweetheart."

"Good, let's get the gloves on," Mia said, calling Glen and Johnny.

Johnny eyed the girls strangely. He helped Carmen with her gloves. "You know she fights dirty," Johnny said, trying to discourage them.

"So do we. Just do as you are told. She asked for it," Carmen ordered. He shook his head.

Glen stared at Mia, "You know you ain't the right girl."

Mia wanted to put him at ease, "Come on, Glen. Do you really think I'm going to hurt them? I just want to give them a little taste of Mia."

"If Falu finds out, he's going to be angry."

She batted her eyes and smiled, "Well, I'm not going to tell him, are you? Come on, Glen, sweetie. Can't a girl have little fun now and then? And you know this isn't going to take long."

"That's what I'm afraid of. I know your strength."

"I promise you no broken bones," she kissed him on the cheek.

Mia warmed up on one side as the twins laughed and carried on across from her. "When I say stop, I mean stop! Don't make me come in the ring and pull you women apart," Glenn announced. When he looked to the side, Tony and Franklin sat on the bench.

"I can't miss this, dude," Tony cried. Glen blew his whistle, and Carmen came charging right at her. Mia threw a combination first to her stomach and then to her face. Carmen fell to the side. Sonia didn't know what had happened. They had worked out a strategy, but it wasn't working so far. Mia started with a little dance step kicking them in the butts and back. The twins charged at her at once, trying to subdue her, but they couldn't get near her. She played with them for another ten minutes, and then Glen saw the gleam in her eyes.

"Mia, you promised!" He yelled. Mia smiled over at him. She landed a straight punch to Carmen's face, blackening her eye. She fell back. "Stop! stop this right now!" Glen yelled as he jumped into the ring, but Sonia kept charging at Mia and grabbed her by the hair. Mia went down on one knee and punched her hard in the stomach. When Sonia lets go, she catches her with an uppercut nipping her nose on the way up, blood everywhere. Glen was caught in the middle as the twins tried to attack Mia, who sat back on the rope.

"Let them go, Glen. They want more, and I have some more for them," Mia yelled. Tony jumped in the ring to help Glen. The twins continued to cuss and scream obscenities.

"I knew this was a bad idea," Glen yelled. Mia left the ring, letting Tony and Glen deal with the screaming twins.

Franklin put his arm around Mia's shoulder and chuckled. "That was great, they were looking for it."

"I've been wanting to give them a little taste of Mia for a week now. I feel energized."

"Unfortunately, I think Falu will be upset," Franklin stated.

"Let me handle my man. I'll be damned if I'm going to let those bitches beat up on me. Shit ain't going to happen."

Peggy set Sonia's nose and was not gentle about it. Sonia yelled every time she touched it. "You two must be the biggest fools getting in the ring with Mia. What were you thinking?" Peggy scolded, finishing up.

Sonia looked in the mirror. Her eyes were upset that she got the best of them. Both eyes were black and blue. "It was two of us. We thought we could take her on."

"Of all the stupid things you could do. Mia's a professionally trained fighter, you're lucky you only have a busted nose, and you Miss tough shit, how do you like your pretty little eyes now?"

"She got lucky," Carmen said, holding an ice pack to her right eye."

"Lucky my ass, you thank your lucky stars she didn't remove it for you," Peggy looked at the x-ray to make sure there were no cracked bones. "Well, it doesn't look like there are any fractures to your eyes."

"Why are you angry with us? We're the ones who got hurt," Sonia whined, spitting out blood.

"Because you're both idiots, Mia is not one of Falu's ex-girls. So, my advice for both of you is to stay away from Mia, she went easy on you. I've seen her spar with more than one man at a time. She is one mean bitch when she's in that ring. If you're thinking of messing with Falu, you may as well dig your graves right now."

"I'm not afraid of anyone. She'll get what's due to her," Carmen said, throwing the ice pack in the sink.

"Well, you've been warned, and if your think you're going to get any sympathy from Falu, don't bother."

Falu was upset when he heard that Mia and the twins were fighting. He found her sitting by the pool drinking a margarita like nothing had happened. He knelt next to her. "What are you doing?"

She smiled, knowing exactly what he was talking about. "You're angry, aren't you?"

He kissed her, "Yes, baby. I don't want you to go to jail for killing one of these bitches. They are not worth it. I know they provoked you, but you should know better."

She touched his face tenderly, "I'm sorry." She replied in a little girl voice, "The offer was just too delicious to pass up."

He kissed her again and smiled, "I know, damn well, you're not sorry, now we went through this before," he held her hands. "You're really strong, and I know your anger can get the best of you. I don't want you fighting unless someone is threatening your life. This was no more than a cat fight not worthy of your skills."

"I… I didn't hit them that hard."

"You hit them hard enough to bust them up, now promise me?"

She put her arms around his neck and kissed him. "I promise on one condition. If they come at me, I will defend myself."

"Alright, I can live with that, but I don't think they're going to be dumb enough to invite you into the ring again." They both laughed.

However, not everyone was laughing, the twins wanted to get back at Mia, and the others made fun of the girls teasing them about Mia's beating. But it wasn't the end. Mia was tortured every time they came around her turning their encounter into a shouting match. When Mia wasn't around the twins, they were where Falu was. It gave him the chance to keep an eye on them, but for Mia, it was a bitter pill.

Falu continued to work long hours, sometimes until late at night, on his important project due to be presented to the Inner Cities. Whenever she got a chance, she would visit Falu to talk to or be near him. Happily, she picked up her small basket from the kitchen and sang her way toward Falu's office. His secretary smiled when she opened the door. "Good afternoon, Miss Mia."

"Good afternoon. I'm here to give my man a break, so why don't you take the rest for the afternoon off."

"Well, there are some things I need to pick up in town. I'll get that out of the way."

"Perfect, you work just as hard as he does."

"He's a good boss. I love him, but double trouble is with him before you go into his office."

Mia turned up her nose. "What else is new?" She smiled and entered his office looking extremely sexy with a white sleeveless sundress. Carmen stood up and looked at Falu. Mia looked at her, "Beat it bitches, vamos… get to stepping. I got business with my man."

Carmen turned away from Mia, who still wore the faded marks from the fight. She would prove to Falu that Mia was the troublemaker, "Well, Falu. We'll see you later when the air is clear," Carmen slammed the door on the way out.

Falu put his head back and chuckled. "Mia, you're a bully."

Mia sat on his lap, facing him. She held his face. "They don't like me, and I don't like them, and it's time they get a piece of what they dish out. They push their way around here as if they own the place."

He kissed her neck, "Sweetheart, you smell so good. Don't give those two a second thought. So, what brings you to my cave?" He was already getting aroused

"I thought that maybe, we can have some lunch and maybe a little dessert later," she whispered in his ear.

He squeezed her tight, "How about some dessert first and lunch later," he pulled on the front of her dress, exploring what was underneath.

"Well, I think I can help you with that. I gave your secretary the afternoon off, and I'm not wearing panties," she whispered in his ear.

"That's my kind of lunch break," he pulled his shirt off. He loved this kind of distraction and welcomed the break. Carmen listened with envy outside the door. She fought the urge to bust in and interrupt them, ruining their time together as they enjoyed their afternoon laughing and teasing each other. Listening to Falu's moans was driving her crazy.

She cussed under her breath and ran down to the bar for a drink to try to drown the lovemaking as she stood outside the door. "Hey, puta, where have you been?" Sonia said, pulling her wet hair into a ponytail.

"We got to get rid of that bitch," Carmen exploded, "I hate her guts."

"What are we going to do? Is there a plan?"

"Yeah, we're going to put pressure on her. I heard Falu was pissed about what she did to us in the gym. So, we are going to provoke her again. She'll get angry and lash out. You know Falu hates bullies. We'll tell him we were trying to be friends, and she freaked out. Sooner or later, he's going to get tired and kick her out."

"I think that's a great idea. You know she'll be here later."

"I know this is where it begins, the end of that black witch."

Mia sat in her own little corner at the end of the bar. Gary filled her glass for the third time. She was going over some new lyrics she wanted to learn. The club was empty except for a few men playing pool. The twins were playing pool, flirting playfully with some of Falu's crew.

Mia ignored their laughter, feeling good, loving the new songs. But her mind was not far from Falu, who came to bed later every night.

Sonia ran up to the bar and sat two seats from her. "Can I get a pitcher, Gary? It's getting hot in here," she looked over at Mia, who was trying really hard to ignore her.

"Well, Mia, what brings you out tonight?" Mia doesn't acknowledge her. Carmen joined her sister at the bar.

"What's taking you so long?" Carmen said out of breath.

Gary put the pitcher of what they were drinking on the bar, hoping they would go away. "Here you go, girls." Gary wanted them to leave Mia alone.

"You know Mia, you could be friendlier. Falu says we're bullies but you are worst than us."

Mia turned to face Carmen. "I am nothing like you, so please, don't put me in the same category as yourselves."

"So, what you're saying is that you're better than us?"

Mia looked at them sideways, "You're a bunch of skanks, and I'm tired of running up on one of you sucking somebody's dick."

"Mia, play nice," Gary said. He knew she had been drinking.

"See, and then Falu yells at us that you're the biggest bully here. You walk around her with your nose in the air because you're screwing Falu. Well, let me tell you about your precious Falu."

Mia interrupted her. "Shut the hell up," she said loudly. "My relationship with him is my business."

"Oh yeah, well, when he gets tired of your ass and kicks you out, then you will understand how I feel. I had him before you did and now look," Carmen yelled back.

"We're only trying to warn you. He's not what you think he is… you know, woman to woman. We're trying to be friendly," Sonia added.

"Are you kidding me? Do I have stupid written on my forehead? You don't like me, and I sure as hell don't like you two. What Falu did before me is in the past, and I live in the future."

"Like always, Mia," Carmen said, creeping closer. "You never like it when we tell you the truth. You have turned him into some puss ass," she said, disgustingly. "He used to be a real man until you came to the picture. But he'll wake up and see you for what you truly are."

Mia jumped out of her chair and walked toward Carmen. "Tell me, smart ass, what am I? What is the truth I'm hiding from?" Ricky heard the commotion and came between Mia and Carmen, getting louder now that Ricky was in the way. "Bitch you don't know a damn thing about me, so shut up!" Ricky was being sandwiched in the middle. Gary alerts Falu and Max. The three continue to shout obscenities at each other, and the louder they become, the angrier Mia becomes. Max was having a hard time holding her back. Falu got Mia in a bear hug while Carmen continued screaming.

"You always blame us for everything. When she's just as bad as us, she bullies us around, and you don't say shit," Carmen yelled.

"Mia, let's get out of here. I'll handle them," he tried to pull Mia out of the door.

"That's the problem. You always say you'll handle things and don't do shit!" She argued, struggling in his hold.

"There you go, Falu! She's turned you into a puss. In which pocket does she have your balls?" Carmen yelled, integrating.

"We were trying to have a civil conversation with her, and she snaps at us!" Sonia whined. Carmen breaks loose from Ricky and swings at Mia before he grabs her again.

"Let go of me, Falu!" He loosened the hold, and she pushed him away. "Choose Falu. It's them or me. If you can't make up your mind, just release me so I can find someone who really loves me," she walked away.

Falu turned his attention to the twins. Carmen was sobbing as her sister comforted her. Falu had never seen either one of the twins cry, not even when they got hurt. "I've warned you two, stay away from Mia."

"Falu, honestly, we were just trying to be nice. Talk to her to try to make friends, and she was nasty. But I know you're going to believe her," she continued to cry.

"Look, your place will be ready in a few days. Stay out of her way. It didn't help the situation that Mia was drinking."

Gary interrupted them, "Boss, it's Tony at the gate. Mia's trying to leave," he turned the monitor on, and Tony was arguing with Mia refusing to open the gate.

"Damn it, tell him not to open that gate. I'll be right there."

They watch as Falu pulls Mia off her horse, wrestling with her and dragging her inside. The twins laughed and high five each other and ran back to their room. "This is the beginning, sister. She keeps acting like this, and Falu will get tired and kick her out!" Carman said, excited.

"But Falu said our place is almost ready. We need more time," Sonia replied.

"That's simple. We can take care of that now. Let's cross our fingers."

Falu refused to let go of Mia, who struggled with him to let her go. "Get out of my way, Falu. I need to ride."

"You've been drinking. You're not going anywhere," he pulled her into a bear hug.

Mia swung at him, wanting him to let go of her. "If you're tired of me and don't love me, let me go and find someone who will. You let these two run through here like they own it, and you expect me to turn the other cheek. Well, I'm not doing this anymore. Call me a bully if you want…I…don't…. care!"

Falu picked Mia up, struggling with her, taking her toward their room. Falu dumped Mia on the bed, wrestling with handcuffing her to the bed. She stopped struggling. The girls had warned her about his temper; she had seen him angry before but never like this. "What are you going to do to me?" She cried.

He stared at her for a moment, "Just shut up and calm down. My advice to you is to stay put. Because it's not going to go well for you," Falu leaned against the door of his room to compose himself. It was a tough night, and all he wanted to do was lie in her arms and let her take him away. "Sleep it off, Mia. I will deal with you later." He returned to the club, "Gary, a bottle of that rum and a glass, please."

"Sure, boss. Are you alright?"

"I will be as soon as I have a few," he saw his brother coming toward him.

"Lord have mercy. What a night! How's Mia?"

Falu took his second shot. "She's alright. I have her handcuffed to the bed so she can calm down."

"You believe the girls that they were trying to be friendly?" He asked sarcastically.

"It doesn't matter, Max. She has to learn to just walk away. These bitches are shitheads. She has to learn how to control her anger. I don't want to visit my woman in jail. Max, I know what anger can do to a person. One mistake, and your life is ruined."

"I understand, brother. I guess we all have a story to tell." Max sat down next to him.

"When she told me to set her free so she could find someone who really loves her… why didn't she just shove a knife through my guts? It would have hurt less."

"Falu, she had been drinking. You know we talk a lot of shit when we're loaded, and those bitches knew she was having a few."

"I will kill him… she would have to go somewhere far because I will be responsible for another man's death."

"Look, a lot of things are said in anger. She loves you, man, sometimes I… I'm envious of the relationship you two have. It's just the talk."

"Well, I know one thing," he took the bottle off the counter. "She's going to learn who is the boss, and it starts tonight." Max watched his brother walk away. He knew his brother's anger, and this was coming from a painful place.

Falu watched Mia from his chair with the bottle next to him. He turned off all the lights except for a small one by the bed. She laid quietly, barely moving. When he took his last shot, he stood over her, taking off his clothes. Mia was afraid but tried not to show it, knowing he had been drinking. He climbed on top of her trapping her with his weight and staring at her. The murderous look on his face made her shut her eyes. "Mia," he whispered in her ear. "I have spoiled you rotten but make no mistake, I will be responsible for your lover's death. No other man will come between us… are we clear?" She wanted to cry. He reached into the drawer and pulled out a knife.

"What are you doing?" She asked, eyes wide and afraid. He didn't answer her right away.

"I'm taking my balls back. Now, this is what's going to happen. You are confined to these grounds, you're not riding Lucky, and I want you to take your meal up here. You can go swimming or work out, and I want you to stay away from those two. Are you digging me?"

"So, you're grounding me like a child?" Her anger flared up again.

"Pretty much. So, start acting like an adult." She reacted to his rules, "And don't you ever mention another man to me ever!" He took the knife and cut off her clothes slowly, forcing himself on her. She tried not to react to his touch or demanding kisses but let him have his way. When he finally takes the cuffs off, he falls into a drunken sleep.

She put her arms around him and kissed his shoulder, "It's going to be a long week, baby."

The next few days were taking a toll on Falu's crew. The more he tried to keep his relationship with Mia from spilling into his work, the more irritable he became. Mia was cold toward him, and though she didn't reject his advances, she fought hard to stay aloof. He would become angry with her if he had to hunt for her when he finished working. Mia would ignore him and shut down whenever he started to fuss at her. He just became angrier.

Falu had a deadline, and he pushed his men hard every day though they were working as hard as they could. Finally, Max snapped, he got tired of his brother's bellowing orders, and the crew looked toward Max to help Falu ease his anxiety. When Max barged into his office, Falu was making the last calculation to his chart. "I need to talk to you," he said, serious enough to get Falu's attention.

"Well, make it quick. I'm taking these numbers down to the construction site."

"Why don't you send them with one of the messengers? What are we paying them for?"

"Because I have to stay on top of these guys or else things don't get done."

"Falu, please…don't go down there, these guys are busting their asses for you, and all you do is yell and scream," he slammed his hand on the table.

"Max, I have three different projects going… I have a deadline with this power grid."

"No, ever since you had that fight with Mia, you have done nothing but bust our balls."

"Max, you're my brother. I love you, but please stay out of my business. Mia is my business, let me handle her. If you can't take the heat, then move aside. I have things to do." He rushed pass Ricky in the outer office.

"What the hell is that all about?" Ricky cried. "All I saw was red."

"I told him to stop busting our balls. I understand he has three huge projects going on, but he's being ridiculous. I need Mia to keep him happy."

"Why is he still keeping her on lockdown?"

"Because he doesn't want her to hurt Carmen or Sonia. You saw the look on her face that night. I'm going to talk to her. Maybe she can tell me what the hell has him so uptight."

"Good luck. I better warn the foreman Falu's on his way to warn them."

Max knocked on their suite and called out to her. She was on the balcony in shorts and a bathing top, reading a book and listening to music. He knocked on the balcony door so as not to scare her. "Hey, pretty lady. May I come in?" He smiled.

"Max," her face lit up when she saw him. "You are always welcomed," he kissed her cheek. "What brings you to my boudoir?" she asked.

Max made himself comfortable. "I came to see how you're doing and to… Look, I know it's none of my business, but what's happening with you two?"

"Why do you ask Max? Did the king say something to you?" She grinned.

"Mia, you are my sanity when it comes to Falu. He is under so much pressure I'm afraid he's going to have a breakdown. Are you guys still fighting or what?"

Mia tried not to laugh but could see his concern, "We're not… communicating. We rarely say two words to each other."

"Honey, as a favor for me. Have sex with him, please do something. He's been such a prick with everyone."

"Oh Max, sweetie, it's not sex. He gets as much sex as he wants… it's the other part I'm not giving him."

"If it's not sex, then what the hell is it?"

"Your brother has a huge ego, and I know just how to stroke it. The connection we have with each other makes our relationship perfect."

Max just stared at her, perplexed, "You women have some secret mojo you put on men, don't you?"

She laughed. "Max, I hate to see you so miserable. I'll tell you what I'm going to do for you. I'll end this tonight."

"Yeah, alright. I know my brother. It will take a few days to get him to calm down."

"Oh- my- God, ye of little faith. You don't believe in me. I tell you what. I bet you five pieces of gold that we will be sitting downstairs in the club… tonight, and he'll be doing a lot of ass kissing."

"Mia, don't play with my emotions. If you can do that, you are the goddess worthy of my brother, but I don't think it's possible. You didn't see how angry he was a little while ago."

"Well, put your money where your mouth is. I shall be collecting my winnings tonight, so don't be late."

"Alright, let's see you work your magic."

Falu snapped when he didn't find Mia upstairs. He raced down to the stables and found her with Lucky. "It's alright, Lucky. I haven't forgotten you. I still love you," she was brushing Lucky when he interrupted.

"Mia, damn it, have you been riding Lucky? I swear to you I will sell her and make you watch."

"Well, hello to you too, and for your information. I haven't ridden Lucky. I just wanted her to know mama loves her," she said in a child's voice.

"Well, get your ass upstairs," he followed her inside and slammed the door. Falu lay back on the bed and closed his eyes. It was a hectic day, and he just wanted some peace and quiet. Mia walked out of the dressing room with a sexy negligée and just a hint of perfume. He loved when she wore the peek-a-boo pink negligee with her pumps. She crawled into bed with him, sitting on top of him. He tried not to laugh. "Do you think you can tempt me with this… sexy pink thing that makes you look hotter than ever?"

"Why don't you ask little Falu? It seems to be having a good time down there," she licked her lips, "I missed you, baby."

He switched positions lying on top of her. "So, you think that having hots, funky sex is going to make me take you off punishment," he says while kissing her neck and breast.

"I say if you're going to punish me, do it the right way, big daddy."

"Mia, you know just how to push my buttons, don't you?" he chuckled.

"I love you, Falu. Let me help you relax." That's all it took to make him forget all his troubles and hurt as they made love. He needed the sweetness of her arms around him, knowing she wanted him just as much as he wanted her. They lay exhausted in each other's arms.

"Baby, you wouldn't sell Lucky, would you?" She asked in a small voice.

"That horse cost me a lot of money, and so did you," He pulled her on top of him, "I'm beginning to think you love that horse more than you love me."

She giggled, "No, my love, she comes in second." She played with the hairs on his chest, "She can't do for me what you do." They laughed and continued to enjoy each other.

That night, Max was shocked when he saw them kissing and holding each other at the club. He shook his head in disbelief. She reached over at Max when Falu went to get drinks for them. "Where's my money?" she smiled.

He counts them out in her hand. "Damn Mia, I want some of that mojo shit you got. Where can I get some?"

"It's a women thing, Max. You wouldn't understand," they laughed.

"Thanks, Mia. You're the best."

"The pleasure was all mine, believe me."

Chapter 14: Runaway

The twins were nervous when Falu summoned them to his office. "Do you think someone saw us?" Sonia asked, afraid of Falu's wrath.

"I don't know, but I guess we'll find out soon enough, cross your fingers," the girls listen outside the door to see if they can detect Falu's mood. They had been staying out of trouble since the last incident with Mia. Carmen knocked on the door.

"Come on in," Falu said. They were surprised that he was calm and in good spirits. Max sat on the side of the desk.

"What's going on? Falu. Is everything alright?" Carmen tried to remain calm.

"Yeah, have a seat. I just wanted to talk to you two about the place I acquired for you," the blood drained from Sonia's face as she looked at Carmen. "Max found a great place for you; it's a nice two-bedroom house, isolated, so you can't bother neighbors with your loud music and your crazy lifestyle."

"Well, that's nice. Isn't it, Carmen?" Sonia said. Trying to sound excited.

"However, there was a little setback," Max added, "It seems that someone broke into the place and had a party. The doors were wide open, and the place was trashed."

"We can clean it up," Carmen said, "sounding excited."

"If it was only that," Max said. "The place was ripped apart, holes in the walls, plumbing busted windows. It is a mess!"

"But we have people working on it to put it back together, and Max and I decided to get you girls a car to get you around."

"That's awesome, thank you," Sonia said, relieved.

"We'll let you know when everything is ready to move you in," Falu explained.

The twins thanked them both and headed to the basketball court. It was the only location that didn't have a camera. Sonia cried when she reached the bleachers. "I thought for a minute, our asses were toast," Sonia said, breathing easier.

"I told you it would work. This gives us a little time."

"Carmen, what if we get rid of her and he still kicks us out?"

"I'd thought about that. If that's the case, we would have to stage something, like if someone came in and beat us up or threatened our lives."

Sonia eyed her sister suspiciously, "Carmen, you're into him again. I hope you're not doing this to get in bed with him."

She put her head down, "I've always had a thing for him, and you know that."

"You had one night with him and look what happened. He didn't even bother to have it with you after that."

"Nay, I lied, we never had sex… he was too high and just fell asleep. Believe me, I tried to arouse him, but he didn't… I just took my clothes off and lay next to him, hoping that when he woke up and wanted to get busy, he just went and took a shower. We looked so good naked. I watched him as he showered. I wanted to jump in with him, but I was scared he'd freak out and tell me to leave."

"So, what makes you think he will want you when she's gone?"

"Well, he no longer has the girls to satisfy his sexual needs. I could be his fallback girl."

"That's a long shot, sister. I hope you're not disappointed."

"Hey, don't you think I have what it takes? I'm pretty, I have guys crawling up my ass to sleep with me.It's possible that once she's out of the picture, he'll start to look at me as a woman instead of Jack's little sister."

"I'm not saying you're not pretty. Hello, we are twins, and we do resemble each other. I just don't want to see you hurt."

"Yeah, it wouldn't be the first time I've been hurt before. So, let's continue with the next part of our plan. We take care of the house, and it should give us a few days. We're meeting with Beth tonight to get what we need to turn him into our sex slave for a night."

The eerie road to Madame Azusa was dark and creepy. *Why anyone would choose to live so close to the swamps was crazy*, Carmen thought to herself. She could hardly see her hand in front of her face. It reminded her of times when she was young, and her family had to run for their lives into the woods, not knowing where they were going. Sonia held on to the back of her sister's shirt, screaming whenever she felt something across her legs. "I'm being eaten alive," cried Sonia.

"We're almost there," Beth said, holding the only flashlight. "It's just around the bend."

"I wish you would have told us we were going into the bayou. We would have prepared better for this," Carman cried, just as afraid as her sister, trying not to show her own anxiety. She had a fear of things crawling around in the dark. Sweat dampened her shirt from her bra and underarms.

"I'm sorry, but she wouldn't give me what you wanted unless she spoke to you, and when she says now, it meant yesterday. Aunt Azusa doesn't have time to fool around." Beth pushed her way through some overgrown bushes. The

French moss was hanging from the tree, making creepy shadows, and sometimes they hung so low it gave the illusion that someone was hiding, waiting to spring forward and drag them deeper into the swamp.

The old house was out of a scary movie, with a front yard and a whitewash wooden fence that needed paint and repair. The tree blew the dead leaves making a rasping sound all around them. Sonia was almost on top of Carmen, stepping on the back of her heels as they walked up the small creepy path of the house. There was a small dirty neon sign on the side window barely visible that read, *Madame Azusa.* Beth knocked on the door; inside, they heard a small scary voice asking them to enter.

The inside was just as creepy and scary as the outside. There was a mixture of mothballs and spices in the stale air. "Aunt Azusa, where are you?" Beth cried. They followed Beth to the back of the house, where candles were lit all over the room. Her alter filled with statutes of every saint in the bible and some that weren't. Every saint had its own powers for the specific task you wanted them to perform. More than one cross was nailed to every entrance, even the front door.

Pictures of angels hung on the walls, pretty and scary angels slaying the devil. She also had black dolls of all different sizes dressed in colorful clothes with turbans, gold earrings, and rows of beaded necklaces of bright colors hanging from their necks. Half smoked cigars lay in an ashtray as if the dolls had been smoking. Madame Azusa was a scary old woman in her late 80's. She was thin with leathery skin that hung and fingers that looked like claws. Carmen looked over at her sister, who was turning pale with fright. Madame Azusa entered wearing an old black Spanish veil covering her pure white hair and red floral dress that hung badly on her frame.

She lived comfortably among her saints and dolls, especially her spirits, who manifested themselves in strange ways every now and then.

"Please sit, my dears," she said in her cracking voice. Beth pulled up another chair for herself. "I hear you want one of my special potions. That sex slave potion is very powerful, and I have to see if you can handle it." The sex potion was no more LSD, an old, forgotten drug.

"Yes, Aunt Zee, these are the girls I was talking about. Can you help them?"

"Do you have something from this person? I don't want to know the name just give me something that belongs to him." Carmen bought out a hairbrush and pushed it over to her. Madame Azusa held the brush in both hands. "Two people have used this brush," she said and mumbled some words in another language. *"Madama spirito todoprodiroso ven a mi spirito."* Her voice becomes louder and louder as her eyes roll back to the back of her head and suddenly, she jumps up. "These two… are powerful spirits. These spirits are not to be messed with. The woman… she is dark… hair, eyes, skin, caramel, and beautiful. She is a Goddess in her own right. God has sent her and a few others to remind us of who we used to be, the curse of vanity took our identity, and now he is restoring us one by one. Only women have the mark. She has a powerful spirit… the spirit of her people." There was a strange eerie silence for a minute. "He is a King among his people," she closed her eyes holding the brush, rocking back and forth, smiling as if she saw someone that was only revealed to her. "I can see him, long golden hair, eyes gray like steel… ay and a body built like a god, the image of his father who was taken to soon stands behind him, guarding his son and the women with brown eyes, long black hair holding his hand, love, lust and they were meant to be together she was born for him."

"But we want to separate them, Beth said, you have the power the… potions to do so," cried Carmen nervously.

"The Madama has spoken," she slapped the table, causing Sonia to jump in her seat, too frighten to say a word.

"Who is this Madama you speak about and how do you know all this," Carmen asked sarcastically.

"She is the spirit of this house, the spirit of the swamp and its people. She is all-knowing when it comes to these matters. Do not mess with this couple, her life is attached to his success, and she is the driving force beside him."

"So, you're saying they cannot be separated. This is crazy. People fall in and out of love all the time," Carmen yelled.

"Young lady, I've been around a long time. I felt the love, passion, and hunger they have for each other. Don't mess what is meant to be," she held her hand out to Carmen. "Give me your hand. There's a lot you can talk about a person when you look into their soul." Reluctantly Carmen lets Madame Azusa take her hands. "Come dear. The Madama wants to give you some advice." But as she held her hand, she went into convulsions. Carmen pulled her hand away as she felt heat coming from the old woman. When Azusa recovered, her eyes grew larger, she stared like a trans, and even her voice became deeper and sounded eerie. "Get out! You wicked child of darkness. You will be a curse if you come against them. Your life will not be worth the ground you walk on. Beware, the demons are after you, child!" She came to, and her voice became normal again.

"Get out! Get out before the Madamo takes you. I saw the lust in your heart for him and the hate you have for her; she is his chosen one. Beth, take them out of here, stay away from them, as far as you can from these two, and do me a favor… never bring this kind of trash into my home again," she said with venom and loathing in her voice.

"I don't believe a damn thing you said. You can fool other people by changing your voice. This is a circus, and you're a crazy witch. No wonder you live out here in the middle of nowhere among the alligators and swamp animals as friends." Carmen shouted, turning red with anger and boldness that even surprised herself.

"Get out! Beth gets this trash out of my house before they anger the spirits more." Beth hurried them out of the house. They stumble through the old furniture and step on a doll as they reach the door. Sonia started to cry with fear, her heart racing as she held on to Beth with a steel grip.

But Madame Azusa didn't want to tell them what else she saw as she held her hand. The evil that leaped from her spirit scared even her. She began to pray out loud, taking the hair from the brush, twisting it into a cross then putting it on the altar. "Great spirits of protection cover these two with your shield, keep the wicket away, keep their love strong to weather the storm before them," for hours, she repeats this prayer until the beads of sweat form on her brow. She kissed her Madama doll and thanked the spirits for covering them from the evil the girls would bring against Mia and Falu.

Sonia was angry as they finally made it out of the swamp covered with sticky stuff from the bushes and trees. Sonia was still shaking from that meeting, unable to get the eerie voice of the old woman out of her head. "I need a drink," Carmen said as she crossed the street to the nearest bar. It was late and the bar was just about to close when they walked in.

The bartender was not happy, "We're closing. Can't you see the guy sweeping and putting up the chairs?"

"I'm sorry, can you sell us a bottle to go? We'll be out of your way, I promise," Beth said, putting her money on the bar. He reached behind him, selling them a pint of rum. She thanked them and they left, walking towards Beth's place where they would spend the night. The streets were eerily silent. It was a hot musty night, and they couldn't wait to get inside after what they had just gone through.

Beth lived in an old apartment rooming house located in what was called the old city. The trio walked over to a woman who was half asleep on the stairs. Every time she nodded off, she'd jump. There was a strong smell of stale beer and garbage in the hallways. The dim yellow light gave off an eerie glow as they climbed the three stories to her studio apartment. The letter 'c' was hanging on with a single nail and the number 3 was painted on. "You live in this dump?" Carmen said, rubbing her arms, "I'm afraid I may catch something."

"It's just temporary. I have my eye on this sweet looking guy who has a real nice place."

The apartment was just as nasty as the hallway outside the door. Beth searched for the light switch. The apartment opened into the small kitchen. It had red and green vinyl chairs and a table. The bedroom was small and dingy. Carmen turned her nose as she sat down on the brown sofa with mix-matching cushions. "Look around you, Sonia. This is how we're going to be living soon if we don't get that black bitch to leave Falu," Carmen said, frustrated.

"It's not so bad after a few drinks. In a little while, you'll think we're in his home," Beth said, laughing. "Get comfortable smoke this joint with me, and we can figure out how to get that woman packing." The girls passed around the bottle of rum and after a few puffs, they were singing another tune. They talked about how much they hated Mia and wanted to get back at her for beating them and taking their meal ticket. A few hours later, they were laughing about how scared they were at Madame Azusa's place.

"So, what's the deal between you and Max? He is one smoking hot man," Sonia asked, blowing smoke rings in the air.

Beth took another drink, passing the joint to Carmen. "I had been following Max for months. You know, trying to get with the same crowd. So, he would notice me, and finally, one day, I had the nerve to ask him for a date, and he said alright. We went to a nice hotel a few times and then one night he invited me to their club. Well, I thought I had it made, and I was blown away. Anyway, we were sitting at the table, the drinks were coming, and we were having a great time. But I noticed that Max kept on asking Mia to dance and it was pissing me off."

"But didn't you dance with him, you know, cut in," Sonia asked.

"I was intimidated. Those brothers can dance. I tried a few times… I couldn't keep up with him."

Carmen laughed. "Their mother was a professional dancer and teacher. I think she even had her own studio for a while,"

"Well, I was jealous. I really liked Max, and I still do. When I got into an argument with Mia, he dumped me. I was so mad I wanted to kill her."

"Wow, I can't believe you had Max in bed," Sonia laughed. "How was it…? I always imagine what it would be like with him between the sheets."

"It was… really good… no, more like a fantasy come true. Let's not talk about him. It makes me angry. So, you have the hots for him too?"

"Don't mind my sister Beth. She's a horny bitch, and she humps anything that hangs," they burst with laughter.

Beth tried to get up and fell back into the ill formed sofa. "Hey, I have something that may help. But it's dangerous. My friend has a few connections and he told me about this drug, they use to put it in people's drinks, and it paralyzes them for a few hours."

"We need something that is going to make him do what we say," Carmen added, trying to open her eyes. Beth stumbled to a heater vent in the corner of the living room. She pulled the grill off and reached down, feeling for a square metal box. She stumbled back, falling to the floor. The girls laughed out of control, feeling the effect of the weed they had just smoked. Beth laughed along with them as she fought to get the lid off the box. When she managed to get it open, it had small envelopes with all the different color pills. Ro-hy-p-nol, that's it, taking a few out of the small envelopes. She hands the pills to Carmen. "Use just one. They are dangerous. It could kill someone."

Sonia examines the small pill in her hand. "Are you sure this is going to do the job? They're awfully small."

"Just make sure you only use one."

Carmen smiled at her sister, "It's on bitch, and your time is limited."

Mia was concerned that Falu would work himself to death. He spent hours working on the solar blueprint keeping him busy. But the twins never failed to get under her skin.

She was always finding their personal things left behind so she could see them. They would wear some of his t-shirts and tie his clothes in different locations. Sometimes leave their underwear hanging on the doorknob. They continued to harass her whenever they were alone.

Falu looked up from his paperwork and smiled when Mia entered his office. His secretary was gone for the day. "Hey, baby, what's up."

"Another late night, I see." She sat in the chair across from him. By the look on her face, he knew something was wrong. "What's on your mind?"

"I'm going to kill those bitches. I told you before to tell them to stay out of my way and leave me alone."

He rubbed his tired eyes. "I'll talk to them, but I told you to ignore them. They're silly women."

"No, not anymore, Falu. I've tried to be the bigger person like Dr. Eli asked me to be. Just walk away is all he would say. Sometimes, Falu, I get so frustrated. Please, baby, I don't want you to go down for murdering one of them, but they are pushing their luck."

He came around the desk and pulled her into his arms. "I understand their place will be ready in a day and then they are out of our hair forever. You still love me? I know you feel neglected."

She pushed his hair back, "te adoro mi amore," she kissed him lightly."

"I love to hear you speak Spanish to me, especially when we're making love," he kissed her neck, making her giggle.

"You're not too bad yourself."

"Listen, I'm working double time to finish this before the Eastern meeting, and I'll be gone for six weeks after that. But I promise you I will make it up to you."

She kissed him back. "I love you, Falu, but I will not share you with anyone. I know what happens at these so call conferences. There's always some whores waiting around to try to snatch themselves some sugar daddies."

"Baby, you don't have to worry about me. You are the only woman I want and love. Why don't you go visit your parents for a few days when I'm gone?"

"I don't trust those heifers around you."

He laughed loudly, "Alright, I get it… hey, meet me in bed. Give me thirty minutes to wrap things up here."

"You're on, baby," Mia hated to see him so stressed out and didn't want to worry about the issues she was having with the twins. Maybe a few days away will cool her down.

It was a memorable night for the couple. They made love by moonlight on the chaise lounge with the balcony door open. The spicy air of New Orleans added to their passion. Their bodies shimmered in the moonlight.

"Marry me, Mia?" he said sweetly.

Mia lifted her head, "You want us to get married?" She giggled.

"Don't you want to marry me?" He asked.

She laid her head on his shoulders, playing with his chest hair and listening to his heart's beat. "I do want to marry you, and I love you. But we just had steamy sex and you may not be thinking with the right head."

He chuckled, "Baby, I want to let you in on a secret. When they first bought you to me, I knew… I knew you would be the woman for me. I felt it right away. Te amo tanto," he kissed her. Mia was always emotional when they spoke about the future. She sat on top of him. The moonlight engulfed her beautiful body.

"If you're proposing, then I except, porque te amo mas que nunca." (Because I love you more than ever.)

He pulled her to him by her hair. "Come to me, she-devil," she laid on top of him, so content and full of love. "Baby, we'll get married after all this is over, so start planning a wedding."

"How long is it going to take for this project to be done?"

"It's supposed to take about a year to complete, but my part should be done in three months, maybe a little more. I have a presentation in two weeks, and then I head out to the project site, which is about a hundred miles from here, for six weeks. After that, I'll be yours, and we can plan a family."

"That sounds nice. I want the girls to be at our wedding. I miss their company when you're so busy."

"So, it's settled. We will be man and wife in three months. I don't want to wait any longer."

Every day Falu worked hard on his presentations, with many components.

The twins knew it would only be a matter of time before he left, and their place would be ready. "It has to be tonight, Sonia. I will distract Lydia. She always brings him coffee when he's working late. Remember to only drop one in the coffee that should do the trick," Carmen hands Sonia the envelope.

Lydia hummed cheerfully, placing the coffee in an oversize mug when Carmen interrupted her. "Lydia, can you help me find something in the cupboard," she looked at Carmen strangely.

"What are you looking for?"

"I want to make this tea. It's supposed to help you sleep. I'm having a hard time sleeping."

While Carman distracted her, Sonia took the envelope with the pills out of her pocket. She held the contents over the mug and jumped when she heard Lydia coming back to the kitchen. "Oh shit," she whispered, unsure how many pills she dropped in his coffee. Quickly she put the rest in her pocket and went out the back way, making sure no one saw her.

Mia woke up in the middle of the night and saw it was after two in the morning. Sometimes, Falu would take a power nap on the sofa. Mia smiled as she threw on her robe and walked downstairs to wake him up and bring him up to bed.

It was a wet and sticky rainy night, and she felt the humidity in the air. There was a strange eerie feeling as she reached the outer office door that was wide open. She found it strange and when she looked under Falu's office door, the lights were out. She felt a strange knot in the pit of her stomach. Slowly she opened the door and gasped. There was Falu sprawled out on the floor naked, with the twins lying next to him. They had their naked breast on him, with their legs intertwined.

Mia could only stare, hoping this was only a dream and that she would wake up and realize it was a nightmare. Tears welled up and a lump in her throat kept her from crying out. She fled with tears streaming down her face. Mia packed a bag, took whatever money she could find, and headed down to the stables. As quickly and quietly as possible, she saddled her horse Lucky and rode down towards the gate. Nelson was fast asleep, and she managed to open the gate without waking him.

Mia threw her hood on and rode blindly through the main street of New Orleans. The streets were deserted as she rode out of the city. She stopped and looked back, sobbing and knowing that she could never come back.

Chapter 15: Voodoo Princess

Mrs. Nelson entered her office cautiously; the door was wide open, which was unusual. Falu was very careful about locking up at night. His office door was slightly open, "Mr. Falu, are you in your office?" She walked towards the door and rapped on it slightly, causing it to open. The odor of liquor hung in the air. "Mr. Falu," she tried to call out to him. She entered his office when he didn't answer and found the three still on the floor. "Oh my God! Mr. Falu," she called out to him with no response. Mrs. Nelson ran towards the Doctors office for help. "Dr. Manny, please come quickly," he saw a look of fear on her face and raced to Falu's office. He was totally confused at what he saw.

"Miss Nelson, please quickly get Max." Dr. Manny was having a hard time trying to wake Falu. The girls were still on the floor when Max walked in.

"What the hell is this shit?" He yelled. The girls were rubbing the sleep from their eyes and trying to cover up.

"Max, help me get him to my office. His pupils are dilated, and his pulse is fast. He's not responding." They moved Falu quickly to the infirmary and started working on him. Dr. Peggy pushed Max out the door. He went to find the twins, who were still in the office putting on their clothes.

He grabbed Carmen by the neck, pushing her against the wall. "What the hell did you do to my brother?" he shook her violently.

"I didn't do anything, I swear," she yelled, trying to pull away from him.

"Both of you better be gone, now!" He bellowed, chasing them out of the room, down the stairs, and through the back door.

Max found Ricky and Tony standing outside of the treatment room. They could hear Dr. Manny and Dr. Peggy shouting instructions to the nurses assisting them. Mrs. Nelson was shaken. She kept on wringing her hands nervously, her face marred with anticipation.

"I'm sorry you had to find him this way," Max said, holding her.

"He looked so pale, and I kept on calling him. I was afraid he was dead."

Max didn't even want to think about that scenario, "Let's not think about such things, and think positive."

"Max, where's Mia? Does she know?" Ricky asked.

"I'll go get her," Tony said, looking at Max and Ricky.

"Thanks, Tony, she's going to freak out," Ricky said, hoping to hear something soon. Tony shouted to Mia and knocked on the door. When she didn't answer, he became concerned that the twins had done something to her as well.

What if something happened to Mia? Tony thought to himself. He opened the door and continued to call out for her, but the room was silent. The only noises came from the balcony outside. He checked the bathroom and the other room. The drawers were open, and clothes were lying all over the bed. Then he radioed the staff down at the stables. Her horse was gone. Tony raced back to Max and Ricky, who were still waiting for word about Falu's condition.

"Where's Mia?" Max asked. Tony was worried and they could see something was wrong.

"She's gone, Max. She must have walked in on them… Lucky is gone too, and no one has seen her." Max wanted to scream, first his brother, now Mia.

Peggy came to the door. The look on her face told the story that she was worried. "Come in, guys."

When Max saw Falu hooked up to machines, he freaked out. "Oh my God," he cried. "What's happening to him?"

"Let's talk in our office," Dr. Peggy said. They followed her into the office where Dr. Manny was waiting.

"Max, he's going to be alright. We got him in time. Whatever he ingested almost killed him."

"Like what? Are you saying he took drugs?" Max asked, alarmed.

"I don't know. It may have been by accident, but this drug was very powerful. He was drugged for sure. I got the report back on what kind of drug it was, and I was really confused. It was made in a homemade lab."

"Doc, Is he going to be alright? All the machines are freaky me out," Max asked again.

"He's going to be alright. Thank God Falu is a strong man. I need you guys to search the office and try to find out how it got into his system."

A few hours later, Falu was sitting up in his bed with a huge headache. Max was almost in tears when he saw him sitting up and fussing at everyone. He sat next to him, "How are you feeling? We were worried," Max asked with a knot in his throat.

"Don't worry, brother. It takes more than a few pills to bring me down. But I still don't know what happened."

"What do you remember?"

"I remember Lydia bringing me coffee like she always does, and everything went black. Where's Mia? I thought she would be here worried," that was one question Max dreaded.

"Mia's…not here, Falu."

"That's right. She was going to see her parents. Has anyone contacted her?"

Max didn't want to tell him that she was gone while he was still recovering. "I have someone looking for her," which was only a half truth. Max had already contacted her parents and had people searching for her.

Falu was not pleased with what happened. The next morning, he was up and at his desk, but he couldn't get a straight answer from anyone about Mia. When Tony, Ricky, and Max gathered in his office, Falu knew something was wrong. "What's going on, guys? You're all shit faced," he stood up. "What's up?"

"Falu… it's about Mia… she's gone," Max said.

"What do you mean she's gone? Where!?" He asked, confused.

"She walked in on you and the twins. She hasn't been seen since."

The blood drained from his face. "Why didn't you tell me," he yelled, storming around the office.

"Because you react like this, like a madman," replied Max. "Now listen to me. We will find Mia. I have people searching for her. Falu, brother, you have to finish this presentation. Leave Mia to us, please hundreds of thousands of people are counting on you."

He sat down and looked at all the work on his desk. "I want my woman Max," he looked at them sadly.

"I know you do, Falu. We all miss her, but you need to focus on this… I promise you, we won't stop looking for her, I swear on our parent's grave."

The atmosphere changed at the Esmeralda Estate. The songbird was gone and Falu was not the same. He refused to sleep in his suite, sleeping in his office or in the men's barracks. His brother and friends worried about his state of mind but kept an eye on him. He was miserable and worked out more than usual. He rarely came to the club and hardly spoke to anyone.

The girls invited him to dinner, trying to get him to open up about his feelings, but he ate and left soon after. The presentation went beautifully and was on target, and he stayed an extra three weeks in the Inner Cities, where he didn't have a memory of his beloved. When Falu returned, he was seen to be himself. He had long conversations with Jesse Quintanilla and some of his friends that helped him with his loss. But he couldn't get Mia out of his thoughts and his heart.

Mrs. Nelson welcomed him with a new office. In his absence, she had his office redone, and he loved it. His crew gathered in his office with champagne to toast the success of the new power grill that was going into production in two months when the weather was perfect for laying the foundation. It was time to celebrate, but the sadness in Falu's eyes could not be disguised. Everywhere he looked brought memories of his Mia. Mrs. Nelson interrupted their celebration. "I'm sorry, Mr. Falu, but Tony needs to speak to you. He is having problems with the twins. I know they have been trying to see you for a few weeks."

Falu smiled, "Tell him to escort them. I think it's about time I address what happened to me that day. Max, Ricky, I want you two to stay. In case I go a little crazy." The girls looked like hookers with their tight clothes and caked on makeup that made them look older. Falu stood in front of his desk when Tony escorted them in. "Au, Tony, please stick around. This won't take long," Falu looked wonderful, clean shaving and smartly dressed.

"Thanks, Falu, for hearing our side of what happened. Everyone was seen to think we had something to do with what happened to you," Carmen tried to explain. They had rehearsed what they were going to say.

"Well, I'm all ears. I'm sure we all want to hear the events of what really happened that night," he didn't even ask them to sit down, and they sense they were in trouble. They achieved what they wanted, for Mia to be gone.

Carmen was nervous, she was on the spot with the others leering down at them. "Well, we saw the light on in your office, so we came to see if we could convince you to hang out with us. The outer door was open, so we just came right in. You were drinking and talking a little crazy. I remember you going to the door and locking the door. Anyway, you said something like, let's get the party started, and so we started to drink, you pulled out a blunt, and after a while, you started to grab me and Falu, you know how much I love you. I've always loved you. Then you said you wanted a threesome. I mean, we were all high Falu, so we went a little crazy. I don't remember much of anything after that," she stumbled with her explanation, hoping he would believe her.

Falu tried not to laugh. Ricky and Max laughed with amusement.

"Well, Carmen, that's one hell of a story. I almost applaud you for that performance, but I know you are full of shit!"

"Falu, I'm not lying. Why would I lie to you?"

"Because you're a lying bitch, number one, I had no alcohol in my system or weed. The only drug in my system was Rohypnol, and it's an illegal drug. And apparently, one of you wanted to kill me because there was enough in the coffee to kill a few people! Luckily for me, I drink my coffee really slowly. If not, I would be six feet under right now."

"But I swear I didn't put anything in your coffee," Carmen argued, trying to sound convincing

He put his hand up, interrupting her. "Right now, it's time for you to shut up and listen. Since you two came back, I have had nothing but trouble from you, and I regret with all my heart that I let you walk through my door. Because of you, I lost the most important person in my life. Why you would do something so hurtful is beyond me? I have been nothing but good to you and this is how you repaid me."

Carmen looked at her sister, "I don't know what you mean…we didn't do anything."

"Stop the bullshit! It's over… you're done… I don't ever want to see your faces around here again. In fact, Tony, do me the honor of throwing these bitches out of my house and out of my city," he yelled so loud they heard him throughout the house.

"But some dangerous people are looking for us. Where are we going to live?" Sonia cried.

"I don't give a rat's ass what you do," he replied. "From now on you both are dead to me.

"Falu, please, I only did this because I love you. I always did," Carmen said sobbing. "Why can't you love me? I'm here."

"You promised my brother you would take care of us," Sonia cried, scared and crumpled on the floor.

He walked up to her, towering over her, "Your parents and your brother were some of the finest people that walked this earth. But you two were spawned from the devil. You two are evil, nasty, and vile. You have ripped my heart out and stomped on it. I don't want to look at your faces ever again, and Carmen, you need the heart to know how to love. Now, Tony, they have one hour to get their shit and leave.

Not one minute more," he turned his back to them. He could hear them crying as Tony escorted them out of his office.

"Wow, now that was severe. Are you sure about your decision," Max asked?

"Had I listened to my woman? she would still be here with me," he turned his face. "Planning our wedding."

"You haven't given up, have you?" Max added.

"At this point, brother, I don't know if she's alive, and I don't know what to say to her parents."

"Please don't give up on her. I know deep inside that we'll find her. She's probably confused and still angry."

"Well, so am I… I can't even tell you how I'm going to act if we do find her."

Max hurt along with his brother, knowing how much pain he was in.

Falu spent most of his time at one of the locations. Women threw themselves at him, but he didn't seem interested. It was his poker night, and Max urged him to join them.

"Come on, brother, it's been ages since we got some of your money, and it will take your mind off things."

"Alright, I think you're right. I can use some downtime. So, count me in."

The club was not the same, the band was a blues jazz, and Max warned them not to play any love lost songs. The club was packed and Falu seemed like his old self, but this time his luck with cards was in his favor. For a few hours, he enjoyed his friends and didn't carry his heart on his sleeve. When his radio started to buzz, "Let it ring," Ricky said, he didn't want to bring him down.

"I have to take this. It may be important," it was the guard Falu who put him on speaker. "What's up, Orlando?"

"Boss, I have Gino out here. He has something important to tell you."

"It's really late, ask him, can it wait until tomorrow?"

"He said it's really urgent, boss. I think you need to see him. He's very adamant about seeing you tonight."

"Alright, bring him to the downstairs conference room. I should be there in a few." They all walked toward the conference room when they finished the last round. Gino stood up when they came in.

"Mr. Falu, I want to apologize for the late hour, but I just got here, and I don't think I could wait."

"It sounds important," Falu replied with caution.

"Mr. Falu, Max, Ricky, you have been a good friend and my best customer. I saw your lady and I wanted to let you know that."

Falu stood up. "You saw Mia. Are you sure it's her?"

"Mr. Falu, there is no mistake about the beautiful Mia, aka Voodoo Princess. I was as close to her as I am to you. But she did not see me."

"Was she with another man? Please tell me the truth."

Gino tried not to laugh. "Yes, if you count the man she was fighting."

"What do you mean?" Falu said, not amused.

"She was in the ring. I had the pleasure of watching her fight, and I must say it was very angry." He handed him a poster.

Falu's heart sank when he saw her picture, and the poster had her in a scandalized outfit, hands in a fist, looking dangerous. "She's only two hours from here," he smiled. "Giddy up, boys. We're going on a trip."

Tony and Gary were only too happy to go scout out the area and find out more information on her whereabouts. At the same time, Falu prepared himself to confront her. He just stared at the poster on his desk. She was in one of her favorite poses. Max poked his head in the door.

"Falu, I need to know what your plans are." Falu took a deep breath. He was upset but yet wanted her back in his arms. "Falu," Max said, trying to get a response from him. "Are you alright, dude?"

"I was just sitting here wondering… what if she doesn't want to come back. I'm going to look like an ass running after her."

Max pulled the chair close to him. "Listen to me, brother. Who said to me that she was yours? You said to me that she was sent here for you. And you waited for her until she was ready to commit to you. Falu, what I saw was not a fly-by-night relationship. It was real. So as your younger brother, who loves both of you… grow some balls and get your woman!"

Falu smiled, "You know me all too well. There's only one thing I worry about. If she's with some dude, I don't know how I'm going to react. I'll be honest."

"That's why we're your backup. She's young Falu and inexperienced. Now, where's my badass brother?" they shook hands.

"I'm ready – ready to get my life back in order."

"That's the shit, man."

Lakeland Louisiana

It was still mid-morning when Falu and his crew entered the main street of Lakeland, a small city hit really hard by the Dark Days. There weren't many activities going on. Most of the stores were still boarded up. The streets were almost deserted except for some older men playing checkers outside of the barbershop in the shade. "Wow, I would have never thought about searching here. I didn't think anyone lived here," Max said.

"It's like a lot of other small cities, trying to survive," Falu added. "Where are we supposed to meet Tony?"

"There's a hotel on the main road on Race and Barrington," Max replied. The Lakewood Barrington was a six-floor rundown Hotel. They walked the granite steps into a large sitting area. There was evidence that it was once very grand. The carpeting was worn, and the furniture was old and mismatched, but it was clean. There were several elderly couples in the lounge area drinking tea and socializing. When Falu and his crew walked in wearing their duster that concealed their weapons, the conversation was focused on them. The young desk clerk was frightened when she saw these five huge men walking toward her. She wanted to hide in the back, and they could tell she was scared. "Sweetheart," Max said in a soft voice, "We're here to meet with some friends. Can you ring their room and let them know we're here?" he winked at her and smiled, which made her more nervous.

"Their names, ah, sir," she asked, fumbling with her register.

"Tony Johnson and Gary Green," Max replied.

She finally smiled. "Yes… I will ring them for you. Ah, we have some coffee and tea by the wall if you nice gentlemen care for some," they thanked her and sat at the small tables by the corner.

Ricky almost gagged on his cup of coffee, "Shit, how can anyone drink this piss water?"

"Oh, come on, it's not that bad. I've had worst," Falu said. "You're getting to be a little prima donna on us," the guys all laughed. Tony and Gary were all smiles when they met up. They shook hands.

"Hey sweetie," Gary said. "Can you open the large conference room for us? Thank you, love." She ushered them into the board room, opening the shades for light and closing the door behind her.

"So, tell me, how is my little songbird," Falu said, waiting for the bomb to drop.

Gary and Tony chuckled. "Man, she is the shit!" Gary said, laughing.

"Do I have to kill anyone?" Falu asked.

"No, boss, the men around her are afraid of her. They said yes and no, Miss," Tony added. "This I can truly say she is… unattached. She wears this chain around her neck with your name on it, boss. We followed her these last two days and have her routine pretty down pack."

"How is she?" Falu asked.

"She looks good. Mia works out almost every day at this gym a few blocks from here. We went to one of her matches yesterday. She's mean and angry and wiped the dog-doody shit out of the guy. I felt sorry for him, but he was talking a lot of shit, and she let him have it," Tony laughed.

"Friday and Saturday nights, she is the main event at this club 'La Coquina' a block away from where she's living. The Voodoo Princess, she's on tonight."

They walked a few blocks to where she was living. It was another rundown hotel called 'The Suites', and people rented the small apartments by the week or month. The glass windows looked as if they hadn't been washed in years. The double doors squeaked as they came in, and Tony and Gary stayed outside as look-outs.

An elderly man was sitting at the desk smoking a cigar and listening to music on a beat-up radio. He took out his gun and laid it out in the open when he saw Falu and Max walk up to the desk. "What can I do for you gentlemen today?"

Falu saw that he had his hand close to the gun on his desk. Max went around to his right and Ricky on his left. "I need some information about someone living here," Falu says, leering at him.

"I'm sorry," he said nervously. "I can't give out that kind of information about our residents. He goes for his gun, but before he does, Falu has him by the collar with a shotgun pointed under his chin.

"Now, let's try this again. I want to know about Mia, aka Voodoo Princess I was told she resides here," the man's eyes grew larger as he started shaking. "Now, my brother here is going to assist me with these questions. Every time you don't answer the question truthfully, he's going to cock his weapon into position, you got that."

"Yes, sir, please don't hurt me," he sat back down.

"Where is her apartment, and is she living with anyone?"

"She's in 1 C, a flight up, looking towards the street," his hands shook.

"Now that wasn't so hard, was it? So now you're going to tell me all you know and don't be stupid and leave anything out."

"You're not going to hurt her, are you?" He asked timidly.

"Look, she's my woman. We had a misunderstanding, and she left. I want her back. Now talk mister because I'm losing my patience."

"What can I say. She's a sweet and beautiful woman. She keeps to herself. Oh yeah, she sings down the street here. Mister, she has no man in her life, I swear to you. One time these three troublemakers decided to pay her a visit. They must have followed her from the fight. The next thing I hear is a loud crack and people screaming. Well, when I ran outside there, they were laying all busted up on the sidewalk bleeding and moaning. She walked outside, pulled one of them by the hair, and said, "Never without invitation, boys," and then she just let go of him and walked upstairs like nothing happened."

"Anything else you can tell me?"

"There is one thing… sometimes I hear her crying, and it makes me sad, such a pretty thing and in so much pain. Now I know she was crying over lost love. Mister, I hope you do get things straight with her, a woman like her shouldn't live in so much pain, and that's all I can say."

"Alright, do you have anything open?"

"Well, sure, he gets up and walks to the keyboard. The apartment right above hers is empty."

"We'll take it. I want the key to her apartment. I know you have an extra key. This is what's going to happen. I don't want her to know we're here. If you even think of breathing a word that we're here, you're a dead man. I will personally torch this place to the ground. All I want is my woman back, and I'm not leaving without her. Got it? Nod your head if you understand. Max, pay the man," Max slapped down three gold and five silver coins.

The old man looked at Max. "That's a lot of money, sir, way more than this dump is worth."

"For your silence," they walk away. Falu opened the door to Mia's apartment. It was small. It went straight into the small kitchen that looks right into the bedroom. Her scent was all over the apartment, driving him crazy. It was clean, and the bedroom had a blue bedspread with a tiny drawer and closet. He opened her drawer that had her personal items. Sexy panties and bras were neatly folded, and her closet was the same everything hung neatly. Falu sat on the bed, looking around the very plain room. He saw something sticking out from under the bed and pulls it out. It was her travel bag. When he opened it and pulled out an envelope with pictures of them together, kissing and dancing. His eyes swelled up with tears. It was finally hitting him, she was here in this very room sleeping in this very bed, and today he would come face to face with her. He stuffed the pictures in the envelope, shoved the bag back under the bed and went downstairs to join his crew.

Le Coquina Club & Bar

Mia's picture was displayed proudly on the billboard. She was in a very seductive pose wearing a Pink mini strapless dress. Her hair in a ponytail and straight bangs, she had a chain around her neck with Falu's name. The outside of the club was rundown. They had to pass a set of double doors to get into the main dance floor. The place was bigger than he had imagined. It had two bars, one in the front towards the entrance and a smaller one on the right side, which had a perfect view of the stage.

Falu and the rest of his crew took their seats and ordered drinks as the band set up and warmed up. Falu was apprehensive about seeing Mia again and what he would do or say when he finally came face to face with her. The club was filling up quickly as the MC started to make announcements and the drinks kept on coming. When Mia walked out onto the stage, Max watched Falu's reaction. She wore a sexy white two-piece outfit looking beautiful as ever. The crowd reacted to her presence, whistling and throwing kisses.

"Is everyone ready to party?" She yelled to the crowd! They erupt, shouting her stage name. The scandalous white outfit looked as if it was sewn on her. Her two background singers flanked her.

Falu turned to Max, "She always did know how to put on a show," he said sadly.

"Hey, are you alright?" Max asked.

"I'm cool, just trying to chill out," Falu replied. He had a great view from where they sat. The floor was packed as she went back and forth from Spanish songs to juicy R&B. The outfits were scandalous as she bumped and grind, and the crowd went crazy. Her slow, sultry song stung him deeply; the wound was still so raw. Those songs she used to sing to him while she was on stage. He knew they were meant for him. *Now, who was she singing to*, he thought to himself. During the intermission, he turned to the bartender, who was enjoying the music. He couldn't take his dreamy eyes off of her.

"So, what's the story behind the songbird?" Falu asked him.

"Man, she's the shit around here. This place was a real dump before she came to sing here, and she's my hero."

"Really, your hero, how's that?" Falu said, pumping him for information.

"Well, she doesn't live too far from here. One night she came for a few drinks. The band was alright, but the singer was really bad. She had been drinking… I remember this because some dude was trying to hit on her, and she punched him in the face. But that's not out of the ordinary around here. She stumbled toward the stage and took the mike from the singer. She turned to the guys and said give me something with a beat. She turned out of the place within a few minutes. People were up dancing and the band kept on playing, and she kept on singing. It was awesome. The next few nights, she came in, and the owner begged her to sing. She picked him up by the collar and said she wouldn't sing in this dump and dropped him on his ass. He chased her and promised to get her a better band and make the place nicer. He's one of those cheap scumbags that don't pay his employees, buys cheap booze tries to con everyone. But she wouldn't take his shit. I saw her snatch him from behind the desk once and I swear he pissed in his pants. He didn't want to pay the girls, and this happened a lot. Yeah, she put a smile on a lot of people's faces, including my own."

"Is she seeing anyone steady?"

"Nah, she still into this guy that broke her heart. What a douchebag! She wears his name around her neck. Men can't get near her. She's angry all the time. They say he was her first and is having a hard time getting over him."

Falu took his jacket off and put his elbows on the bar. The bartender looked at his tattoo with Mia's name on it. He was scared when he saw how big and menacing Falu was. His crew glared at him.

"You're him, her… man," he said, wiping the bar nervously. "Sorry about the douchebag comment."

"Where is her dressing room?" He looked into Falu's eyes and knew he was not someone he could mess with, and the others dwarfed the bouncer they had.

"You won't hurt her, will you? She's a nice person."

"Why would I hurt my woman? We just need to talk, that's all, you get me?"

"I understand… her dressing room is down that hallway, third door on your right before the back door exit."

"Good boy, now I won't have to kill you," Falu smiled at him.

Mia was tired when she finished for the night. She shared a dressing room with Penny, who lived in the apartment next to hers. Penny was one of her backup singers who had a great voice. She was a shy petite woman with huge blue eyes admiring Mia. Mia encouraged Penny to sing her heart out and was the only woman she let in on her heartbreak with Falu.

Mia tried to push back the depression that seemed to be her unwanted companion. When she was on stage, she left her heart. But when she sang songs she used to sing to Falu, it made her feel even worst. "Mia, why don't you go with us to Gilly's? I hate to see you all tore up every time we finish a set." Gilly's was an after-hour bar hang-out, a real dive.

"Penny, you know I can't go to those places. I always end up fighting with some asshole."

"Well, that's the fun part," Penny laughed.

"I'm sorry... I wouldn't be good company for anyone," Mia said, removing the makeup from her face.

"Mia, when are you going to let go? It's killing you," Penny said, watching Mia's eyes fighting back the tears.

"You don't understand, Penny, we shared more than super-hot sex, and we connected in a deep way. Who knows, maybe someday, but it's going to be a long time before I can move on." She went into the small dressing room where they changed. Carefully she took off her clothes, hanging them carefully. She changed into her black dress and shoes, needing to have a drink and take a walk.

There was a hard knock on the door. "Who the hell is that?" She asked, annoyed. Penny was in shock when she opened the door.

"Mia… I think you better come to the door."

"Whoever it is, get rid of him or her," she brushed her hair. "I'm not in the mood."

"No, Mia, I think you better get this," Mia was frustrated. Sometimes, men would come to her dressing room to ask her out. "Really, Penny… " Falu was in the door's entrance as Penny cringed against the dressing table. Mia was speechless. He pulled her out of the room into the hallway. "Oh my God!" she yelled.

Falu had a murderous look on his face. "We have to talk!" he grabbed her and threw her over his shoulder like a sack of potatoes.

Mia reached out to Max, who was following them. "Max! Help me!" Falu kicked open the back door. The rest of the crew followed Falu down to the apartment building. People stared as he carried the struggling Mia. "Falu, you're insane," she screamed.

"Max, you better open that damn door before I kick it in," Max ran ahead of them and opened the door to her apartment. He set her down, cornering her against the refrigerator. "You're killing me, woman!" He yelled at the top of his lungs. She could see anger in his eyes. Mia threw herself against him, kissing him. He opened his mouth to capture hers. For a moment, everything stopped. He was lost in her arms, remembering how wonderful it felt, her embrace, the taste of her kisses, and the scent of her body.

She whispered in his ear. "I missed you so much," he turned to Max, who was standing by the door, not knowing what to do next.

"Max, close the door behind you." His eyes were dark with anger. He held her against the refrigerator again. "Is this what you want to do, shake your ass at a bunch of horny men? You left me to die!" They could hear him yelling throughout the building. She pushed him away from her, walking into her small bedroom, not knowing what to say to him. "You put me through hell!" He grabbed her to face him.

She broke his grip on her. "You think you're the only one who suffered! When I saw you laying there naked with those... those two skanks all over you, the smell of booze and weed in the room, I wanted to die!"

"I was set up. I almost died and when I looked for the woman who confessed she loved me, you were gone! Sometimes I wished I had died."

"I didn't know. All I saw was you on your naked back, and they were all over you. I just stood there for a few minutes just staring at this nightmare."

"Why didn't you beat us up and react like you would normally?"

She sat down on the edge of the bed, "My mind went back to a really dark place. I wanted to go downstairs and get a butcher knife and cut you all into tiny pieces... but then I remembered what Doc said to me during one of our sessions, and that's what I did. I didn't walk away. I ran," she said, sobbing. "I grabbed some of my things and rode Lucky out of... of the city. I let him take me wherever she wanted to in any direction. I needed money, so I did what I knew how to do best, fight and sing." He knelt next to her. "I... wanted to come back a million times, crying myself in pity. I missed you so much," she sobbed. "I needed you... but I didn't know if you wanted me back."

He could tell how much pain she was in because he was feeling the same torture. He forced her to look at him, "Why would you think I didn't want you back? I ask you to marry me." He stood up and walked to the window, trying to shut out all the pain he suffered when he was told she was gone. "It was a setup, Mia. I lay there between life and death. All I wanted was for my woman to comfort me and she was gone. I felt like shit! How was I going to go on without the woman I adore?" Mia came behind him, holding him around the waist, kissing his back. He pulled her around to face him, his tears mixed with hers as he searched for her lips.

She clung to him, "I never thought I'd see you again," she said. He pulled her back to the bed.

"I'm not leaving without you," he pinned her under him. "I don't care if I have to take you back kicking and screaming." They kissed and immediately, it was as if they were never apart. He kissed those sensitive places that drove her insane. Soft moans escaped her lips, and she let herself fall into a sea of pleasure. She removed his shirt, wanting to feel his naked body against hers again.

"Mia…who have you been with?" he whispered, feeling her stiffen beneath him.

She pushed him off her, "Is that all you think about," she stood up. "Who I was screwing… you asshole!" she screamed at him.

"I wanted to know. Mia, you're a passionate woman. We had sex almost every night anywhere."

"Shit, you think that sex is the answer to everything! I'm not like you, Falu! Maybe you can drown your sorrows in sex, but I can't. You ruined me! When a man would approach me, all I would do was compare him to you!"

He held her by the shoulders. "I just needed to know, that's all. I haven't slept in our room because… it was too painful. All your shit was everywhere, that damn pole we used to… you know."

She wanted to slap him.

Falu finished taking off his clothes and stood in front of her. She could not resist touching his chest, tenderly remembering all those times she laid her head against his chest, listening to his heartbeat. A flood of emotions entered his body as he touched her breast, watching her nipples harden kissed them tenderly, "Mia," he whispered. "What have you done to me." She slipped off her clothes slowly, watching the lust in his eyes. They found themselves in bed, taking all the frustration out on each other in the heat of wild passion.

"I missed you so much," tears mingled with kisses. "I hated you and loved you at the same time," Mia sighed.

"Don't talk, baby. Let me get my fill of your kisses that drive me crazy. Te amor mujer."

Mia clung to him as they lay in each other's arms, happy that he was in her arms again. She kissed his chest, "I think everyone in the building heard us," she said, kissing him.

"So, when did that ever bother you," he pulled her closer.

"Because you were so loud," she giggled.

"It doesn't matter. All I care is that… that you still love me, and I'm taking you back home where you belong."

Mia sat up in bed, "Falu, I can't leave."

"What do you mean you can't leave?" he jumped out of the bed.

"I have a contract to perform for another three months."

"If you think I'm leaving here without you, you're insane. You are leaving with me tomorrow." He started to put his pants on.

"Where are you going," she grabbed her robe.

"You listen to me, I am not leaving you behind, and I want you to promise me that if anything like this ever happens to us again. You don't run… I don't care if you find some woman hanging onto my dick. We will work it out because this should have never happened. I love you. There is no one else. Mia, the woman who stole my heart," he held her.

"I promise," she sealed her promise with a kiss, "Come back to bed."

"I'll be right back, baby. Keep the bed warm for us," Falu headed towards the door.

"Where are you going?!" she yelled after him, screaming as he ran downstairs. Max appeared at the top of the stairs. She smiled at him. "Max, help me get this fool from leaving," she yelled.

Max pulled her back up the stair and turned her around, "I missed you guys."

"I missed you too," he pushed her hair back. "When are you going to learn about Falu?"

"He's so pigheaded. Max, your brother's irrational," she smiled.

Penny opened the door shyly when she heard them talking. "Is everything alright?"

"Penny, come and meet my best friend Max," she held her hand out to him.

"One of my backup singers, Penny Garcia – Bradley," Max held her hand longer than normal, "Ah, why don't we go inside before we wake up everyone else," Mia finally suggested.

"You have a great voice," Max said, trying to be friendly to the shy Penny.

"Thank you. It was Mia who encouraged me to sing in public. I used to hear her singing, and I wanted so much to come and knock on her door. One night I heard her crying, and I worked up enough courage and knocked on her door to see if I could help."

"Yeah, we stayed up all night, and when I found out she could sing, it's like we were connected right away," Mia explained.

Penny sighed, "Now, what am I going to do without you? Old clown face will go back to paying us when he feels like it."

"Why don't you come back with us unless you have ties here, New Orleans has some great clubs and if my brother or I refer you, I'm sure we can get you some nice gigs?" Her eyes lit up. She turned her attention to Mia, who was smiling.

"I think that's a wonderful idea, Max. He's right, and with Falu and Max backing you, the gigs will come rolling in."

Penny's face was flushed with excitement. "What about Mr. Falu… what will he say about me tagging along?"

Max started to laugh, "Oh God, that was funny. Mia has Falu wrapped around her finger. He'll do anything as long as she agrees to come back with him."

Falu appeared at the door, grinning, "Are you guys talking about me again," he said as he pulled Mia into his arms. "No more contract, you're free," he kissed her neck.

"What did you do…? Falu?" she looked into his eyes.

"I gave him an option he couldn't refuse," he squeezed her tight.

"Falu, this is Penny. She kept me from jumping off a cliff. She's coming with us," she said, kissing him.

"You're one of the backup singers? Nice to meet you. Now I have some business with my woman," Max chuckled, that was Falu's cue for them to get out. Falu picked Mia and carried her to the bed. "We have a lot to talk about. I never want to feel such pain again."

She kissed him passionately. "I never meant to hurt you, I saw red, and I had to get away. I'm so happy you're… you're here next to me, loving me once again."

Falu felt the chain around her neck with his name. "You don't need this anymore," he pulled it from her neck; "You have me, now."

For hours, they talked and cried, and in between the bouts of tears and regrets, they had passionate sex until they were exhausted. They held each other as they slept, wanting only to feel the comfort of each other's touch.

Chapter 16: Home Again

Penny didn't understand the dynamics between Mia and Falu's relationship. They displayed their affection for each other publicly. She didn't know whether to be embarrassed for Mia, who didn't seem to mind when Falu rubbed her hiney or put his hand down her shirt.

They stopped at a small Inn for lunch. Penny sat alone, eating a burger and fries, when Max sat with her. She smiled shyly. "Are you alright?" he asked, knowing she was alone with Falu taking up much of Mia's time

"Yes, everything is wonderful," she smiled, wanting to feel part of the group. "However, I was wondering about Mia. Is she going to be alright? Your brother seems so possessive," she giggled. "Last night, I was embarrassed for her, they were so loud, and those walls were like paper."

Max chuckled, "Don't worry about Mia. She can handle my brother. She'll tell him to back off if he comes on too strong. We're used to their… open affection."

"Wow, I was blushing in my apartment," she laughed.

"They have a very unique love connection. If you're going to be around us, you better get used to it. Especially when they get on the dance floor to a slow song, it's better to look away. It's like a prelude to sex with those two. My mother was a dancer, and my grandmother had a dance studio. My parents were great dancers. On their 20th anniversary, my parents danced the tango that had everyone on their feet, it was magical."

Penny looked down, afraid to look at Max. "I can vouch for how much she loves him. She cried something terribly. I was afraid she would do herself in on some nights after we left work."

"Yeah, they are born for each other, but what about you...? Do you have someone who is going to come looking for you?"

She opened her eyes, surprised with his question. "Um, no one special. There was this one man I dated once. He scared me, so I didn't want to go on the second date. He would come around me, trying to have a relationship with me. He hounded me for weeks until I gave in. That night we had sex and it was very painful. He didn't care when I told him to stop. He said I should get used to it. I tried to discourage him. I told him I didn't want anything more to do with him, and he laughed. He just made himself my boyfriend. Harry Miller, he was a regular at the club. I was so afraid of him. He would come over and demand sex. He would bang on the door so loud that the owner gave me a warning. That if the loud banging continued, I would have to leave because the other tenants were complaining."

"Did he rape you?" Max asked.

She turned away, embarrassed. "It was forced, I tried to get him to stop, but he said that I was his woman and I better get used to it. It was very crazy; all I could do was pray to God that he would find someone else and leave me alone. One night after work, I locked the door and wouldn't let him in… I thought I was going to die. I hid in the closet, praying he'd get tired and leave. But he kicked in the door and went crazy looking for me. When he opened the closet, I started to scream. He slapped me and busted my lip. I tried to get away as he started to rip my clothes off. There I was, alone, with no family or friends that could help me since I had just moved to that town. I just prayed. I knew he was going to kill me at that moment when he had his hands around my neck. I was crying and begging him to stop. I closed my eyes, hoping he would finish. He laughed and said, 'I know you like it rough and that's the way I like it baby' and then I heard him scream.

Mia had him by the hair, pulling him away from me. He was swinging at her, but she kicked and punched him in private. The screams were awful. The neighbors watched in disbelief as she beat the shit out of him. She threw him down the stairs and I swear she killed him. He struggled to get up, his face was all bloody, and he looked up to where Mia was and ran down the stairs. I never saw him after that."

"I'm sorry you went through that experience. I can assure you that will never happen under our watch, and Mia does not like bullies. I'm glad she was there for you."

"She saved my life. I could never repay her for all the things she has done for me. I'm looking forward to something new and wonderful."

"Don't worry, we'll take care of you," he smiled, and she almost lost her mind.

The staff threw a party to welcome Mia home. It was an emotional celebration for her. When the girls came, she broke down crying along with them. Penny was immediately embraced by the girls and made her feel welcome. But Mia felt anxious because Falu was going away, and she had separation anxiety.

Falu held her tight as she cried in his arms. "Baby, if I can take you with me, I would," he kissed her neck."

"I know you have to go, but I just got you back and now you're leaving me."

"Hey, now you have time to plan a wedding, which will take a lot of your time."

"You still want to marry me, baby?"

"Muñeca, whatever you want. You're my reason for getting up in the morning, and when I see your smiling face... I know without a shadow of doubt that you're the woman I want to spend the rest of my life with, te amo," he kissed her teary face.

"Marry me now, Falu. I don't want to wait until you come back." He squeezed her tightly.

"Whatever you want, baby. Why don't we send for your family, and we'll get married in a simple ceremony? Later on, we can celebrate."

She smiled up at him. "I like that, I have this huge ring on my finger now and all I need is the band to make everything official."

Tina stood in for Mia and Max for Falu. She looked beautiful in a simple mini white dress, matching stiletto. The crew whistled and clapped when she walked towards the anxious waiting Falu. They exchanged the sweetest vows making her promise to obey him, proclaiming their love for each other and what kind of future was in store for them.

"Alright, my wife. Wow, that's real. I mean… real. You'll be my wife forever," they kiss tenderly. They continued to make plans for their future, playing around with baby names. They wanted children and didn't want to wait.

The day Falu departed, Mia cried her heart out. Penny stayed with her while Max and the crew accompanied Falu and Ricky as far as they could. The road to where the new power grill would be built was very dangerous, and he had to go on ahead on horseback. It was on top of a mountain.

Max called it the top of the world. They waited until Falu and Ricky were out of sight before they turned back.

Mia spent a few weeks with her parents and helping Ponyboy with his new pets and horses. After the third week, Mia became homesick, missing her surroundings. She also wanted to see if there was any chance to pay Falu a visit. She rehearsed some songs with Penny noticing that Max was always hanging around Penny, protecting her and showing her around. But Penny never mentioned her feelings for Max.

Mia cornered Max one day when he was going to the construction site and wanted to tag along. "Please, Max. I got to see him. I'm going crazy."

"Mia, it's so dangerous. If something happened to you, Falu would never forgive me."

"Max, you know me. I can handle myself. I want to see my husband." He understood her feeling of missing his brother also.

"Alright, but you have to listen to me, you promise?" she nodded, agreeing. He couldn't deny her a thing and hugged her, "I know you miss him."

"We didn't have a honeymoon. I need him, Max."

"Alright, give me two days to set everything up."

It was a sunny day when they traveled toward the construction site. Max was surprised that the roads were redone, and they were able to travel without any problems. Max sent word to Falu that he had arrived and needed to see him urgently. He was happy to see his brother and was anxious to find out how his wife was getting along. "Man, I'm so happy to see you, little brother," they embraced. "How's my wife?" It was still strange to him when he referred to Mia as his wife.

"She's good. She is handling herself. However, there is a problem with one of the stonemasons. He's in your office."

"Alright, look, I don't know how long this is going to take, so I don't know what you want to do."

"I'll be at the site. I want to see what's going on… oh, you have two hours. I want to get back on the road."

"Not a problem. I'll try to make this quick." Falu was surprised that his lights were dim when he turned them up. Mia was sitting in a seductive pose, wearing a silk sleeveless dress on his desk. "Oh my God!" he said excitedly, locking the door behind him. "Oh baby, what a surprise!" he chuckled, squeezing her tight. "I missed you so much." She held on to him, feeling his strong muscular chest against her.

"I had to see you. To make sure you were alright," they kissed passionately.

"Baby, we have two hours so let's make the best of it," she dropped her dress. It didn't take much for them to be on the couch in his office. All the stress melted away as she came alive in his arms. They couldn't get enough of each other, and their passion was only matched by the love they had for each other.

"Baby, I love you so much I couldn't wait for another day to see you."

"I'm glad you came. I hated leaving you. But this was a wonderful surprise." They lay in each other's arms. He held her from behind, playing with her breast. "How is everyone back home?"

"Alright, except for Max. He and Penny have been getting close, and that worries me."

"Why? I know he likes her a lot?"

Mia took a deep breath. "Falu, I love Max, but I don't want Penny to get hurt. She's been through a lot. Max… he's a hound dog, just like you were."

Falu chuckled, "Well, it's too late. They like each other. Max knows she's a nice girl," he kissed her shoulder.

"Can you talk to him? If I say something, he's going to think I'm being paranoid."

"Alright, I promise," he pulled her towards him. "Now, let's get busy. We have a time limit," they laughed.

Mia was satisfied seeing him for that brief time. She was satisfied and was her old self again. She continued to do what she loved. During one of her workouts, she became lightheaded. Gary was concerned and ordered her to go see

Dr. Peggy. She dragged herself to her office, tired as if she had no energy.

Dr. Peggy was glad to see her. "Mia, sweetie, what's going on? How are you feeling," she smiled. Mia was one of her favorite people.

"I'm feeling really tired and lightheaded. Maybe I'm lacking some vitamins."

"Alright, let's take some blood and see what's going on," they chitchatted for a while until the blood results came back. "Um, Mia, looks like your problems will be over in nine months," Mia was shocked, "You are pregnant."

Mia was speechless for a moment. "I'm… pregnant. She jumped up and down, hugging the Doctor.

"Congratulation, sweetie. Let's find out how far long you are?" Peggy had her lay back down, checking the ultrasound to see how big the baby was. Mia looked at the screen. "Looks like maybe ah, six weeks."

"Oh my God, which means I got pregnant in my apartment. No wonder I've been so moody and emotional. Oh, Peggy, I'm so happy. I'm going to be a mama and Falu is going to be a papa. Please don't tell anyone. I want him to be the first to know besides us. Sure, it's going to kill me, but I think I can wait." Mia ran to her room to look at her belly. She rubbed her flat stomach. "My baby, my baby," tears roll down her cheeks.

It was hard for her to wait for Falu to return. She stood by the window, anticipating his arrival. When the caravan of trucks came through the gates, she ran to the door like a schoolgirl waiting for her boyfriend. His crew clapped, watching them kiss. "You are feeling like a million bucks, baby," he said, squeezing her.

"You better make that two million and change your name to big papa."

"Big papa…," he had a confused look on his face.

"I'm pregnant," Falu looked down at her belly, going to one knee. He kissed her belly, laughing. He couldn't wait to shout it from the rooftop. He was going to be a father. He had Mia, now his wife, and a child on the way. That night he and Max got drunk to celebrate. Max was thrilled he was going to be an uncle.

Mia couldn't wait to go shopping for maternity clothes. She took Penny with her wanting to pick out some clothes for the baby. They chatted along and had lunch. Gary was also caught up in their silly chatter. He laughed along with them. Mia had a strange feeling she was being watched but struggled it off as baby paranoia.

Their wedding celebration was the event of the year. Solana took charge and made sure that her daughter was not going to overdo herself. Gerry insisted on making her a dress for the occasion. The festivities went on into the early morning. Falu carried her upstairs to their suite. When he opened the door, the girls had decorated the room with pink roses and apple juice on ice since Mia couldn't drink. It was a night to remember for the couple. They danced to a beautiful love song as Falu sang sweetly in her ear. There was no one else in the world but them.

He held her for a long time, kissing her belly as Mia played with his hair. "You are beautiful and you're mine, all of you and baby too." He tried to listen to the baby's heartbeat.

"It's too soon, Papi."

"It's never too early to kiss my son," he smiled.

Rufus' Saloon

Rufus was a place where most of the prostitutes hung out. It was located two miles outside the city limits. Carmen and Sonia waited at the table. The cheap candles hid the sleazy décor, dirty walls, and pictures hanging since before the Dark Days. It was a hot sticky night and the cheap whiskey made them sweat. Sonia moved uncomfortably, unsure of the two men they agreed to meet with. "What time did they say?" Sonia asked for the fifth time.

"They should be here any minute," Carmen said, pouring herself another drink.

"I'm not sure about this, Carmen. We hurt Falu so bad the last time and now they're married. I'm nervous. I don't like these guys."

"Look, Sonia, stop bitching, or haven't you noticed we're living in a shit hole. We need this money, now shut the hell up." Carmen was getting annoyed at her sister. Sonia wiped the sweat from her forehead with a napkin when she noticed the two men looking straight at them.

"Oh my God, Carmen, here they come."

"Just let me do all the talking, alright." Sonia was too scared to speak. Ivan and Edgar sat across from them.

"I heard you two lived in the Esmeralda Estate. We can pay for any information you two can give us. We just need to know the safest way to get in and out," Edgar asked.

"Well, how much are you willing to pay? We have expenses," Carmen asked, feeling them out to see how much money they could get from them. Her eyes were already glassy, but her greed came into play.

"Money is not a problem. We can pay. We just want Raven Moon back where she belongs," Ivan replied.

"You won't hurt her, will you?" Sonia added. Carmen cut her a dirty look.

"Raven Moon is our Goddess. Why would we hurt her?" Edgar said, taking offense. "She was stolen from us as a child. Now she has to take her place among her people. It will take a bit of convincing, but she will become accustomed to her new surroundings and position."

Sonia looked at her sister, pleading. "Well, as long as no harm comes to her and that's where she belongs… I guess I could help you get back what belongs to you," Carmen smiled.

"So, you can help us then. Can we count on you?" Ivan asked.

"Yes, I can show you how to get in and out without being detected. Did you bring something to bargain with?" Carmen asked, not trusting them.

"We have. Now, what do you have to give us in return," Edgar replied, smirking.

"There's a wooden gate overgrown by shrubs, down beyond the stables. My sister and I used to sneak in and out without being detected. There is a garden no one uses anymore. It leads to an old road. Mia rides close to that side of the gate every morning. She can be taken that way."

"What do we need to open the gate without making noise?" Ivan asked curiously if the gate needed to be taken apart.

"This," she pushed the key in the middle of the table. "I lifted the key from Tony one night when I wanted to meet a friend. What is this worth to you?" Edgar pulled out a small bag full of silver and copper coins.

Her eyes lit up, "Good, I will draw you a map. Now, do we have a deal, gentlemen?"

"Yes, but only if you show us the way. I don't want to get caught and have the big guy coming after us."

"Alright, we can do that," Carmen laughed.

Mia kissed Falu and waved at him as he left to meet his crew at one of the construction sites. She felt alive, the humidity was low and she wanted to take Lucky for some fresh air. She spoke to some of the young boys who kept the stables clean and fed the horses. She was thrilled. Motherhood gave her a wonderful glow. Her mind was on her baby. She remembered her mother buying up materials for the baby's first blankets and clothes. They couldn't wait to be grandparents. She took Lucky on a second turn around the court when she felt a sharp pain on the side of her neck. She pulled it out, watching it fall from her hand as she too fell backward into a sea of blackness.

It was afternoon when Jason looked at the clock. He was worried. Mia had been out for six hours. She never rode Lucky this long and in the heat of the afternoon. "Kenny, have you seen Mrs. Mia? It's not like her to stay out this long. I'm going to check on her."

"I'll go with you. I hope she's alright," Kenny said, running behind Jason. Lucky was wandering around alone, and Mia was nowhere in sight.

Kenny started to panic. "Oh my God, Jason, where is she?" Jason ran his fingers through his hair, frustrated.

"We have to alert security," Jason cried. The whole estate was in an uproar. Tony met Falu, Max and Ricky at the door. Falu took a deep breath and took control of the situation.

"I found this on the courtyard," Tony said, handing Falu the dart.

"Oh God," Falu started to breathe erratically, and Dr. Manny was concerned.

"Falu listen to me… look at me. You're no good to her if you can't keep it together." Falu ran outside to catch his breath. He raced back to where Mia went missing. Raymond, the head security foreman, was already gathering information.

"What can you tell me, Raymond?" Max asked as he followed him around. He looked up to see Falu standing over him.

"Boss, I found footsteps. By the size of the shoes, I'm positive it was two males and maybe a female."

"Tony, please contact her parents. I think I know who took her," Falu said, taking control after the initial shock.

Chapter 17: The Return of the Goddess

Mia was in and out of consciousness. She was wrapped in a blanket pinning her arms to her sides. She was loopy and disoriented. They could hear her call out to Falu above a whisper. Her mind was in a fog, wondering what was happening to her, lapsing back into darkness. Ivan was concerned he may be giving her too much medication. "Edgar, are you sure this is necessary she doesn't look good?" he felt her forehead.

"We have to keep her sedated, or else she'll be trouble. You want her to wake up and start to fight us. You remember what she did to us before."

"Yeah, but are we giving her the right dose? I don't want to kill her before we get her home."

"Just keep an eye on her. We'll be home in ten hours if we don't run into trouble."

Ivan stared at the helpless Mia. Now that he had a chance to see her closeup, he understood why Falu was in love with her. His heart swelled with feelings for the exotic beauty. He touched her hair and kissed her when Edgar was busy driving. "What are you doing?" Edgar scolded him.

Ivan was startled. "What do you mean?"

"Mia is to be my bride and you're kissing her, Butthead!" Edgar cried angrily at his brother. "You're disrespecting me."

"Why does she have to be your bride? She should be able to choose!" Ivan argued.

"Because it is going to take months before she agrees to stay with us. I am the eldest and she will be my wife. I will marry her, bed her and she will be obligated to stay with me."

"I will challenge your claim to her, and you already have two wives."

"Look, Ivan, she is mine. I claimed her years ago when we first saw her. If you don't like it, take it up with Pop. Plus, you don't have the balls to fight for her if that meathead comes looking for her."

Ivan stared at Mia. Every now and then, her eyes would open and close, trying to focus on what was happening, calling out Falu's name. "Even in her dreams, she speaks his name. Do you think he'll come for her?"

"That is why we shall keep her hidden. She will be kept in isolation until she agrees to become part of us. Right now, they are scrambling, wondering where she has gone. It will take a few weeks to figure out where she is. By that time, it will be too late. She will be pregnant with my seed."

"Yeah, I can see your crazy wife going along with that. How many times has she been in a serious fight with Anita? Huh, how are you going to keep Anita silent when she's the biggest gossip in the community?"

"Let me handle Anita. She's not as crazy as people make her out to be. She's just very jealous. Everything is planned. Once we have a meeting with Pop, she will be moved to a secluded place. Even if he comes looking, he won't find her. We covered our tracks, so what do we have to worry about."

"She's so beautiful," Ivan couldn't resist touching her hair. He bent down, kissing her lips. Edgar pulled over abruptly, opening the door on Ivan's side of the car.

"Get out!" He wrestled Ivan pulling him out of the vehicle onto the ground. Ivan fought back and the brothers fought over the lovely Mia for the next few minutes. Edgar overpowered Ivan punching him in the mouth. He went crashing into the ground. Ivan wiped his mouth with his hand tasting blood.

"You will pay for this," Ivan cried with disgust.

"You are going to pay for your stupidity. You're taking advantage of an unconscious woman. But if you want to fight for her, I'm ready. I've waited years to get my hands on her, fighting her family, so if I want to fight my brother, I accept the challenge. In the meantime, keep your damn lips to yourself. You drive, I don't trust you."

The brothers drove in silence the rest of the way. Each taking turns to get home as soon as possible. Edgar watched over Mia, who was beginning to feel clammy to the touch. He cut the sedative in half, afraid they were hurting her.

It was getting dark. The streets would be deserted when they arrived at the big house. They saw the porch light come on. Jario opened the door for his sons. "Quickly take her upstairs. The room is prepared." Jario watched with glee as they laid Mia on the bed. Aurora Jario's second wife was shocked when she saw Mia. She had heard about her but never thought she would ever meet her.

"Get her undressed and into something comfortable." Ivan proceeded to help Aurora. "Are you insane?" Jario yelled at Ivan, pulling him away from her. "Give her some respect. She will be our goddess. The ladies will help her," he turned to Aurora. "Get Lisa to help you with her. Make sure she's secured for the night."

Jario met with his sons in the main living room. He was not expecting them to be successful. When he saw their vehicle drive up and flash their lights, he hobbled to the door. Jario looked from Ivan to Edgar with pride. "I'm proud of you both. I have to be honest with you. I didn't think you two could pull it off. Now, did you take all the precautions we spoke about?"

"Yes, father. It will take weeks before they figure out what happened to her," Edgar replied, smiling with confidence.

"Good, this will be the first place they will look, so as soon as we get her under some control, she will be moved to her new home. I have already contacted someone who will brainwash her into staying and taking her role as a goddess."

"How are you going to convince the elders and committee members to go along with our plan? Surely they will ask questions," Edgar asked.

"They will not know until she is ready to be presented to them. We will move her in the middle of the night."

"I want to challenge my bother for her hand. It is the law," Ivan blurted.

Jario was surprised. "You want to challenge your brother. Well, that's pretty bold. It is already settled that your brother will be Raven Moon's husband. But if you have the balls to fight him for her, I will not stand in the way." He noticed the swollen lip. "It seems as if you already got in a fight."

"Yeah, he caught me off guard. That won't happen again," Ivan said, cutting his eyes at his brother.

"Raven Moon is a worthy prize, and so was her mother. It was my fault I lost her. I let her rejection of me get in the way and instead of wooing her. I took her brutally and that was a mistake. Raven Moon should have been my daughter… he stole her from me. Now Mia is ours, and she will give us beautiful children and restore who we are. One of you will bring great power to our community and our people. Throughout the years, we have lost respect among our people. Now, it's time to show them that we are the Warlords. We have power. Let us show these people who we are!"

It only took a few hours for Naphtali to reach the Esmeralda Estate, where Falu waited patiently for his in-laws to arrive. He had scouts in the city and found the confirmation he was waiting for. Max was surprised his brother took on a calmer approach to this crisis. Within a few hours, everyone was ready to go. Solana and Pony Boy refused to stay behind. It was clear to him that his sister would be returned back to her family. Solana was never prouder of her son.

Naphtali plotted a course to the place he called home as a boy, where he grew up and met his wife. Where they still had family who missed them and wished they were back. But the dark cloud made it impossible to be with the family they loved. Solana's parents are still strong and healthy and live in the community, making a difference in many organizational developments.

Solana's father was an advocate of bringing charges against Warlord Jario and his family. Some of the committee members' elders were tired of the brutal tactics that Jario and his sons afflict on those who don't see eye to eye with them.

Some of the riders were showing signs of fatigue and needed to rest for the long ride in the morning. They rode their horses, taking shortcuts they couldn't take with their automobiles. They stopped at a hotel in Georgia. The place was clean, and they had a helpful staff that helped them settle for the night. The owner's sons took the horses to be fed and boarded for the night. The stress was evident on everyone's faces. Solana worried about Falu's mental state. He seemed to calm, and it scared her. "Falu, hey, what are you not telling me? Your control demeanor speaks louder than words," she wanted to tell him she will be all right.

He smiled at her. Mia favored her mother in so many ways. "I'm afraid I won't be able to control myself. They took my wife from my own backyard. I know someone helped them. They are not that smart. That is what's troubling me. I failed her, just like I failed to protect my mother."

"Falu, this is not your fault. This is an old grudge that should have been settled a long time ago. It is partly my fault. I was afraid… afraid of losing my husband. You see, he still had these vengeful feelings inside of him from what happened to me. When Mia learned what they did to me, she vowed she would make them pay. I knew she would go through with it and I begged her not to go anywhere near that family. That is why we moved around so much. She is so much like her father. They are angry with us because they felt we kept Mia away from them. This family lives in their own power-hungry reality. My parents were the ones who told us to get her away from them as far as possible. Once they discovered her, it was like nothing else mattered to them. The Warlord Jario is obsessed with her, claiming she should have been his child, which is crazy. I never wanted anything to do with him. He was a cruel man and I loved Naphtali. So now he wants her to mate with one of his oddballs sons."

"Mom," he called her. "I'm going to kill them. I just want to put that out there. I killed the man who murdered my mother with my bare hands. I feel the same rage I'm feeling now."

"Oh son, please don't say that. Killing them will not serve anything. They would go down as warriors, fighting for the woman they should have had. Now humiliation, that's the weapon of choice. Beating them in front of everyone would be their hell for the rest of their lives. I don't think Mia would like for you to have blood on your hands over her. It's a terrible thing to live with. Think Falu, and I know you will do the right thing. This matter will be settled tomorrow when we get her back," She put her hand on his arm.

Falu looked down. Deep in his heart, she was right, but the pain was still there, and the anger will not subside. It was a long night for Falu, tired and frustrated, not able to sleep, wondering about his Mia and how scared she must be. By morning his attitude changed. He thought about what his mother-in-law shared with him. After a good breakfast, the crew was ready to move on. They still had a long way to go.

Mia woke up in a panic; the room was dark, and the blanket they wrapped her in restricted her movement. She tried to remember what happened, but all she could remember was the pinch on her neck. The door creaked open. Mia turned her head to see who was standing at the door looking at her. She didn't recognize the silhouette in the dark. "Who's there? Somebody, help me." She cried. Lisa knelt by the bed and motioned to be silent. "I need to use the bathroom. Please let me out of this."

"Everyone is still asleep, keep it down, or they will come," said the young girl. "Here, let me help you to the bathroom." Mia's legs were like rubber. She had a hard time standing on her own. She looked around the small room, trying to piece out what was happening or where she was? She panicked when she noticed that the windows had bars.

"Where am I, and why can't I move my legs?" She tried desperately to get answers from the girl.

"My name is Lisa. You are home, don't worry, nothing will happen to you. You are safe. We will take care of you."

"This is not my home. Who are you, people? Where's my husband?" She said, breathing erratic. She could feel her head spinning, white spots before her eyes. She hung on to

Lisa, who was a little thing, to help her back to the bed. "Help me, Lisa. I can hardly move. What have you done to me?" Mia said, shutting her eyes and trying to think. But her thoughts were muddled, and she couldn't focus. Her legs and arms did not work trying to pull herself up and she would flop back down. Tears stung her eyes as she lay helplessly waiting for someone to give her some answers. Lisa tried her best to help Mia get comfortable, using all her strength to pull her onto the bed. Lisa was afraid for the pretty woman they called Raven Moon. She looked towards the closed door. Soon the whole house would be awake, and they would send her away to do her work.

"Mia, you are in… the community of Manati, in the house of Warlord Jario Perez-Augustine. They bought you here to be their Goddess. I don't know much more."

The drugs they used to keep her still were racing through her body. She cried, not knowing her anguished about her situation, but she felt so weak, hardly able to move.

She tried to get Lisa to understand her dilemma, "Lisa, you have to help me get out of here. I have family, grandparents Senior Juan Vega-Rivera, tell him I'm here please," she begged. Her voice was no more than a whisper. Lisa looked at the door nervously.

"I'm a prisoner in this house just like you, but I will try. I can't promise you anything." Mia cried harder, she thought of her family, Falu and the baby she was carrying. Lisa tried to calm her down. "Please try to understand." The door busted open as Sabrina stood by the door glaring at Lisa.

"Puta sucia, what are you doing here?" She grabbed Lisa by the hair and pushed her towards the door. Lisa hit her head on the doorframe.

"I was helping her to the bathroom. What are you doing here? You're not supposed to be anywhere near her."

"Don't tell me what to do bitch! I just want to welcome my new sister into the fold. So shut up!" Lisa scrambled to her feet and disappeared into the dark hallway. Sabrina smiled at the helpless Mia. She tried to close her eyes, pretending she was asleep.

"I know you're awake, so don't pretend," Sabrina laid next to her, contemplating her next move. "So, you're this royal bitch everyone is talking about. What makes you so special, your eyes?" She put her finger close to Mia's eyes in a menacing fashion. "Maybe it's your black hair or that sweet skin color which anyone here can get if they stay in the sun longer. Hum, I really don't see what the big deal is about you. You have breast, I have breast, we have the same thing between our legs," Mia turned to look at her. "Your eyes are starting to freak me out. I just want you to know something. Ivan is my husband, and I won't have you screwing him." She added, threatening her.

Mia rolled her eyes. "Look, sister. I don't want your man. I have my own husband help me get out of here, and I swear you won't see me ever again."

Sabrina rolled off the bed and walked towards the window that faced the side of the house. She moved the curtains watching the men take off in their vehicle. "I wish it was that easy, sister," she said with bitterness in her voice. "You will be forced to marry one of them and that's the way it is." Sabrina walked back to Mia and straddled her on the bed. She bent down, almost touching her face. "Stay away from my husband. I know he has the hots for you, but if you want to live, turn him down."

Mia could feel her anger rising. "Get your nasty ass off of me. Your breath stinks and you smell like rotten fish. I don't want your husband. If he comes near me, I will kick him in the balls." Sabrina balled up her fist to strike Mia when Aurora appeared at the door carrying food.

"Sabrina, don't you dare! You're not allowed here now. Get out!" Aurora stood her ground.

"Don't worry bitch. We'll be seeing each other again very soon. Just remember what I said." Aurora waited for Sabrina to leave and sat the tray on the small table next to Mia's bed. She helped Mia sit up.

"I'm sorry about her. We call her la loca, because she has major anger issues. I bought you some food so you can regain your strength," Aurora was a sweet woman. She was the third wife of Jario and was not treated very well by his second wife, who left two years ago. Aurora was afraid of everyone.

"What am I doing here? And what the hell was I given that I can't even stand up on my own?"

Aurora lowered her eyes. "The medication they gave you was too strong. You had a bad reaction."

Mia rolled her head back, "Oh my God, you people are destroying my life. I'm pregnant! And you guys shot me up with drugs. Is everyone crazy around here?" Mia yelled, dropping back into the pillows. "I swear to God if anyone of you hurt my baby, I will hunt you down and kill every one of you!" Aurora didn't know what to do. The blood drained from her face with fear. She heard different stories about Mia and what a furious fighter she was.

"I don't think it would hurt the baby. It was… it was just a mild sedative. They just gave you too much. The effects should go away in few hours. Raven Moon, I didn't know. Please believe me. I'm just following orders," she said, frightened. "Eat something. It will wear off the effect sooner."

Mia could only stare at Aurora as she hand fed her oatmeal, eggs and toast. It tasted like cardboard in her mouth. But she needed to regain her strength in order to get away. "I want to talk to Jario. I want to go home."

Aurora's hands shook as she wiped her mouth and set the tray on her lap. "I'm so sorry. I do what I can."

"I'm sorry that you're caught in this shit. Do me a favor and… tell that bitch to stay away from me. She'll be eating meals through a straw next time." Whatever Mia drank made her drowsy again and she fell back asleep. When she woke up, Jario was standing at the foot of her bed, watching her sleep. They chained her to the bed by her ankle.

"Good morning, Raven Moon. How are you?" He said excitedly.

Mia tried to focus, but her thoughts were still foggy, "How do you think I feel? I was kidnapped, drugged and now I'm chained to this bed by a bunch of nuts!" She yelled.

He laughed, "Look, I know it's not the ideal situation, but we went through a lot to bring you home. To where you belong…"

She interrupted him, "I belong with my husband… I have a home, who gives you no right to force me to do what I don't want!" She shouted loud to see if someone from the outside would hear her screaming.

"Hey, I know you are upset, just calm down and listen to me. I know you think I'm this monster, and what I did to your mother was inexcusable. I was young and didn't take rejections well. But I loved her, when I kissed her, and she slapped me in the face, I just saw red. Let's put the past behind us. Now the reason you are here is because this is where you belong with your people. Had your mother and I married, you would have been my daughter. As Warlord, I do not acknowledge your marriage to an outsider. One of my sons will fight for your hand in marriage and whoever wins will be your husband."

Mia was shocked, "Are we living in the dark ages or what? Jario, I'm married to a tribal man and in love with my husband. He will come for me. We're having a baby, and I'm pregnant."

It was Jario's turn to be shocked. He had not expected pregnancy to put a damper on his plan. She could tell he was getting angry. Jario could never hide his anger. "You'll come to understand that what we are doing is fixing the way things should have been. You are a Goddess to be worshiped, the one to restore our people."

"You are nuts. My husband and family will come for me!"

He smiled, "By the time they figure things out, you will be on our side and married to one of my sons."

"You'll never get away with what you're doing. I'm begging you, let me return to my family. Release me," she tried to get through to him.

Jario just looked at Mia and left the room, dragging his leg. He had gout, so he walked with a cane when he had a flare up. He called for Aurora. She stood outside the door before entering. Lately, all he does is complain and yells about everything.

"Jario, you called for me?"

"Yes," he answered in a foul mood. "Have a seat, I just heard some disturbing news about Mia, she's pregnant and that's not good. I want you to go down to the Botanica, tell Jamie what we need to get rid of this baby. He'll know what to do, ah, make it fast," his discomfort showed on his face.

Aurora started to shake, "Jario, this is against the law. You can't do this without her knowledge. She will figure it out. Please don't do this," she begged.

"She can't have someone else's child. I don't have the time or patience to argue with you. The only seed I want in her belly is our bloodline! Now go and do what I said! She will abort tonight. Tomorrow morning, I will deal with her. She will learn soon enough that I rule."

Jario sat down in his office, wishing his leg would stop hurting. He sat in silence for a long time until his first wife Freda pushed open his door. Jario was startled. "This is why you wanted to send me away? Why is Mia in this house and caged like an animal? Jario, have you lost your mind?" She yelled.

Jario sat back on his chair and rolled his eyes. The pain in his leg was pulsing. "You knew the plan from years ago when we discovered her. Now our family will be complete. Are you on board?"

"No, I'm not and I'll never be. You want to force that beautiful woman to marry one of your loser sons," she shook her head. "I'm glad my children are not here to see just how far their mighty father has sunk. Send that poor girl home, Jario. Do the right thing for once."

"Don't tell me what to do, woman! I'm still the man of this house and the Warlord of this community, so don't forget who you are talking to," he yelled as veins in his neck pulsing.

Freida was the only one who was brave enough to confront him since her children were not in the picture. "Jario, what do you want with this young girl…? Are you lusting after her?"

Jario turned away from her. "Don't be ridiculous! She's beautiful and will make a good match for one of the boys. However, if I was a few years younger and didn't suffer from this damn gout, who knows, a woman like her… needs a strong hand."

"You're such a fool! You couldn't have her mother, so now you want her daughter, Jario. What has happened to you?" She said, trying to reason with him

"Watch who you're talking to. I can still put you in your place!"

"I thought I was talking to a man of honor. Oh, I forgot that was never on your resume. Everything you ever did was done by force. You beat me until my son was old enough to threaten you. Solana Vega was bold enough to say no to you, so you beat and raped her. Bravo, for her and her husband who took her away from here and from you. Now you want her daughter since you can't have her for yourself. However, let's face it. You're not the man you used to be. All those years of drinking and whoring have caught up to you. So now you want your deadbeat sons to mingle with her blood. How far will your obsession go? I won't have any of it. I'm leaving for good."

Jario snatched her by the arm and squeezed it. "You're not going anywhere. You're my wife and you do what I say. There's no one here to defend you from getting a beat down."

She pulled away, "There is someone. Your days of beating me are over. I took it a long time because of my children. But my children are out of your grasp and doing well. I'll stay until I see Mia back safely with her family," she left him standing in the hallway.

"Stupid bitch," he said as she walked away. Her words hit him like a bullet, sitting back down and putting his leg on a chair to ease the pain. He had never seen Mia up close, just in blurry pictures. But now that he had a chance to see her face to face, he felt a stirring in his loins for the young beauty. He realized why his sons wanted to fight for her hand in marriage. Memories of another beauty flooded his memory. "Solana," he whispered. Jario was already married at the age of seventeen to Freida, but Solana wasn't his choice from his father how he hated the cruel bastard. When he died, Jario took all his pictures, clothes and anything that would have reminded him of his father and burned it. He was hard on the young Jario. The beatings he endured were brutal. His father, Jario Senior, wanted his son to be hard and he succeeded.

When Jario was older, they would get into fist fights. He and Freida had been married two years when Solana caught his eyes. She was beautifully fresh and exciting. He wanted her, but she always turned him down and her father was always around, making sure the young men stayed away from his baby girl.

Jario was obsessed with her thick reddish blonde hair, green eyes and full lips of Solana. He loved her personality and how sweet she was with her students. She would hug them and would tell them how special they were. Something he longed for from his own mother, who was just a shell of a woman. He would wait for her to dismiss her students and follow her home. It would infuriate him when she refused him. Jario tried to control his temper in front of her, not wanting her to be frightened of him.

He was crushed when the news that she was dating Naphtali came to his attention. His father called him a gutless puss, not going after the woman he wanted. Gathering his confidence, Jario went to talk to her father with a proposal in mind. The minute her father answered the door, he was met by an antagonizing stare. "Jario, what brings you to my door?" Don Manolo asked, very guarded.

"May I speak to you? It's an important manner if you please." Jario said nervously. Don Manolo phase at the door before he allowed him to enter. Dona Isabel sat next to her husband on the sofa. "I'm here to ask for Solana's hand in marriage."

Don Manolo gave him a peculiar look, "Are you kidding me? Is this some joke? Solana is spoken for. They already have wedding plans and you're already married."

"I know, but as you see, my wife has not been able to give me children. Our law states that we can have more than one wife if the first wife agrees. I love Solana. I have for a long time. I understand she is engaged but think about who can give her a better life. My father is the Warlord, and it will be passed to me. I can protect her and give her whatever she needs. Our family has great connections." Jario was not prepared for the brutal response.

Dona Isabel sprung from her husband's side, "I think you better leave Jario." He looked at her, confused.

"Was not my proposal clear? What else can I offer you? My feelings for her are sincere."

"Jario, I suggest you set your eyes on someone else. I rather she is an old maid than mixed with that devil's blood of yours," she said, determined.

"I think my wife was clear. You would be the last man on earth I would have my daughter attached to. My daughter is happy. She will marry Naphtali. He has proven himself worthy of her and she loves him."

"Don Manolo, I will have Solana one way or another," he got up to leave.

"Jario don't darken our door again and stay away from my daughter," Dona Isabel said in a demanding voice. She knew his family was trouble if someone showed fear. Jario remembered the humiliation he endured taking his frustration out on the rest of the family. But he wasn't finished when he tried to speak to her, and she refused to bother him. Jario grabbed her, wanting to force her to come with him breaking into the house. But she fought back when he tried to drag her way. In his anger, he beat and raped her. When he was finished, he was afraid of what he had done to her. Wanting to comfort her and tell her he loved her. A neighbor saw him running away. Jario was shunned for a year after his fight with Naphtali. His father beat him, breaking his arm as a lesson for losing to Naphtali.

When his father died, Jario did what he always promised he'd do. Piss on his father's grave, refusing to even put a grave marker to honor his memory. Jario hated to think about his past. He couldn't help but be who he was, living with a madman. His anger was always on the surface, waiting to explode at any unfortunate event.

Mia was part of that past he wanted to correct, remembering her mother and the humiliation she imposed on him. The rejection he felt forced him to go after her. The harsh words from her family about the mixing of blood rang in his mind for years as if his father tainted his blood. Now her blood will mix with theirs, the child that should have been his. The goodness will pass from her to his seed, pushing out the vile stench of his father.

His grandchildren will be great. They will be looked upon with greatness and not carry the stigma of their parents, an abusive father and a condescending mother. Jario wanted to erase the ugliness that overshadowed his life. Mia was his answer. His status and importance in the community will be elevated.

Freida was angry. She had only returned to gather her things and retrieve the money she had been stashing away for years. Mia created a problem for her. She knew his sons were just as violent as their father and would force Mia if they could. And then there was la loca, Sabrina had mental and anger issues and would try to go after Mia. Freida would stay and take over the care of Mia and figure a way to set her free.

Mia woke up startled, sweating in a panic. She tried to get out of bed, looking for her clothes. Her legs felt like lead. She used her hands to move them. Her ankle was swelling up where the chain was making it difficult to move. She tried to find something to open the lock, but there was nothing she could use to attempt to jimmy it open. Tears ran down her cheeks, wishing she was home safely in Falu's arms. She wondered if they knew where she was and what had happened to her.

Mia jumped when the door suddenly opened, thinking it was that crazy woman who had attacked her earlier. Fried was upset. She bought another tray of food for her. Mia watched this other woman suspiciously. "Mia, my name is Freida. I'm the first wife." She set the tray next to her bed. "Listen to me closely, my dear. Don't drink anything they give you. I have a jug of water for you. I bought you some food you must try to eat. Tonight, I will try to get the key to get the chain off your ankle."

"Why should I trust you?"

Freida smiled, understanding her reasoning. "I know what they plan on doing with you. When I found out you were here, I had to stay. You see, I would have been on my way far from here. But... I couldn't get the good conscious leaving you here. Tomorrow night they plan on moving you to a compound away from everyone secured in the woods. I have a pair of pants, a shirt and a pair of shoes. I'm going to leave them in the top drawer. I will remove the lock from the bathroom window before I leave, it is small, but you can fit through the window. I will put a trash can in front of the window so you can step down. Make your way to your grandfather's house, which is over five blocks from here. I'm being watched, so I have to be careful."

"Why are you helping me? What are you getting out of my escape?"

"I knew your mother, and to be honest, I always envied her. She had Jario's heart, as black as it was, he really loved her. I will try my best to get you out of this hell hole. Remember, do not drink anything they bring you. It is laced with a sedative to keep you doped up and easy. Here is a bucket in case you need to dump the drink. They will be looking to make sure you're drinking it. Here is water. If you get thirsty, I'll hide it behind the table."

"Thank you, Freida. I just want to go home with my husband and family."

"Then you're married? Why is he trying to marry you off to one of these losers?"

Mia was confused, "They are not your sons? Who are they?"

"Hell no, their mother was the second wife who ran off with someone and left them behind. My children are good, thank God. I sent them away to school. One more thing, beware of the crazy one. She will try to hurt you. She's very disturbed and afraid everyone wants to take away her meal ticket. Hit her hard if she comes near you."

Mia smiled for the first time since she woke up, knowing she had an ally in the house of horrors. It was only mid-morning. She ate all the food and drank some of the water Freida bought her. She was starting to think clearer now, and the feeling in her hands and legs were beginning to return. She lay quietly staring at the ceiling wishing time would pass so she could get out and track her family down. There was a slight knock on the door. Ivan poked his head into the room, but she pretended to be asleep. She could hear him coming close to her. Sitting on the edge of the bed. He pushed her hair away from her face. "Raven Moon, I love you," he said. She tried not to react when he touched her breast. Ivan laid on top of her trying to kiss her. "Raven Moon, you will be my wife," he felt his hair being pulled back.

"Get your filthy hands off of me, you son-of-a-bitch!"
She pushed him off her. "I will take your balls and twist them
in knots if you come near me again!" When he stood up, she
could see how aroused he was. He stared at her, surprised.
Sabrina appeared at the door, enraged when she saw his
reaction.

"What are you doing in here," she glared at Mia, who
was more alert than earlier that morning.

"Give your man some ass woman so he could leave me
alone," Mia yelled.

Sabrina bounced on him, kicking and scratching him. He
grabbed her by the neck and knocked her down. "I'll kill you
bitch, now get out of here!" he yelled at Sabrina, "Don't
come back here again." He turned his attention back to Mia.
"You will be my woman, like it or not." He dragged Sabrina
out of the room by her arms.

"In your dreams, asshole. I'll kill you first before I let
you touch me!" Mia could hear them screaming at each other
all the way to their room on the third floor.

What a nightmare, she thought to herself.

She was asleep when she felt a pinch in her arm. When
she looked up, Aurora had given her an injection. Mia
panicked, wanting to be alert when she fled tonight. "What
the hell are you doing to me?" Mia cried, grabbing her by the

hand. Aurora didn't expect her to be alert. She had to think fast.

"It's just a B12 shot to give you strength," her eyes wide with fear.

"Please leave me alone! I don't want you around me anymore," she said sternly. Aurora didn't realize she was so strong. The drug in her juice was wearing off.

"Would you like something to drink? Or something to eat maybe," she said timidly.

Mia shouted at her. "Listen to me, just leave me the hell alone."

Aurora backed out of the room, turning on a small night light. "I'm sorry, Raven Moon, try to eat something and rest." She closed the door on the way out. Mia didn't touch the food, afraid it may be tainted. She cried silently, waiting for the sun to set so she could escape this house of torture. All day she heard someone screaming or crying. Another hour went by, and she started to feel lightheaded. Her mouth was dry. She reached for the water Freida had bought. Then her heart sank when the door opened, and Sabrina appeared at the door, her right eye was turning colors and her neck had marks from where Ivan grabbed her. She walked towards Mia slowly and sat at the edge of the bed. Mia watched her closely. She turned her head in a peculiar way. "Ivan said he loves you," tears rolled down her cheeks. "He said that if he wins your hand that I would be out the door. I can't let that happen. Sabrina reached behind her, feeling for a hammer, "He said you were… how did he put it, exquisite," she knelt beside Mia, who was very still. "How much would he love you with your face bashed in!" She raised the hammer to strike Mia, but Sabrina didn't know that the effect of the drug was wearing off. They wrestled for control of the weapon. Mia punched her really hard in the stomach knocking the air out of her, punching her on the side of her face causing Sabrina to fall off the bed.

"You are one crazy bitch. Now get out before I kill you!" Mia shouted, but Sabrina charged her like a wild woman. Mia grabbed a small lamp and bashed her over the head. The lamp exploded into pieces. Mia took the cord from the lamp and began to choke Sabrina, trying to scare her. Sabrina didn't think Mia was that strong. Sabrina was turning red when Mia let her go and kicked her off the bed. She could hear Sabrina crying on the floor by the door. When the door opened, Freida was shocked to see Sabrina crying on the floor, holding her head when she turned on the light.

"Mujercita loca, oh my God, what are you doing here?" Freida said, trying to stand her up.

"She wants my man. I'll kill her first," she cried.

Freida shook her, "Girl, nobody wants your deadbeat husband. Now go to bed before he wakes up and beats you senseless. Go now clean yourself up and get upstairs before he discovers you gone."

"You won't tell him I was down here, will you?" she asked, sounding like a wounded child.

Freda treated her more like a child, "No, this is between you and me, dear. Go to bed and pretend this never happened. Go on now." Sabrina turned to Mia before she left and stuck her tongue out, shutting the door behind her.

"Did she hurt you?"

"No, but I think I twisted the wrong way. My stomach is hurting."

Freida didn't like the way she looked. When she felt her forehead, it was clammy to the touch. "You don't look good, honey. Is there anything I could do for you?"

"I'll… be fine. I just want to get out of here. Aurora gave me a B12 shot and now my stomach is starting to feel funny."

Freida worked, trying to open the ankle chain without hurting Mia, "I made them a special dinner. I put sleeping pills in the soup somehow, it didn't work on Sabrina. I guess we need a bat to knock that one out." Freida rubbed her ankle, trying to get the blood flowing. Mia sat on the side of the bed, lightheaded and still weak. "Mia, the bathroom window is unlocked and opened. The lower roof will allow you to jump down without injuring yourself. When you get to the end of the garden, make a right, go three blocks you'll see a playground on your left. At the end of the gate, make another right. Go five blocks on Nation Street you'll see your grandparent's house. Can I help you dress?"

"No, you've done enough, and I don't want them to get suspicious. Thank you, I can handle it from here. Just keep the crazy girl away from me. I won't be easy on her next time."

"Don't worry. She won't bother you anymore tonight. You hit her pretty hard," she gave her a strong hug. "I'm sorry this happened to you. I will be gone by tomorrow morning. I rented a home for my children and me. I have stashed away enough money for ten years to support us."

"Thank you again, Freida. God must have been on your side, surviving this madhouse."

"I'm going to lock the door from the outside. It's still early out, so be careful."

Mia's head was spinning and the pain in her stomach was getting worst. The second she put her feet flat on the floor, she felt blood running down her legs. She stumbled towards the dresser holding on to furniture, leaving a trail of blood all the way to the bathroom. She sat on the toilet, clamping down on a towel as waves of pain eased her body. She sobbed into the towel, knowing she was losing her baby. A half an hour later, the pain began to ease, and she managed to clean herself up. She thew-up in the bathtub feeling her stomach in knots. In a cold sweat, she leaned against the wall trying to compose herself.

The window was small, but she managed to squeeze herself through the small opening. The roof was slanted, and she was able to reach the lower level using the trash cans as steps. The house was silent as she crept her way towards the garden, out of the gate, holding on to the fence to keep steady. Her legs shook as she tried to walk, and the pain in the abdomen came back in spasms. Slowly with all the strength she could muster, she made her way toward the park. The three blocks seem like miles. She kept on telling herself she had to get as far as she could from the house or hide so they wouldn't come after her.

The view of the park was just ahead. The dim light shined on the small park with its basketball court, swings, monkey bars and some benches. Mia dragged herself towards the bench to rest. She saw spots in her eyes, and her head was swimming and unfocused. Afraid of being caught, she lowered herself under the bench to rest until she gathered enough strength to go further. Mia felt her heartbeat racing closing her eyes to slow down her heartbeat like she was taught. Within a few minutes, everything went black.

Chapter 18: Revenge

Justin watched that no one was looking, sneaking a lighter into his pants pocket. It was his father's poker night. The drinks were plenty. They were bragging about who was the better player making fun of when they made mistakes. Justin enjoyed his father's Friday night poker game. His mother was relaxed, focusing on the game and not hovering over what the kids were doing. "Dude, I'm kicking your ass this next game," Victor said, shuffling the cards.

Kumar looked at his four stacks of chips and smiled, "Vic, you always say that, but it's nice that you have such high hopes," he chuckled.

"Put up and shut up, man. Say goodbye to your money, dude," Victor teased. Justin motioned to his brother Paul who stood by their uncle Kumar. Justin pointed to follow him outside.

"What's up?" Paul said, wondering what his brother had in mind.

"Let's throw some hoops."

"It's getting late, Mom's not going to let us go out."

"I'll ask her if it's just for a few minutes. I have something to show you." Justin knew this was the best time to ask her mother; they were drinking, and she was in a great mood.

"Mom, it's summer. Can we go to the park for a little while," he begged.

"Come on, Alissa. He is fourteen, almost a man. Let them have a little fun," Kumar said, winking at him.

"I try to tell her that she's got to cut the apron strings and stop smothering them, they are growing boys," Victor added.

"Alright, just for an hour, if your asses aren't back in an hour, I'm coming for you… Alright?" she gave them the famous 'don't make me come for you' mother look.

"Thanks Mom, we'll be back in an hour, I promise." Justin ran out the front door and down the stairs where Paul waited. The boys ran the five blocks to the park. It was dark and deserted, with only the floodlights illuminating the playground and benches. They walked towards the monkey bars. "Look what I got," Justin said, pulling out a small pipe.

"Where'd you get that at?" Paul asked, fascinated by the old pipe.

"It was from grandpa. I was helping him clean out the attic. It was in some old boxes he told me to throw away. He doesn't know that I took it."

"It's cool, but we don't have anything to put in it," Paul said, fascinated by the carving on it.

"Come on, let's go over to the bench. I took some of the Pop tobacco to see if it works. You want to try it?" He smiled, hoping his younger brother took the bait to try it first.

"Yeah, I know it smells bad, but they keep smoking it, so there must be something good about it," Paul said, curious about what it would taste. The boys walked towards the bench when Justin was scared by the movement under the bench. "Ay shit, it must be a raccoon or something," they jumped off the bench.

"No, Justin. It's too big, maybe it's a dog, it may be hurt," Paul cried. He was an animal lover. The boys inched toward the bench when they saw a hand.

"Oh, shit Paul, it's a person," Justin said, kneeling down. "It's a girl, Paul and she's still warm. We have to get help."

Paul was scared, "Who is she?" he said in a panic.

"Help me pull her out and bring her in the light." They carry her the best way they could from under the bench.

"Justin, I've never seen her before."

"She has a tag, M.i.a Raven Moon. Raven Moon! Paul, it's Raven Moon! Our cousin, get help. I'll stay here with her hurry, get Pop hurry!"

Paul stumbled a few times before he got some memento under his feet. Looking to see if there was anyone who could help him. Paul was out of breath when he interrupted the card game. "Pop, come quickly. It's Raven Moon, she's in trouble!"

"Raven Moon?" Kumar sprung from his chair. "Are you sure, Paul?"

"Yes, we know how to read tags. Come quickly, she's hurt." Everyone sprung from their seats, turning over the table and chairs and running towards the park where he left Justin. Justin cradled her head on his lap, hoping she would open her eyes.

"Mia, please wake up," he whispered, his voice shaking with fear that she may not make it. Mia's eyes fluttered, trying to focus, falling into unconsciousness.

Victor reached her fist, checking her pulse, "It's strong. We got to get her to the house."

Kumar picked her up, carrying her towards the house. He was emotional when he saw her, "What is she doing here? Where is her husband?" He cried, carrying her like a baby. When he laid her down, there was blood on his hands. "Justin, run and get Dr. Michael, tell him it's an emergency," Kumar tried to revive her, but she was not responding.

Victor was crying, pacing around the room, not knowing what to do, "I called your parents, Victor. They should be here. Kumar, is there anything we can do until the doctor gets her," Alissa said, taking charge. She examined her to see where the bleeding was coming from. "There are no wounds. She must be hemorrhaging. She needs to go to a hospital."

When the doctor examined her, he was concerned she was not responding to anything he did. Mia's lips were pale as she was rushed to the hospital. Cries of despair and anguish were heard through the hospital from the family. They watched helplessly as the nurses and other technicians ran in and out of the room. Alissa comforted her mother-in-law, who could not stop sobbing. She held her rubbing her shoulder, "Mama, she's going to be alright. You have to believe that."

"Where's my daughter? Something has happened to her as well? You know she wouldn't let Mia come all this way without her."

"I know this is a big mystery, but don't worry, we'll find it out soon enough. Why don't we say a little prayer for her?" The two women stood and held each other, praying for Mia and the rest of the family.

The men conferred away from the women, who were too hysterical and emotional, "Something is not right here. Falu would not let her out of sight. I have a bad feeling about this," Kumar said, frustrated, "He is very protective."

Victor was becoming just as hysterical as the women. "What if something happened to the family and this was the only place she can come to? What happened to my sister and her husband? God help me, I think I'm going crazy."

Julio one of the investigators and a close friend put his hand on Victor's shoulder. "Calm down Victor, we need to not jump to conclusions. Look I know this is hard for you, but I need your head on straight right now," Victor shook his head.

Señor Manolo tried to keep it together, "Julio, don't you think it's strange that my granddaughter just appeared from nowhere hurt. It's a long way from New Orleans to North Carolina. Where is the rest of the family?"

Dr. Michael interrupted them. "How is she?" everyone asked at the same time, bombarding him with questions.

"She's going to be alright," there was the sound of relief throughout the room.

"Did she say anything?" Victor said, hoping they could get information about the rest of the family.

"All she said was… they killed my baby. She was hysterical. We had to calm her down. Ah… and we did manage to stop the bleeding, but she may need a transfusion. We're waiting for the blood work to come back. We need to find out what she was given in order to determine how to precede."

"She lost her baby?" Señora Isabel asked, fighting the tears.

"I'm sorry Señora Isabel, but the baby is gone. We'll know more in a few hours," Dr. Michael hated giving the family the bad news.

"Can we sit with her?" Señor Manolo asked, wanting to be close to his granddaughter.

"Yes, but let her rest. She lost a lot of blood. If anyone wants to donate blood, it would be helpful."

Señor Manolo was quiet for a moment and Victor knew what was on his mind. "Papa, what are you thinking?"

"That son-of-a-bitch finally did it. Wasn't it bad enough that he violated your sister? Now he had to get his hands on my beloved granddaughter, who was kept away from her family because of his obsession. This stops here."

"Señor Manolo, please don't go half cock to his house. Let us handle this," Julio said, trying to keep things from getting out of hand. "If they are behind this, we need more details. Sit with Mia, she's going to need her family when she awakens.

Falu was desperate, a major storm kept them from moving forward and they had to take shelter in a small town. He tried several times to communicate with Kumar, but most of the lines were down. Falu became irater as the hours passed and was not able to move. Pony Boy sat next to him. The young boy idolized his brother-in-law.

Falu looked down at the young boy, "What's on your mind, buddy?"

"Falu, I know you're worried about my sister, but she's the smartest and the strongest woman I know. I have to believe that she is alright." Falu looked at the thirteen-year-old. He looked so much like her. They had the same nose and facial shape.

"So, you think your sister is invincible?"

"The first time I saw her fighting with men, I was scared. They were taller than her. Some dude was trying to break into our house. We were cleaning out some traps all morning. I was teasing her because I caught the biggest rabbit. We saw two men trying to break down the door. My mother was the only one in the house. I watched my sister pick up a stick and run towards these three men. She fought them like she was three people kicking and punching so fast I couldn't keep up. The men kept on fighting, but she didn't give up. Then my mother appeared at the door with a rifle and shot two of them in the leg. They ran away, and when father and Kumar returned, they went after them, but I don't know what happened. I guess what I'm trying to say is that she's good. She's a great fighter."

Falu patted him on the back, "I know, but even the best skillful fighter needs help sometimes."

He smiled up at Falu. "I want to be like you, Falu, when I grow up. You are strong, but you also have something that makes you special, just like my father... you care. You have a good heart."

"Well, thank you for the compliments, coming from a thirteen-year-old. I am honored. I love Mia and would gladly give my life for her."

"You two are one hell of a force. I got your back, don't worry," Pony Boy smiled.

"Falu!" he turned to see who was calling him. "The weather broke. We should be ready to go by daylight," Max said, knowing it was the best news they've had since they started to travel. Falu could see the strain on Solana's face. It's been three days since Mia was taken and she was worried about her even though she tried to present a strong demeanor. Deep inside, she was afraid for her daughter and her husband was not helping. The crew pushed hard as they reached the North Carolina border. Their plan was to go to her parents' house first and proceed from there.

It was early evening when the thirteen riders reached Palo Manati. There were few people in the streets as they made the right turn towards her family home. The porch light was on when they reached the house. Solana ran through the house, calling for her parents. The rest of the crew searched the property. Solana started to panic, "Where could they be? Something must have happened to my parents," she cried. They stared at the two black cars that stopped in front of the house. "Solana, Naphtali!" Julio waved at them. He hugged Solana.

"Mia's is alright. She's in the hospital. The whole family is with her," he turned to Falu. "You must be her husband. Julio, It's a pleasure to meet you," he shuck his hand, "I'm one of the investigators. Climb in. I will take you to the hospital."

"You go ahead, sweetheart," Naphtali said, "I want to get the men settled."

"Naphtali, your daughter needs you. I need you," she knew her husband what was he planning to do.

"She's right, Mia is my wife, and we'll do this together." Falu said, "First, I have to make sure my wife is well."

Naphtali smiled, "I promise. I just want to get the men to settle. I will be there in a few minutes."

The tears started to flow again when the family gathered together. They were relieved to see that the rest of the family was safe. Solana made all the introductions as the family welcomed Falu and Max into the family. Victor held on to his sister for a long time. They hadn't seen each other in years. "You look great, sister. Where's your husband?"

"He'll be along shortly. You know him. He has to get his head together."

Falu was not one to wait for anyone as he paced around the room, waiting to see Mia. The doctor finally made an appearance, "You must be the husband. She's been asking for you."

"How is she?" He asked nervously.

"Mia is going to be alright. She's a strong woman. We had to wait until we found out what kind of drugs she was given."

"Wait," Falu interrupted. "She's pregnant. How will that affect the baby?"

The doctor looked seldom, "Mia lost the baby." Falu's emotions exploded, "Please, I understand you're angry, she was given a dose of this old medicine called Coumadin mixed with something else which we couldn't identify and at first... it aborted the fetus. She's getting a blood transfusion. The thinner blood made her lose a lot of it. Physically she will recover completely, but emotionally, she will need her family's support."

"When can I see her?" Falu said, fighting back the tears of anger.

"The grandparents are in there with her right now, give us a few minutes to get her settled."

Solana sobbed in Falu's arms, "She wanted that baby so bad. All she talked about was her baby."

Falu tried to keep it together, but deep inside, he was screaming with pain and anger. "Don't worry, Mom. We'll have other babies for you, I promise."

Naphtali had to be held down by some of the men. His anguished cries were heard through the hospital floor. "I will kill him once and for all! I swear to God." It took them a few minutes to get him under control. Pony Boy was scared, afraid of his father's reaction. He had never seemed his father in such a rage.

"Papa, you're not helping," he said, widened eyes and anxious.

He pressed his son to his chest, "I'm sorry, son. I don't mean to scare you, but you children are my life," he whispered, holding his tender face between his hands.

"She is my sister. We need to do this the tribal way and restore honor to our family. I don't want to lose my father." Naphtali embraced his son, knowing he was afraid with so much anger and emotions flying around.

Falu took a deep breath before he entered Mia's room. Her grandparents gave him a quick embrace, and Señora Isabel kissed his cheek. "She's been asking for you," she whispered as they stepped out. Mia had her eyes closed when he approached the bed, the sounds of the machines ringing in his ears. Tears ran down his cheeks. She looked like a sleeping beauty waiting for her prince to wake her up. He sat at the edge of the bed. Her hand was cold to the touch, he bought it to his lips.

"Baby, come back to me. I can't live without you, Te amor," he whispered.

Her eyes fluttered a little before she opened her eyes. "Falu," she reached for him. He held her in his arms, unable to stop the tears. "I lost the baby, I tried to protect our baby, and I failed," she sobbed in his arms. "I'm sorry," he wiped the tears from her face.

"I know, baby. It isn't your fault. Someone gave you something," he rocked her in his arms. "I'm so glad you're alright. I love you so much."

"I didn't know if you knew where I was. I prayed you would find me," he laid her back down.

"You know I would search under every rock to find you. Your parents are here. Can you tell me what happened?" She blinked a few times, staring at him, knowing just what he'll do.

"I want to go home. I want to forget this place. I want my husband, a family, and your children. I don't want you going to prison island. Falu, I can't bear to be without you." He kissed her lips. He already knew what had happened.

"I promise you I will not go to Prison Island, but this will be solved before we leave. It will be resolved in a tribal way. I'm going to let your parents have a few minutes with you. Your father is not doing well," he kissed her again. "I'll be back. I know the investigator needs to talk to you, alright. I'm here and I'm not going anywhere… yet"

She smiled, "Alright, love you, Falu, please don't leave me." He blew her a kiss, not wanting to break down in front of her.

Max and Ricky comforted him. "It's time to think, smart brother. We'll bring these fools down, but we can't go crazy without getting the facts. I'm here for you, brother," Max said.

Señor Manolo sat across from Falu. He had never met someone like him in his life and admired his strength and determination. But he knew behind the wall of muscle and strength laid an angry man. "Falu, I have sent some of our committee members who have been working with me to have Jario and his band of degenerates removed from their responsibilities as Warlord of this community. He's a tyrant, and we're tired of his incompetent leadership."

"Why hasn't he been removed? He should be voted out."

"He has family members that refuse to vote against him and a few others who he has bullied to vote his way. They feel we didn't have enough proof to have him and his family removed. But now it's a different story. Unfortunately, my precious granddaughter is paying for his obsessions. He has always been fascinated by her and now he has crossed the line. We have proof of kidnapping and murder."

The look on his face was scared of what he would do and what was on his mind, "You tell your council members that

I claim my right to challenge him. It is my right under tribal law."

Jario ran from room to room, looking for any signs of Mia. He roared at the family, pushing and breaking things along the way. His sons searched the surrounding area looking for traces of her or where she could have gone. They found blood in the bathroom and were concerned she may be injured somewhere.

"We have to find her, you pigs! Everything is arranged to move her tonight. She couldn't have gone far." Jario limped towards the back door, frustrated. He kicked the door with his good foot. "Damn it to hell!" He grabbed Ivan by the shirt, "Find her and bring her back," he said, pushing him away. For hours they searched for her, tensions were high, and the women huddled together, frightened as they watched Jario go from one extreme uncontrollable fit of rage to another. Aurora was afraid he was going to have a psychotic breakdown.

Sabrina stumbled down the stairs, where the family scrambled to understand what happened. She smiled to herself, knowing why they were going crazy this morning. *Serves them right*, she thought. Without anyone noticing her, she snuck upstairs and locked herself in her room. She lay back in bed, laughing out loud. From the attic room, she could hear yelling coming from downstairs. Last night before she went in to attack Mia, Ivan made it clear that when Mia became his wife, he would get rid of her. She attacked him, trying to scratch his face, but he held her wrist, twisting them and knocking her to the floor.

Ivan picked her up by the hair and shook her. It was common for them to have drag-out, beat-down fights and then have sex afterward. She remembered watching him sleep and it infuriated her that the woman sleeping below would take her place.

After Freida chased her out of Mia's room, she hid in the darkness, watching Freida leaving the room and locking it behind her. Her eye was throbbing when she touched the tender area. She knew Freida was up to something. For a long time, she had been discontented with her life with Jario. Quietly Sabrina followed her. She was used to sneaking around the house in the dark like a mouse. She stopped outside Freida's room, which was a small room off the kitchen. Freida chose to sleep away from the rest of the family. Sabrina tried looking through the keyhole, pressing her eye against the door. She heard drawers opening and closing. However, her curiosity was overwhelming, wanting to know more about what Freida was doing. It wasn't long before Sabrina was outside on her tiptoes, peeping into Freida's window. Freida pulled out three bags from a secret hiding place in the closet. Sabrina struggled to see what she was doing when she heard a commotion coming from the second-floor window. She watched with fascination as Mia rolled over to the edge of the second-floor roof and lowered herself onto the trash cans.

She giggled, following and watching as she stumbled down the path towards the park. Mia disappeared from her sight for a moment when she reached the park. She waited to see what Mia was doing and hoped she would disappear. Sabrina moved from one place to another, careful not to go into the light until she heard voices.

At first, she was angry that the boys found Mia before she did, but then she realized that Mia was gone, and she could keep her husband. Sabrina smiled with glee. She stayed behind the trees as people came and carried her away. Sabrina erased any tracks that Mia made and headed back to the house. By the time she came back to the window, the light was off and Freida's car was gone. "She did it," Sabrina laughed, and she knew all the suffering that Freida endured marrying Jario, who never let her forget she came second in his life.

She opened the back door as quietly as she could and went back to her room. Ivan was in the same position she had left him. She cuddled next to him, satisfied that Mia would not come between them. She would play stupid, giggling to herself. That's what everyone thought she was anyway.

Ivan busted in the room, rummaging through the closet. "What's going on? I heard your father screaming at everyone," she could see the fear on his face.

"Do me a favor and stay upstairs, Sabrina. Mia is missing and father is outraged. Our plans have changed."

"What are you going to do?" she asked innocently.

He pulled out his rifle, making sure it was loaded, "We have been summoned by the council and father wants us to present a strong force. So please stay out of the way, I don't want you to get hurt."

"Alright, I'll stay upstairs. No one will even know I'm here," she smiled sweetly.

"Good, now be a good girl and don't answer the door. If anyone comes asking questions, just don't say anything," she nodded.

Jario had Aurora shoot him up with painkillers so he could put on his boots. He was determined to walk with his sons to the civic center where they were summoned. He saw stars when he finally shoved his foot into his boot. His four sons watched with panic, wishing he would stay home. Troy and Orlando looked at each other, wondering what they had gotten themselves into. They were working on the hideout when they were ordered back. The two younger sons were not part of the kidnapping but were part of the plan to rehabilitate Mia for the family.

Jario was sweating by the time he laced his boots. When the pain medicine kicked in, he was able to stand up.

People began gathering outside the civic center, knowing something happened to bring the Warlord and his sons out. Jario walked into the lobby where they met Manolo, and three other committee members. Behind the double doors came Julio with four of his officers. Jario turned to look at them, holding his rifle by his side.

Julio walked up to him, "Jario, I see you are up to your old tricks again. We have Mia and she was hospitalized."

"What does that have to do with us?" Jario said with a smirk.

"Don't play games with me, Jario. You and your boys will be arrested. But before I take you away, you will face your worst nightmare," Julio laughed out loud.

"I am the Warlord here. You can't arrest me," Jario said with a grin.

"Not anymore, Jario," Manolo said, coming from behind Julio.

"You again, shit. I should have known. For years, you have been trying to destroy my family and you failed. You failed with my father, and you will fail with me. Mia came with us willingly. We didn't hurt her or molest her. If she said we did, she is lying."

Monolo's face was red with anger, "Your lies and intimidation are not going to work anymore."

Julio couldn't believe the lies coming from him, "You know what, I'm going to let you convince her husband to his face that his wife willingly left with your punk-ass sons."

"Who gives a shit about her husband? He doesn't scare me. You should know better than that, I'll take on all you, bitch," he smiled.

"I would reconsider that if I were you," Julio said. "We're doing this the tribal way. First there are some people who want to talk to you before we proceed."

Julio ushered them to another room, where the women waited. They noticed that Jario favored his other foot. The three women waited. Solana turned to face Jario. He was surprised to see her. His heart skipped. She was still beautiful, with just a hint of gray along her temples. Her eyes were still vivid. "Solana," he said, surprised.

"Hello, Jario," she walked up to him and slapped him across the face, he hung his head.

"I guess I had that coming," he grinned.

"My husband is under guard. They are trying to keep him from killing you for what you did to my daughter."

He straightens his posture and laughs. "You know Solana, she should have been our child. She belongs to us, to this community."

"Shit, only in your dreams. I don't understand where you ever got this motion that I would be with someone like you."

"I loved you, Solana. I still do, and she would have made our family stronger."

"Really? You think you could ever create someone as beautiful as she? You're pathetic and a coward. The only reason I moved away from this community where I grew up and my family was because Naphtali would have killed your sorry ass. So, what was your plan, we're going to erase the rape and all those years of harassment."

"Solana, she belongs with her people. This is her home with us," he was getting loud.

"No! She belongs with her husband. She is no one's property." The women walked out of the room, disgusted by the five men. His sons couldn't believe she spoke that way to their father and walked away unharmed.

The council was made of five men and five women, ranging from 32 to 74 in age. Two of Jario's family members avoided his glare as they walked into the room. The ten council members were accompanied by five officers and Mia's family. Jario and his sons sat in the middle. After reading the charges against them, Jario laughed hysterically. His sons were nervous as they had joined him.

"What proof do you have, one woman's statement against what, the five of us, and our women they will testify that she came with my sons willingly and then got scared because she was afraid that her family would find out. This is a joke. She knows where she belongs," he glared at some of the council members, trying to intimidate them with his presence. Mia's family held hands for support. Victor squeezed his wife's hand, trying to stay calm.

Julio came from behind the table and stood in front of him, "Jario this is the end of the road for you and your family. But in fairness, you will explain to her husband how Mia became your prisoner in your house. You see, her ankle was bruised from where you had her chained to the bed, and the drugs you gave her to keep her sedated made her lose the baby she carried. Doesn't sound like a woman who came willingly, right?" Julio said. He nodded to his men to allow Falu, Max and Richie to enter the proceedings. Everyone turned around to watch the three huge men walk towards them. Jario's younger sons looked at each with fear on their faces.

Jario stood up. Falu towered over them, entering the circle where the five stood. They had their weapons at their side. They could only stare at the intensity in Falu's eyes. Falu stared him down. "So, you're the big bad boogieman who kidnapped my wife?"

Jario swallowed hard, "I don't recognize this marriage. She is a tribal woman, and is bound to our laws."

Falu ripped off his shirt, his muscle glistening as he displayed his tag. "My father was the WarLord of the Rivera Tribe in New Orleans, we are equal. Our national tribal Carter allowed me to challenge and avenge the death of any family member. You violated my home, and you will pay."

"So, the big bad Falu is going to beat up an old man. I'm not afraid of you, bring it on."

"No, you are absolutely right. What satisfaction am I going to get from beating a cripple-ass man like you? Your sons came into my home without permission. I'll take them both on… both at the same time."

"Jario laughed out loud, "Alright, you're on. My sons are highly skilled fighters. We accept your challenge."

Falu turned to the council, "Let the council and the witness note, they have accepted my challenge in front of the witness and the tribal council. We'll settle this the tribal way."

Frank Armstrong, the head councilman, stood up, "As the head of this council if there is anyone who opposed this proceeding, speaks now. If not, we will convene in two days. According to our laws, he or she is to be made whole, this is the law, and it shall stand. This meeting is adjourned."

Jario laughed out loud as he hobbled to his feet. He refused any help from his sons, letting everyone see he was still in charge as he walked home between his sons, as his foot screamed with pain.

Ivan had to cut open his boot to get his foot out. Beads of sweat poured from his body. The family gathered together to plan on how they were going to bring down Falu. His younger sons sat quietly, confused by their father's actions. "Damn it, what a time for this gout to fare up," he screamed.

"Pop, why did you let that woman hit you?" Orlando asked. Jario looked down at the floor. It was something he wasn't proud of.

"It's a long story Orlando. She was… a woman I fell in love with. I asked for her hand in marriage, but she was already promised to someone else, and I did the unspeakable. I took her by force, hoping that her father would make us marry, but it backfired. I was young and stupid. I never forgot her and even now, when I saw her, my feelings for her came back like a flood."

"Mia's husband is a big dude. Do you think we can take him on?" Troy is wondering what the outcome will be.

"I'm not going to lie, boys. It's not going to be easy to defeat Falu, he is stronger than I imagined, and his brother is just as strong. We have to plan."

"I'll fight him first," Edgar stated eagerly.

"Edgar you and Ivan may have a chance if you fight him together. But I have other ideas for the mighty Falu. He will come at us if we don't stop him. If we're going to prison, it's going to be for a reason. It's not for taking something that belongs to us. Mia belongs to us and her mother… should have been mine."

Sabrina couldn't resist hearing what the men were whispering and planning. Like always, she put her ear to the door that separated the living room and the kitchen. "You better come away from there before someone catches you," Aurora whispered, scolding her.

"Be quiet, woman. How are we ever going to find out anything if we don't sneak around and listen? What do you think is going to happen to us if they go to prison?"

"You don't think they're going to prison… do you?"

"It's a possibility, Aurora. They committed a crime, bringing that woman here. Now we are all in danger of losing our home."

Aurora sat down at the table, wondering if what Sabrina said was true, "Where did you hear this?"

"Well, if you would pull your nose out of your ass, you may hear what the hell is going on around here. I overheard them talking outside. This is serious. Now they're planning something against some dude name Falu."

"That's Mia's husband, Sabrina… I think you are right. This is not going to be good. We should make plans of our own."

"My advice is to play dumb. You know how Jario gets when he's frustrated."

"I've been playing dumb since I married him. Keep your ears open and let me know what you find out. Jario doesn't talk to me about his affairs."

Mia recovered and was released from the hospital. The women in her family pampered her. They fought over who would take care of the overly emotional Mia. Her grandmother always won, holding her and soothing her anxiety about Falu and his challenge. "Your husband has every right to fight for your honor and the death of your unborn. He is a tribal man at heart."

"Abuelita, you don't know him. Falu has these fits of rage he can't control, and I don't trust them. Do you think they will go into that fight in a good fate?"

"I know me, Vida, but not even God coming to earth will change their mindset. Our men are very proud, and their women are like gold to them. They will do what they think is right. We must have caution when it comes to that family."

When Falu entered the room, Mia dried her eyes, "Well I guess you two lovebirds have a lot to discuss. Try to rest, dear," she kissed his forehead before she left them alone.

Falu sat on the edge of the bed. He took her chin in his hand, "Are you still not talking to me?"

She perched her lips, "I just want to go home and put this behind us," she said with trembling lips.

"I know baby," he kissed her. "They will pay for what they did. For years, they've been getting away with shit, but not anymore. They will go to prison after I beat the shit out of them and only them."

"Baby, I have no doubt of your fighting abilities and strength. I just don't trust them. I'm sure they would have realized by now that you can take them, and they must be planning something."

"Trust me, my love, just know that I have to do this, and they are done around here." He takes her in his arms, squeezing her gently. "I love you more than life, Mia. I promise we will have a family."

She tried to hold back her tears, "It hurts… I wanted our baby so bad."

"I know love, so did I. Tomorrow, we'll put all this ugliness behind us. We'll spend a few days with your family. I know they missed you all these years."

"Please, I don't want to lose you too," she said sadly, holding him tight.

Centro Plaza

Crowds began to gather at the plaza where the match was going to be held. Extra officers were on hand to keep everyone in line. Mia refused to stay behind and with Max on her heel, she made her way toward the plaza. "Max, I just can't wait at home wondering what's going on."

"I think you should be in bed resting," he argued.

"I've rested long enough. Please, don't make me out as one of these weak women."

"Mia, I can see the concern written all over your face, so don't try to fake it. These two guys are pussies compared to the men my brother has fought. I watched him beat six guys bigger than these two punks into a pulp."

"I know what he can do and so do they," she cried. "They are dirty fighters, Max. Do you really think they will go into that ring clean handed?"

"That's why, we're here. They will be searched, and so will the rest of the family. If I let you go, please sit with your family and for heaven's sake, do not jump in. I know you. Now, promise me," he glared at her. She pouted, crossing her arms. "Mia, please promise me to let us handle this," he said forcefully.

"I promise," she replied halfhearted.

"For some reason, you don't sound convincing. Now, swear to me you will not jump in," she gave him a dirty look.

"I hate you, Max," she said. "I swear, what else do you want me to say?"

"I want you to have confidence in your husband, and you may hate me right now, but if anything happened to you. I would blame myself for not keeping your ass in bed."

"You know, I don't really hate you, Max, don you?" She said, hugging him.

He chuckled, "I love you too, smartass."

Mia found her family and sat next to her grandfather. She was amazed at all the people that showed up to watch the fight.

Sabrina watched from her window as the men left the house towards the plaza. Jario tried his best to limp alongside his sons. But right away, she sensed something wrong while the men walked toward the plaza. Orlando slipped away from the others. He was carrying something on his back. She hurried down the stairs, almost falling down the last set of stairs. Sabrina ran down to the intersection where they separated. Down the next blocked, Orlando walked towards the taller buildings. She followed him, watching him jam open one of the exit doors up the stairs. The building faced the plaza perfectly. Orlando hesitated on each floor. His hands were shaking and sweating as he took each step towards the roof of the 10th story building.

Falu entered the arena without a shirt in shorts; his chest glistened as he flexed his chest and arm muscles. His gray eyes were like steel as he took his stand across from the brothers who were seen nervous. He tied his hair back and grinned. After the announcer gave his statement, the bell rang. Ivan came running into him like a raging bull. Falu blocked him and grabbed him by the neck with one hand. Ivan struggled to get free, Edgar came around him, punching him from behind, but Falu turned suddenly and slammed Ivan into his brother. They both fell with force.

Orlando positioned himself on the roof. He had a clear aim from where he was. His hands shook as he tried to get a clean shot at Falu, who was moving too fast. Orlando took a deep breath and tried to focus. He nearly pissed in his pants when he heard his name. "Orlando, what the hell are you doing?" Sabrina cried, shocked at why he was he holding a rifle.

Relieved to see it was only Sabrina, "What are you doing here?"

"I followed you, fool. Don't do this Orlando. You're a good guy. How could your father ask you to do something like this?"

He looked at her wide eyes nervously, "I have to do this. Father said it would save my brothers."

"Don't you understand, you will go to prison for the rest of your life… you are too good for this. Please, I beg you, don't.

"Sabrina, you don't understand. If I don't do this, my father will kill me and I will shame the family."

He took aim again, sweat was affecting his eyes. His brothers were getting beat badly, all he saw was blood. He finally got a clear shot at Falu's back. He squeezed the trigger and fired, but Sabrina pulled him from behind and the shot went into the air. They struggled with the rifle and another round escaped into the side of the building. People ran for safety, and they scattered in all directions. Max picked up Mia over his shoulder into one of the buildings as he went back to help others that didn't know where the shots were coming from.

"Sabrina, now look what you did!" He tried to find Falu, but people were going crazy looking for shelter.

"Let's go Orlando, it will take time to find out where those shots came from. Come on," she yelled at him, pulling him along. They rushed down the stairs hoping no one saw them on the top of the building fighting over the rifle.

Julio and his men were all over Jario and his sons, who needed medical attention. Troy was knocked out cold when he jumped in to help his brother. Jario could only sit and watch as his sons got beat. There was an officer with his weapon pointed at his head at all times.

When the commotion was over, Jario was taken to jail along with his sons after they were treated. Ivan suffered a broken arm, and his eyes and lips were bleeding. Edgar was treated for a broken jaw. His face was a bloody mess. He lost some of his hearing. Falu had him by the neck when the shots were fired.

Falu was frantic looking for Mia, in the middle of screaming people looking for shelter. She ran into his arms. "It's over, baby. You won, please. You won."

"I'm alright. It's time to heal and move on." She kissed him as he lifted her off her feet. "Let's go home, woman."

Epilogue

Mia and Falu spent the next few days with the family before they headed home. The judge found Jario and his sons guilty of kidnapping and imprisonment. They found out that Jario was going to have his leg amputated. He was removed from his title of Warlord and could not pass it on to his sons. Because of his health, he was sentenced to house arrest for the rest of his days.

His sons were sent to the Inner Cities, Prison Island, with their families. Away from their father's influence, they began to find themselves. Edgar entered a training program for higher learning and discovered he had a teaching gift. He took classes in History to become a teacher. Ivan found he was good with his hands, he enjoyed fixing things and took advantage of most of the classes, learning how to fix small and large engines. Sabrina received medical attention, she needed help with the bipolar condition she had suffered from most of her life. Now, she was stable and couldn't wait to be a mother.

The brothers had plans when they were released to find a new path in their life. They felt free to live their lives as they pleased, without someone barking at them and making all the decisions that affected everyone. They discovered a new world and they intended to live in it. Ivan often wondered about his father. Sometimes he would catch himself saying some of the things he spouted and would stop. He vowed not to become his father and a bitter man.

No one ever found out who fired those shots that day. Sabrina made the crying Orlando promise not to tell anyone what happened on the roof. When his father asked, he simply told him that the doors were jammed, and he couldn't get in.

Jario regretted so many things in his life. All he had was his title and now it was taken from him. His wives were gone except for Aurora, who was too scared to leave. His children were gone and the family he depended on turned their backs on him.

Victor was named as Warlord of Polo Alto. It would be passed on to his older son, who found it to be the most amazing thing in the world. The community had a lot to celebrate. The tyranny that kept their community in fear was over, broken and never to rise again.

Mia's family settled back in the community they left behind. They traveled between the two homes. When Mia gave birth to her precious little girl, her mother was there to meet her new granddaughter. Falu lost his heart to his baby girl. They named her Esmeralda, after his mother.

So many things had changed. Max and Penny were married, hoping for a child of their own. Blanca and Betty were planning a double wedding. Tina hired an accountant for the apartment complex, and after a while, he captured her heart, and they began a loving relationship.

Falu ruled the city with an iron fist, but in return, New Orleans became the rich city it once was. The smooth jazz soulful sounds that once echoed throughout the street came back. The spirit of the nightclub and the drum of the Latin beat invaded every corner with the rich salsa rhythm.

Mia couldn't stay away from her passion. She loved to sing and had a huge fan base. Whenever she was featured, it was standing room only along with Penny, her faithful backup singer. Among the crowd at reserved tables were Geraldine and Nico's happy faces. They continued to make clothes for Mia for the stage.

Carmen and Sonia never came back to New Orleans. They worked for a low budget brothel, still looking for that sugar daddy that would take care of them.

Mia gave Falu two sons, each as bullheaded and brawny as their father. Little Reyes and Falu junior were the spitting images of their father. Falu could now look out into the city and feel pride in all he and his family work hard for. He looked out on his terrace, watching the lights from the city. "There you are. I just put Esmeralda to bed. The boys are asking for you," Mia held him pressing her face against his back.

"Do you think my parents are watching from heaven?" he said, putting his arms around Mia and kissing her neck tenderly.

"I think they are, and they are proud of you and Max. You made your father's dreams come true."

"I wish they were here to see our children and see what a wonderful wife I have."

"Ah, yeah," she giggled.

"Remember, this is where I said you would be my wife and you laughed at me."

Mia wiggled in his arms, "Alright, fat head, it's time to put your little monsters to bed, and they want you to tell them some ridiculous story about you and some dragon."

Falu laughed loudly, "Te amo mi amor," he said, capturing her lips. They fought hard and loved deeply, embracing the future ahead of them.

The End

www.ingramcontent.com/pod-product-compliance
Lightning Source LLC
Chambersburg PA
CBHW070346170726
48291CB00001B/200